THE FATAL PICNIC

THEIR NEAREST AND DEAREST

TWO NOVELS BY

BERNICE CAREY

INTRODUCTION BY CURTIS EVANS

Stark House Press • Eureka California

THE FATAL PICNIC / THEIR NEAREST AND DEAREST

Published by Stark House Press
1315 H Street
Eureka, CA 95501, USA
griffinskye3@sbcglobal.net
www.starkhousepress.com

THE FATAL PICNIC
Originally published and copyright © 1955 by Doubleday & Company, Inc.,
New York. Copyright renewed January 6, 1983 by Bernice Carey Martin.

THEIR NEAREST AND DEAREST
Originally published and copyright © 1953 by Doubleday & Company, Inc.,
New York. Published in an abridged digest edition by Mercury Publications,
New York, as *The Frightened Widow*. Copyright renewed February 12, 1981
by Bernice Carey Martin.

"Murder Most Real" © 2021 by Curtis Evans

ISBN-13: 978-1-951473-34-1

Book design by Mark Shepard, shepgraphics.com
Proofreading by Bill Kelly
Cover art by Fred Zimmer from the original edition of *The Fatal Picnic*

First Stark House Press Edition: June 2021

THE FATAL PICNIC

The Mallory family gathers for a picnic at the park. It looks like a perfect day for it, and they all start to arrive, ready to feast and play. Then Uncle Maurice shows up. Maurice of the sadistic tongue and crude humor. His wife Esther puts on her usual brave face, but no one is pleased except the kids, who love his antics. Most of the family have good reason to hate Uncle Maurice. He swindled Jocelyn and Marvin in financial deals. He found out about Fred's affair, and holds it over him. He torments Alison every time he sees her, belittling her unmercifully. Even his son, David, hates him, and with just cause. Maurice has spread so much poison among the Mallorys, it really comes as no surprise when the shots ring out…

THEIR NEAREST AND DEAREST

Salinas lettuce grower Stanley West is found murdered at his desk, shot in the chest with his own gun. At first they police are completely baffled. West had many visitors that day, but who dropped in on him that evening with such a grudge that could only be settled by murder? His wife Laverne becomes their first suspect, simply because she is his wife. Chuck Willet, a slightly shady real estate friend who wanted West to back him in a local political bid, could have been upset when West wouldn't support his campaign. Hal Schmidt owned him a lot of money, and might have wanted to cancel a debt. But then Laverne's daughter Patty tells the cops about a young man she had been dating, a young man from the worker camp whom her father didn't approve of. And the cops know they have their man. Or do they?

Bernice Carey Bibliography
(1910-1990)

Novels:

The Reluctant Murderer (1949)

The Body on the Sidewalk (1950)

The Man Who Got Away With It (1950)

The Beautiful Stranger (1951)

The Three Widows (1952)

The Missing Heiress (1952)

Their Nearest and Dearest (1953;
abridged as The Frightened Widow, 1954)

The Fatal Picnic (1955)

Stories:

He Got What He Deserved (*The Lethal Sex*, 1959)

MURDER MOST REAL
BY CURTIS EVANS

In May 1955 the local community theater of the town of Los Gatos, California, securely nestled in the foothills of the Santa Cruz Mountains south of San Francisco, presented a staging of English playwright Janet Green's *Gently Does It*, a murder play which had hit the boards on Broadway two years earlier, after having generated substantial business the previous year in London, under the title *Murder Mistaken*. Like the smash success *Dial M for Murder* (later adapted by Alfred Hitchcock into a posh film starring Grace Kelly, Ray Milland and Robert Cummings), on whose heels *Gently Does It* had swiftly followed, the latter play was a sophisticated British murder melodrama ringing yet another variation on the perennially popular, if a tad shopworn, plot of a wicked husband scheming to bump off his naïve wealthy wife. A minor character in *Gently Does It* is housemaid Emmie, resoundingly stolid and dim in the grand tradition of servants in condescendingly classist British mysteries. ("[P]roperly subservient and sufficiently stupid," is how an American reviewer in the *Harvard Crimson* snootily described the character after seeing a performance of the play in Boston.) In the Los Gatos production Emmie was played by Bernice Martin, the wife of a local high school history teacher and herself a "well-known mystery author," the local newspaper noted, whose latest—and, as it transpired, final—mystery novel, *The Fatal Picnic*, would be published later that year in the fall. Before World War Two, Bernice Martin, then Bernice Fitch (or, to use the name under which she wrote her novels, Bernice Carey), having an ironic taste for performing in traditional British mystery plays, had been as well a member of the local acting company in Salinas, California, the setting of Carey's *Their Nearest and Dearest* (1953), the mystery which immediately preceded *The Fatal Picnic*.

Both of these accomplished although long out-of-print crime novels, which in milieu, characterization and social attitude differ vastly from the stereotypical British mystery of book, stage and screen, are now available again, in the form of another fine twofer volume from Stark House. While Bernice Carey did not explore the mean streets of Raymond Chandler and Dashiell Hammett, she nevertheless intrepidly ventured down suburban lanes and other, decidedly less well-off thoroughfares, where credible characters—everyday people like you and me, not aristocrats glumly inhabiting crumbling country houses or starlets thoughtlessly partying at tony Hollywood mansions—commit murder for all-too-believable reasons. Carey's crime novels afford a bracing change indeed after one has been restricted to a steady diet of what Raymond Chandler derisively dubbed "week-end chichi" mysteries—that deadly, once seemingly endless procession of tales concerning inevitably fatal country house parties where death is variously dealt out by cardboard cutout houseguests by such posh means as jewel-encrusted Florentine stilettos, Queen Anne dueling pistols and curare-tipped darts, all for the most impeccable, if improbable, of motives.

When editor and book reviewer Avis DeVoto—wife of historian Bernard DeVoto and a friend and influential promoter of prospective cookbook author Julia Child—reviewed Bernice Carey's "excellent" mystery *Their Nearest and Dearest* in her weekly "Thrills and Chills Dept." column in the *Boston Globe*, DeVoto highlighted what she deemed the author's "extraordinary ability for projecting, without a trace of sentimentality, her understanding of what are called 'the little people.'" ("[A] phrase this column abhors," the patrician DeVoto hastily added.) Two years later, in her notice of Carey's *The Fatal Picnic*, which she also highly recommended, DeVoto similarly commented, "Miss Carey has a flair for lower middle-brow talk and behavior equaled by none." Although both of the Carey novels in this volume tell compelling tales of murder—and *Their Nearest and Dearest* is graced with the author's finest example of a classic murder puzzle—what may linger most in the minds of readers after finishing them are the moving stories of the "little people" who finally felt compelled to commit murder (and in some cases actually did so). These characters' lives intensely matter to us for a time, because the author with consummate, unobtrusive skill compels us utterly to believe in their reality. They come off neither as puzzle pieces nor puppets, but rather flesh and blood people who feel real pain. To borrow from Shakespeare, if you prick them, they will bleed.

Reviewing *Their Nearest and Dearest* in January 1953, leading American crime fiction critic Anthony Boucher praised Bernice Carey for absorbingly depicting the community of Salinas, California while simultaneously integrating this background "perfectly into an unusually strong murder story." At the end of the year Boucher would include *Their Nearest and Dearest* in his annual list of the year's ten best mysteries, along with these acknowledged genre classics: Ira Levin's *A Kiss Before Dying*, Josephine Tey's *The Singing Sands*, Michael Gilbert's *Fear to Tread*, Guy Cullingford's *Post Mortem*, Edward Grierson's *Reputation for a Song* and Ross Macdonald's *Meet Me at the Morgue*. Carey's "mature, adult whodunit" was, the critic avowed, "the best yet in [the author's] distinguished series of realistic novels."

In an eventful year which saw the death of Soviet leader Joseph Stalin and the coronation of the United Kingdom's Queen Elizabeth II, the first Soviet explosion of a hydrogen bomb and the formal conclusion of the Korean War, the triumphant scaling of Mount Everest by Sir Edmund Hilary and the retributive American execution as spies of husband and wife Julius and Ethel Rosenberg, *Their Nearest and Dearest* yet managed to set Salinas tongues wagging. Ultimately Bernice Carey divulged to the Salinas *Californian* that she was one and the same as the housewife Bernice Fitch who had resided in Salinas from 1931 to 1942 with her first husband and later as well the couple's two young boys, Bill and Danny. The fact that Salinas sat up and took notice of the new novel is not surprising; aside from the natural interest derived from the fact that someone had bothered to set a novel in the small though rapidly growing community (Salinas' population in 1950 was shy of fourteen thousand, not a great deal more than it had been a decade earlier, yet that number would more than double, to nearly thirty thousand, over the course of the Fifties and more than double again, to nearly sixty thousand, during the Sixties), there was the fact that Carey took a hard and unsparing look at racism, sexism, class antagonism and sexual vice, including prostitution, in her former home town. In 1942, the year Bernice Carey left Salinas, the town with much local publicity had shuttered its houses of ill repute, under threat from the United States military, which was concerned about soldiers from nearby Fort Ord contracting sexually transmitted diseases from local working girls.

Their Nearest and Dearest studies the events which follow the fatal shooting of Stanley West, President of the Golden West Produce Company, a Salinas lettuce packing plant, late one night in his office. In form a classic whodunit problem is presented to the reader (one which successfully kept this reader in suspense until the end), with a wealthy man mysteriously slain, if not in a country house, at least in an enclosed location. Yet Carey's novel diverges widely from much classic mystery in its realistic, sympathetic treatment of characters all along the social, racial and gender spectrums.

Much of the novel focuses on Stan West's not unreservedly bereaved widow, Laverne, who was ashamedly aware that Stan had been, and likely still was, unfaithful to her and has herself been carrying on a spot of hole-and-corner adultery with a prominent Salinas defense attorney, Brian

Rhodes, who has been strenuously urging her to divorce Stan. Thirty-eight-year-old Laverne, who married young at the age of nineteen, has gradually become disillusioned with her marriage (like the author had in real life with her first union), despite having born her husband three children, sardonic eighteen-year-old Patty and coltish thirteen-year-old twins Kerry and Terry, the latter of whom Carey doubtlessly modeled on her own sons, both of whom were around the same age. (The novel is dedicated to the pair.) When the local police pay a call at the upscale West residence—the Wests have a swimming pool, a basement "rumpus room" and a black maid, Lulu—to inform her of Stan's murder, she cannot recall much about the night before, on account of all the "social drinking" in which she indulged. (The amount of casual drinking and smoking among the Salinas upper crust in this novel is prodigious.) However, she fears that Brian impetuously might have resorted to murder as a way of finally taking his relationship with her to the next level, as it were. Meanwhile daughter Patty expresses concern that her boyfriend Rex Maffey, a handsome and ambitious packer in the lettuce plant whom she had been rebelliously dating in defiance of her prejudiced father, might have been tempted violently to remove a major obstacle to his social advancement.

There are other interesting characters in the novel as well (some of them potential suspects), like Rex's older sister Bonnie, another packer at the plant, who has had to shoulder too many family burdens for too long; Chuck Willett, a somehow socially semi-respectable realtor and local vice king (i.e., he owns the town's whorehouses and gambling dens), who has been struck with an itch to run for political office; Earl Fowler, the company accountant who has been spending exorbitantly on his and his family's mid-century modern suburban domicile; and Hal Schmidt, another, hard on his luck "lettuce man" whose note Stan was contemplating calling in, and his breezy wife Joan, Laverne's best friend.

At its core, however, the novel is an immensely absorbing tale of the belated coming-of-age of a jejune wife, Laverne West, whose mind finally matures only after her masterful and controlling husband's death. The story is powerfully abetted by the author's keen eye for social detail and talent for tart cultural and political observation, the amount of which she packs into a short novel of some sixty thousand words is nothing short of astonishing. (Modern mystery writers should take note.) Rereading *Their Nearest and Dearest* I was reminded of the 2002 film *Far from Heaven*, which brilliantly critiques the stultifying cultural norms of the Fifties; yet remarkably Carey's novel appeared nearly half a century before director Todd Haynes' critically acclaimed revisionist film, in the very heart of that constricted decade. In my mind's eye when I read *Their Nearest and Dearest* I could easily imagine actresses Julianne Moore and Patricia

Clarkson, both of whom received Oscar nominations for their performances in *Far from Heaven*, as, respectively, Laverne and her blunt best friend Joan, although the same-sex dalliances of Moore's husband in the film, played by Dennis Quaid, admittedly have no counterpart in the book. However, the socially progressive Carey does bring race, so important an aspect of *Far from Heaven*, into *Their Nearest and Dearest*, as she had in several of her earlier novels, most notably *The Body on the Sidewalk* (1950).

Carey does this in the form of Laverne's maid Lulu, who at first seems a very minor character but ends up playing a pointedly memorable role in the tale. Although she may have drolly portrayed a stereotypically "dumb" British maid on stage in Los Gatos, Carey makes clear that Lulu is no fictive black maid of yore, noting that "she differed as much as it was possible to from the fat, ungrammatical, invincibly jolly stereotype of the female Negro servant of fiction and the movies." There was much social ferment astir even in the buttoned-down decade of the Fifties, to be sure, and, in her own modest but far from unimpressive way, Bernice Carey was part of crime fiction's social vanguard.

Bernice Carey's social progressivism is much in evidence as well in her eighth and last crime novel, *The Fatal Picnic*, which, upon its publication a little over two and a half years after *Their Nearest and Dearest*, in September 1955, was praised by Anthony Boucher as "another ironic and realistic study [by the author] of middle-class murder." Although in this novel Carey narrows her social telescope to descry a group of middle class relatives picnicking at a California state park, the number of characters in the novel is actually vast. While perusing the first chapter readers may well pine for the presence of a family tree, that not incidental adjunct in classic mysteries, where murders of wealthy relations for bounteous inheritances abound; but things soon settle down as Carey focuses on the major characters/suspects in the murder of their toxic in-law Maurice Egstadt, the proverbial fly in the ointment—or in this case, ant on the potato salad. Rarely have I read a murder mystery in which I felt myself wanting to see someone actually get whacked more than I did the odious Maurice Egstadt.

Following the first chapter, in which Carey introduces over a score of Mallory kin and gives readers their first awful glimpse of the all-round egregiousness of Maurice Egstadt, an unexpected "guest" at this year's picnic and the husband of Esther, the baby among the second generation Mallory siblings, there are six chapters which provide back stories on why a half-dozen individuals—Esther's devoutly religious spinster sister Jocelyn, her "successful" brother Fred, her carpenter brother-in-law Marvin Nelson (sister Bea's husband), her bank clerk niece Alison (daughter of her late brother Arthur), her and Maurice's schoolteacher son

David Egstadt and, finally, Esther herself—had particular reason to want to see Maurice put down in the ground for good. The reader quickly perceives that Maurice is a jolly sort of sadist, constantly and calculatedly belittling others, including his wife Esther, although she perennially makes excuses for his poor behavior, much to the disgust of adult kinfolk. (Conversely Maurice with his joking ways and bluff buffoonery is popular with young children, although one notices that creepily he cannot seem to keep his hands off little girls.) Only over the course of the novel do readers come fully to appreciate Maurice's utter perfidy, however, as incident after baneful incident is revealed, like peeled back layers of a rancid onion. When Maurice is felled with a gunshot, the police, upon their arrival at the fatal picnic, soon receive a confession to murder—but are they really getting the whole truth of the matter?

In *The Fatal Picnic* Bernice Carey eschews the pure puzzle narrative in favor of a more unconventional crime novel structure, but she continues to employ her keen eye for cultural detail—particularly, to my mind, on the question of women and marriage, as seen through the characters of Jocelyn, Alison and Esther. Esther provokes steadily increasing exasperation with her seemingly inexcusable idiocy in constantly making light of her husband's appalling actions. Why does she act so? For her part, twenty-eight-year-old Alison's demeaning urgency (if not desperation) to avoid becoming an "old maid" like her Aunt Jocelyn is palpable (and painful) as she contemplates the state of her fledgling relationship with tentative new boyfriend Orville, peacefully napping beside her at the park:

> What a commentary on my life, she thought ironically, twenty-eight years old and a sleeping man is an oddity to me. … We learn that Orville had been married once and divorced. As an eligible man, he had been calculatedly considered by all the single girls in the bank, by the unmarried salesgirls and waitresses all through the business district, and by half the unattached female schoolteachers in town. Alison knew Orville had dated a number of girls during his year in Coast City. She hadn't dared to hope that she would become one of their number. Alison—at twenty-eight—had almost given up hope. Wherever one went, it seemed as if there were always more single women than men.

The classic detective novel that ascended in both the United Kingdom and the United States in the years between the two world wars often was patterned after a highly stylized, deliberately artificial design, as was, Raymond Chandler's militant claims notwithstanding, its opposite number, the hard-boiled gumshoe mystery that became increasingly popular from the 1940s onward. In Bernice Carey's fiction, however, readers refreshingly got to see crime as it more genuinely might impact *them*—not with ingeniously convoluted or viscerally violent killings, solved variously by flippant men-about-town or wisecracking private dicks, but with simpler crimes committed out of quiet desperation, solved by plain—though never, in Carey's hands, prosaic—people.

As journalist Nancy Barr Mavity, herself a former scribbler of "Golden Age" detection fiction, wrote in "No Ruts on the Road: Los Gatos Writer Roams Far," an *Oakland Tribune* review article on *Their Nearest and Dearest* which managed to take shots at both Raymond Chandler and his aesthetic adversary John Dickson Carr:

Bernice Carey, in short, is a writer who will not be 'typed.' Her plot imagination is fertile and ingenious, and needs no props of reliance on blood-and-sex stimulation, the locked-room-puzzle, or highly specialized and recondite scientific lore. If, in the extremely various circumstances she contrives for them, her stories have a common denominator, it is that what the characters do springs naturally from what they are. If this includes murder, it is only what you might expect after you have found out—but not before: as, in real life, we often respond to some unforeseen conduct among our acquaintances with an initial "How surprising!" quickly followed by, "But, come to think of it, he (or she) always had it in him (or her)."

In other words, not *murder most foul* (to borrow the clichéd title of a painfully arch 1964 Miss Marple mystery film, for which Agatha Christie herself deserves no opprobrium), but *murder most real*—at which Bernice Carey was both a pioneer and a past master.

—March 2021
Germantown, TN

Curtis Evans received a PhD in American history in 1998. He is the author of *Masters of the "Humdrum" Mystery: Cecil John Charles Street, Freeman Wills Crofts, Alfred Walter Stewart and British Detective Fiction, 1920-1961* (2012) and most recently the editor of the Edgar nominated *Murder in the Closet: Essays on Queer Clues in Crime Fiction Before Stonewall* (2017) and, with Douglas G. Greene, the Richard Webb and Hugh Wheeler short crime fiction collection, *The Cases of Lieutenant Timothy Trant* (2019). He blogs on vintage crime fiction at The Passing Tramp.

THE FATAL PICNIC
BERNICE CAREY

This book is affectionately dedicated to
Margery Wells Empie
By "Her Author"

ONE
The Family

No one expected Maurice to be at the picnic. Esther had told Beatrice on the phone that he was in Southern California on business. When those already gathered around the picnic tables looked up and saw that Maurice was one of the quartet advancing from the direction of the parking lot laden with cardboard cartons and emitting glad cries of greeting, various members of the family suffered pained reactions, some silently, some audibly.

"Oh *no!*"

"So *he's* going to be here."

"You wouldn't think he'd have the nerve!"

"I thought for once," Beatrice said, "we'd have a nice peaceful day."

"Now, Bea, you be nice to him—for Esther's sake."

"I'm getting sick and tired of putting up with that man for Esther's sake."

It was Bea who had issued the call for a family reunion—in honor of her daughter and son-in-law who were visiting from Chicago on a two-week vacation.

Bea and her family had driven out early that morning to reserve a good spot in the park. The location they had taken possession of was around the first bend in the road after the entrance. To the south, screened by a clump of madrone trees, another picnic site was occupied by a Portuguese family. To the north a graveled area ran in toward the creek bank, and before noon it was filled by parked automobiles. Some fifty feet to the east the bank fell away steeply, the upper branches of the sycamores below rising above its brink like an uneven hedge.

A rough path led down this embankment through protruding roots and dusty bushes to the bouldered stream which flowed out of the small dam to the north. Beyond the dam lay the swimming pool, with man-made sandy beaches on both sides of the pent-up water and diving boards protruding from the top of the dam.

From the site Bea had chosen the pool could be reached either by skirting the parking lot to the north and descending a set of wooden steps further along, or by clambering down the rough path opposite their tables and dodging among the boulders which shored the stream.

Diagonally across the road to the north through a small grove of buckeye trees lay the baseball diamond; and beyond that, around two more curves in the road, were an open-air dance floor equipped with a juke box, and a shack dispensing hot dogs, ice cream, and soda pop.

As the morning advanced there was much kissing and exclaiming beside the three tables which had been pushed together in the shade of two giant live-oak trees some twenty yards from the road winding along the creek bed through the park.

The children of the party were, as Bea remarked resignedly, "all over the place"—in the pool, climbing downstream from rock to rock, racing around the as yet deserted dance floor, getting in the way of a ball game being organized by a group from Local 17 of the Plasterers' Union who were gathered for their annual barbecue at tables near the pavilion.

"I told them to all be back here at one sharp," Bea complained, "but you'll see, we'll have to go round up every last one of 'em."

One young matron had spread a tarpaulin near the further oak and laid out a blanket on it for her infant son. In a folding canvas chair in the shade of the nearer oak, an old lady generally addressed as "Auntie" watched from under a starched gingham sunbonnet the relatives who darted past her from time to time. A sixteen-year-old girl and a seventeen-year-old boy came wet and nearly naked from a dip in the pool and got to chasing around the table, shooting olive pits at one another, a game which was terminated abruptly when one of the pits hit a six-year-old female cousin spang in the middle of the forehead, educing yowls of anguish from the victim.

A middle-aged man extricated himself from the main cluster at the end of the table and approached the water faucet, where he exchanged greetings with a brother-in-law, who glanced toward the rank of automobiles to the north, with a nod at the long wine-red Buick with its sporty tan top. "Thought you was driving your own car down, Fred."

"I thought so too," Fred replied glumly. "Me and Jane were supposed to stop and pick up Esther, because everybody thought *he'd* still be gone. Well, he was back home, and nothing would do, Maurice had to take his car. Like to blew my ears off. Couldn't roll the windows up. 'No sense in having a convertible if you don't take advantage of the fresh air.'"

"Guess you made good time from Valdale," the other drawled with a laconic grin.

"You ain't kiddin'. Thirty minutes flat. I'm still shaking like a leaf."

"C'mon, have a beer to settle your nerves." They walked over to a galvanized tub where brown bottles crowded half submerged around a square of ice.

Aunt Esther was holding onto the hands of the guest of honor. "It's so nice to see you, Flo. And"—her eyes turning to the self-conscious young man beside the girl who was a stranger to most of the family because Florence had met him when she was working in San Francisco—"to meet your husband—at last. We've all heard so much about you, Steven. If only you hadn't taken dear little Flo clear back to *Chicago* to live! Couldn't you get transferred or something out here so we could see you once in a while?"

"I'm afraid not," Steven mumbled awkwardly.

"If only," Esther was proceeding vivaciously, "David could have been here today. Couldn't you drive down to see him? It's only about a hundred miles south. He'll be just sick at missing you."

"But David's coming to the picnic, him and Renée," Florence returned in a surprised tone. "Didn't you know?"

The face of David's mother went strangely blank as Florence spoke. It was only for a few seconds, and then Esther was again the sweet, good-natured aunt being oh so happy over seeing her own dear kinfolk again.

"What a nice surprise!" she chirruped. "I must run and tell Father. We had no idea—" She started away, patting one of the ubiquitous children on the head and stopping to kiss the elderly great-aunt who crossed her path.

Steven looked after his aunt-in-law with a puzzled expression. "What gives? She looked scared."

Florence shrugged. "I thought it had all blown over. 'Father,'" she explained in a mimicking tone, "never did get on very well with Junior—that's their son, David. You know, I told you. And when Dave married Renée, that tore it. They weren't speaking for quite a while. Aunt Esther is afraid Uncle Maurice will be rude or something and embarrass everybody."

Florence turned to a woman who was setting a bowl of potato salad on the table. "Seems like Aunt Esther didn't know Dave and Renée were coming."

The other straightened and tendered Florence a meaning look. "I know. Isn't it awful? It's all your mother's doing. When she heard Maurice wasn't going to be here, she called the kids up and invited them. Thought it would be nice for Esther, give her a chance to see David without the old man around."

With an oblique glance toward the group of men around the beer tub whom Maurice had joined, she added, "Somebody ought to kill that man," and broke off to scream shrilly down the length of the table at a small girl who was standing on the plank seat, leaning across the place settings with one pudgy hand in the top of a jar, "Sharon, get away from those pickles! You hear me?" She sighed plaintively. "Honestly, that kid! *Loves* dill pickles. Just loves 'em. You want to be sick before it's even time to eat?" she scolded her offspring, who was sprinting toward the bank, clutching a fat green cucumber.

Florence looked off toward the road where a two-door sedan had just pulled into the row of parked cars. A young woman in short slacks and a plaid shirt was getting out on the side away from the driver's seat.

"Oh," Florence exclaimed. "Good! Here's old Alison, bless her heart." She paused and peered toward the machine. Bea had come up beside her daughter, and Florence surmised aloud, "That's him, I suppose?"

"Yeah, that's Orville. She didn't want to ask him, everybody else being family, but I just up and gave her a good talking to. 'For goodness sake, why not?' I said. 'He's got nothing else to do. He'd enjoy it.' And then she starts fussing around about wouldn't it be kind of *obvious*, asking him to a family doings, as if she was hinting that he join up. And I just told her—"

But Florence had hurried around the table and was running between the stove and the water faucet, crying, "Allie, Allie, you old son of a gun. Am I glad to see you!"

They hugged each other with inarticulate cries, more like sisters than cousins. Alison had indeed been like an older sister to Florence, for she had lived with Bea and Marvin Nelson since the death of her own parents when Alison was twelve and Florence six.

The girls had hardly finished assuring each other how well they looked and getting Florence introduced to Orville before Aunt Esther came trotting forward to kiss her niece and acknowledge her own introduction to the stranger who stood smiling helplessly in an attempt to appear at ease.

"It's good to see you," Alison told her aunt kindly. People always seemed to feel obliged to speak kindly to Aunt Esther.

Then, as her glance fell on the men by the tree, the smile withered on Alison's face. "Oh," she said, "I thought Uncle Maurice was away."

"Got back late last night," Esther rejoined ever so brightly. "Wasn't it lucky? I was so disappointed, thinking he couldn't be here. And guess what?" Her vivacity increased as if at a sudden needling from within. "David is coming too! Isn't that wonderful? The whole family."

Florence spoke to Orville with good-natured mockery. "Yep, you're going to meet the whole damn family."

Aunt Esther addressed the man archly. "Don't pay any attention to her. If I do say it as shouldn't, we're a wonderful bunch. The nicest people I know. You'll look a long ways before you find a family that sticks together the way we Mallorys do."

Orville was a slender man of medium height, in no way handsome, but on the other hand in no way ugly. The women found now that when his smile came spontaneously rather than merely dutifully Orville's face took on a surprising magnetism.

"Well," he said, glancing toward the tables, "you can say one thing, there's a lot of you."

Florence turned and surveyed the scene. "Mamma estimated, counting babies, there'd be over thirty here today."

"And to think," Esther mused with simulated wonderment, "when Mother and Daddy came out to California thirty-five years ago there was just them and us five kids, me and Bea and Jocelyn and Fred and your poor dear father, Alison. And now look how many of us there are."

"Well, of course, Cousin Helen and Cousin Wilbur came out on their own after the war," Florence pointed out. "Grandma and Grandpa Mallory had nothing to do with that. Even so," she concluded pensively, "families do sort of—spread, don't they?"

"You'll never get everybody straight, Orville." Alison laughed nervously.

"Well, I've got a start. Florence here is your cousin, and Mrs. Egstadt is your aunt."

"Now you just call me Aunt Esther," that lady beamed coyly.

"Florence," Alison said abruptly, "do you want to help us get the stuff from Orville's car? I brought a cake."

"Oh," Esther bubbled gaily, "there's Jocelyn! I was wondering if Jossy would get away to come." With the full skirt of her nylon shirtwaist dress flying back against her legs, Esther took off in the direction of an angular woman bearing a large wicker basket in both arms.

The women, of sundry ages and dressed variously in cotton house dresses, slacks, and tight denim shorts, moved officiously along the tables, hindered by the long plank seats affixed to the sides, setting out bowls of green salad and platters of cold fried chicken and plates of deviled-egg sandwiches. Coffee boiled over the sides of huge granite coffeepots, and casserole dishes of spaghetti and chili beans bubbled on the blackened grate above the open fire in the cement-sided stove. Men lounged on the crisp dry leaves at the edge of the bank, smoking and drinking beer and discussing values in secondhand cars, interrupting themselves occasionally to fetch and carry at the demand of their womenfolk.

Orville Gray stood around wondering perpetually what to say next. Bubbles of family reminiscence rose up in the surrounding conversations, to burst into exchanges of information about the number of children or cases of serious illness now being enjoyed by persons who were apparently not present on this occasion. Orville was sure that he would never sort out the names or the degree of kinship to Alison of the persons gathered around the tables.

As he toyed with this reflection a large man with rugged features and sandy hair combed thinly backward across a freckled scalp approached Alison from behind with clumsy, playful stealthiness to clasp his big hands roughly around her upper arms, bellowing simultaneously, "Smoky, old sock, ol' sock! How's the glamour gal?"

Orville noticed the strange expression that came over his new girl friend's face. It was obvious that Alison had instantly recognized her frolicsome assailant, and that gaiety was not her immediate response. Carefully she marshaled up a composed expression and turned in the man's grip.

"Hello, Uncle Maurice."

The big man, whose short-sleeved rayon shirt had a pattern of golf clubs, tennis rackets, and badminton birds sketched in violent chartreuse and purple hues on a coral background, brought an arm around the girl's shoulders and held her captive against his side while his eyes boldly sized up the startled Orville.

"So this is the latest one, eh?" Uncle Maurice laughed heartily. "Can't keep track of 'em. This kid has a new man on the string every time we see her." He chucked Alison under the chin. "Ain't that so, glamour girl?"

While his eyes and ears registered this byplay Orville's mind was dealing with the reflection that Alison had probably never impressed anyone as a glamour girl and that Uncle Maurice's persistent reference to her as such only served to underline the ways in which Alison differed from the current stereotype of female perfection. It was also quite clear that the man's insinuation that there was a succession of male escorts in her life was not calculated to have the effect of strengthening the girl's claims to charm but of diminishing them. The implication was only too clear that Alison could not hold a man. Seeing the pain in her eyes behind the perfunctory smile Alison was using as a foil against Uncle Maurice's chaffing, Orville felt a surprising rage dispelling his usual composure.

Florence's voice came to him. "Uncle Maurice," she said dryly, "is the family wit. Or so he thinks."

Alison was trying to make a dignified escape from the man's embrace. "This is my uncle Maurice," she said breathlessly, "Mr. Gray, Mr. Egstadt."

"Just call me Unc," the humorist chortled blithely, and with the flat of his hand struck his niece so soundly between the shoulder blades that she involuntarily lurched forward awkwardly. "Smoky'd like that, wouldn't you, Smoky?"

Orville achieved a sickly grin and an unintelligible mutter.

Florence intervened with generous intentions, lifting the painted tin cover from a cake resting on the paper tablecloth. "Oh, Allie, you brought one of your marvelous banana cakes. Yummy, yum-mee!"

"Sure you really made it with your own lily-white hands?" Uncle Maurice chuckled with a leer and turned his countenance upon Orville. "Allie ever tell you about the fried chicken she took to the box social, and the fellow that bought it got so enthused he almost proposed—till Bea let it slip she'd fixed the whole lunch for Allie because the kid here couldn't hardly boil water fit to drink. That boy sure cooled off, didn't he, Smoky?"

At that point a teen-age girl who had not yet greeted Uncle Maurice mercifully hurled herself at him from the rear, and he turned to chase the girl gleefully through the crowd.

Dully Alison watched the subsequent cavorting, thinking that it was odd:

Uncle Maurice went over big with the kids. They took his clowning and rough-housing ecstatically. It would probably be some years before young Peggy began to tremble inwardly at the sight of him.

Alison heard Florence speaking to Orville. "We always let strangers know as soon as possible that Uncle Maurice is no blood relation to the rest of us. It would be awful to think he was hereditary, like big ears or web toes."

Orville smiled politely and addressed Alison. "Why does he call you 'Smoky'?"

A slow flush dyed Alison's somewhat sallow skin. "It's an old family joke," she said nervously. "I—I've forgotten exactly myself." Abruptly she looked to the side and exclaimed, "Oh, here's Aunt Jocelyn. I don't think you've met her."

Jocelyn was the spinster of the Mallory family. No one really enjoyed her company, but she was fiercely respected. "Such a *good* woman." Jocelyn was sternly religious, having been converted some years back from the prevailing somewhat casual family Methodism to an evangelical sect with intransigent views about the Bible. Aunt Jocelyn engendered a somewhat nervous feeling among her relatives by her insistence that the end of the world was imminent and that their own wickedness was a contributing factor in this eventuality. Even Uncle Maurice restrained his boisterous good-fellowship when it came to Jocelyn. There were more reasons for his avoidance of his wife's spinster sister than simply the quality of her personality; but her righteous imperviousness to his ruthless jocularity would have been enough to account for Maurice's restraint where Jocelyn was concerned. There wasn't much fun in baiting people if you couldn't get at least a little rise out of them.

Jocelyn Mallory was the only woman present wearing a hat. It was a beige straw affair with a turned-up brim and polka-dotted veiling. She also had on a rayon print dress in subdued tints, and sensible black oxfords.

"How nice you look," Alison remarked when she had introduced Orville.

"I had to come straight from church in order to make it in time," the older woman volunteered seriously, and inspected the others through rimless glasses. "I don't suppose you two took the trouble to go this morning."

"I'm afraid not," Alison confessed weakly.

"Oh well," Aunt Jocelyn said resignedly, and let the subject lie there drearily between them.

Cousin Helen's voice rose piercingly, directed toward her twelve-year-old son. "Bradford! Bradford Farmer! What have you got?"

Everyone turned to look at Bradford. It was obvious that what he had was a shiny new rifle slung in one arm.

"Didn't I *tell* you," Helen wailed, "you could *not* bring that gun to the picnic?" Turning, she singled out her husband, who stood nearby. "You see,

Wilbur, I told you. I told you it was a mistake to give that kid a gun for his birthday. He'll maim somebody for life before he's through."

Maurice spoke up in a jovially chiding tone. "What's the matter with you, Helen? Every boy should learn to handle a gun. Makes a man out of him."

"Not on family picnics he shouldn't handle no gun. He keeps it loaded all the time."

Cousin Wilbur gave Cousin Maurice a sour look, and started for his mutinously pouting son. It was apparent that Cousin Wilbur wished Cousin Maurice would keep his nose out of other people's domestic disciplinary problems. It didn't help matters that Maurice Egstadt was the only member of the family to own a gun aside from hunting rifles or shotguns. Maurice always carried a .32-caliber revolver in the glove compartment of his car. He was, in fact, rather boastful about having a permit to carry a gun—because he was on the road so much.

"But, Maurice," Cousin Helen had protested one time, "you'd never actually use it on anybody."

"You're damn right I would. Anybody gets funny with Mr. M. J. Egstadt and they'll never live to try their tricks on anybody else."

So far as anyone knew, Maurice had never had occasion to "teach somebody a lesson" with his gun, but his relatives suspected that he would have welcomed a good safe excuse to do so.

Opening the rear door of the sedan parked at the edge of the picnic area, Wilbur laid the rifle on the floor. Turning, he glared at the children who were within hearing. "Any of you kids touch that gun today and I'll tan the seat of your britches." He looked down at Bradford. "I oughta take the hide off you right now. You were told not to bring that rifle."

"Cousin Fred said he'd give me some pointers on target shooting," Bradford muttered.

"He said that someday he'd take you out to the Rod and Gun Club rifle range," Helen pointed out with asperity. "You don't have target practice in crowded public places."

Just then attention was diverted from the Farmers' problems by Bea's apprehensive moan, "Oh my goodness, here they are! I'd better go warn them *he's* here so they'll be prepared."

David's little English sedan had just pulled in at the other end of the picnic site, down the row of cars parked in an inward-facing file parallel to the road. Beatrice, her rear end waggling frantically in the faded denim pedal-pushers someone ought to have dissuaded her from wearing, made for the machine where a young couple were disembarking.

"Just in time," Beatrice called as she came near. "We're going to sit down to eat right away. I'm so glad you could come."

Their embraces of welcome were a warm, triangular affair, kisses landing haphazardly on flushed cheeks and chins.

"We didn't expect him," Beatrice said with desperate cheeriness, "but your father is here too, David."

The handsome young man regarded her stonily. "You said they weren't coming."

"He wasn't—your father. He was in L.A. But he got back."

"You gave me to understand Mom wouldn't be here either," David said accusingly.

"Well, I thought that would be a nice surprise for you, Esther being here," Bea said weakly.

"It isn't. I don't want to see either one of them."

"Oh dear. Has something happened? Something else, I mean?"

The young woman spoke levelly. "Do they know we're coming?"

"Why, yes. I told Esther, and she was tickled to death." Determinedly Beatrice became cheerful again. "Oh, come on now. Let's all let bygones be bygones for today. After all, everybody's here. That makes it—well, just social. And," she concluded triumphantly, "it's not like being in the same house. Outdoors like this."

"We're leaving," David declared flatly, his full lips closing in a narrowed line.

The dark eyes of his wife rested first on David, then shifted to the distant tables, and finally returned to Aunt Bea. "I'd like to speak to David alone for a minute."

"All right. But—Davy—please. Let's not have a fuss. Everybody will think it's queer if you turn right around and go off again. And I did want things to be nice for Flo and Steven."

She moved away reluctantly, with a backward glance at her nephew's stormy face.

"Look," Renée said in a low voice. "We're stuck now, might as well make the best of it."

"You can sit at the same table with them, after what he did!"

"They'll know we walked out. He'll know then that we know what he did. You've never refused to at least be in the same crowd where he is. It would be a dead giveaway. Do you want to give him the satisfaction? Didn't we agree it was better if he thinks he got away with it?" Her voice was low and husky, importunate. "You know we figured it this way—if he thinks he got away with it, maybe he'll be satisfied, leave us alone in the future."

"It's my mother I can't stand to see," David growled.

"I know. But think how enraged he'll be if we walk out and the whole family knows it's because of him. He'll be so furious he's liable to try something else—something worse."

"This whole attitude—it's appeasement," David grumbled. His eyes lost their look of angry preoccupation as he regarded his wife painfully. "All right. If that's what you want. But God! I hate to see my mother."

"We can't blame her too much. She doesn't know what he did."

"People deserve blame for stupidity," he snapped. But he turned and pulled the picnic box from the back seat.

Peggy Nelson came running to meet the couple. Her eyes rested admiringly on Renée, whose sleek cap of black hair gleamed in the sun, framing her olive-skinned face in little pointed scallops.

"What a darling outfit!" Peggy ejaculated, eying the tight black cotton pants laced in white just above the shapely bare calves of Renée's legs.

"Hi, Dave," she greeted the tall young man with his cap of curly brown hair tousled from the breeze of driving.

The newcomers were exchanging embraces with Florence and meeting Steven when Esther came cooing toward them, arms outstretched. "I was so happy to hear you were coming."

Renée turned her cheek to catch Esther's kiss. David did not lower his head nor move his arms as his mother put her hands on his shoulders and managed to reach his chin with her lips.

"'Lo, Mom," he said woodenly.

Amid the turbulence of greetings and unpacking of food which followed, Esther stood still, at a loss. But apparently she decided to overlook the rebuff she had met with and was soon busily making inefficient motions about place settings for the newcomers. After all, Esther had had long and expert experience in overlooking things she did not wish to recognize.

On the bank where the men had gathered in the shade of one sycamore whose roots had caught hold near the top of the incline, loud, argumentative noises were becoming noticeable. The men lay with shoulders propped against a log at the edge of the bank or, with arms clasping knees, sat on the papery leaves which mingled with the powdery dust underfoot.

"Oh my goodness," Beatrice said, "we'd better break that up and get to the table. They're talking politics again. I do wish they wouldn't. It makes me so *nervous*."

The Mallorys were solidly of the Democratic way of thinking, except for Fred; and they blamed his defection partly on Jane, who came from a long line of conservative small-town business people, and partly on the fact that Fred had become the most prosperous member of the family by way of his successful paint contracting business, thereby gradually coming to take a dim view of "coddling labor" and "government interference," activities which he ascribed to the Democratic party.

Any gathering of the relatives was likely to degenerate into a political argument where much misinformation was exchanged with dogmatic assurance and where prejudice was proclaimed in the name of pure cerebration.

It was a source of exacerbating annoyance to Fred that his political views gained support in only one quarter. Maurice was also a Republican. Fred would rather have stood alone in noble martyrdom than find himself handicapped by such an ally. The others took it for granted that naturally Maurice would be an enemy of the country's welfare and progress. It was doubly painful, however, that the renegade Fred should always be supporting the same candidates Maurice did.

When Maurice was present no one really enjoyed a good loud debate filled with non sequiturs the way they did when they had Fred cornered by himself. The men's anger at the obtuseness of the opposition took on a sharper and more choleric quality when Maurice was mixed up in the discussion.

So it was with relief that they raised their heads at the cries of "Come and get it!"

Maurice advanced upon the groaning board at the far end from that where his son and daughter-in-law were climbing into their places. Standing with one foot inside the plank seat, one outside, he called with jocund facetiousness, "Hi, Junior. I see you made it up here in that little limey rattletrap of yours."

David raised his eyes incredulously, and involuntarily nodded a response.

"Hi, Renée," the irrepressible man added and, without waiting for a reply, lifted his other leg over the plank and dropped heavily into place, seizing a knife in one hand, a fork in the other, and banging the table with their handle ends. "Well, I'm here. What's holding things up? Let's eat!"

"Oh, Maurice, can't you ever behave yourself? Always cutting up," his wife reproved in a laughing tone that was supposed to give the others their cue that this wasn't really uncouth manners on Maurice's part, just boyish good spirits. Even those closest to Esther in the family could never be sure whether she really did think her husband was a regular card or whether she acted as she did to cover her humiliation at his behavior.

"Squaw keep mouth shut when Big Chief belly empty," Maurice enjoined with mock ferocity. "Squaw bringum food. Big Chief eatum."

Peggy and Fred's Leo and three younger children giggled delightedly, and Esther retorted playfully, "Now you just wait for everybody else, or I'll Big Chief you." She appealed archly to the adults getting settled near them, "Isn't he the limit?"

Several people smiled halfheartedly. You couldn't let Esther down, had to make a show of playing up.

Grant Nelson, Bea's son, said jokingly, "Somebody stick a drumstick in his mouth. That'll shut him up."

In riposte Uncle Maurice tilted a tray and dumped six liverwurst sandwiches into Grant's plate, to the practically suffocating amusement of every child in the party.

With Maurice and Esther at one end of the long picnic board and David and Renée at the other, conviviality burgeoned with more freedom from constraint than might have been expected. Sunlight wavered capriciously through the boughs overhead, causing those at the north end of the table to do a certain amount of shifting to get into the flickering shade; for the sun had outsmarted the original layout and in its northward movement managed to glare down on the heads of those sitting at the corner.

One could not say there was conversation. Many words were hurled back and forth through the warm, slightly dusty, coffee-scented air, but they consisted mostly of such ejaculations as:

"Flo, did you have some of Aunt Jossy's bread-and-butter pickles? They're simply dee-licious!"

"Hey," with heavy jocularity, "how about passing that chicken this way for a change! Whatta you think you're doing at that end of the table, gonna hog all the best parts?"

"Alison, you're not eating a *thing*. Here, have some of Aunt Jane's potato salad. Honestly, Jane, I don't know how you *do* it; I always make a pig of myself over your potato salad."

"It's the mustard. And just the right amount of pimiento—"

"Bea, did you make these beans? Well, I want your recipe—"

"Peggy, see if Aunt Sarah got a piece of the breast—"

"Sharon, no *more* dill pickles—"

"Did you say Cousin Vera was expecting her *fifth?* In October? Well, I just don't see how they make out. We can't hardly get by with just three of us—"

"Oh, I meant to tell you, Esther, I had a nice long letter from Aunt Frannie. She hasn't been a bit well—"

"Well, I just told Lester, if I don't get a dryer before the rain starts this winter, I'm just going to send every stitch to the laundry. Lil Huston next door got one, and she just wouldn't be without it—"

Uncle Maurice handed the jello to Cousin Wilbur in such a way that Wilbur stuck his thumb and three fingers into the whipped cream clear to the first knuckles. In withdrawing and shaking the fingers some of the cream got flipped onto Uncle Marvin's new nylon shirt, which he'd never worn before, and another drop landed in Orville's eye, much to the consternation of the relatives nearest him. But the children were fit to burst, laughing.

Looking back on the dreadful day afterward, various members of the family remarked wistfully, "Well, anyhow, the dinner was nice. Everybody having such a good time. I remember thinking at the time how lovely it was, all of us being together and laughing and jolly."

TWO
Jocelyn

Rising up through the froth of jollity into the minds of several in the party were bitter memories and present anxieties.

Jocelyn Mallory had found herself sitting so close to her brother-in-law that she could hear Maurice's raucously bantering voice and see his powerful hands as they moved out to spear passing tidbits with a predatory fork.

Grab, grab, grab. So typical of Maurice's character. If it were not that she had always been so fond of her delicate little sister Esther, and if it were not that Esther was technically innocent of complicity in the perpetuation of her spouse's sins, Jocelyn would never have maintained the cold civility she had granted Maurice all these years.

When others of the family in private conclave of two or three declared disapprovingly, "I don't see how Esther can be so blind. How can she defend him against everybody the way she does?" Jocelyn did not share their real or pretended mystification. The obvious answer, "Well, I suppose she loves him," was not the whole story. Jocelyn, the unmarried one, knew better than the others why and how in Esther's situation a woman could deceive herself into loyalty.

Maurice was, unevenly but in the long pull reliably, a good provider. So far as anyone knew, he did not chase other women. He was not a drinking man. And he did not beat his wife. Physically, that is. The beating of sly ridicule couched in terms that disguised it as affectionate teasing left the victim ashamed to take offense. It was easier to interpret the barbed raillery as an inverted compliment.

And he was a man, a husband. You were not alone, and you were not helpless against the world when there was a husband between it and you.

When Esther was first married none of them had hated or even particularly disliked Maurice. Jocelyn's eyes fell on Cousin Helen's little boy across the table, saw the titillated expectancy on the child's face as he watched Uncle Maurice, waiting for the next practical joke or broad verbal quip. Just as children were captivated by the excitement he gen-erated—in their immaturity being incapable of deeper judgment of human behavior—so most adults were, on short acquaintance, taken in by Maurice.

Jocelyn herself had found the man stimulating during his brief courtship of Esther. The constant joshing of Big Sister, the boisterous, ostensibly affectionate clutches at and wrestlings with her person had seemed like naive masculine high spirits. At least when someone was teasing you, they were noticing you; and everybody likes attention. It took a little time to become aware of the small wounds Maurice inflicted sharply down deep in his victims' sensibilities; for the sense of gratification one experienced at being the object of this bluff creature's banter had a temporarily anesthetizing effect.

Jocelyn had grown tough with the years, however, and eventually could have remained aloof, have rebuffed the man decisively to protect herself against these gadfly hurts, if he had not chosen to inflict a blow where it did lasting and concrete damage to her life.

Jocelyn had never expected to be an old maid. Sardonically she reflected to herself that for this at least she couldn't blame Maurice. Even now she was not sure how it had happened that she alone of the three Mallory girls had not found a man. Somehow it had always been that the ones she could get she didn't want and the ones she wanted she couldn't get.

Jocelyn was the middle child, between Fred and Alison's father, Arthur, who had been killed in an automobile accident. After Jocelyn finished high school she went to work in the Penney store in Los Alegres, and when she had been there for six years she realized with some dismay that all the other children were married, even Esther, the youngest. Jocelyn was the only one living at home with Ma and Pa.

Then Pa developed a heart ailment that forced him to retire from his job with the Pacific Gas and Electric Company, for whom he had worked so many years, and about the same time the arthritic condition which had bothered Ma off and on began to get worse, until the first thing they knew she couldn't go up and down stairs and found any movement increasingly difficult. Pa was incapable of keeping the housework up decently; and after many and sometimes heated conferences it was decided that Jocelyn should stay home and look after the folks. With Pa's pension, and the ten dollars per month per family the other kids promised to contribute, and the rent for the two upstairs bedrooms which they decided to let to nice quiet schoolteachers, and with the occasional day's work Jocelyn obtained at the store during sales or busy seasons, everything would work out fine. And the other children all agreed that when the folks died the house should go to Jocelyn.

Jocelyn had not objected to this arrangement. It was less confining than working steady in the store; and her wages had been so low that it was small sacrifice to give them up and take over the management of the household finances. Furthermore, the prospect of inheriting the four-bedroom family home promised future security.

After the folks died she rented the third bedroom and made out nicely by continuing to serve as an extra saleswoman at the store on Saturdays.

When she rented the front downstairs bedroom to Mrs. Witherspoon, Jocelyn did not think much about it. The Witherspoons were a childless couple who owned a ranch several miles out of town, and Eustacia Witherspoon had always been considered a little odd—flighty, sort of.

When Eustacia became a widow she leased the ranch and looked around for a place to live in town. The Mallorys' front bedroom with its bay window and nice little writing desk and chintz-covered easy chair was just what she wanted. And it was within walking distance of downtown; that was one big advantage.

"I don't ever want to do another tap of housework as long as I live," she told Jocelyn saucily, and blinked her mascaraed eyelashes girlishly. Mrs. Witherspoon's pale pink hair escaped in frail cylinders from under a dainty white hat; and at her other extremity plump ankles bulged a little in the embrace of the white kid ankle straps of high-heeled sandals.

"I just want to relax and enjoy myself. I intend to go to the movies every time the bill changes and eat out downtown every single night."

Jocelyn agreed to let Mrs. Witherspoon prepare her own breakfast at the house.

"All I have is orange juice and coffee and toast. But it's just too gruesome to have to get up and into a girdle and make-up and shoes and all to go out for it."

Jocelyn charged Mrs. Witherspoon ten dollars a month more than she would have anyone else and hoped for the best out of the arrangement.

Mrs. Witherspoon exhibited an immediate taste for sitting in the living room and "visiting" with her landlady. Jocelyn circumvented this inclination on the part of her "guest" by retiring to the platform rocker in her own sunny back bedroom, listening to the table radio while she crocheted afghans for Christmas presents, or reading the *True Confessions* magazines, which were her secret vice.

It was impossible to escape Mrs. Witherspoon in the morning, however. After her meager breakfast she would station herself at the kitchen table, drinking coffee and smoking cigarettes and looking grotesque without lipstick or eye make-up, her head compressed into a billiard-ball shape by the coarse lavender hair net she slept in, her feet cozy in red leather moccasins bordered with white fur.

Jocelyn became the recipient of innumerable autobiographical confidences which covered Eustacia's childhood, youth, and subsequent connubial situation with Ralph. Quite often Mrs. Witherspoon would become lachrymose over her present solitary state.

"I envy you, Miss Mallory," she would declare mournfully, "with your sisters and brothers all living near you. Everybody always says what a wonderful family you are, get along so well together. 'The Mallorys are so close,' people always say."

"Yes," Jocelyn agreed mildly, "it is nice having your people near."

"You know, living here in the old home makes me feel sort of part of your family—in a way." Mrs. Witherspoon uttered a self-conscious laugh. "Do you want me to tell you something? You'll think it's awfully silly. But you know, sometimes I sort of pretend you're my sister. It gives me a good feeling, even though I know it's just make-believe."

Jocelyn regarded her roomer with softened eyes. The woman was a fool and a bore, but you couldn't help feeling sorry for her. Mrs. Witherspoon had enough money so that she didn't have to worry about sheer survival. But that was all she did have. Otherwise the poor woman's life was rather vacant.

"That's—uh—sweet of you," Jocelyn rejoined with some embarrassment.

On another day, after she had been in residence for several months, Mrs. Witherspoon, in discoursing upon her financial affairs, which she constantly referred to with naive candor, observed archly, "You know, I won't have a single heir when I die. Isn't that strange, when you stop to think of it? And I've been thinking that the closest thing I have to a family is my pretend sister." She regarded Jocelyn with an expectant smile.

After that remark, somehow Jocelyn began to feel more tolerant toward the tiresome little woman. There were acres of fine apricot orchards on the ranch, and the buildings were solid and up-to-date. Gradually Jocelyn found herself treating Mrs. Witherspoon more like a sister. When ladies came for afternoon coffee, Jocelyn invited Eustacia to join them; she took her along to family dinners at Thanksgiving and Christmas, occasions upon which you just couldn't leave the poor thing sitting at home alone.

If it had not been for this sisterliness which had sprung up between them, Jocelyn might have sent Mrs. Witherspoon packing when the older woman's weakness became manifest. In her little shopping trips and excursions downtown for dinner Eustacia discovered what fun it was to drop into the Hotel Caballero bar for an occasional cocktail. The bartenders, both local boys she had known for years, kidded with her and made her feel happy; and there was almost always a lone beer drinker or two who would permit Mrs. Witherspoon to engage him in conversation. She found the Rodeo Room a very cozy spot in which to kill time. This patronage of the Caballero bar might have proved a fairly innocent diversion except that through these calls Mrs. Witherspoon belatedly discovered the agreeable effects of alcohol to be irresistible.

The first time Mrs. Witherspoon had to hang onto the porch railing with both hands as she struggled up the front steps Jocelyn became alarmed. And when she found later on that Eustacia had taken to keeping a pint in her room so that she could have a little nip now and then "to settle her nerves," Jocelyn decided she would have to do something about it.

Dr. Henderson had attended most of the Mallory family for most of their lives; and Jocelyn appealed to him. In his office she came right to the point. "There's nothing wrong with me, Doctor. It's my roomer, Mrs.

Witherspoon."

Succinctly she described Eustacia's growing addiction. "Dr. Resnick was their doctor," Jocelyn went on, "but since he died Mrs. Witherspoon hasn't been seeing anyone regularly. She goes to that chiropractor on Fourth Street sometimes; but that's the extent of it. So if I can get her to come to you for a checkup, will you please, Doctor, scare the daylights out of her about drinking? Tell her it's curdling her liver or paralyzing her kidneys or something. I simply cannot have an alcoholic on my hands."

The physician smiled. "I can't promise to frighten her, but I can with a clear conscience inform anyone that excessive intake of alcohol is damaging and that in special cases even small amounts can be downright dangerous."

"Can't you arrange to make Eustacia one of those 'special' cases?"

"I'll do my best to talk her into greater temperance. That I can certainly do in good faith, no matter what her present physical condition is."

Mrs. Witherspoon had so little to do with her time that she proved easily amenable to the idea of an afternoon call at Dr. Henderson's office.

"Just for a checkup," Jocelyn encouraged. "I go in myself regularly once a year. That way you feel safe."

After the call Mrs. Witherspoon confided ruefully, "There's nothing really wrong with me, it seems, except my liver isn't doing *just* what it ought to. And the doctor says I have to cut down on drinking, just one cocktail before dinner and a nightcap occasionally if I feel I must. Oh dear, and I *have* come to enjoy a few quiet drinks now and then, to relax me."

"Well, the doctor knows best," Jocelyn averred smugly. The physician's advice put a temporary brake on Mrs. Witherspoon's consumption of "little nips"; and Jocelyn conscientiously set herself to making greater efforts toward keeping Eustacia amused. She taught her to play gin rummy, and a few games before bedtime became a nightly ritual. The winter that Mrs. Witherspoon contracted pneumonia Jocelyn visited her religiously at the hospital and tended her faithfully through convalescence. The older woman still bored Jocelyn. Frivolous elderly women who had their thinning hair dyed an unsuccessful strawberry blond, who wore high-heeled slippers with platform soles, and who fancied off-the-shoulder blouses and jangling silver bracelets just weren't Jocelyn's type.

But Mrs. Witherspoon paid more than anyone else for her room and she was getting older all the time, thus bringing closer for Jocelyn the fascinating prospect of someday owning and either selling them or living off the income from all those lovely acres of rich valley land with their potentially valuable frontage on a main highway.

Maurice and Esther were still living in Los Alegres then, and David was a serious, handsome little boy. Naturally Mrs. Witherspoon met Maurice in the course of her association with the family. From the first she was greatly impressed by Esther's husband. Maurice flirted outrageously with "the old girl," and Eustacia never caught on that he was thereby crudely making fun of her. But Jocelyn did, and she found it irritating.

One winter Mrs. Witherspoon bought a pair of shiny black rubber rain boots with a red band around the top and little leather tassels, each of which was decorated with a tiny silver bell that tinkled when she walked. It was then that Maurice chose Puss-in-Boots as her nickname. Eustacia glowed fatuously, and loved it even more when Maurice shortened the pet name to Puss.

"Sickening," Jocelyn stated privately to her sister Bea.

And Bea returned, "Honestly, I feel embarrassed for her. Can't she see he's poking fun? An old woman like that."

In his presence Jocelyn stoically pretended not to notice her brother-in-law's underhanded baiting of her paying guest.

But when, one evening after Mrs. Witherspoon's long recuperation from pneumonia, Maurice brought the woman home at ten o'clock, holding her with an arm about her waist, the while Eustacia grinned foolishly and gazed upon the world with glassy eyes, Jocelyn broke her silence.

"Wait in the front room," she commanded Maurice curtly.

"I can't hang around," Maurice demurred plaintively, "Esther's expecting me."

"Wait for me in there, or I'll be over to your house and have my say in front of Esther."

So Maurice lingered sulkily while Jocelyn got Mrs. Witherspoon to bed, a procedure interrupted twice while Eustacia had to be supported into the bathroom, there to be good and sick.

Jocelyn entered the living room speaking. "What do you mean, taking that poor old thing out and getting her drunk?"

"*I* got her drunk! All I did was run into her downtown this afternoon and ask her if she wanted to go for a drive over to Coast City. I had some business over there; and I thought the old gal would enjoy getting out."

At that time Maurice was trying, not too successfully, to be a real estate broker. His explanation of the trip sounded reasonable.

"She didn't get in that shape just from going for a ride," Jocelyn retorted sharply.

"So I got held up, and we had dinner over there. I phoned Esther to tell her I wouldn't be able to get home for dinner," he explained virtuously.

"I see. And after dinner you bought Eustacia all the booze she could hold."

"How was I to know she couldn't hold her liquor?"

"Maurice Egstadt, you ought to be ashamed of yourself! You could tell she was getting soused. You could have brought her home."

Maurice had been lounging with offensive negligence in the deepest overstuffed chair, and now he lifted himself to his feet belligerently.

"Look here, what right do you think you've got to be laying down the law to me? Or to anybody else, for that matter."

"Mrs. Witherspoon lives with me, and she's all alone in the world, and it's my duty to look after her; that's what right I've got. And if you had any sense of decency you wouldn't take an old woman out and pour liquor down her!"

"Now, you look here—" he blustered, glowering.

"No. You look." Jocelyn boldly took the truth in both hands and stretched it a little. "Mrs. Witherspoon is allergic to alcohol. Dr. Henderson told her to lay off it. If she takes too much it might kill her."

"Well, how was I to know she can't take a cocktail or two, and a few highballs after dinner? Look at me; am *I* drunk?"

"No, but you're not a frail little woman who just got over pneumonia a few months ago. And you're not in your sixties either, like she is."

"So O.K. Now I know. You don't have to act as if I was trying to bump the old dame off."

"Well, I just wanted to impress it on your mind. After all, I'm the one has to look after her when she gets sick."

Mrs. Witherspoon felt terrible the next morning; but by the second day she was her usual chipper self. She even seemed a little complacent over her dissipation as she recounted the evening's highlights to Jocelyn, who listened in a somewhat dour manner.

The fact that she had survived a good soaking drunk and the subsequent hangover seemed to embolden Mrs. Witherspoon into gradually slipping back to daily visits to the Rodeo Room. But as far as Jocelyn could tell, Eustacia refrained from caching any more bottles in her bedroom, nor did Maurice openly take the woman pub-crawling again.

One Sunday, however, when Jocelyn was entertaining the family at two o'clock dinner, which she did conscientiously once every six months, she became quite certain as the day progressed that Maurice had a flask with him and that he and Eustacia were acting like naughty children, mischievously slipping apart from time to time for a "quick snort," as Maurice would inelegantly term it.

Although her manner remained cold and even more prim than usual, Jocelyn was beside herself with fury. She couldn't blame Mrs. Witherspoon too much. To Eustacia's simple mind this was just an amusing game thought up for her delectation by that enchanting, fun-loving man.

But Jocelyn had no illusions as to Maurice's motives. He was slyly taunting his hostess by flouting her wishes.

Even so, Jocelyn never tumbled to what Maurice was really up to. His double-edged flattery of the old lady, his covert egging her on to drink more than she ought, Jocelyn had put down as simply the way Maurice was.

He knew it annoyed his sister-in-law, and he was constitutionally incapable of refraining from tormenting another person if he saw an easy way of doing so.

Mrs. Witherspoon had been with Jocelyn for over eight years when she died. Her death was rather sudden. She had entered the hospital for a minor operation, and two days after the surgery a blood clot struck her heart.

Jocelyn was honestly grieved. She had grown fond of the silly little creature. And used to having her around. But she could not deny a certain feeling of relief. In many ways she had been as tied down by Eustacia Witherspoon as if she had been legally responsible for the woman.

And now she was free. She did not have to consider Eustacia's comfort, did not have to worry about keeping her entertained, nor about leaving her alone for a few days or a week.

Jocelyn tried not to think too joyfully about the land which would soon be hers. The town had been growing out that way; motels and supermarkets and roadside inns were creeping down the highway toward the old Witherspoon place. One new subdivision had already sprung up nearby. Jim Lucas, the attorney who had served both the Mallorys and the Witherspoons for many years, telephoned to ask Jocelyn to come into his office at three the day after the funeral.

Jocelyn had to hold herself deliberately to a sedate pace as she walked down Main Street and around the corner on Hydrangea Street. She felt like striding along with a jaunty swing. Guiltily she pulled her face into sober lines as she mounted the stairs to Jim's office. She was sorry, really sorry for Eustacia, and she would miss the poor little thing. But it was stimulating to be an heiress.

When the secretary ushered her into Lucas's private office, Jocelyn was surprised to find Maurice sitting back with legs carelessly crossed in one of the chairs that faced Jim's across the desk. Maurice made a show of rising when his sister-in-law entered. At least he uncrossed his legs and brought his buttocks a few inches off the chair seat.

Mrs. Witherspoon must have mentioned Maurice in her will, some trifling bequest to demonstrate her virtual hero worship of the man. Jocelyn settled back composedly to hear Jim Lucas read the document he brought out of a folder on his desk. When he had finished, she just sat there, numb. Her eyes moved like mechanical things, to rest for a second or two on Maurice's smugly grave face.

The beneficiary of the two-thousand-dollar life-insurance policy had been Jocelyn, with an agreement that Miss Mallory would pay Mrs. Witherspoon's final hospital and funeral expenses. Jocelyn had known this. Already the commitments were made; and there would be about two hundred dollars left over. At her death Mrs. Witherspoon had possessed some three hundred dollars in a checking account in the First National Bank. This came to Jocelyn. But the ranch went lock, stock, and barrel to Eustacia Witherspoon's dear friend, Maurice Egstadt.

Jocelyn caught the commiserating glance Jim Lucas sent her from under his lashes as he carefully folded the document.

Maurice spoke unctuously. "This certainly comes as a surprise to me. I had no idea the old girl thought so much of me." He shook his head, sighing lugubriously.

Jocelyn looked at him dully; then she stood up, holding her black cotton gloves pulled out tightly in both hands.

"If that's all, Jim," she said hollowly, "I'll be going."

Maurice rose in clumsy haste. "Let me drive you home."

"No," she said, "I want to walk."

When she had gone out the lawyer observed, "This has been a shock to Jocelyn."

"To me too," Maurice asserted defensively.

"Yes?" the attorney said dryly.

In her living room at home Jocelyn sat in the center of the davenport with her hat and coat on, her handbag in her lap, still holding the pair of gloves, which she had not put back on all the way home.

Gradually the stunned feeling was wearing off. She twisted the gloves as if she were in pain. Then she threw them aside on the cushions, pushed her handbag off her lap, and lifted her hands to remove the stylish black straw hat she had bought for the funeral. She laid it on the end table and automatically smoothed the rolls of hair rising from her forehead. She pushed the black gabardine coat back on her shoulders and stared with increasing awareness in her eyes at the coffee table in front of her.

Oddly enough, her first anger was at herself. She pounded her fist into the palm of her other hand.

How could she have been so blind? Why had she not seen what he was up to and circumvented him somehow? It was imbecilic not to have suspected Maurice's attentions to Mrs. Witherspoon. The very fact that he had treated the woman more decently than he did most people should have alerted Jocelyn. She clasped her temples in her hands and cried silently to herself, "How could I have been so stupid!"

Right under her nose that monster had made away with *her* inheritance. Played up to the silly creature, flattered her, helped her to obtain liquor when Jocelyn made it difficult—who knew, perhaps even made love to her.

Slowly her rage turned fully on Maurice. Jocelyn rose and moved jerkily, frantically, about the room, uttering an occasional moaning cry. Eight years! Eight years of playing nursemaid, giving up her own time, being bored, getting up nights to look after the woman when she was ill, inflicting Eustacia on Jocelyn's own friends, some of whom had even quietly dropped her from their social calendar because they didn't want to be bothered by that odd Mrs. Witherspoon, who was certainly no asset to anyone's social orbit but who seemed to have to go everywhere with Jocelyn.

And the future. The bright, beautiful future based on owning the Witherspoon property. The ranch had provided for Eustacia with her narrow, unimaginative tastes. It would have kept Jocelyn in far more fulfilling style. And now she was left just where she had been before, with only this house and a few days' work a month at the store. And eight years older. Thirty-seven now.

She had never really hated anyone in her life; but now Jocelyn learned what it felt like to hate. With mild astonishment she realized that she could understand—something she had never really comprehended before—how one human being could kill another. It was a form of self-defense, really.

The rest of the family, when they heard what had happened, were horrified. To a man, they were on Jocelyn's side.

Fred, with a brother's license, even told Esther what he and the others thought of it.

"It's a damn shame," he fumed. "Poor old Joss, putting up with that crackpot all this time, and then Maurice coming in and scooping up the gravy. I don't know how you can sit there and defend him, doing such a thing to your own sister."

"Now, Fred Mallory," Esther protested with unconvincing spirit, "don't you talk that way about Maurice! Is it his fault if the old lady adored him? He treated her like a human being, and she appreciated it."

"Bullshit," Fred rejoined coarsely.

"I'll have none of that kind of talk from you, Fred Mallory. You can just apologize this minute."

"Apologize hell. What kind of a woman are you anyway, letting that big four-flusher get away with money that your own sister earned, fair and square?"

"As far as that goes," Esther retorted with specious defiance, "we had every intention of doing something for Jocelyn, maybe buying the house from her for a good cash price with what we get out of the ranch. Maurice and I discussed it—"

"Big deal," Fred grunted.

"But," Esther continued aggrievedly, "after the way she's been talking about Maurice, trying to set everyone against him, he doesn't feel like doing a thing for her. It has hurt him dreadfully, Jocelyn's attitude, the way she acts as if he was dishonest or something. After all, under his bluff exterior, Maurice is very sensitive."

"Bull—" Fred began, and altered the epithet to "Bulloney!"

Esther's eyes had filled with nervous tears, and she cried out desperately, "None of you understand Maurice. You're all just jealous—because he's so—so forceful and—and virile."

Her chin was trembling as she gazed at her brother imploringly.

Fred regarded her, baffled. "By God, Esther, I just don't understand you." And with that he let the matter drop.

Among the family, however, they discussed the affair with hopeless non-comprehension.

"How she can defend that man," Bea complained, "is more than I can see. And Esther was always fairly bright. Did better than the rest of us in school, for that matter."

"He's got her buffaloed. Like under a spell," Fred observed gloomily.

"Not, I must say," Bea went on primly, "that Marvin and I were really surprised. After *our* experience," she added meaningly, "we ought to have known nothing was too low for him to stoop to."

"Well, after this," Jocelyn put in bitterly, "I think we ought to drop him permanently. Naturally I'll never speak to that—that—*toad* again as long as I live. And I'll be very disappointed if any of the rest of you ever go near him again either."

"I suppose that's how it will have to be," Bea said regretfully, "although poor Esther isn't really to blame. She hasn't any more influence than—than a mosquito on that man. And David is such a lovely boy. It's just too bad to shut him and Esther out of the family."

"Too bad," Fred said mordantly, "he doesn't just up and die."

Bea sighed. "That's the kind just never *do* die. They just go on and on making everybody else miserable."

Maurice had the grace to keep out of his relatives' way for several months. His real estate business had been limping badly; but now he was suddenly the big man of affairs, making trips to the county seat and even to San Francisco. As soon as the estate was settled, he began negotiations to sell the ranch. At first he had thought of setting himself up as a subdivider, hacking the orchards up into one-acre plots and making a deal with some contractor for building ranch-type houses for sale; but a prosperous middle western farmer who had sold out back East and decided to try his luck in the milder climate of California appeared magically on the scene, prepared to pay thirty thousand dollars cash for a good ranch; and Maurice could not resist such a juicy lump sum, more than any of the Mallorys had ever possessed in cash or ever been worth in property.

"It won't last long; you'll see," Fred pronounced gloomily.

Maurice bustled around importantly for several months, looking for a good opportunity in a business way. When he found an opening that he considered suitable to a man of his present means, it was in Valdale, twenty miles inland from Los Alegres. He bought into partnership in an agricultural produce packing firm and looked forward to becoming a vegetable tycoon.

"That's good, that is," Bea's husband Marvin said scornfully when he heard of the new enterprise, "him not knowing a potato from a turnip, hardly."

By the time the Egstadts moved to Valdale the breach in family relations had already begun to close up a little. Esther had determinedly refused to recognize the hostile chill among her relatives. She continued to telephone their houses—just to see how they were. She went on dropping in on Bea, despite their tearful quarrels on her first few visits after the reading of the will. And she deliberately used Junior, as Maurice persisted in calling David, as a wedge to keep the family contacts open. Even Jocelyn could not slam the door in her nephew's face when he bounced up the front steps, bringing a sheaf of chrysanthemums Esther had sent. David played frequently with his cousins Alison and Florence and Little Bea, and their parents could hardly close the door against the likable boy who was only dimly aware that his folks were in bad with the rest of the Mallorys.

Finally one day Esther bravely marched right in to Jocelyn's kitchen, opening the door without knocking.

Jocelyn looked up startled from where she was kneeling beside the cooler, getting out apples for sauce. She came erect slowly and said, "I wouldn't think you'd have the nerve, Esther Mallory."

Esther's face quivered. "Jocelyn, we can't go on like this. We've always been so close, you and I. Think how poor dear Ma would feel if she knew her girls had become estranged," she gulped emotionally.

"Ma would understand perfectly," Jocelyn said coldly.

And then Esther began to cry. She put her hands over her face and stumbled to a chair beside the table.

"Please don't treat me like this, Joss. I can't stand it. It's awful, having everybody hate me, when I haven't done a thing," she sobbed. "Was it *my* fault that horrid old woman got a crush on Maurice?"

Jocelyn stared down at her younger sister helplessly. After a moment she burst out in exasperation, "Oh, shut up, Esther! You know I never could stand to see you cry."

"I'm so mi-i-iserable," Esther whimpered. "My family means so much to me, all of you; and *I* never did anything." She put her head down on her arms and wailed softly.

Jocelyn let out an exasperated breath. It was true. Esther hadn't actually done anything. Being fair, Jocelyn admitted that Esther had probably been as thunderstruck as she herself had been when she learned of Mrs. Witherspoon's bequest. It would simply never occur to Esther that Maurice had been scheming and plotting against a member of her own family. Esther would be incapable of believing such a thing of Maurice.

Jocelyn's lips tightened angrily as she stood gazing at her sister's heaving shoulders. It was pathetic, and horrifying, to think of your own little sister being married to that odious man and being so unaware of her own fate. In spite of herself, Jocelyn felt pity for Esther. She gritted her teeth and touched the bowed shoulders in their cardigan sweater.

"Pull yourself together, Tess—" She halted, and her lips drew back from her teeth in an annoyed grimace as she heard the old pet name escape her lips. "I'll fix you a cup of coffee," she said abruptly.

Esther raised her head and dabbed at her cheeks with her fingertips. "Oh, Jossy, I've been so unhappy. I can't bear to be on the outs with you."

"Just one thing," Jocelyn warned severely, dumping coffee into the silex. "Keep that man away from me. I'll not be responsible for what I might do if he ever crosses my path again."

"I'm sorry you're so bitter," Esther said plaintively, adding hastily as she caught her sister's baleful glance, "I know you can't help it, dear. We'll just not talk about it," she finished with too-sudden cheeriness.

Jocelyn gave her sister a cynically wondering look. For a girl who had been so bright in some ways, it was incredible that Esther could be so dull in others.

With time and the new twenty-mile distance between the Egstadts and the rest of the family, most of them settled down into a grudging acceptance of Maurice's occasional presence among them. Esther was so almost hysterically determined to maintain amicable relations that it was impossible not to give in, little by little.

Even Jocelyn relented on the second Christmas after Eustacia's death and accepted the invitation to Fred's and Jane's dinner, knowing full well that Maurice would be there. In the crowd of children and garrulous adults, they avoided one another's eyes and managed not to have to speak directly to each other. Afterward Jocelyn felt sourly noble and martyred over her generous Christian spirit.

The whole family noticed a change in Jocelyn after what came to be recollected as the Witherspoon Trouble. She began to evolve into the typical Old Maid Aunt, a little more tart in speech, a little more narrow in opinion, a little more prudish in behavior. No one was really surprised when Jocelyn left the Methodist Church and joined the Messengers of God. Although they all spoke as if it were a seven-day wonder and as if they could hardly believe it, somehow, deep in their hearts, they had been prepared for some such development in Jocelyn's life.

At first she attended a few services with her old school friend, Ida, who was married and had four children and lived down the street with her husband, who was the custodian at the high school. Ida had grown dowdy from childbearing and struggling to make ends meet on George's inadequate salary; but in her religion she seemed to find something that gave life color and zest. Jocelyn could not help seeing that Ida was really a happy woman.

The Messengers of God disapproved of almost everything—liquor and tobacco naturally, playing cards, social dancing, the theater in all its forms, and even many organized sports. They were absolutely certain of the imperishable correctness of their own version of the Bible's message to mankind and completely intolerant of other faiths based on the Holy Writ. As far as the Messengers were concerned, the Presbyterians and the Catholics, for instance, had no more prospects in the future that came after death than did atheists or Mohammedans.

Jocelyn slipped with surprising ease and rather frightening fervor into the Messengers' strait jacket of self-denial in worldly things and certitude of infallibility in spiritual matters. She was willing to expatiate at length to her restive kinfolk on how she had been reborn by faith; and she missed few opportunities to do evangelical work among them. They were constant recipients of pamphlets and tracts spreading the gospel as the Messengers of God saw it.

As time went on Jocelyn came more and more to view the world as a place infested by the forces of evil in human form. Maurice Egstadt, naturally, was one of the most dramatic examples of the satanic presence.

Here, today at the picnic, it was brought home to Jocelyn more vividly than ever before what an embodiment of wickedness the man was. She had always felt a sympathy for poor little Alison; and Jocelyn winced for her niece's sake as she was forced to sit by helplessly, watching the man poke sly fun at the girl in the presence of her new young man. Jocelyn lowered her eyes in shame to avoid seeing Maurice's lewd behavior as he pinioned young Peggy to his side with an arm about the child's waist while she squealed and kicked hilariously in a sham attempt to escape.

Jocelyn had hardly been able to look at her sister Esther after the arrival of David and Renée. It was too painful. Jocelyn could tell that something was wrong, much wronger even than usual, and that beneath her desperate social pretense of gaiety Esther was strained almost beyond endurance. It was ghastly to watch your own sister go on for years struggling feebly like a dying moth on a pin.

Jocelyn had thought at the beginning of the meal, just after they had all wedged themselves in hip to hip and elbow to elbow down the long benches, that she would lose her self-control and lash out verbally against the detestable man.

Cousin Helen had raised her voice to propose tentatively, her eyes flicking toward Jocelyn, "Anybody want to say grace?"

And Maurice had roared. "Grace! O.K. I said it. Everybody dig in."

Even now as she recalled that galling moment when there had been self-conscious titters in Maurice's vicinity, Jocelyn heard him speaking once more. "God'l'mighty, Fred, don't take all the pie. The rest of us want a bite too."

Blasphemy, that's what it was. God ought to strike him dead where he sat, remove his loathsome presence from the company of decent people.

THREE
Marvin

Stray shafts of sunlight struck gleams from the sides of glass pickle jars and the scumming surfaces of coffee cups. Flies darted at the littered plates, and crusts formed on the cooling contents of the half-empty casserole dishes. The diners, gorged and lethargic, complained humorously, "I'm stuffed, absolutely stuffed."

"It's a sin to overload your stomach like this. But I *will* do it."

Mothers screamed after the children who were already trooping away toward the water, "Don't go in now! I'll let you know when the hour's up. Brad, keep out of the sun! Betty, don't forget the salve for your nose; it's peeling just terrible."

The women made halfhearted gestures toward cleaning up the mess. From her place at the table Bea listlessly gathered the plates within reach and scraped them into an empty salad bowl. Cousin Helen fitted plastic covers over dishes miraculously still containing usable food.

Maurice climbed out of his place, belched, and stretched. "I'm gonna lay down and let my victuals digest." He ambled toward the tarpaulin where Little Bea's baby was asleep in its bassinet. "Us babies," he chortled, "gotta have our naps."

"Don't wake him up," Little Bea admonished.

Maurice turned toward Peggy, who was pulling a striped beach towel from the gear piled under a tree. "Wanta join your old unc in a siesta, Peggy girl?"

"Nope, Leo and I're going to take a sun bath."

Peggy's father, Marvin, lifted his leg over the bench and walked away to the bank, where he stood alone, looking down through the foliage to a glimpse of the purling stream below. He lighted a cigarette, shook the match out carefully before dropping it, and made his way down the path to sit on a flat-topped rock beside the water.

He looked unseeingly at the hand which held his cigarette. Anyone could have guessed it was a carpenter's hand. The heavily callused palm, the enlarged knuckles, the coarse scabs on the back from abrasions left by violent encounters with lumber, the broken fingernails with purple bruises covering the moons on three of them. It was a strong hand, one whose fingers had recently curved and then clenched with the desire to commit violence.

It was funny how you could go along, refusing to let your mind dwell on unpleasant subjects, preventing yourself from feeling the emotion certain people evoked by their mere presence, deliberately putting aside your hatred so that it would not interfere with your getting along smoothly with what you had to do—and then all of a sudden find yourself helpless to refuse, to prevent, to put aside, finding yourself overwhelmed by the bitterness and antagonism you had consciously caused to lie dormant and innocuous.

Like the sickening bitterness of unexpected heartburn it had come back to Marvin today, the memory of that long-ago experience when he had had his eyes opened to Maurice Egstadt's real character.

He had got over it, never thought of it if he could help it. Even the details of what had happened he had managed to dim in his memory. But he had been taken, and taken good. His resultant humiliation and resentment had never grown indistinct in recollection.

It was at about the time when Mrs. Witherspoon came to live at Jocelyn's. The whole family was still accepting Esther's husband with naive tolerance and only some slight irritation at his blustering, taunting air of superiority. Maurice had just gone broke in an ill-fated venture as the local agent for a national concern which sold household insulation. They gathered that there had been some trouble about getting along with the salesmen, but the family had never looked into the situation closely, just accepted Maurice's and Esther's offhand explanations of why Maurice had "given up" the business.

Subsequent events had educated the family to the fact that Maurice almost inevitably terminated his business connections with some kind of a mess that generated inclusive ill will on the part of all concerned. For instance, the vegetable-packing business he had entered so confidently had in a little over a year wound up in a dissolved partnership and considerable animosity and a substantial financial loss for Mr. Egstadt. He had remained in and around the produce business ever since, however. At the moment Maurice called himself a "produce broker," whatever that meant. Nobody inquired too closely as to Maurice's business activities. They were all mordantly aware, however, that all the Egstadts had left to show for the money from the Witherspoon property was the house they lived in at Valdale.

Back there when Marvin got involved with Maurice in a business way, the latter had managed to obtain a real estate broker's license after his disappointment as an insulation magnate. Not much seemed to be coming of this new career either; but one Saturday afternoon Maurice roared into the driveway at the Nelsons' in one of the ostentatiously large motorcars he always sported, even if it had to be a ten-year-old model. On this day he had a hot proposition to lay before Marvin.

It was early summer and they sat in the patio out back while Maurice explained the project he had in mind. He had run across a lot at the edge of town that he could pick up "for a song." His idea was simply this: why didn't old Marv come in with him on building a house on the lot? Maurice could work along with him as a helper, and they could put the building up dirt cheap, not having to hire any union labor since they would be doing the work themselves *for* themselves. Then on the proceeds of the sale they could find still other cheap lots through Maurice's "connections" and build more dwellings and sell *them* and eventually be really in the business of building and selling on a big scale. When they got to the stage of larger operations Maurice could handle the business and financial end of things and Marvin could supervise construction, and they would really clean up.

"How you going to get the money for materials?" Marvin inquired dubiously. "I can't raise anything. We still got a big loan to pay off on this house."

"Now, don't you worry about that. I'll handle the financial end of things. I already bought and paid cash for the lot. It's a good investment, whether we build on it or not. I'll double my money on it in two-three years."

"Where'd you get the cash to buy it?" Marvin asked bluntly.

"Cashed in an insurance policy of Esther's. She saw it was a steal that we couldn't afford to lose out on."

"But that still doesn't give you the money to build. You can't raise enough on the lot alone to even lay the foundation; and, between the two of us even, we couldn't get enough credit from any of the building supply companies around here to start construction."

"I got that all figured out. Our house is clear, and I'm willing to get a loan on the place and gamble it on this deal. What do you think of that?"

"Well, it's your home. If you want to mortgage it."

"So you see all you have to do is supply the brains and brawn when it comes to actual construction. And believe me, Marv, I'll settle down and work right along with you. I'm no carpenter, but I can fetch and carry and pound a few nails without bending 'em. What d'you say? It's a chance to make a nice little lump sum with no investment on your part except a couple of months' work."

"How much would I get out of it?"

"We'll split the profits. Of course, seeing's how I'm the one putting up all the cash and will be putting in time as a laborer too, maybe you'd see your way clear to giving me a little the edge in the divvy-up." He laughed jovially and slapped Marvin's knee.

So Marvin drove out to look at the lot with Maurice. His imagination became active, seeing the five-room ranch-type house with garage attached nestling against the big white oak which had been preserved on the lot.

It took him a day or two to give in and embark definitely on the partnership. After all, he had a sure, steady summer's work at union pay and union hours with the contracting firm, Connelly and Weed.

When they were putting in the forms for the foundation Fred Mallory stopped by to speak to Marvin, who was digging away alone in the hot sun.

"Where's your partner?" Fred drawled.

"He'll be along in an hour or so. Had to drop in at the bank when it opens at ten, and had to take care of a few details at the lumber company."

"I see." Fred talked casually for a few minutes and finally asked unconcernedly, "You guys got a partnership agreement or anything drawn up?"

"No. Little job like this, it's not necessary to go to a lot of expense for lawyers and stuff. We don't want to complicate things more'n we have to. Might run into a lot of red tape, and trouble with the union, and so forth."

"I see. How's it set up then?"

"Well, technically it's Maurice's lot, and he's building his own house on it; and I'm just helping him. That way, you see, the union can't kick. Nobody's being hired. Then when we sell her, Maurice'll just make me a present of half the profits."

Fred surveyed his brother-in-law speculatively. "If it was me," he said flatly, "I'd get Jim Lucas to put something down in black and white so if any—uh—differences of opinion came up you'd have something to fall back on. I don't exactly like the look of it with everything being in Maurice's name."

Marvin pushed back his white carpenter's cap and wiped his forehead with his hand, leaving it streaked with grime.

"Hell, Fred, you can't be so fussy with a relative. Makes it look as if you didn't trust him. It ain't as if it was strangers. He wouldn't try to pull no funny business on his own brother-in-law."

"O.K. But remember what I tell you. Blood ain't thicker than water where the old green stuff's involved." He settled the belt of his trousers and turned toward the pickup truck parked by the road. Fred was working as a painter at the time; and he volunteered jokingly as he moved away, "I'm on my way in to the shop to pick up more pigment. This old dame we're doing a house for, seems as if her idea of heliotrope—that's the color she's doing her bedroom—ain't the same as the boss's idea of heliotrope."

For three hot months Marvin slaved over the little house, nine hours a day and eight on Saturdays. He balked at Sunday work. A man had to rest sometime. His young son Grant came along on many days, lending a hand wherever he was able. Even little David lugged sawhorses back and forth and swept up litter and brought more nails or found the level for Uncle Marvin when it was misplaced. Maurice put in an average of about a half day of manual labor for every one that Marvin put in. His multifarious business responsibilities were a continuous irritating interference to his ardent desire to work on the house—or so he let on, anyway.

Electricians and plumbers had to be hired to meet building inspection standards, and the price of plywood went up before they got their order in; but they kept fairly well inside Marvin's original estimate of costs.

He did a lot of figuring on pieces of scratch paper at home; and toward the end, when the inside paint was going onto cupboards and woodwork, Marvin informed Bea a bit ruefully, "Well, if we sell for ten thousand and do it pretty soon, I figure I'll have made not quite the union scale. That is, if you figure as if I'd been paid for overtime."

"Well, you have to look at it," Bea said reassuringly, "as a start toward better things. Someday," she added fondly, "you'll be in a position like Mr. Connelly, building and selling right and left with scads of people working for you."

Marvin grinned deprecatingly. "I've been thinking it over, and I think our best bet for the next investment would be to buy up some older house and modernize it and put it in A-one shape and sell it for twice what it's worth."

"Shame on you, you old profiteer," Bea chided banteringly.

The last two weeks of work on the house Maurice performed no physical labor. Showing the property to prospective buyers naturally took a lot of time. He would lean on the side of the prospect's car with his head in the window, talking for an hour or so after the party had looked at the house.

They were lucky in that almost simultaneously with the application of the last lick of paint Maurice found a buyer who had enough cash to pay down so that the bank would give a loan for the balance, leaving the partners with the selling price in cash.

Since the property was in Maurice's name, and since he handled the business side of things anyway, all Marvin had to do was sit back and wait. The whole Nelson family went camping at a state park in the Sierras, using up the last of their savings to do it. Marvin needed a little vacation.

A few evenings after their return Maurice breezed in triumphantly and beamingly passed a crisp check to his brother-in-law. "There you are pardner," he said. "Your share of the loot."

With a smile Marvin scanned the slip of gray paper. The smile died out into a puzzled frown. The check was for one thousand dollars.

"Actually, your share came to nine hundred and fifty-six dollars and twenty-five cents," Maurice elaborated genially, "but I didn't think you'd kick if I made it an even figure."

Marvin raised his eyes. "How did you arrive at this figure? The way I worked it out, I was supposed to get seventeen-fifty, give or take a dollar or two."

Maurice's eyes opened wider in innocent astonishment. He reached for his inside coat pocket. "I got the figures right here."

Marvin was looking down at the check, and he spoke in a thickened voice. "This ain't even wages. I could have done better than this workin' regular hours for Connelly and Weed."

"Well," Maurice protested patiently, "that's the chance you take, being in business for yourself. Here," he said reasonably, proffering a sheet of yellow, lined paper, "it's all broken down."

Marvin took a step back and sank into an armchair, his eyes on the paper. The pained lines between his brows deepened as he read.

"What's this?" he demanded, looking up. "Interest on your investment."

"Well, my God, man, I put my own dough into the lot and put my own house up as security. I ought to get some compensation for that, oughtn't I?"

Marvin gave him an incredulous look and returned to the figures on the paper. He let out an outraged breath and put a trembling finger on another item.

"Broker's fee!" he ejaculated hoarsely. "You're paying yourself a *commission?*"

Maurice looked pained and bewildered. "Why, certainly. After all, I put in a lot of time finding the lot in the first place and keeping up an office where buyers could find me. And general professional expenses."

Marvin thrust the paper from him violently, and it fluttered to the floor.

"O.K. If that's the way you want to play it, I'm putting in a bill right now for wages at the union scale. With overtime. Good thing for me I kept a record of my time."

Maurice regarded him with grieved eyes. "There was nothing in our agreement about you getting *wages.*"

"You're a fine one to talk about agreements! The way I remember it, we were going to split the profits. Well, I don't call this any fifty-fifty split."

"Who said anything about fifty-fifty?" Maurice cried in astonishment. "My God, man, I put up the money, take all the risks, handle all the paper work and legal end of things, and besides that do a day laborer's job, day in and day out, and you expect to get fifty per cent of the profits! What d'you take me for?"

Marvin stared at the man, astounded.

Coldly Maurice picked up the hat he had tossed on an end table and nodded at the check Marvin had discarded on the arm of the chair.

"That's my final offer. Take it or leave it." He pulled himself up with offended dignity, hat in hand. "I must say I never expected this kind of treatment from my own brother-in-law." With the air of one wounded to the quick, Maurice turned and left the house.

Speechlessly Marvin stared at the door.

Bea had been out at a neighbor's, and when she came in from the rear of the house she found her husband sunk in the armchair with his chin on clasped hands, his expression ferocious.

"Marvin, what's the matter?"

"The son of a bitch," he growled, "the goddamned, stinking son of a bitch."

"What's happened!" Bea's eyes were frightened. Her mild, good-natured Marvin didn't talk like this.

He picked up the check and shoved it blindly toward her. "Look at that."

He rose and tramped heavily back and forth across the floor. "A thousand dollars, almost a thousand dollars," he cried hoarsely, "that miserable bastard took out of the profits and kept! Paid himself for this, paid himself for that." He kicked at the yellow sheet still lying on the rug. "Look at it. Just look at it. Hell, if we were going to play that way, I could charge him something. Not only my wages. That would be enough. But who drew up the plans, made the blueprints, figured all the specifications? I could put in for an architect's fee. Who figured every last goddamned sliver of material, down to the final doorknob and tenpenny nail? I did, that's who."

Marvin wheeled on his wife with contorted features. "D'you know what he's done? D'you *know?* He's made me scab for him; that's what he's done. Got his goddamned house built without paying the union scale for labor. Boiled down, that's all in Christ's world it amounts to!"

"Marv, your language," Bea murmured, and squeezed back in her chair, frightened.

"I'd like to kill him," Marvin said hoarsely, and stood before the picture window, running a hand roughly through his hair.

"Couldn't"—Bea cleared her throat with difficulty—"could you— maybe—go to the union? Put in a claim? Or —or something?"

"How can I? He didn't hire me. I walked right up and gave him my time." He shook his head futilely. "Maybe I could talk to Jim Lucas about it, bring suit on my own."

"Oh dear." Bea bit her lip. "It would be awful, a lawsuit in the family. And he'd lie. He'd lie himself blue in the face. About us. The scandal. And poor Esther. She'd feel terrible."

"Poor Esther, hell. It's time she found out what kind of a heel she's married to." He sighed morosely. "Fred was right. I should have had something on paper."

They spent two or three days talking it over—between themselves, and with Fred, and with Jocelyn sitting in once. Peppery Jane was all for going to court, but Fred thought such a course would be useless and expensive, and "the girls" hated to see "poor Esther" put on the spot; and besides, family squabbles made so much gossip and notoriety in a small town.

It was finally Marvin himself, after his first wrath had subsided, who put the quietus on the whole thing. He was a peace-loving man and an ethical one. It was for the latter reason that he hesitated to take up his problem with the union lawyer. In his heart he knew he had attempted to evade union practice by working on the house in the first place without a previous guarantee of proper pay for his labor.

"I might as well face it," he said wearily. "I was taken. But good. I should have had sense enough to have a written agreement before I ever picked up a hammer. He outsmarted me, the dirty louse; and there's nothing I can do but take my medicine like a man."

Bea had it out with Esther, "in no uncertain terms," she told other members of the family. Bea was less inclined to handle Esther with kid gloves than Jocelyn was. Bea was fundamentally kind but not sentimental, and she had always been inclined to step down hard on Esther's "airs."

The day Esther came tripping up the walk for the first time after the "fuss," Bea met her grimly and, as she held the door open to let her sister in, declared accusingly, "I should think you'd be ashamed to look me in the face, Esther Mallory."

The "girls" all had a tendency to ignore the changes of status made by matrimony and in moments of stress to address one another by their common surname.

"Oh, Bea," Esther exclaimed ingenuously, "I know the boys have had some silly argument over business, but do we have to let it affect our private lives? Men take those things so much more seriously than they really warrant."

Bea planked herself down in an occasional chair and eyed her sister severely. "*I* call it serious when your precious Maurice cheats us out of nearly a thousand dollars."

Esther had come to rest on the sofa, and she threw up her hands in a prettily despairing gesture. "There, you see it's all some misunderstanding, Marvin blaming Maurice, and Maurice all upset and brooding because *he* says Marvin accused him of dreadful things."

"H'mph," Bea grunted, at a loss for a moment in the face of Esther's guileless aplomb.

"*I* never understand money matters," Esther stated frankly, "and you never had any head for business either, Bea Mallory; so you and I might just as well keep out of it and say no more about it. Let the boys sulk at each other if they're bound to until they get over it. It's no use for us to get mixed up in it. Whoever's in the right or wrong of it, you and I both know that neither of us had anything to do with it. I know you wouldn't cheat me, and you know I wouldn't do anything against you; so what's the *point* in us fighting?" Esther finished plaintively.

Bea regarded her sister, nonplused. Even though she had no qualms about quarreling with Esther, it was often like this. The younger girl twisted everything around somehow. Slippery, she was. Wouldn't face facts, that was Esther's trouble, and got what facts she did get hold of so jumbled up that the other party found herself all mixed up in them before the argument was well started.

"Do you want me to come by tomorrow," Esther was asking sunnily, "to walk over to the church with you for the Circle tea?"

"No," Bea snapped defeatedly. "I'll go by myself. I don't want to even see you anymore."

"Oh, Bea, now don't be childish."

Bea's lips pressed together and her cheeks seemed to puff out as if she were about to explode. But that was the way Esther was, didn't know when she'd been insulted. Within two months the good-natured Bea was on the usual casual terms with her sister again. They just didn't mention the "misunderstanding," and by tacit consent kept their husbands apart.

Marvin's bruised pride was soothed by the knowledge that all the rest of the family were on his side and saw Maurice in his true colors. For the next few months, roasting Maurice became a favorite pastime when any of the relatives got together.

"I just wouldn't have believed—"

"Of course, he always did impress me as crude. Loud, you know—"

"But who would have thought he'd be so lowdown—"

"Well, Esther's the one gets my goat, pretending she doesn't *know*—"

"How she can have any respect for such a crook—"

When Marvin was not in the gathering there were sometimes remarks of another tenor.

"Well, Fred warned him, stood right there on the lot before the foundation was even in, and told him—"

"*I* think Marv should have sued—"

"Sometimes it seems as if some people just ask to be taken in—"

During this time the relationships of other members of the family with Maurice were in an uneasy state. It was really not their business, and you could hardly refuse to be civil to the man, especially when Esther was along. Nobody blamed her. They really rather pitied the girl.

The first time he met Maurice face to face on the street Marvin ignored his ex-"partner's" stiff "Hello, Marv," and walked past as if he had neither seen nor heard.

But inevitably he met Esther—in his own house, downtown, at church affairs; once he had to sit in the same pew with Maurice at a funeral, and one evening they were forced to play cards at the same table at a P.T.A. benefit whist party. It was no use. Marvin suffered the gradual resumption of normal though strained social contact with the unscrupulous man.

Now, after all these years, no one would suspect from the way he and Maurice behaved that there had ever been anything seriously wrong between them.

But Marvin had never really forgotten the betrayal of his trust. Everything that had happened in the intervening years had grooved his resentment deeper into Marvin's being.

Maurice had blundered on, always the "businessman" in one way or another, never demeaning himself with downright manual work, always maintaining the badge of the white collar, sporadically belonging to the high-toned organizations like the Elks and the Lions Club, driving his nearly-new, showy automobiles, talking big, acting big.

Marvin tried to tell himself that actually he was a more successful man than Maurice. He had mastered his trade, was considered one of the best carpenters in his local, a man you could put anywhere on a construction job and who would deliver the goods with flawless craftsmanship. He owned his home, owed no man a dollar, had brought up a larger—and a happier—family than Maurice had. And his conscience was clear. To his knowledge Marvin had never done any man an injustice or an injury.

But it had always been hard work, accompanied by worry and strain. No matter how much he made, it was never enough for everything the family wanted and needed. There were always the rainy months when work was scarce. And the layoffs at every slight economic slump.

Meanwhile Maurice had never seemed to work hard. He might be thousands of dollars in debt, yet he still sashayed around in well-pressed tailored suits and starched shirts, and he always came out of his financial setbacks somehow, self-confidence as glossy as ever. It boiled down, Marvin supposed, to the fact that Maurice invariably made a good showing, acted as if he were entitled to be considered in a higher social class than his plodding, working-stiff brother-in-law; and people were subtly affected by this assumption of superior prestige.

With a shock Marvin had seen this phenomenon demonstrated this very day, and by his own son Grant. The boy was drifting at the moment, looking for his place in the world. He was working in a service station but not with the thought of remaining in that line. While the men gossiped before dinner Maurice had clapped the boy on the shoulder and offered, "Tell you what, son, I'll keep my eyes open over in Valdale, see if I can't use my connections to find an opening for you, some kind of work where a bright boy like you can have a chance to get ahead. You don't wanta plug along being a wage slave all your life."

Marvin had regarded the man with sardonic scorn. The big success handing out advice. And then his eyes had fallen on Grant. The boy's expression was hopefully respectful. Grant knew what everybody in the family thought of that big blowhard. The youngster even concurred ostensibly in the common judgment that Maurice was a heel. And yet, in spite of himself, in his youth and his yearning for the symbols of success, Grant was involuntarily impressed by the older man's braggadocio.

To Marvin it was sickening. There was no doubting the sincerity of Maurice's offer. The big four-flusher would try to induce some business acquaintance to give the boy a chance. Maurice loved to be a benefactor, even though it usually wound up with his negating the original good turn by taking unfair advantage of the creature he had befriended.

His bluffness, his heartiness, his very ruthlessness seemed to have a strange, insidious appeal to the young. Today Marvin had noted this with fresh clarity in the case of sixteen-year-old Peggy. Maurice's playful wrestling, the overtly innocent physical contact the man kept making with the girl's nubile body, his heavy-handed teasing seemed to have a stimulating effect on the girl. Peggy, too, knew from hearing the rest of the family talk that no one really liked Uncle Maurice; but it was obvious that in spite of her imperfectly understood knowledge of his unpleasant character she was irresistibly drawn to the man.

It was not that Marvin feared his brother-in-law had overt intentions of actually corrupting the girl's innocence. Even Maurice was not that low. He satisfied his repressed lust for young female flesh by this socially innocuous physical playfulness.

But the recognition of Maurice's basic impulses filled Marvin today with almost unbearable revulsion. With one part of his mind Marvin registered a startled surprise at the violence of the feelings which had suddenly welled up in him. It might have been only yesterday that he had railed at Maurice in the living room over the dirty deal he had been given in the affair of the house.

Why this onslaught of emotion should have come upon him just today, Marvin did not know. Perhaps so many reminders had lifted their heads. Perhaps so much evidence of Maurice's villainy had been on display in so brief a space of time. His needling of poor Jossy by making fun of Cousin Helen's well-meant offer to have the blessing said before they ate. His sly but brutal persecution of Alison, whom Marvin thought as much of as he did his own daughters. The cold, set anger on David's face, more acute today, Marvin sensed, than he had ever seen it before.

It was almost as if some hidden power were directing the searchlights of exposure on the man on this bright summer Sunday, showing him up for what he was in lineaments no one could mistake.

After the meal Marvin had withdrawn almost in self-defense, as if he did not trust himself. He felt as if some slight incident might dissipate his self-control and throw him, in a physical frenzy of destructiveness, upon the man he had hated for years with a hatred that he thought had shrunk with disuse but that, it seemed now, must have lain there deep within himself, fattening and growing like some monstrous fetus.

FOUR
Alison

When Uncle Maurice retired to the canvas under the tree, Alison breathed more freely. At least he was silenced temporarily. And before he came booming back into the party she hoped to have maneuvered her new beau out of his way. With luck she might keep Orville beyond the sound of Uncle Maurice's voice for the rest of the afternoon.

Alison did as much as she thought was her duty in clearing the tables and repacking food. Then she proposed offhandedly, "Shall we go for a walk, Orville? Explore the park?"

"Good idea. I need to walk off some of this dinner. We can go swimming when we get back."

Unobtrusively they wandered off through the parking lot to the road. To Alison's relief, no relative marked their departure and offered shrill comment, as she had half expected.

They followed the road to the park's north boundary, cut down to the stream and crossed over it by leaping from one rock to another. Then they took the trail south, skirted the beach over the dam, and, a short distance below their own picnic site but on the other side of the stream, came upon a small shaded area where dry sand lay alongside a deeper pool formed by a bend in the creek's course. Just above this spot there was easy passage over the water by means of reasonably flat stones lying diagonally across the stream bed.

As he settled down beside her Orville observed lazily, "A person wouldn't think that just a few rods away there were several hundred people, would you? We could be in the middle of a wilderness."

Alison tilted her head. From upstream came faint, shrill echoes of human voices around the swimming pool. Through the treetops on the opposite bank, a wave of shouting drifted muted from the baseball field.

"Of course," Orville added practically, "you can hear signs of people in the distance, but they don't seem to have any connection with the sounds here—the squawking of that blue jay, for instance, and the rushing of the water, and the rustle of the leaves."

"I know what you mean. It seems stiller by contrast." She put her head back and sighed. "It's so restful, isn't it?"

He had stretched out with his check on his arm. "Yeah, makes me feel like taking a nap."

Alison wriggled herself backward until her shoulders rested between two rounded boulders whose sides met at an angle. "Why don't you?"

"Doesn't seem very polite." He grinned up at her.

"I'd like it," she said lightly, "if you went to sleep. I could just sit here and daydream and not feel I had to make conversation, and yet I wouldn't feel all alone and scared a bobcat or a rattlesnake or something would jump out at me. By myself in the woods I'm always a little nervous."

"Well," he returned jokingly, "if a snake rattles or a wildcat jumps, don't hesitate to scream."

"I'd probably have to chase it away from *you* before you came to enough to know what was going on."

On this bantering note they exchanged a few more sallies, and Alison noted that his eyes were closing frequently and for longer periods each time. When she saw that he had finally fallen asleep, she studied the man's face intently—the long thin nose, the soft fringe of brown lashes, the jaw a little slack in repose, the slightly crooked line of his lips now softened and parted. She couldn't remember, it occurred to her with some surprise, ever watching a man sleep before.

What a commentary on my life, she thought ironically, twenty-eight years old and a sleeping man is an oddity to me.

Her eyes shifted to the still water in the bend before them. Its dark surface was picked out with golden, glittering sequins where the light struck glancingly through the tremulous leaves above.

It was only a month since her first date with Orville, although she had known him to speak to for almost a year. They had become acquainted during coffee breaks at the corner drugstore between the chain grocery where Orville was a clerk and the bank where Alison worked. He had been transferred to Coast City from another store in the chain, and he had prospects of someday being promoted to a managership, probably in still another town. Orville had been married once and divorced. As an eligible man, he had been calculatingly considered by all the single girls in the bank, by the unmarried salesgirls and waitresses all through the business district, and by half the unattached female schoolteachers in town. Alison knew Orville had dated a number of girls during his year in Coast City. She hadn't dared to hope that she would become one of their number. Alison—at twenty-eight—had almost given up hope. Wherever one went, it seemed as if there were always more single women than men.

After Orville had taken her out three times in two weeks, Alison analyzed the situation thus: He had been disillusioned once in women as a result of his broken marriage. He was shy now of the more flighty, vivacious girls and of any sign of flashiness or predatory behavior in women. Therefore he found Alison Mallory reassuring. She was diffident, conservative in dress and appearance. It wasn't a very flattering summation; but Alison was so grateful for any attention and companionship from a presentable man that she could not feel chagrined over having won Orville's company for the negative reason that he was not afraid of her.

Alison was finding herself more and more drawn to the man; he was in her thoughts almost incessantly. She would have liked to tell herself excitedly: "I'm in love! Really in love!"

Other girls she knew were always going off into such transports, broadcasting to their friends the excruciating state of their emotions, whether the state proved lasting or not.

But Alison no longer dared to admit such feelings to herself, let alone to other people. Twice in her lifetime she had felt like that about a man: This is it! I'm crazy about him! The first time she had been seventeen; and the boy had let her down out of this ecstatic stratosphere by callously dropping her cold for a new girl who burst upon the high school in a tempest of titian curls and tight sweaters and jingling charm bracelets and the latest snappy catch phrases.

Then there had been Frank when she was twenty-three. They went steady for a year, and Alison had expected any moment to become engaged. Frank was an automobile salesman and had lived in Los Alegres all his life. Even Alison's relatives agreed that he was "cute" and a real go-getter. He had an accepted status in the family as "Alison's boy friend."

Frank had liked Uncle Maurice the best of all Alison's relatives. "He sure is a kick," Frank used to say. He always listened, impressed, to Uncle Maurice's opinions on business, on politics, on personalities. "I wish I had half your Uncle Maurice's get-up-and-go," Frank would sometimes declare admiringly.

"He's an extrovert all right," Alison would respond weakly. She couldn't criticize Uncle Maurice to Frank because it would have reacted against herself. But it worried her that Frank was so taken in by the big oaf. For Alison had recognized for some years that Uncle Maurice hated her. She felt it as definitely as she would have a cold draft between her shoulder blades.

At first she had painfully wondered why; and then, when Uncle Marvin had the trouble with Uncle Maurice over that house they built together, Alison found out the main reason why Uncle Maurice couldn't abide her.

Aunt Bea, in her wrath over the rooking Marvin had taken, was letting off steam to Alison, who was in her early teens at the time. They were cracking walnuts together in the kitchen, in preparation for a cake.

"I'm beginning to see now, Allie," Aunt Bea had grumbled bitterly, "your father was the only one in the family with a lick of sense. He never had a bit of use for Maurice, not from the very beginning. I never mentioned it to the rest of the family because your father asked me not to. But he talked to me about it. He begged and pleaded with Esther not to marry that man. The rest of us just thought Arthur was being persnickety when he made critical remarks about Maurice when him and Esther were going together. And after the wedding Arthur never uttered one syllable against Maurice. What was done was done, he figured, and we might as well make the best of it."

Aunt Bea sighed with reminiscent eyes. "Your father was a fine man, Alison. Quiet, and kept to himself and never said much. He was a great reader too, always had his nose in a book. Being the oldest the way he was, we all had a lot of respect for him. I don't think he'd of ever even told me about the talk he had with Esther, except one day he drove me over to Valdale to shop and, riding over, just the two of us, we got confidential the way people will sometimes; and he told me how he went to Esther and just begged her to postpone the wedding for six months, to give herself time to get better acquainted with Maurice. Naturally Esther wouldn't listen.

"I remember as if it was yesterday Arthur saying to me as we rode along, 'She can't see it now, Bea, but I tell you it's a tragedy for Esther to marry that man.'

"And I said, 'Oh, he may not turn out so bad. I'll admit he's kind of loud and sort of a bully sometimes—'

"And I'll never forget the way Arthur lifted one hand from the steering wheel with sort of a brushing movement and said, 'It isn't his crudity and bad manners. It's deeper than that. Maurice Egstadt is one of the most thoroughly vicious men I ever saw. And in the worst way. Because he can't help himself. He *has* to hurt people. It's his way of handling life. Some people can be mean and cruel and ruthless deliberately, because they've made up their minds that's the way to get what they want. And some people embrace vices—promiscuity with women, or gambling, or drinking, or whatever, because that's what they think is fun. They deliberately choose to do those things.

"'But this Egstadt isn't like that. He thinks he's God's gift to humanity. He thinks he's the bighearted benefactor of everybody he comes in touch with, and God help the person that can't see his behavior toward them in that light. I won't say he's crazy, but there's something like an insane person's view of the world in the way his mind works. He has a completely distorted conception of himself and other people, and that's what makes him dangerous. He'll destroy Esther. You wait and see. I don't know just how, but he will. Nobody can accept him and live with him and get away safe. I hate to see this happen to Esther. She's always been such a happy little girl, so gentle, and affectionate, and—and hopeful.'"

Aunt Bea halted and fell silent, her eyes on the walnut meat she was disinterring from its shell. "Like yesterday," she said slowly. "I can hear him saying all that."

Alison had listened tensely, more absorbed in what was being revealed about her father than in the details of the story Bea had told. "He must have been a smart man," the girl said softly.

"He was. Arthur was the best." Bea brushed a tear from her lashes. "Maybe not the kind of smartness that lets people get rich, but shrewd about people." She smiled mistily at the girl. "I don't know why, but he was always partial to me. Used to call me 'Bea-bea.' The main reason I insisted on having you when he and your mother died was that I knew Arthur would feel better knowing you were with me than with any of the others."

The sun had crept around to send its rays against the rocks where Alison leaned, and she put her head back, eyes closed, the sun on her face.

It was more than just Bea wanting her though. It was that the rest of them hadn't really wanted their orphan niece. At least not very much. And Uncle Maurice had not wanted her at all.

A kid twelve years old picked up more than the adults realized. Bea and Marvin had taken her in temporarily the day of the accident that took her parents' lives. She had been at school, and the principal had sent a message to her room that Alison was to go to Aunt Bea's right after classes. Her mother had been alone in the world, and so Alison had only her father's people to go to.

She slept on a cot in the room that was Florence's. Grant had a room of his own, and there was one more bedroom, Aunt Bea's and Uncle Marvin's. It was just a bungalow, with small, tightly organized rooms. A little girl lying tense and frightened in the dark when the others thought she was asleep heard a great deal through the lath-and-plaster wall between herself and the living room.

Jocelyn was willing to take Alison in, but Grandma and Grandpa weren't well, and maybe—a child around the house too—it might be pretty hard on Joss and the old folks. But Alison knew that Jocelyn wouldn't have minded having her.

Uncle Fred really wanted her; he loved Arthur and would have felt good to bring up his brother's daughter. But although Jane was willing—my goodness, yes, she was willing—but after all, little Bea was a boisterous eight, and Leo was a baby in arms, and Jane really had her hands full.

Anyway the others did not seriously consider giving Alison to Fred and Jane. It was the woman of the family who would have the real responsibility, and Jane was no blood relation to the child. Not that anyone had anything against Jane. But still—they did, behind her back, sometimes make sniffing remarks about Fred's wife. They wouldn't come right out and say Jane was high-hat, but she was painfully proper, and the Mallorys sensed with mild resentment that Jane considered her husband's people rather common. They ate on oilcloth to save laundry, and some of the Mallorys' friends were—well, just not the sort of people who did you any *good*, people who sat on their front porches in their sock feet and drank beer straight out of the bottle. Jane did try to keep up *standards* and made an effort to live nicely.

Esther probably actually wanted the little girl more than any of the others did. And Maurice knew it. After David, Esther would never have another baby. It would have been company for her to have a girl in the house and pleasant to have a sister for her little boy.

But Maurice had come out flat-footed from the beginning, "We'd be tickled to death to take the kid—nothing I myself would like better—but for Esther's sake I absolutely refuse to risk it. Esther's not strong, and the extra work would be too much for her. I wouldn't feel right if I let her take on that much of a responsibility."

In a family conclave at Bea's which did not include the Egstadts, Jocelyn snorted scornfully, "Esther's not strong! She's never been sick a day in her life except for flu and a few colds."

"Well, of course," Bea put in, "she did have to have that hysterectomy after David was born."

"So what," Jane chipped in. "It left her in better shape than ever. Actually," she added with a well-bred giggle that took the vulgarity out of the quip, "the operation should have been good for her nervous system. At least now she doesn't have to wear herself out worrying every month for fear she's pregnant."

It was only later, after Aunt Bea told Alison of the talk with her father about Uncle Maurice, that Alison fully understood why he had bluntly refused to take her in. Esther, in the first flush of married love, would have confided to her husband that Arthur had tried to prevent their union. Alison knew that her own and the Egstadt families had seen little of each other during her childhood. A coolness had undoubtedly existed there, even though its reasons were prudently concealed from the family in general. But it was natural that Maurice would under no circumstances have accepted into his home the daughter of the man who had tried to "do him dirt."

So it was Bea and Marvin who were appointed the girl's legal guardians. There was a small insurance policy with Alison as beneficiary, and by squeezing every penny it would support her through high school.

Alison always remembered gratefully that while all the rest of the Mallorys were giving voice to excuses and reasons for not taking her, not once did Aunt Bea and Uncle Marvin advance any of their own. Yet it was they who had the most crowded house and the most children to care for, if you counted Peggy, who was even then conspicuously on the way.

Uncle Maurice's antipathy might have been modified if Alison had shown the sort of attitude he liked and expected from young people. But she had never been able to demonstrate enthusiasm for the rough, tumbling playfulness to which he subjected all weaker beings. His teasing never filled her with the half-apprehensive, half-pleasurable nervous excitement it seemed to bring the other children. He frightened Alison, and Uncle Maurice could tell that he did, and it annoyed him. He couldn't bear being avoided and disliked.

Where Frank was concerned, Uncle Maurice's animosity showed definite results. Deliberately and patiently he undermined Alison's status in the young man's eyes. The constant merry derision, the denigrating remarks on her personality, her clothes, her physical attributes, had a cumulative effect. It was a tribute to Frank's independence of taste, Alison reflected sadly, that he continued to like her as well and as long as he did.

The final blow to Frank's respect for her was delivered, she decided afterward, when Uncle Maurice confidentially informed Frank of his reasons for dubbing Alison with the nickname "Smoky."

The relatives all knew of the incident, but no one else in town did, for Alison's kinfolk kept the story sympathetically to themselves. Even Uncle Maurice saved it to use sparingly, recounting the tale with a leer only when it would really work effectively against the girl.

It happened when Alison was eighteen. As a special treat in the summer after graduation from high school she was permitted to make a trip by bus to visit Great-Aunt Sarah's family in Los Angeles. Sarah was Grandma Mallory's sister, and she lived with her son, Cousin Helen's brother, and his family in a suburb of the southern metropolis. Cousin Hubert had a daughter Alison's age, and this daughter, Eloise, put herself out to entertain her cousin Alison from up north.

Eloise, however, proved to be not quite Alison's type. She had, it seemed, a whole flock of swains who all appeared to drive hot rods and wear leather jackets and smoke cigarettes chain-fashion. Alison was astonished at the way Eloise led her elders around by the nose. She talked back to her parents freely, brooked no interference as to the number of evenings per week that she could go out or the hours at which she should return home. She wore lots of eyebrow pencil, and false eyelashes, and indelible lipstick in violent shades of red. Eloise had several pairs of "falsies," and six formal evening frocks, and a closet floor full of shoes that ranged from saddle oxfords to fragile gold sandals with four-inch jeweled heels.

Privately Eloise put Alison down as an awful square, but she resigned herself and nobly did her best to show the country cousin a good time for the week she was there. On Saturday night Eloise took Alison to what she said would be a "beach party" at Balboa. Alison never did see the beach. The car full of young people drove directly to one of the flimsy frame cottages which lined the streets of the seaside resort, to be welcomed by the quartet of boys who had rented the cottage for the week end.

A portable record player blared constantly during the ensuing festivities, the refrigerator was stuffed to capacity with cans of beer, and joy reigned more or less unconfined. Alison spent most of the evening evading the pawing attentions of the "date" to whom she had been assigned. She nursed along a can of beer for over an hour, and smoked two or three cigarettes to keep her hands occupied, and wished miserably that she were back home in Los Alegres. The music made her head ache; she had no talent for screaming the fashionable nonsensical phrases which comprised the substance of all conversation; and she had no taste for close physical contact with the boys when they asked her to dance on the ten-foot-square area available for terpsichorean activity.

At the height of the noise and confusion someone passed her a cigarette, and Alison allowed the donor to light it for her. She thought it tasted funny, but the beer had tasted funny too; she never drank beer, didn't like the flavor. And her mouth was dry and musty-feeling from the unaccustomed smoking she had already been indulging in. She supposed her palate was affected.

In a few minutes Alison became aware of an unwonted euphoria. She began to laugh at everything the others said, and she felt like dancing. It struck her that she just didn't give a damn, and she surrendered to an uncontrollable urge to broadcast the fact.

"I just don't give a damn!" she announced loudly to no one in particular.

It was at that point that two uniformed policemen appeared at the door. The officers had arrived in a squad car in response to a complaint from a nearby cottage whose tenants really had come down to enjoy the sand and the sun and who wanted enough sleep during the night so that they could do so the next day.

The officer sniffed at the heavy blue air and made a quick revision of their intentions. A message was radioed in to send the patrol wagon. The local police, already harassed beyond endurance by the crowds of roistering teen-agers in their streets, were good and ready to make an example of some of them; and in this case the unmistakable scent of marijuana in the air was the last straw.

Alison found the whole thing hilarious. She remembered winking at the matron at the station and blowing kisses to the arresting officers.

The next day there were headlines in all the metropolitan papers: "Teen-age Gang Held on Dope Charge." "Beach Resort Cracks Down on Juvenile Delinquents." Out of deference to the families involved, no names were mentioned.

The next day Alison actually felt like both a Delinquent and a Dope Fiend. An irate Cousin Hubert had collected his charges early in the morning, lecturing them furiously all the way home. Eloise sulked and muttered defiantly, but Alison cowered and felt crushed.

In Los Alegres she started to cry the minute she saw Uncle Marvin waiting for her in the bus station. But it was heartwarming to find that all the folks were merely sympathetic. Naturally Cousin Hubert, full of righteous indignation, had telephoned the whole sordid story to Bea and Marvin. Alison found herself looked upon as the Innocent Victim. It was Eloise who incurred the Mallory family's outraged censure.

Eloise was "no good." She'd "come to a bad end; you wait and see." "I always thought Hubert and Fran were too easy on that kid."

As it happened, Eloise had later married one of the very "delinquents" who attended the ill-fated party. He was now a steady employee at an aircraft factory in Burbank, and they had two children and a house of their own. Eloise was a stand-by in the P.T.A. and took the lead in "cleaning up" the comic-book stands in their neighborhood when the local mothers became alarmed after being told repeatedly in other publications that undesirable comic books were corrupting their children.

All her folks in Los Alegres understood how bad Alison felt over having been arrested and held in jail and made to appear in juvenile court, and they tactfully and tacitly agreed among themselves to say no more about it and thus to help the poor kid forget.

All except Uncle Maurice. For once he didn't dare fly in the face of all his in-laws by spreading the story broadside around town as he would gleefully have liked to do. He had to content himself with insinuating smirks as he addressed Alison as "Smoky," or sometimes, for the sake of variety, "Birdie," short for "jailbird."

It was the most humiliating experience the girl had ever had. She could not smugly load all the blame on Eloise as the others did. Nobody had forced her to drink the beer and continue to smoke up the reefer after she noticed that it was affecting her. After the way the family had taken her in and loved and protected her when she was thrown upon them, an orphan, she had a responsibility to be worthy of their care and generosity. She had no right to bring disgrace upon them by being publicly labeled a juvenile delinquent. The incident left a wound of guilt that quivered to painful life again every time Uncle Maurice covertly taunted her with references to the occasion.

Alison had used to dream sometimes of having Uncle Maurice helpless and in her clutches; and she would go at him ferociously with both fists, lustful to hurt him and hurt him, to pound and pound at his evil face until it was a shapeless pulp. And the horrible part of the dream was that, forceful as was the drive behind her blows, her fist never connected, never quite reached his taunting face. It was so frustrating a dream that she would wake up tired and with a feeling of self-revulsion.

Alison was shocked when she learned that Uncle Maurice had maliciously related the whole story to Frank. If their intimacy had progressed, Alison would eventually have told him the story herself, as an instance of a traumatic experience in her girlhood. But it was not the kind of gossip you forgive other people for repeating to one's friends.

Frank had grinned at her oddly as they sat in his car in front of the house after a date one evening.

"The other day Maurice told me why he calls you 'Smoky.' I had no idea you got so gay when you were safely away from Los Alegres. Maybe I've been misjudging you. I guess you're more of a live one than I thought."

Alison stared at him transfixed. "He told you about that party in Balboa?"

"And how! Must have been quite a wingding."

"The old—the old—" Alison wasn't accustomed to the use of violent epithets, and she had to search for a word. "Why, the old bastard! Talking about me behind my back!" For once she wasn't thinking about the impression she might be making. Her resentment toward Uncle Maurice overrode everything else.

"Oh, come on now," Frank protested. "What's so bad about him letting me in on a little family gossip? After all, it was nothing so terrible, getting picked up at a wild party. It could happen to anybody. Just throws a slightly different light on you, that's all."

"That's just what he had in mind," she retorted in clipped tones. "He'd do anything to belittle me."

"I think you're kind of unjust to Maurice."

"Nobody could be unjust to that man. I hate him," she added vehemently, "hate him."

Frank looked puzzled. He was obviously thinking that he must not have understood Alison very well. First he finds out she has hidden potentialities for "low" behavior—drinking and getting high on marijuana and running around with a fast crowd when she got away from local supervision. And being hypocritical about it in the bargain, pretending to be so proper and concealing this phase of her past. And then exhibiting this violently vindictive attitude toward a swell guy like Maurice Egstadt—who was thinking of buying his next car from Frank.

Alison and Frank drifted apart after that scene. He could not conceal a vaguely suspicious, watchful air; and Alison could not suppress her latent irritation with Frank for defending Uncle Maurice as he always did.

She blamed her uncle for the affair's expiration. Maurice had firmly planted in Frank's mind the idea that Alison harbored a suppressed appetite for vice, and Frank seemed never to quite trust her afterward. It was as if he believed she were being somehow dishonest when she was her usual retiring, inoffensive self.

It was all very well to tell herself, "Well, if a man doesn't trust you, allows a stranger to influence his conception of you, you certainly wouldn't want to marry such a person."

So it was a flaw in Frank that he was small-mindedly and provincially uneasy at the suggestion that his girl might not be in her heart the model of virtue and conventionality he wanted in a wife. But Alison had already come to the clearheaded recognition that a girl of her qualifications was not going to find perfection in a lover. Frank had failed her in this instance, but she accepted somewhat cynically that whoever she loved would probably fail her in some way.

She tried desperately to keep things as they were between her and Frank, but it seemed as if the more she put herself out to please and hold him, the faster their relationship deteriorated. Afterward she suspected that she had tried too hard, had made him feel pursued and fearful of a too keen possessiveness on her part.

When she heard that Frank had taken Virginia Abbott to the Elks' Club Ball and been seen playing golf with Mildred Devore the following Sunday, Alison felt terrible. She had thought she couldn't stand it. She wanted Frank—his smile, his chummy way of saying things, his strong hands, the little caressing ways of making love to her.

When she was forced to acknowledge to herself that it was hopeless, that he had dropped her for good, Alison made up her mind. She applied at the bank for a transfer to the branch in Coast City. She would meet new people—and by "people" she meant men—she would have a little apartment of her own and be looked upon as a sophisticated "career woman" rather than as just another small-town girl living at home. And she would get away from Uncle Maurice. Since he had cheated Aunt Jossy out of Mrs. Witherspoon's money, the talk was that he was thinking of moving to Valdale, but that was only twenty miles away. Another twenty-five between Los Alegres and Coast City wouldn't do any harm.

In so far as the quest for a mate went, moving to Coast City hadn't done Alison any good. It was true, she was not tormented by Uncle Maurice, but that was a minor relief. She became twenty-four, and twenty-five, and twenty-six, and still she had no steady boy friend. Other girls either got to the eligible ones first, or the ones she knew simply did not think of asking the efficient, reserved Miss Mallory for a date.

Alison's desperation grew as the years advanced relentlessly toward thirty. She wanted a mate; it was as simple as that. Mating was a social and biological need, and Alison did not want to be cheated out of it by her own deficiencies and the circumstance that females outnumbered males. She did not worry about love. Alison had faith that she could come to feel a strong, lasting emotion for any man who was congenial and fairly decent and not definitely unsightly. But first she must find the man.

She looked down at the sleeping Orville with gentleness in her eyes. And now she had found him. There had been no nonsense about love at first sight. She had estimated the man dispassionately and found him worthy. Ever since, her pent-up emotions had been growing in tenderness and desire.

She still did not quite dare expose herself to the danger of failure and loss by permitting herself to label her feelings passion or love. She needed more indications from Orville that he seriously cared for her before she could allow her nascent emotions to burgeon and mature.

But it was becoming harder all the time to maintain this discipline over her emotions. Less than an hour ago sheer animal feeling had threatened to dissipate the limits she had imposed on the scope of her desires. As they descended a steep slope in the trail, Alison had slipped and Orville caught her in his arms. Casually, he had pulled her closer then and kissed her lingeringly. His lips were warm, his chest firm and steady. Through the material of her shirt she could feel the warmth of his hand against her back.

Warmth and steadiness, the firmness of flesh and bone and muscle to lean upon. Only her timorous mind, leaping to the fore frantically with reminders: "It isn't safe. You don't know how he feels. He may mean nothing at all by this caress. He might scorn you afterward if you reveal your pitiable need of his love," kept Alison from clinging with a mute, physical plea for more and more of his warmth and strength.

So her responding kiss had been controlled, her withdrawal from his embrace casual, her manner unconcerned as they resumed their hike.

Recalling those moments now, she was disturbed. It was frightening to realize how close she was to the danger of caring so much that the pain would be unendurable if he did not come to want her as much as she did him, if she lost Orville too, as she always seemed to lose the ones she had the effrontery to love.

If she had known that Uncle Maurice would be present today, she would never have invited Orville.

With almost his first words Maurice had renewed his usual campaign to belittle her in the current prospective suitor's eyes, to make her seem like a subject of ridicule rather than of desire. Common sense might argue that the crude attack of one boorish individual could have little permanent effect on a sensible man's opinion of a girl. But Alison knew that she walked a precarious tightrope in first establishing the intimacy which might eventually bind a new boy friend to her more securely. She had neither beauty nor a striking personality with which to overpower a man. Hence she needed all the favorable conditions she could muster to make herself seem worth while in his eyes. And the picture of her that Uncle Maurice deliberately projected on the potential lover's mind could be poisonously disruptive to the frail new relationship which was forming.

Actually, of course, there was not much the loathsome man could do in one day to queer her with Orville, but Alison feared Uncle Maurice so poignantly that she could not feel easy in his presence even for a few hours. She told herself sensibly that it was a neurotic fear, that it was weak of her to let the man affect her so intensely.

But verbalizations were powerless against the anxiety his presence generated.

Alison clenched her fists in the warm sand and raised her eyes, looking over her shoulder toward the opposite bank, where a few yards away the gross creature was probably sleeping off his gluttony. Rebellion gathered in Alison's heart. It was absurd and humiliating, being so dominated emotionally by apprehension and repugnance of another human being. She must not allow herself to knuckle under like this. For the sake of her own self-respect she ought to face up to Uncle Maurice, not cringe and slink away under his attack.

She folded her lips together to keep from speaking aloud the words that swelled in her throat: "Just one more crack, just one, and I'll let him have it!"

Alison did not particularize in her mind just what she meant by "letting him have it."

But she was experiencing a feverish determination to have done with this emotional cowardice in regard to Uncle Maurice. It was as if something had tightened and tightened within her and suddenly snapped.

Irrelevantly she thought of Aunt Jossy, rigid and opinionated and sour. That's what could happen to a single woman, especially one who knew she had been cheated.

Alison looked down intently at the relaxed, sleeping man, and she had not only a yearning desire to touch him hungrily, but she felt protective and—how strange—maternal toward him. Timidly at first she acknowledged these feelings which strove pathetically for acceptance in her thoughts. Then she grew bolder. She set her jaw and admitted fiercely, "I want him. I love him, and I want him to love me. And I will not let anything turn him against me."

With abrupt but quiet movements she rose and took a step toward the edge of the water, staring toward the hidden picnic site. She did not intend to take any more. No more "Smoky," no more cracks about her cooking or her way of living or her lack of sex appeal. She was not a child, nor yet a mouse to be played with. She would assert herself, show some backbone and dignity. It might make all the difference in other phases of her life if she were able once and for all to stand up to and vanquish the ogre who had haunted her girlhood, not only by specific persecuting actions, but by spreading his influence like a miasma through her subconscious being.

FIVE
Fred

Fred took part in the exodus to the beach after the picnic dishes were put away. He had swimming trunks under his faded denim pants, so it was easy to prepare for the water. In fact, by the time the others got in Fred was ready to come out.

"I've reached the age," he told Cousin Wilbur jokingly, "when fifteen minutes is enough of a swim for me."

So the others were still splashing in the pool when Fred gathered up his outer garments and the underwear he had brought along and retired to the flimsy dressing rooms on the bank above. When he emerged, Fred took his wet trunks to Maurice's car and hung them on the door handle to dry. He moved out between the cars and surveyed the picnic site idly. It was deserted except for Maurice supine on the shaded canvas with his mouth open. Across the distance Fred surveyed his brother-in-law with distaste and turned away, deciding to watch the ball game for a while.

He pulled a cigar from the pocket of his loose sport shirt and lighted it as he walked meditatively along. It had certainly not been to his taste to drive over with the Egstadts. He and Jane were glad to pick up Esther, but Maurice had been an unpleasant surprise.

Fred, almost alone of the family, had never had an open break with Esther's husband. As the others said, Fred had been too smart for Maurice, had never allowed himself to become entangled in any kind of business dealing with the fellow, never laid himself open to being cheated as Jocelyn had done, and always refused to let Maurice's barbed joking rattle him visibly. Not that Egstadt hadn't taken his full quota of digs at the "successful" brother-in-law, insinuating that the brand of paint Fred used was inferior, that Fred overcharged his customers, that he unfairly underbid his competitors. Maurice made none-too-subtle fun of Jane's efforts to live well and to mingle with "nice people," denigrated every addition the Fred Mallorys made to their household furnishings and general standard of living.

Maurice irked Fred and Jane; of that there was no question. But they discussed him between themselves and concluded that there was only one way to handle such a character and that was to ignore his oafish behavior. They suspected that jealousy was at the root of Maurice's veiled resentment toward them. As Fred's business prospered, Maurice became ever more envious and resultantly broader in his pseudo-humorous criticisms of their mode of living.

But Fred was very fond of Esther. When it came right down to it, he liked her better than he did his sisters Jocelyn and Bea. Jane, too, found Esther more socially acceptable than the somewhat frumpy Bea, who refused to take any pains with grammar and diction, or the narrow-minded Jocelyn, who could not but be a figure of fun to Jane's more sophisticated friends in the fashionable village of Mountain Springs.

So for Esther's sake they bore with her husband, refusing to let him get under their skins.

In the past month, however, Fred had found himself in an unexpectedly vulnerable position, and he was angry with himself because of it. All his life Fred had been a fairly circumspect person where women were concerned. Since his marriage he had taken it for granted that he loved Jane. Sometimes, it is true, he had wondered if it wouldn't be better if Jane were a little softer, less quick to defend herself against anything she fancied as derogatory treatment from her husband—if it wouldn't be nicer if she were more, in fact, like his sister Esther; that is, docile and ever ready to look on the good side of her husband rather than to cheerfully point out his faults. But Fred had never seriously questioned his affection for Jane nor been consciously unfaithful.

He was a little surprised at himself over the way he had succumbed to Gracie's attractions. Not for a minute did he consider his feelings serious. But there was no question about the illicit desires the girl had called forth.

Gracie was a waitress at a restaurant on the main street in Valdale. The Sunny Spot Café had tables along the street windows and a long counter with stools. Its largest volume of business was in hamburgers and french fries, although a Merchants' Lunch was available daily. Fred often stopped in for a quick bite and thereby got on friendly terms with the counter girl.

Gracie was in her twenties. She had tawny, natural blond hair that, despite the change in fashions, she still wore in a nearly shoulder-length bob. Her greenish eyes were set almost imperceptibly at a slant above prominent cheekbones, and she applied lipstick generously. Although she was slender, her arms were plump, and Fred noticed that there were dimples in her elbows. For some reason he found this irresistibly appealing. Gracie usually wore the collar of her uniform turned back down past the top button of the bodice. This led to fascinating glimpses of the curves on either side of the groove in her flesh that rose above what was presumably a tight brassiere under the crisp white smock. This alluring declivity was especially apparent when she bent over the ice cream containers or leaned forward to rinse out glasses in the sink beneath the counter.

All Fred realized at first was that he enjoyed exchanges of repartee with Gracie when he dropped in for pie and coffee, a custom which soon became a daily one. He was even somewhat surprised when Gracie accepted his first invitation to go out with him. Their dates soon became another regular custom, discreetly handled and, on Fred's part anyhow, a delightful diversion. The fact that Gracie would accept little presents, like money for a new suit she was dying to buy at the Valdale Emporium, did not diminish Fred's enjoyment of the relationship. After all, he was twenty years older than the girl, and married. So she could not expect any permanent rewards for being nice to him. It was no more than right in Fred's eyes that he should help the kid out occasionally to get the nice things she wanted.

Fred had practically no guilty conscience as far as Jane was concerned. She need never know, and he was depriving her of nothing she wanted. He was careful not to be seen alone in public with Gracie. Not for the world would he have hurt Jane by letting himself become the subject of gossip which would put her in the humiliating position of a wife who could not keep her husband faithful.

Maurice sometimes stopped at the Sunny Spot for coffee and doughnuts, and if they happened to meet there, Fred was scrupulously cordial. Then one day as they sat side by side at the counter, both idly contemplating Gracie as she bent with her back to them, getting pies out of a low shelf, Maurice nudged Fred and muttered with a salacious grin, "Wouldn't mind having a piece of that. Heh, boy?"

Involuntarily Fred scowled at his brother-in-law. "How about getting your mind out of the gutter for a change?" he snapped.

Maurice pulled his face down comically. "Oh-ho! Hit home, did I? You have got your eye on this chick."

Fred surveyed him coldly. "Why don't you grow up?"

After that if he saw Maurice's car parked nearby, Fred did not enter the Sunny Spot. There were times, however, when it was impossible to avoid an encounter with the man. Maurice would come in while Fred was halfway through his coffee, and then with winks and leers and raising of eyebrows and twisting of lips Maurice would convey his thoughts in regard to the girl busy behind the counter. Fred had instantly regretted his sharpness that first day when Maurice made his remark about Gracie. His annoyance had revealed too much. So now Fred attempted to be blandly uncomprehending as Maurice mouthed his lecherous insinuations.

"Must be something in here you go for," Maurice observed raucously one day as he swung his leg over the stool beside Fred.

"Only place in town you can get decent pie," Fred returned equably.

Then, just last week, the worst happened. Gracie had Mondays off, and quite often she and Fred spent an hour or so on that afternoon at a place called The Gables, three miles out of town. It was an old family mansion of the nineties which had been converted into a sort of night club. The house had gables in plenty and just about everything else too—cupolas, bay windows, railinged porches, and extensive incrustations of ornamental shingles and carved woodwork. The bar, located in what had once been the family sitting room, remained open all day, and there were rooms on the second and third floors which could be reserved for private use by trusted patrons.

In the evenings one might find representatives of the community's best people drinking and dancing in the former dining and drawing rooms of The Gables, but there was a tacit understanding in the area that respectable women did not visit the old mansion until the dinner hour.

As, with Gracie beside him, Fred departed from The Gables by way of the rear driveway late one afternoon, he had the bad luck to pass Maurice Egstadt turning in, presumably for a cocktail and a game of dice poker with the bartender before he proceeded home for dinner. Maurice waved, grinning broadly; and Fred had no hope that his brother-in-law had failed to recognize Gracie.

Sure enough, the next time they met on the street Maurice chuckled lewdly. "Ain't you the sly one? Never would have thought it. No sir, never would have suspected old pillar-of-respectability Fred. Wonder what Jane would have to say about all these goings-on."

Fred suddenly felt as if he were choking and realized that it was with rage. He controlled himself determinedly and replied coldly, "Don't jump to conclusions."

But when Maurice left him Fred found himself cold with apprehension. He knew very well what Jane would have to say at even the hint of such "goings-on." And Fred quailed at the thought. He'd never live it down. Jane would have him reduced to virtual slavery for life if she got something like this on him. And furthermore, he did not want to cause her the pain the knowledge of his infidelity would inflict. From the start he had not wanted to hurt Jane. But this overmastering and unfamiliar—unfamiliar in recent years anyhow—obsession had incomprehensibly taken hold of him, an obsession with Gracie's dimples, and that fascinating white valley at the opening of her blouse, and those full, ripe-colored lips, an obsession that led to desires he seemed unable to resist—that he didn't even want to resist.

Fred cursed himself for having laid himself wide open to Maurice Egstadt's malice. Especially when he had always felt smugly that Maurice might put things over on people like Marvin and Jocelyn, but not on Fred. Fred was too smart for him.

On the way to the picnic today as they passed The Gables Maurice had nudged Fred with a knowing smirk and a jerk of his head toward the back seat where the girls and young Leo were sitting. All the rest of the way Fred had simmered with rage and frustration.

As he walked toward the ball-field bleachers, Fred mused upon the man he had just seen lying asleep under the tree. Privately he had always been faintly contemptuous of the other members of the family who had let Maurice upset them so seriously. Little Alison, for instance; the kid had always been neurotic about Maurice. You could tell by looking at her that Maurice scared her. Fred had often thought: Why doesn't she stand up to him? He had often reflected in similar terms about Esther. Why didn't she tell the big stiff off once in a while? Just let him cross my path, Fred had told himself grimly, and I'll show Mr. Egstadt a thing or two.

But now that Mr. Egstadt was preparing to cross his path Fred found himself strangely helpless. It seemed as if Maurice attacked only when his prey was in a position where it couldn't fight back. It was this, Fred realized now, that made Maurice so malignantly potent.

Rather sheepishly Fred recalled how he had pooh-poohed Arthur's distress over Esther's getting involved with the man.

"I tell you," Arthur had complained, "I hate to see Esther marry him. He's one of the meanest men I ever saw."

"I don't know about that," Fred had rejoined, "but I know he's one of the biggest fools I ever ran across. I hate to see her fall for a big bag of wind like that too, but it's her life. It's none of our business."

"I know. There's nothing we can do, really. And you're right, he is a fool. That's probably one reason he's mean. He resents people who have more on the ball than he has. And practically everybody has. He's got an inferiority complex as big as a house; and you watch, he'll take it out on Esther."

"If she's bound and determined to make her bed with a slob like that," Fred had protested impatiently, "let her lie in it."

When the others went into their tirades against Maurice's latest piece of villainy, winding up inevitably with the despairing comment that they just couldn't understand how Esther could tolerate that man, Fred had usually kept to himself his own cynical interpretation of Esther's loyalty. Maurice probably gave her a good time in bed, and sheer physical satisfaction kept her apathetic to his faults in other fields of behavior.

Now he experienced a much-belated twinge of guilt. Perhaps if he had added his voice to Art's and talked to Esther straight from the shoulder, they might all have been spared the burden of Maurice all these years.

On the other hand, it was Esther's life, and she seemed satisfied with it. Except of course where this trouble about David and Renée was concerned. That had hurt Esther terribly, the way Maurice had acted over David's marriage. It seemed as if that was the first time Maurice's behavior had really got to her. Fred knew Esther was unhappier about the breach between Maurice and David than she ever let on. Poor little Tess. She had been an awful cute little girl.

Much as he tried to concentrate on the ball game, Fred could not get

Maurice out of his mind. The creature kept returning in one connection or another. It troubled Fred to discover that he was hating the man, too, as personally and as irrationally and probably as violently as Marvin or Jocelyn did. Hatred of Maurice seemed to be an emotion that, once you let it get a toe hold, moved in on you in an overwhelming manner. It was probably because Maurice stimulated your resentment in ways that left you with no means of concrete counterattack. For one thing, he picked things like this affair with Gracie to throw at you, and there was nothing you could do about it but sit around generating frustrated animosity. For another thing, Esther always stood between Maurice and his victim. If you fought back openly at Maurice you would hurt Esther even more than him, probably, and none of them wanted to cause pain to Esther.

SIX
David

After dinner David and Renée went with the other cousins of their own age down to the swimming pool. Little Bea's husband carried the baby, and Florence and Steven got into their bathing suits at the flimsy bathhouse among the trees.

"The young married set," Little Bea laughed as they lounged in the shade near the bank.

They chatted companionably, exchanging news of their jobs, their housing problems, and budgetary difficulties.

"I hate to see us all getting so scattered," Little Bea regretted. "I understand you're going to be teaching clear down near San Diego next year, David."

"That's right."

"I thought you meant to stay in Dos Rios and get tenure in a year or so."

"I decided not to get in a rut quite so early in the game."

"Bea's folks want us to move over to Mountain Springs where they live now; but I figure we're O.K. right here in Los Alegres," Little Bea's husband put in. "They're only thirty miles away, and we'll get along better if we aren't too close."

"You've got something there," David rejoined shortly.

He only hoped that he and Renée would be safe with nearly four hundred miles between them and his folks.

After they had done some swimming and dressed once more, David and Renée went back together to stow their bathing gear in the car. The picnic site was deserted. Maurice no longer slept under the tree.

Renée glanced toward the west where the sun was getting lower. "Maybe we should think about getting started."

"It's O.K. with me."

All afternoon they had avoided a tête-á-tête with Esther. When she had joined the "young married set," her son and his wife had chosen that moment to take a dip. Afterward Esther had merged into the group of older women who sat together a little out of the main flow of activity, leaning on collapsible back rests, gossiping and watching the lively crowd around the bathing area.

As he floated in a quieter corner of the pool David brooded over his parents. Lying in the sun to dry off afterward at the edge of the wooden platform around the diving tower, his mind continued with undisciplined persistence to come back to his father and mother.

He was Maurice David on his birth certificate, and to this day his father insisted on calling him by the fatuous "Junior." Esther, in rare defiance of her husband's example, had begun to call him David when she learned during the boy's adolescence that he hated being "Junior." This little defection on his mother's part had disproportionately affected the father, David sensed, created even more antagonism toward the son, who had already proved a disappointment to Maurice in many ways.

His early childhood David remembered as a reasonably happy one. His father had favored him with a tolerant acceptance, playing with him a little too strenuously for comfort at times, but on the whole showing a real though rather flaccid interest in his offspring. Maurice had always been too busy with his shifting business interests and his more stimulating relationships with adults to be deeply concerned with fatherhood. Very small children bored him. It was as if he granted Esther her boy as if he were a doll to keep her amused and pacified. Instinctively, until he was nine or ten, David had imitated his father, used him as a model. But when his own natural temperament began to assert itself he paid less and less attention to the man of the family. He found in the music teacher at school and his home-room teachers, who for several years in the latter grades of elementary school happened to be men, the idols with whom he could unconsciously identify himself.

In the seventh grade, when there was an opportunity to take music at school, David chose to play a flute. It was one of the collection of instruments the school provided.

"The flute, for God's sake," Maurice had erupted. "Why in hell the *flute?*"

"Because it makes such a pretty little noise."

Maurice turned choleric eyes upon Esther. "A pretty little noise! If you have to play something," he demanded, "why not the saxophone or a French horn or drums? Something with a little guts to it."

The boy looked bewildered, but he reiterated, "I wanta play the flute."

Esther timorously bought David a flute of his own for Christmas, and

Maurice made fun of it. David's feelings were hurt by Maurice's scoffing: "Tweet, tweet, tweet! What are you, a little bird?" But in spite of his wounded sensibilities, David caressed the new instrument in the secrecy of his bedroom and blew into it fondly. He still liked "the pretty little noise."

Maurice became really offensive in his remarks when David refused to go out for football.

"But I don't like running into people and being pushed and shoved," the boy protested.

"Athletics are an essential part of education," Maurice declared pompously.

Esther interposed nervously, "But, dear, he's awfully good at tumbling. Remember the demonstration he was in during Public Schools Week. That's athletic, develops their muscles and things."

"And I'm on the swimming team," David added hopefully.

"Tumbling," Maurice snorted. "Swimming! Girls can swim."

"Not as good as me," David maintained stoutly.

Maurice's manner toward his son was coldly disapproving for quite a while after that and laced with constant sarcasm. But young David, to his own surprise, found that he didn't mind so very much. By keeping out of his father's way and crowding his days and evenings with the company of his boy friends, he could almost shut his father clear out of his thoughts and also out of his emotions. And his mother was a quiet rock of loyalty in the background. He was perceptive enough to recognize that, while she never defended him openly against the man's attacks, secretly Esther was on her son's side. When he was older David realized that Maurice was also frustratedly aware that, though his wife publicly concurred in his opinions, this was not necessarily an indication of her private views where the boy was concerned. And David realized later that this situation encouraged in Maurice a gnawing antagonism toward both of them.

Now in maturity David could analyze better the changing relationship between himself and his father. When he had been a little child, "Junior" was simply another of Maurice's possessions, like his car or his real leather armchair or his wife, and as such the lad was naturally an object of approval—as any part of Maurice would be to Maurice. But the more the child became individualized and emerged as a separate personality, the less the older man could tolerate him, especially as it became more and more apparent that the boy was far from a carbon copy of his sire, which Maurice had unconsciously expected David to become.

Maurice had been pleased to refer excessively to "my boy up at Cal" and "Junior's fraternity brothers" when David went to the university at Berkeley. But when Maurice learned that David had elected to become a teacher and was majoring in education, he nearly blew his top.

"Who ever got rich teaching school?" he demanded. "Teachers make a living. That's all you can say for it. Don't you want to get somewhere, be somebody?"

David prudently refrained from arguing with his father. But when the boy persisted in preparing for the teaching profession, Maurice laid down the law. If that was all the ambition Junior had, Maurice was damned if he'd finance any more college for him. So David worked two summers in the cannery and during the school term got an evening job ushering in a movie theater near the campus, thus paying his own way the last two years of college.

He did it quietly and without defiance, but he could see now that this behavior on his part had tipped the scales of his father's hatred. Hatred was a strong word, but at last David had to admit to himself that it was the only term to describe what his father felt toward him.

Renée had brought Maurice's animosity to a culmination. David brought her home for a weekend in the spring before he graduated. Esther seemed quite taken with the girl. Oddly enough, she had almost always liked David's girl friends, often taking the girl's side in little tiffs and mis-understandings that came up. It was almost as if she "identified" with the girls.

Maurice had been sarcastically polite to Renée, and David had inwardly writhed at the slanted remarks his father made, perfectly innocuous on the surface but with an implied raising of the eyebrows.

David should have recognized ahead of time that Renée was everything his father regarded askance.

First of all, she had a "foreign" look, and Maurice's most ordinary conversation teemed with expressions like "wop" and "dago" and "cholo." Orientals were all "gooks" to Maurice. Worst of all, Renée's father was Jewish, a fact which Maurice had drawn out of the girl within the first hour. Afterward he informed David cynically, "I knew it the minute I looked at her. They can't fool me." And her mother, as the girl's name indicated, had been French. People of that nationality were invariably "frogs" to Maurice. To make matters worse, since her mother died when Renée was ten, the girl had been brought up by an aunt who was a Catholic, and Renée had rather fitfully attended that church, an institution which Maurice was firmly convinced had iniquitous designs on civilization as he conceived it.

Furthermore, Renée was obviously an intellectual. She even brought a book on psychology with her to read for relaxation on the weekend. Maurice distrusted "highbrows." And Renée was a liberal—or "radical," as Maurice expressed it. She did not, for instance, think that the whole Roosevelt family was inherently wicked, as Maurice did, and she brazenly informed Maurice that there were some good things about socialism, even as practiced in "Roosha"—Maurice's deliberately derogatory pronunciation.

The next time Maurice saw David after that weekend he made incessant fun of that long-haired "furriner" the boy was running around with.

When David told his mother that he and Renée were engaged, he felt a quick sympathy for Esther as he discerned the terror that came into her eyes.

"You like Renée, don't you?" he asked gently.

"Yes. Oh yes, I thought she was very attractive. And bright. And she isn't a frivolous type. I think she probably has a lot of common sense tucked away in her. But it's your father I'm thinking of. He's going to be terribly—disappointed. Renée isn't—well, isn't the type of girl he hoped you would marry."

Maurice was more than disappointed; he was outraged and at vocal length. David held his tongue and tried to keep his own anger under control. He had learned to do that, for his mother's sake.

When Maurice saw that his wrath, his ridicule, his scorn were having no effect on this perverse offspring, he delivered an ultimatum. "If you're bound to make a fool of yourself and mess up your whole life by marrying that foreigner, I wash my hands of you—for good! Just don't bring her around me. She's not coming to my house so the whole world can see what a fool you've made of yourself."

David, white-faced, got up and left the room. A man could not knock his own father down, and whatever he said would only make things worse for his mother. Dad would take it out on her even more than he was sure to anyway, with fulminations against David and accusations against Esther for having raised their boy to be a disgrace to his family.

They were married quietly at City Hall in San Francisco, with only a fraternity brother of David's and Renée's best girl friend present. On their way south to the small town where David was to teach in the fall, they stopped and spent the afternoon with Esther. David had telephoned his mother ahead of time so that she would expect them.

Esther was wearing her newest and best summer dress, a pale green linen trimmed with ecru lace, and her hair had obviously been freshly set at the beauty parlor. She greeted the newlyweds effusively, aflutter with excitement.

The best china coffee cups and an angel-food cake with a toy bride and groom on one side and a cluster of pink-icing roses on the other were set out on the tea wagon in the living room. When David saw them he wanted to cry. Instead, he put his arms around Esther and buried his face in the scented waves of her fresh coiffure so that the women should not see the helpless tears in his eyes, tears that were not for himself but for Esther, who would have so loved the fuss and preparation of a real wedding for her son.

When he raised his head, tears were running down the sides of his mother's nose, and Renée had turned away so that they could not see her face.

Esther brushed childishly at her cheeks and quavered in what was meant to be a light tone, "I guess it's true what they say: people always cry at weddings. It's not that I'm really sad. I know you're both going to be so happy." She moved into the room. "But sit down now, and we'll have a nice visit. I thought of asking some of the folks over. I know they all want to see you. But you have so little time, and I just decided to be selfish. I wanted you all to myself."

As her voice ran on, high and light but intense, Esther had perched on an occasional chair. "I'm so disappointed your father couldn't be here," she stated airily, "but he just *had* to be in Los Alegres this afternoon on business."

David felt a momentary irritation at his mother's determined hypocrisy, a saving antidote to the maudlin emotion which had threatened to overwhelm him a few moments before.

Esther was back on her feet, and from the dining table visible through the archway she brought a large package wrapped in yellow paper and elaborately decorated with pale blue ribbon. Proudly she set the box on Renée's lap.

"A little present for your new home."

"How nice." Almost shyly Renée touched the broad, sheer ribbon bow.

"Well, open it," David enjoined heartily.

As the bride laid aside the heavy white envelope tucked under the ribbon, she murmured, "The wrappings are so beautiful I hate to undo them."

David leaned toward her as she lifted the white lid to reveal a pink wool bed blanket. Esther beamed as they exclaimed and thanked her. Renée put the box on David's lap and came over to kiss the woman gratefully.

David pulled the fancy white card from its envelope, running a finger over the raised satin surface of the bride's dress on the front of the card. As he opened the folder, before he could read the verse, he saw the handwriting in violet ink at the bottom, "With love and best wishes from Mother and Dad."

His teeth caught the inside of his lower lip until it almost hurt him. Acquainted as he was with his mother's almost illimitable capacity for dissimulation, this instance of it was well-nigh unbelievable. "—and Dad." David was certain that Maurice neither knew of nor had authorized the purchase of the expensive blanket. But Esther would keep up the pretense of family harmony, no matter how obvious its absence. David didn't know whether to admire her determination or berate her silently for moral dishonesty.

When they said good-by Esther wept openly, clinging to David, kissing him repeatedly. She blew her nose and wiped her eyes and turned to Renée, her hands on the girl's arms, speaking hoarsely, "Please—don't misunderstand. I didn't want to break down like this. I just can't help it."

Her voice was becoming steadier, and she met the girl's eyes appealingly. "It isn't that I'm—sorry you two are married. I want David to be happy, and I can see that he is." As she spoke the next words there was a withdrawn look in her eyes, and her voice was lower, "It's just—I feel so alone now."

When the young couple were in the car headed south David said after a silence, "Poor Mom, she tries so hard."

Renée spoke slowly, honestly. "I like Esther. Basically, I think she's a nice person. But she's weak."

"Who wouldn't be?" David responded bitterly.

Renée regarded his profile thoughtfully. "You've done very well, d'you know that, coming out of it as well as you have, practically unscathed? I think we have to give Esther part of the credit for that."

"I guess," David said dryly, "the main thing wrong with her is my dad."

Renée shook her head in perplexity. "I keep trying to understand it. But it's difficult. I can't see myself ever refusing to see anyone as the person really is, no matter how much I didn't want to."

"Maybe she sees things in him that the rest of us don't," David retorted cynically.

"That may be."

That winter Bea and Marvin took a trip to Southern California to see Cousin Hubert and Fran. They would go right through Dos Rios where David was living, and Bea tentatively suggested to Esther that she might go that far with them and they could pick her up on the way home.

Esther's face lighted up; then it dimmed. "I'd love to! But I'll have to think it over. I'm not sure I can get away right now. I have so many social commitments. I'll phone you in a day or two."

Bea was not taken in by the "commitments." Esther had to find out if Maurice would let her go without raising hell.

To Esther's own surprise, he consented after only token resistance and, of course, continuing derisive comment about her stupidity in wanting to go at all.

Esther seized encouragement wherever there was the slightest pretext for thinking it was warranted. She took this scornful acquiescence as a sign that her husband was softening toward the kids, wanted to re-establish contact with his boy. She determined to be as unobtrusive and tactful as she could possibly be. Give things time, and everything might straighten out of its own accord.

Renée was surprised at her mother-in-law's gaiety during the four days she spent with them. When she spoke of it to David, he smiled contemplatively.

"I never thought of it, I guess. Mom was always full of fun and cheerful like this, as I remember her. But I guess it was when we were alone together that she was like that. Naturally, as a boy, I saw her by herself a lot of the time. But you've only met her in a group. The day we stopped by after the wedding was an exception, an emotional occasion when all three of us didn't feel quite normal. Somehow I must have just taken it for granted that when Dad was around, or some of the relatives or friends, Mom would tighten up, that there'd be a forced note to her gaiety. I suppose I just thought of this strained air as 'company manners.'"

Renée had found a job working mornings as bookkeeper for a small warehouse firm, and Esther happily did the housework while her daughter-in-law was out. They lunched together and went window shopping and took short drives in the afternoon to view the local points of interest. Renée found herself becoming genuinely fond of the somewhat naive older woman.

Esther had let it be known with a guileless casual air that "Dad" was "so pleased" that she had this chance for a little holiday and a visit with "the kids." After that, no one spoke of Maurice.

The day before Bea and Marvin were to pick her up, Esther and Renée were working together remodeling a skirt for the girl. The click of scissors, the rhythmical back and forth of needles and thread gave rise to a cozy, confidential atmosphere. Esther fell to reminiscing about David's birth and the reasons that she had been able to have no more children; and Renée found herself confiding her own hopes about a family—how soon, and how many, and her intentions of following the procedures, when the time came, of having a "natural birth," which was all the thing now.

After David's remark about the change in his mother's demeanor when she was in groups where Maurice was present either physically or in the consciousness of Esther and the others, Renée had felt a more poignant sympathy for the woman, and it imbued her with a desire to give more of herself to Esther, as if to comfort David's mother by drawing close to her.

And so the first thing Renée knew she was telling Esther about her own past. "My mother was an actress—in pictures. Not a very successful one, but she worked pretty steady up until a year or so before she died. It was peritonitis after an operation that killed her." The girl frowned and bit off the thread close to the seam she was turning. "She lived hard," Renée said slowly. "It's an awful thing to say, I guess, but, for me, it was probably just as well I had to go and live then in a quieter, more normal home. Mother's apartment wasn't a very suitable place to bring up a teen-age girl. Not that she was immoral or anything. But she lived at a high pitch. Irregular hours, lots of parties and drinking. My aunt's home seemed dull afterward, but it was more wholesome."

"I understand your parents were divorced."

"Yes."

"That always makes it difficult," Esther said gently.

Renée wove her needle through the thick material, conscious of a growing impulse. Esther had come to seem something like a mother to her, and Renée felt a childish need to let go and be a little girl unburdening her thoughts to a kind and understanding maternal figure.

"You know who my father is, don't you?" Renée ventured. "Or no, I suppose David wouldn't mention it."

"Who is he?" Esther repeated.

"You've heard of Carl Myer?"

Esther frowned. "I do seem to have heard the name."

"He's in prison right now."

"Oh! How terrible for you."

The girl shrugged. "Oh, he's not a common criminal. He's one of the Communists convicted in the trials last year, and things are worse for him because he jumped bail and was caught later."

Esther stared at her with anguished compassion. "You poor child!"

Renée gave her a strange look. "You needn't feel sorry for me because of *that*. He's doing what he thinks is right, and I shouldn't be surprised if he isn't happier—in jail—than most people are out of it." She drove her needle through the material. "What I hold against him," she went on bitterly, "is that he was too busy saving the world to be a good husband to my mother and thereby possibly to save her life. She was too run-down and—dissipated, I suppose you could say—to withstand any complications after the operation she had to have. If she had been rested and physically in good shape, I don't think she'd have died.

"And he was too busy being a revolutionist to give any of his time or love to me, even when I felt so lost after Mother was gone. He came to see me exactly three times since I was ten years old. Those are the things I hold against him, not his sins against the government; I could forgive that."

"Why, I never dreamed—" Esther said helplessly with a worried look at the girl's brooding face.

Suddenly Renée smiled. "Don't be upset. Actually I hardly ever think about my so-called family. It's very likely I shall never set eyes on my father again. I don't know why I even brought it up. It's just"—she grinned—"you're sort of disarming. Made me feel like getting things off my chest."

"I'm glad," Esther said earnestly, "that you feel that way toward me. It makes me feel—included." She smiled gratefully, but Renée detected an uneasiness in the woman's expression.

"No one knows," she said quickly, "that I'm Carl Myer's daughter. I don't consider it anyone's business. And it's meaningless anyway. My parents separated when I was five. You won't mention it to anyone?"

"Of course not."

After Esther had gone home Renée told David of their talk. He frowned and said slowly, "I wish you hadn't told her about your father. If she tells Dad, it will be the final nail in your coffin as far as he's concerned. He'd probably see to it that we never got to see Mother again."

"But she knows that, doesn't she? She'll see that it's not the sort of thing to tell him. Because she really wants to patch things up among us all."

"She ought to see it. But you can't tell about Mom. Where people are concerned, she's downright stupid sometimes."

"But surely Esther will know instinctively that the last thing in the world I would want is for Maurice to know anything more about me than he has to. She likes me, I'm sure she does."

"I should think she'd know that much."

"I don't know what got into me," Renée said ruefully. "I guess it was the atmosphere of 'just us girls letting down our hair.'"

A month and a half later the superintendent of the school district called David to his office for an interview. Mr. Harris was a tall, stocky man with thick, sandy hair and a bluff manner. He smiled frequently, but his gray eyes had a gritty look. As David entered the office with its windows overlooking the green football field in the distance, Mr. Harris turned on the moderately cordial smile he used for teachers; but there was an unmistakable gravity in the tone of his voice. Mr. Harris prided himself on his forthright ways. A busy superintendent, he always said, should come straight to the business at hand. His time was valuable.

"Good afternoon, Egstadt. Sit down. I received a letter this morning which has disturbed me no end. It struck me the first thing to do was to talk to you direct, man to man. So far," he finished portentously, "no one else has seen it; and I hope we can straighten the whole thing out here and now, with no need *for* anybody else to be drawn in."

There was always a slight uneasiness in the mind of a teacher to whom Mr. Harris sent a summons, but David had approached the office more in curiosity than anxiety. At this point, however, apprehension invaded and took possession of him, and it was the more potent in that David had not the slightest inkling of what he was to face.

He accepted the typewritten letter Mr. Harris handed him across the desk and scanned it with feverish haste. After the first paragraph David's eyes dropped to the signature: Maurice Egstadt. He had known almost as soon as he started to read, but still the sight of the handwriting was an almost physical shock. He read on with his face turning a curious, pale gray shade.

Mr. Harris had watched David surreptitiously, and as he noted the color of the young man's skin he averted his face and gazed out toward the bluish hills beyond the athletic field. When he heard the paper rustle as David laid it on the desk, Mr. Harris looked back and asked, "Who is this man? A relative, I presume, since it's the same surname."

"My father."

Mr. Harris had trained himself to meet almost any crisis with an imperturbable countenance, but now he looked taken aback. "Oh." He paused uncomfortably. "I'm sorry."

"He doesn't like my wife," David said dully.

"So it seems." Mr. Harris picked up the letter and read a few lines with a slight puckering of his lips while David sat motionless, his face slack and stupid-looking.

The writer began by enlarging on what a friend he had always been to the public school system and how he had wrestled with his conscience and finally come to the conclusion that as a public-spirited citizen he could do no other than what he was now taking pen in hand to do. (He seemed in the fervor of literary creation to have overlooked the fact that instead of taking pen in hand he was obviously setting fingertips to typewriter keys by way of the hunt-and-peck system.)

It was the writer's painful duty to inform the superintendent of the Dos Rios schools that the daughter of a convicted traitor to the United States Government was the wife of one of its teachers, a woman whose background was further complicated by a dissolute mother whose loose life in the theatrical profession had contributed to her early demise. The writer felt that it was unfair to the people of Dos Rios to have such a woman exerting her pernicious influence on an instructor in their schools and furthermore undoubtedly mingling with their children via the P.T.A. and student activities, especially since the woman in question had in the writer's hearing expressed views similar to those entertained by her incarcerated parent. Anyhow, he just thought the superintendent should be forewarned, in case adverse publicity ever struck his schools through the revelation that the daughter of the notorious Carl Myer was lurking in their midst under false pretenses.

"I suppose it's true," Harris said casually. "Carl Myer is your father-in-law?"

"I've never seen the man," David said dully. "But he's my wife's father."

Harris shook his head and sighed as he let the letter fall to the desk top. "We get crank letters every so often. I always find them distasteful."

David's face was resuming its normal hue, although it was still pale. He swallowed, and his eyes rested on the superintendent with more life in them. He waited.

Mr. Harris said sadly, "This puts me in a very awkward position."

"My wife's parents were divorced when she was five years old. She has seen her father perhaps a dozen times since. As for her sharing his political views, that's absolutely ridiculous. I doubt if she even knows what they are."

Mr. Harris shook his head sympathetically. He smiled philosophically. "I have never subscribed to the belief that the sins of the fathers should be visited upon the children. If this were just a matter between you and me, Egstadt, I assure you we could approach the whole thing very differently. But you see the spot I'm in, don't you?" He touched the paper with a fastidiously rejecting finger. "The intention of the letter is that I should bring the contents to the attention of the trustees."

"Is that necessary?" David asked thickly.

"That is my dilemma," Mr. Harris replied rather unctuously. "If I do not mention this unsavory incident to the Board, and if the facts of your wife's history should become public, and if Mr. Egstadt then made it known that I had been cognizant of these facts all along, you see the position it puts *me* in, don't you? One of not having been open and aboveboard with the trustees."

David regarded the man blankly.

"On the other hand, if I call this letter to the attention of the Board members, I am putting *them* on the spot, no matter how all of us would look at the matter individually. They are elected officials, responsible to the community. And if unpleasant publicity ever did arise in connection with your wife's—er—connections, the citizens of the district would rightly feel that the trustees had not been completely straightforward in ignoring this communication and saying nothing of it."

Mr. Harris gazed regretfully toward the emerald turf beyond the windows. "You know what small-town school politics are. The opposition at the next School Board election would distort and pervert this whole matter of the letter and the Board's knowledge of it and their silence about it." His expression grew even more ruminative. "There's the bond election coming up too. And you know how some of the taxpayers are, ready to leap on *anything* to discredit the administration. And we *do* need a new swimming pool. And the band uniforms are a disgrace."

The flesh on David's face looked as if it were some sort of clay which had suddenly hardened into a permanent mold. "You mean," he demanded bluntly, "you think I should resign?"

"Oh, my dear boy, no. Nothing of the kind. But I have been trying to think of this from your point of view. It's tragic that this situation should exist in your family—between you and your father, I mean. And it seems to me that if perhaps you would find a position in another school, more distant from where your people live, and where *that* superintendent had not been subjected to such a missive as this, perhaps this animosity in your family circle would have died down by next fall. Mr. Egstadt has obviously gotten his hard feelings off his chest by writing me. It's very likely he will let the matter drop now, just won't work up enough steam again to do such a thing twice. In the meantime, as I said, perhaps the breach between you will close a little. Time heals all wounds, you know," he concluded with a bland, wise smile.

"If the wounds don't kill the patient first," David said harshly.

It was after six o'clock when David got home that night. Renée thought nothing of his tardiness. An emergency faculty meeting, an unexpected coaching demand, a call on the parents of a problem child—anything could delay a teacher after hours.

David had been walking since he came down the steps of the high school's main building where the superintendent had his office. He had considered not telling Renée of what had happened. It would be kinder not to burden her with the sordid incident. But David knew he couldn't bear this alone.

Their dinner cooled and remained uneaten on the stove. Renée reacted with fury. She wanted to throw things and break furniture and slam doors. She stamped about the house, her voice raised in incoherent ejaculations. Along with Maurice, Mr. Harris took his share of vilification.

"I could publish the whole story on the front page of the *Gazette*," Renée stormed, "and practically nobody in Dos Rios would give a damn. A few people would cluck and want to run me out of town on a rail, but most of them wouldn't see anything to be worried about. But that pusillanimous old Harris is so anxious to get in trustees that will eat out of his hand when the election comes up that he won't take the tiny risk of any controversy over the wife of a teacher he hired. It makes me sick! And as for your father, I could kill him with my bare hands."

When the excess of Renée's emotional energy had been worked off she sat on a hassock in their small living room, hugging her knees tensely, her eyes fixed wrathfully upon a stripe in the cheap green fiber rug.

"Don't keep saying," she snapped at David, "'How could he do such a thing?' I know how, and *why*. He wants to drive you out of teaching and into some racket where you'll make a lot of money so you'll be doing what he always wanted you to in the first place. He thinks this little stunt will make you so discouraged you'll quit. And he wants to break us up. He figures you'll work around to blaming *me* for your having to give up teaching, because it was on account of facts about my life that you got in trouble. So then he'll have had his own way all the way around. And besides all that, he's purely and simply getting revenge for your having crossed him. He's punishing you for disobeying him."

David was lying back on the studio couch which was the room's principal piece of furniture. He put both hands over his face and rubbed it savagely. "It isn't him I care about. So he's a son of a bitch. So I've known that for some time. It's Mom. She told him. Deliberately handed him the ammunition against me. I feel—I feel—" he made a strangled sound and finished weakly, "Betrayed."

Renée sighed heavily, closing her eyes. "Well, she didn't mean to. It's like you said. She's not bright in her dealings with people."

"This is more than stupidity. If she won't even use her head for a moment to protect me from him, it shows that she doesn't really give a damn about me."

Renée rose and moved about jerkily. "That craven old chicken-livered hypocrite Harris is right about one thing though. Distasteful as it is, the best thing we can do where your dad is concerned is bow our heads and take it. Maurice has had his fun. He'll know why we're leaving Dos Rios. Maybe that'll be enough to satisfy him. Maybe by next fall we'll be old stuff to him. He'll be all wrapped up in conniving against somebody else, and he'll figure, 'Oh, what the hell, I showed those kids they couldn't get away with flouting me. Why bother with them anymore?' And just go on sharpening his weapons against whoever he has it in for then."

All this took place about a month before school was out. From then on they had not answered any of Esther's chatty letters. Presumably she thought they were just lax about correspondence.

SEVEN
Esther

All afternoon Esther had kept a distant eye on her son and his wife. Beneath her brightly social manner she was so deeply disturbed that her thin façade of artless affability threatened to break at any moment. It was much easier to overlook unpleasantness and wait for time to dull the edges of the animosity which had caused it when the protagonists were less closely entwined in her own emotions than David was. She could tell that the children were annoyed with Dad again and that this time the displeasure was so voluminous that it had swept out to include her. Usually when some of the folks misunderstood Maurice they set his wife aside in their thoughts on a little island of assumed innocence. It was deeply disturbing to sense that this time the children had reserved no such isolated space for her.

She saw David with the towel around his shoulders, shaking hands with Steven and Little Bea's husband, Lester; and she saw the girls in the group kiss Renée, who, held her own towel in one hand and swung her bathing cap by its strap in the other. Out of the corner of her eye Esther watched the couple ascend the steps and disappear into the trees in the direction of the dressing rooms. It was apparent they did not intend to return to the beach.

They were leaving without even saying good-by.

Esther could no longer keep up even a pretense of participation in the conversation of the women around her. They were going exhaustively into the pros and cons of cold-packing versus pressure-cooking as a method for putting up fruit this summer.

Jane informed them smugly, "Of course I don't can anything anymore. I just pop everything into the deep-freeze."

"All of us don't have freezers," Jocelyn reminded her tartly.

Esther rose. "I think I'll go up and see what's happened to that husband of mine," she announced lightly. "He oughtn't to sleep *all* afternoon."

When she was out of earshot, Bea muttered, "Let sleeping dogs lie, I always say."

"It's been so nice and peaceful without him around, hasn't it?" Jane murmured ruefully. "But where are all the rest of the men?"

"Fred said he was going to watch the ball game," Jocelyn volunteered, and sniffed, "Ball games—on the Sabbath!"

The other women exchanged resigned glances.

When Esther reached the Mallory picnic site, Maurice was gone from his napping place under the tree and David and Renée were heading toward their car, fully dressed and carrying their damp swimming clothes.

Esther hesitated for a moment, her face crumpling with distress. Then she squared her shoulders and made her face smooth out. She called out gaily and waved as she hurried past the tables.

"You leaving already?"

The young couple had turned. They stood still, facing her.

"Yes," David said.

Esther smiled with playful reproachfulness. "Without even saying good-by to your old mother?"

David surveyed her calculatingly and then spoke abruptly. "I think we should say good-by. You might as well have it straight. This is good-by, Mother."

They were at the outer edges of the oak tree's shade. Sunlight fell in dancing fragments through the leaves, making a grotesque pattern on Esther's stark face.

"I don't know what you mean."

Anger steeled the man's voice, anger to sustain him in the difficult task at hand. "I'm through, that's all. I don't ever want to see either you or that husband of yours ever again."

Esther put her hand to her throat. Her eyes went to Renée and back to David. "Why?" It was a whisper. "What has Maurice done?"

"Not just 'Maurice' this time. I can take anything he can dish out. God knows I've had enough practice. This time it's you."

"What have I done?"

David stared at her inimically, and suddenly he reached for the billfold in his hip pocket.

"David, no—" Renée spoke.

"I've just made up my mind," he interrupted her harshly. "It's time she found out what she's married to. You've been protected long enough," he said to Esther. "You're no better than he is. In fact, in some ways you're worse."

There was a stricken, uncomprehending look on the woman's face as her eyes rested on the stiff sheet of paper David was unfolding. "I took this photostat myself in the lab at school. Mr. Harris kindly lent me the document so I could do so. Read this, and then see if now you can come out blameless in your own eyes the way you've always magically managed to do all these years."

Esther's eyes fled blankly over the photographed letter. She lifted them to David's face and then, holding the paper in both hands, bent her head and reread. She let it fall to the ground and put both hands over her face to muffle a faint moan. "No, oh no."

"You gave him this information," David told her inexorably. "You handed him the ammunition to attack me."

"David, please," Renée said sickly.

She could rant and fume and slam doors when they were alone with their anger, but she could not openly turn her indignation upon the woman and have to stand by to watch Esther suffer. But David's pain had penetrated beyond reason.

"You always cravenly convinced yourself the other people he hurt were unjust, that they exaggerated. You always made excuses. It was easier— and safer—for you to shut your eyes, fool yourself, than to admit you were married to a cruel, vicious, heartless man. Well, deny this! Deny your part in it!"

Esther met his gaze beseechingly. "I did. I did tell him—about Renée's family. I thought if he knew what a hard time she'd had, how much unhappiness there'd been in her life, it would soften him toward Renée, he'd be more willing to—to accept her and eventually come to like her, as I do. He was softening, I know. He let me come to visit you, didn't he? That showed he wasn't bitter anymore."

David had bent to retrieve the letter from the dust. He was folding it back into his wallet as his eyes rested cynically on the woman. "It showed," he said bluntly, "that he was morbidly curious about our affairs. He hoped you'd bring back some tidbit he could use to make trouble. And that's just what you obligingly did."

"But, David, I didn't mean—"

"Don't ever let me hear you say 'I didn't mean' again. It doesn't make any difference what people 'mean.' It's what they do. And you've aided and abetted that man in his cruelty to everybody else in the family ever since you married him. I could overlook and even forgive your disloyalty to other people you love, your own blood kin; but when it's your own son you'll sacrifice on the altar of your cowardice, it's too much. I can't condone nor forget it. A man has a right to expect loyalty from his mother above everybody else in the world, even his wife. But you're not even a mother. You're nothing! You're—you're just that man's plaything—"

"David!" Renée cried. "Control yourself; you're going to pieces—"

"Be quiet," he snarled, and turned on his heel, away from both of them, his face distorted with unbridled rancor.

Dazed yet tortured, Esther stared after her son. Renée spoke with helpless misery. "He can't help it, Esther. It—it just all boiled up, seeing you and feeling so bad the way he does." She continued desperately in the face of Esther's stunned incomprehension. "You must look at it this way: David loved you so much that when he felt you had betrayed him in favor of Maurice he lost all sense of proportion. This outburst, he couldn't help it—"

Still gazing after David, Esther put out her hand toward the girl, moving it up and down slightly as if to shush her. "Yes," she muttered abstractedly, "yes."

"I'm sorry," Renée said miserably. "Good-by, Esther."

"Good-by."

The girl had gone only a few steps when Esther's voice halted her.

"Renée!"

"Yes?"

"That letter. You saw it? The original?"

"Yes. David brought it home to show me before he returned it to the superintendent."

"It wasn't a trick? Some hocus-pocus? It *was* Maurice's signature?"

"There wasn't any trick. You might as well face it, Esther. Maurice wrote that letter."

Esther nodded. The leaves cast shifting shadows on her face. She turned away from the girl wearily.

At the end of the picnic tables she put one hand on the rough boards as if to support herself. Slowly she sank onto the corner of the seat. She did not look around to see whether the youngsters got into their car to drive away or not. She sat with her hands lying open on the weathered table top and stared ahead of her unseeingly. Another part of her mind seemed to rise out of the numbness which had permeated her being. This stranger within looked back, reviewing.

Images, fragments of scenes, bits of fact came drifting up and sinking back in her mind. Maurice had showed up in Los Alegres, a stranger, all those years ago when she first met him. He drove a La Salle car that was several years old. He was the agent for miniature-golf-course equipment and had been attempting to promote some kind of amusement park at the edge of town. Esther remembered vividly how robust and virile and well dressed the new young man in town had been. All the girls were in a twitter over him. Maurice Egstadt was not handsome in a John Gilbert sort of way, but his large blunt face had a sexy, male quality that was more potent than clean-cut beauty. Esther had felt triumphant when he took to dating her in preference to the other girls.

She soon learned the salient facts about his life. Maurice's family consisted of two older sisters living on the east side of San Francisco Bay, but even then he seldom saw them. One was married, one not. The single girl taught physical education at Mills College, and the other's husband was a lawyer in Oakland.

"Snobs, both of 'em," Maurice had pronounced them. And Esther had developed a mental picture of the women who had brought Maurice up as prim, social-climbing types incapable of understanding a high-spirited, vigorous little boy, always making impossible demands in the line of decorum and scholastic accomplishment until the child had fled them in desperation. Rejected, that's what he had been, Esther had deduced sentimentally, a rejected little boy.

She had seen the sisters, Amy and Charlotte, perhaps a dozen times since her marriage. They were always courteous but reserved. They made it plain that they encouraged no intimacy with their brother. And yet Esther had to acknowledge that if it weren't for what Maurice had told her of their niggardliness and the puritanically high standards of behavior they had insisted upon for him Esther would have been taken in by "the girls." They would have impressed her as kindly, sensible, intelligent women who were, it was true, self-consciously socially correct.

Once when money was tight before David's birth, Esther had suggested appealing to one of "the girls" for a loan.

"Not on your life," Maurice snorted. "They've never quit harping on the money they loaned me to go to business college on. Just because I quit before I finished they take the attitude I flunked out, and got sore because I couldn't pay 'em back then and there."

Esther prudently refrained from asking if he ever *had* paid them back.

"They're always throwing it up to me how they spent what the folks left, bringing the three of us up, and how they both worked their way through college doing housework and taking care of kids after school, and why couldn't I get a part-time job? Hell, I was younger than them."

Although Maurice had only the most formal relations with his closest kin, Esther became very much aware as the years went by that he was secretly proud of his sisters. He had many ways of making it clear to her that *his* people were of better quality, higher class than *hers*. Who among the Mallorys had married a successful attorney and had a four-bathroom house in Piedmont? Who among the Mallorys was a professor at a high-toned women's college? Who, in fact, in the older generation of Mallorys had ever even gone to college? The turn his pride took had hurt her feelings for a while until she managed to make herself see that it was a form of compensation for the poor boy, a way of bolstering his self-confidence.

Through all the friction which had developed among her own relatives and Maurice, Esther had found reasons to explain the trouble and therefore to exonerate her husband. As a bride, she had smarted sometimes when Maurice's kidding had made her feel ridiculous before other people, but she had known it was his way of showing possessiveness, a way of telling people, "Look, this woman belongs to me; I can tease her because I know she loves me. The way she will take so much off me shows how sure I am of her."

In a peculiar, painfully pleasurable way Esther had been gratified by Maurice's rough banter at her expense. It was his way of publicly claiming her; and what woman does not like having a man display his proprietary interest in her, even if it is in the somewhat unorthodox way in which Maurice chose to do it?

For years she had kept reminding herself of the reasons that Maurice and David were not as close as father and son ought to be. Maurice wanted his boy to fulfill his own dreams of what a young man should be, and David had failed him. Esther had continued to feel sympathy for both, to divide herself up, giving to the man with one hand, to the boy with the other, figuratively not letting the right hand know what the left did.

Understanding the reasons for Maurice's conduct, she had been so sure she was being perspicacious and wise when she told him of Renée's unhappy childhood. Maurice, with "the girls" who had been such a disappointment to him emotionally, would feel drawn to his daughter-in-law in sympathy with the unfortunate choice of parents fate had dealt to the girl. His resentment and dislike would soften, and one day they would all be a happy family group, woven together by common understanding of one another's problems.

Esther had always been able to conjure up reasons for believing everything was as she wished it to be. It had been more difficult when she was first married. There had been times when unwillingly she recalled the things Arthur had said to her; but with practice it had become easier and easier to convince herself that what she saw as reality was what everybody else would see if their eyes weren't too befogged with emotion to take in the true interpretation of events.

Esther had managed to create for herself what she thought was a steady, calm emotional balance. She had prided herself on the way she refused to let things upset her, on her lack of "nerves." Other people might yell and scream and quarrel as Jocelyn and Bea had done when they disagreed with Maurice; but she, Esther, had always been able to rise above such pettiness, to be—in her own eyes—the philosophical, all-forgiving little Christian character for whom to know all was to forgive all.

And now, catastrophically, the reasons would not come when she summoned them; no explanations crowded forward to mitigate and extenuate her husband's conduct in this last episode which had so unsettled his son.

Esther sat alone on the end of the plank, lost in the dry air, her figure patterned grotesquely by the slanting light that sifted through the faintly trembling leaves above her.

A few minutes before David and Renée returned to the picnic area Maurice had awakened and, after stretching and yawning thoroughly, wandered off in the direction of the ball diamond, where he stood watching the play for a few moments before ambling off toward the rest rooms on the other side of the field. When he came out of the toilet room he halted again to observe the game and then headed back toward the picnic site to see if there was any coffee left.

Meanwhile Fred Mallory had become bored with the baseball game and had himself returned to the picnic area, intending to fish a beer bottle out of the tub and take it to the beach, where he would join the others.

He saw Esther sitting at the end of the table and approached her with a word of greeting. As she turned her face toward him, Fred sobered and inquired anxiously, "Is something wrong, Tess?"

She continued to regard him as if she had not heard.

"What are you doing?" her brother demanded.

"I was thinking of Arthur," she said tonelessly. "You remember our brother Arthur."

"Of course I remember Art." Fred pushed back his denim cap by its long visor.

Esther looked away vacantly. "He warned me."

Fred frowned and moved closer. "What's the matter, Tess?" In his Hawaiian print shirt that hung loose over his prominent belly Fred looked rather like a pregnant woman.

Esther raised her eyes with an impatient flutter of expression. "Go away, Fred. Don't bother me."

"Are you all right?"

She moved her head restlessly. "Leave me alone."

Forgetting his impulse for beer, Fred studied his sister frowningly for a moment and then walked slowly toward the cars in the parking area.

"Upset, poor girl," he thought, "over David and Renée. Something worse than usual going on between them." He scowled and jammed his hands in his pockets, wondering what Maurice had done now. Maybe the four of them had had a big row.

"That bastard," he said to himself.

Esther got up slowly and wiped her face with her hand. She walked across the picnic site, taking the same direction her brother had.

EIGHT
Aftermath

Quite a few people heard the shot. In fact, there were some who insisted they heard two. But no one attached any particular importance to the noise. The family who held temporary title to the adjoining picnic site and who would have been the best witnesses were dispersed throughout the park, enjoying themselves. The leafy trees all about were a muffling agent. It was very noisy around the baseball field. A man was sliding into third base while an effort for a double play was going on at first and second, and the stands were screaming wildly. At the pool there was constant commotion, little boys shrieking as they jumped spraddle-legged, holding their noses, off the diving tower, children engaging in splashing water fights, mothers yelling at offspring who ventured too near the deep end. Two cars were passing one another at the turn near the Mallory picnic site. The occupants of both heard an echoing, explosive noise over the sound of their own two motors, but they assumed it was another machine backfiring. Other merrymakers took it for granted that someone was illegally taking pot shots at rabbits or ground squirrels or blue jays in the surrounding woods.

When Peggy and Leo came along the roadside, licking ice cream cones they had bought at the stand, they were weightily exploring the question of whether it paid to "go steady" or not. Leo could, with a tenth-grader in Lincoln High in Valdale, but he wasn't sure that he wanted to get roped in. As they edged between the cars lining the road, they saw Uncle Maurice lying on his face near the open stove. With startled ejaculations they ran to him, and Leo turned the man by his shoulders. Both youngsters gasped. Dirt, and blood from a hole in the forehead made the face almost unrecognizable. With a shudder Leo let go, and Maurice's face sank into the soft dust once more.

The two young people stared at each other. Peggy opened her mouth to scream; then she closed it quickly, clenching her teeth. Her lips parted, and she said thinly, "I mustn't scream."

Leo put one hand against his stomach and swallowed fiercely. "I'm gonna be sick," he panted.

"No!" Peggy cried. "Don't. Don't!"

"Shut up. You'll get hysterical." Leo looked around frantically. "Where is everybody?"

Peggy's eyes darted about in panic and fell on the gun lying on the powdery soil near the table. She moved toward it apprehensively. Leo was taking deep breaths, trying to stave off nausea.

Peggy knelt and picked up the revolver. "Look," she breathed.

Leo came to her fiercely and grabbed the weapon. "Haven't you got any sense? Don't touch it. Fingerprints." He looked down at the gun he was grasping tensely and laid it on the table.

"He was murdered," she whispered, aghast.

They looked at each other speechlessly before their eyes slewed toward the figure on the shaded earth.

Just then Marvin surmounted the bank behind them. Peggy gave a gasping cry and ran toward him, hurling herself into his arms.

"Oh, Daddy, Daddy, it's Uncle Maurice! Somebody killed him!"

When Marvin came closer and saw the body his face went white. "What are you kids doing here?" he snapped.

"We found him," Peggy wailed, "and the gun. There!"

"What in the world is going on?" demanded a voice behind them, and they turned to see Aunt Jocelyn crossing from the parking area.

From then on there was confusion, but a confusion they somehow managed to confine to their own party. The park manager appeared shortly; a call was put in from his office to the sheriff in Valdale; the family converged upon the scene; the manager and two of his employees helped Little Bea's husband and Steven to patrol the immediate vicinity and keep the curious away; Little Bea and Flo corralled the children and herded them down to the stream, where they could neither hear nor see what was going on above. It seemed only a matter of minutes until a county police car which had been patrolling nearby had reached the park in response to a short-wave message. The two deputy sheriffs brought a semblance of order and quiet to the scene. Someone had thrown a blanket over the corpse, and Fred had put the gun in his pants pocket for safekeeping.

It was Bea who finally ran her eyes over the frightened, dazed faces and demanded, "Where's Esther? Has anybody told her?"

Everybody looked frantically at everybody else as if they expected anybody to be Esther. But she was not there.

"Oh God, she's wandered off somewhere," Bea moaned. "She'll hear it from some stranger."

"Maybe she went to the toilet," Jocelyn said, "I'll go look."

"Break it to her gently," Bea called after her sister.

"Where's David?" somebody asked.

"They've gone." Flo wrung her hands. "We ought to get them back.

They won't know, and they'll get clear home and have to turn around and drive all the way back. Oh dear, oh dear!"

The last ones to arrive on the distraught scene were Alison and Orville. When the man had awakened from his refreshing nap, Alison had been kneeling a few feet away, letting the water flow past one of her hands in two rippling wings.

"I must have slept," he said groggily.

Alison straightened and waved her hand to dry it, glancing at the watch pushed up on her wrist. "About an hour." She smiled.

He shook his head, widening his eyes to clear them. "I had no idea. I thought I just dozed off a few minutes." As he sat up, Orville apologized ruefully, "I'm afraid I'm pretty dull company."

Alison stood with her hands in the pockets of her slacks and looked down at him with a frankly tender smile. "Not at all. I enjoyed it, just sitting here quiet and peaceful."

Orville clasped his hands around his knees and squinted up at her. It struck him that Alison did look more relaxed than usual. There was a subtle difference in the tone of her voice and in the quality of her smile. Something less guarded, as if she were letting herself go, or as if she had rid herself of some hidden anxiety. It must have done her good just to sit there in the sun with no company but the water and the trees and the birds.

It was Flo who rushed toward them as they came into sight on the steps up from the stream. "Have you see Aunt Esther?" she demanded.

"No. What's the matter?"

"Hasn't anybody told you?"

"Told us what?"

"Uncle Maurice, he's dead."

"Dead," Alison repeated. "Uncle Maurice?"

"Yes." Flo uttered a sound like a sob. "Murdered. And now we can't find Aunt Esther. And David and Renée are gone. And the police are here." She drew a shuddering breath.

"How was he killed?" Orville demanded.

"He was shot. With his own gun from the car. Uncle Fred went and looked in the glove compartment. And it's gone. And anyhow everybody knew it was Uncle Maurice's own gun. And the detective that just got here from the sheriff's office, he's furious because everybody handled it and Uncle Fred touched the knobs on the glove compartment and everything. So fingerprints won't do any good. And he thinks some of us did it. He as good as said so."

Flo's forehead puckered, and she put hand over her mouth.

Alison's face was still and thoughtful. "How strange," she said abstractedly. "I've felt—different—the last hour or so. Relieved. Almost as if something had told me he was out of the way."

Flo gave her a sharp look, quickly snapping out of her own state of nerves. "Get hold of yourself, Allie. I know it's enough of a shock to make any of us talk crazy, but we're all being questioned. You want to be rational when that man talks to you."

Orville gave Alison a worried glance. Then he looked toward the tables where groups were standing about. He picked out the man in a quiet sport suit and a tan straw hat who was speaking to Fred Mallory. A man in his shirt sleeves was taking a picture of something on the ground.

Bea called to Florence, and the girl hurried away. Stiffly Alison stepped forward. Impulsively Orville put his hand on the girl's arm. He spoke in a low, hurried tone, not taking time to consider his words.

"Look, Alison, when they question you, don't tell them I slept. Say we sat down there and talked, necked, did anything. But don't mention my nap."

She regarded him blankly.

"I could tell," he continued impatiently, "you hated the man. They must all know it, and in a thing like this that's bound to come out. So there's no use leaving yourself wide open."

Alison's expression became more sentient. She studied him and then said softly, almost wonderingly, "You want me to have an alibi?"

"You may all need one," he said gruffly and, with his hand still on her arm, moved forward toward the others.

The detective in charge was trying to get all the information he could before the party scattered to their separate homes. It had so far been impossible to set the exact moment of the shot. Peggy and Leo had found the body between four twenty-five and four-thirty. Fred thought it was around four-fifteen when he came to the picnic area and saw his sister there. His guess at the time seemed to be fairly close when compared with the guesses of others who had seen him come down to the beach at what Fred said was immediately after his leaving Esther.

The detective's name was Wilson. In contrast to the bereaved picnickers he seemed disturbingly calm, not to say phlegmatic. It soon became evident, however, that he considered it highly suspicious that the murdered man's wife and son and daughter-in-law had been on the scene apparently just prior to the shooting and had now vanished. No one knew the license number of David's Austin sedan, but Wilson had notified the highway patrol to pick up the vehicle, which was by now presumably heading south on the 101 Highway. Wilson suspected that the little English car would also contain Esther Egstadt and that within the trio of its passengers lay the solution to his case. Meanwhile, all he could do was collect facts from the others while the photographers did their work and the coroner hauled the body away. Wilson was not bothering about motives or the dead man's personal standing among his in-laws. That could come later. He had enough on his hands at the moment in obtaining the physical facts of the late afternoon events. With most of the adults present it was necessary to start with the picnic dinner and work right on through.

Wilson eyed Marvin Nelson and stated, "Egstadt was your brother-in-law. Right? Now when did you last see him alive?"

"When he left the table a little after two and went to lie down."

"How did you spend the afternoon?"

"Resting. I sat down by the stream for fifteen-twenty minutes after I got up from the table; then I wandered around, up by the swimming pool, over past the ball diamond, watched a horseshoe game on the other side of the pavilion for a while."

"Alone all the time?"

"Most of the time. I stopped to talk to some of the folks on the beach awhile and ran into some fellows I knew up at the other end of the park. I had a beer with a couple of guys at the plasterers' picnic."

"I understand you came up from the creek by those steps there just after the kids found the body. Where had you been just previous to that?"

Marvin wrinkled his brow in recollection. "Well, after I had this beer I spoke of, I headed back to the beach. Talked for a minute to some of our folks there and then just sort of meandered along downstream and back up here."

"Who of your party were on the beach when you reached it?"

"Well, let's see; there was my wife, and Cousin Helen and Wilbur, her husband, and Aunt Sarah, and Jane, and all the young folks except David and Renée and Peggy and Leo. Fred showed up a few minutes after I did."

Wilson consulted his scrawled notes. "What about your wife's sister, Jocelyn? I notice you didn't mention her."

"I met Jocelyn at the head of the steps as I went down."

"Did she return while you were there?"

"Not as I remember."

"I've been asking everybody this. Did you see or hear any signs of arguments or bad blood between the deceased and anybody else during the day?"

"No," Marvin answered with a straight face.

"Know of anybody that had it in for him?"

"No."

When Wilson cornered Jocelyn next, he inquired bluntly, "Where did you go when you left the beach late this afternoon?"

Her face drew together primly as she replied coldly, "I went to the ladies' room."

"The one by the dressing rooms or the one on the other side of the ball field?"

"The one nearest the beach."

"How long were you there?"

"I hardly think that's any of your business," Jocelyn retorted frigidly.

"Everything any of you did this P.M. is my business," the detective said tersely. "How long were you there?"

"Possibly ten or fifteen minutes," Jocelyn answered with a slight flush, and added curtly, "I had to wait my turn."

"Other women in the place saw you there?"

"I presume so. If they weren't blind."

"What did you do between the time you came out and the time you showed up here right after the discovery of the body?"

"I sauntered out to the road and stood looking about for a few minutes. Then I made my way back through the parking lot over there. I stopped on the way to check my car to see that it had not been molested."

Her eyes followed the detective's hand as he jotted down notes. Jocelyn looked disapproving. An account of her trip to the toilet was hardly the sort of thing she considered necessary to record officially. She almost told him so, but delicacy restrained her.

Wilson looked beyond Jocelyn to where Alison and Orville had been joined by Florence. "Now who the hell are they?"

After following his gaze, Jocelyn regarded the man sternly. "I don't think profanity is necessary." He looked a trifle startled, and she added, "That is my niece Alison and a friend."

"Big family, aren't you?" Wilson remarked in a pained tone, and set off to intercept the newcomers as they approached the tables.

Jocelyn joined the group huddled miserably on the bench, facing outward, their spines resting against the edge of the table.

Jane looked back over her shoulder at the men carrying Maurice's remains toward the waiting ambulance. She put a handkerchief to her lips and sobbed into it, once. Then she looked at the others with swimming eyes. "Poor Maurice. I know he had his faults, but you can't help feeling sorry—now."

Jocelyn gazed at the retreating men. Her face was stern, her stance erect. "I don't think grief is in order. I look upon this as a judgment of God. 'As a man soweth, so shall he reap,'" she quoted. "I cannot but feel that a higher power has taken a hand here. And it is not for us to question the will of the Almighty."

Fred had been sitting with elbows on knees, head in hands. He looked up irritably. "Don't talk foolish, Joss. God may not have had any use for Maurice Egstadt, but I'm damn sure that whoever fired that shot doesn't stand in very good with Him right now either."

"Don't be flippant," Jocelyn snapped. "He has told us in so many words that the wicked shall be cut down, root and branch—"

Bea twisted her hands together and broke in with an anguished quaver, "I wish they could locate Esther. Something may have happened to her too."

"You don't think—" Fred exclaimed gruffly.

"I don't like it," Bea reiterated. "People don't just vanish."

"They're looking for her," Marvin said soothingly.

The harassed manager of the park came bustling up to the group, his straw hat jammed too far down on his head. "We just got a phone call at the office. They picked up the young couple forty miles or so down the highway. They're on their way back here now."

"Was Mrs. Egstadt with them?" Fred demanded.

"They didn't say. A motorcycle cop phoned in the message for Wilson."

"Maybe they'll know something," Bea mumbled.

Wilson returned to the group by the table. "Young Egstadt and his wife should be here in half an hour or so. I want the rest of you to stick around until I've talked to them. Then I can probably let you all go home."

They regarded him with lackluster eyes, and Bea asked weakly, "My sister, Mrs. Egstadt—"

"No sign of her yet. She doesn't seem to be in the park. Two of our men are working downstream, and we're going to check the roads around here now."

He appraised Esther's uneasy relatives with speculative eyes and glanced toward Cousin Helen, who had built up the fire with her husband's help and was preparing to serve revivifying hot coffee. Wilson made his way to the stove, where Helen was lifting a dripping bag of grounds from the big pot. He estimated that he might get slightly more unbiased comment from one who was only a cousin than from the brothers and sisters.

"That looks good," he said genially. "Mind if I have some?"

Helen reached for a paper cup on the cement ledge around the fire box and poured it full of coffee.

"I understand," Wilson observed offhandedly, "that Mr. Egstadt and his wife didn't get along too well."

Helen dropped the lid into place on the pot and met his eyes deliberately. "Esther worshiped the ground her husband walked on," she stated shortly.

"H'm. Must have been somebody else that had it in for him then."

"Us Mallorys," Helen said distinctly, "are very close. Anybody'll tell you that. It wasn't one of us did it."

Inwardly Wilson sighed. So it was going to be like that. Family solidarity. All of them protecting each other and lying like hell in the process. They had already—deliberately, it looked like to him—tampered with the evidence, passing the gun around from hand to hand. He was not discouraged, however. It was just that solving the case would take longer than he had hoped would be necessary. In a public place like this, witnesses were bound to turn up—people who had heard and could swear to the time of the shot, for instance, someone who had seen a person leaving or entering the area at a crucial moment. It might be tomorrow or the next day before the significant testimony turned up, but it would come. And there were still the son and daughter-in-law and the wife to be questioned.

Florence helped Helen serve the coffee, and together they excavated among the picnic boxes to find some drying sandwiches and battered cake. A few of the waiting "witnesses" ate a little in nervous bites, but most of them just drank their coffee with an air of witlessness.

Alison and Orville withdrew from the others to sit on the log by the bank as they drank their coffee. Alison regarded the man curiously and then, holding her cup in both hands, asked impulsively, "Do you think I left you this afternoon while you were asleep?"

"What makes you think I'd think that?" he returned gruffly.

"Because I did, you know, for a few minutes. I got restless and walked out on the rocks in the middle of the stream. I even took off my shoes and waded a little on the other side where it was shallow."

"So what?"

"I thought maybe you thought," she persisted, "that I had come up here and had a row with Uncle Maurice and killed him."

He met her eyes levelly and inquired in a low voice, "Did you?"

"What would you do if I said I had?"

He looked away and, after a brief, unhappy pause, replied, "I don't suppose I'd do anything. I'd have to figure you had good reason."

Breathlessly Alison studied his averted face. She set her cup beside her on the log and touched his wrist. "You can relax," she said. "I didn't."

He sighed. "Well, thank the Lord."

Alison smiled, openly adoring as her eyes rested on his face. Orville covered with his the hand that still lay on his wrist, looking down at her attentively, a little puzzled.

"It's wonderful," she said softly, "to have someone willing to stick up for me and stand by me, even if they thought I was a murderer."

He grinned. "I guess I must kind of like you."

Alison felt no fear that it wasn't safe to do so as she told herself exultantly, "I'm crazy about him."

Over by the tables Florence said to her aunt Jane, "It looks as if this time Allie really has made it. Look at them, mooning at each other in broad daylight."

With a glance at the pair Jane observed tartly, "A fine time to be sitting around holding hands, with her uncle on the way to the morgue."

"Let's face it," Florence returned cynically. "Nobody's going to go into a decline over the loss of Uncle Maurice."

Jane was sitting on the bench with the girl standing beside her, and now she looked up and spoke tautly, her voice lowered. "It's just beginning to penetrate with me, now that I've got over the first shock of knowing Maurice is—gone. Somebody killed him, and that somebody is one of us. Have you thought what that *means*, Flo?"

Florence passed a hand through her purposely tousled-looking hairdo. "I haven't thought of it. Don't want to." Her lips pushed out in a pout. "I couldn't bear to have any of our folks convicted of killing that man. It—it just wouldn't be fair. After the way he's provoked everybody."

Marvin had been sitting behind them on the other side of the table, his arms lying flaccidly on the boards. Staring at the backs of the two women's heads, he turned over in his mind what he had just overheard.

He was only now beginning to feel the real horror of what his own first reaction had been when he saw Maurice lying there lifeless. Relief and triumph had mingled in the involuntary thought, "He's out of the way at last."

Revulsion at himself had been creeping slowly over Marvin ever since. He had tacitly condoned murder, that's what he had done. Which made him no better—made him worse, in fact—than the man he had hated. They had all thought Maurice a monument of iniquity, yet this turn of events showed that there was one among them even more unprincipled than the man who was killed. For murder was the very culmination of cruelty and wickedness. That Maurice himself had created these impulses in his executioner was no excuse.

Marvin was invaded by a great weariness and distaste for life that such things could be. There was no safe place for hatred in human affairs and yet its presence seemed inevitable.

When Fred had snapped Jocelyn up on her interpretation of the afternoon's event as an act of God, it jarred her more than she at first realized. Over the years it had become reassuring to enclose herself in the precise conviction that on the one side were the Devil and people like Maurice, on the other Jocelyn Mallory and God. She had been instantly able to bring up quotes like "Vengeance is mine," and "An eye for an eye, a tooth for a tooth," as insulation against the horror of what had happened. But the words of the irreligious Fred had unaccountably opened up a path in her mind down which crowded other quotations, "Judge not that ye be not judged," "Turn the other cheek," "Do unto others as you would have them do unto you."

Unconsciously Jocelyn fought against these reminders of another facet of her lifelong religious orientation. She felt more secure, wrapped in the self-righteous conviction that her God also hated creatures like Maurice and would approve of the elimination of such vileness on His earth. Jocelyn did not want to have to hate the perpetrator of this deed. And yet if this act against Maurice was as wicked as its victim, and if she was to remain safely wrapped in her cocoon of certainty about right and wrong, she must now turn intransigently against the one who had killed the man.

Jocelyn moved about with tense officiousness, finding cans of milk for coffee, washing cups, unpacking and then repacking the jumbled picnic boxes on the pretext of finding supplies.

NINE
Solution

There was a general sense of relief when David's little car nosed into the now almost deserted parking strip beside the road. The erstwhile picnickers were beginning to feel the nervous strain acutely; even the children, despite the administration of sandwiches and ice cream cones and soda pop, were becoming rebellious. They didn't want to stay on the cooling beach any longer.

All the way back David had driven like an automaton. Through the shock of the information the motorcycle policeman had given him and Renée, what came uppermost to their minds was the simple question of what had happened after they left the park. They seemed incapable of any thought or feeling other than this tense curiosity.

David strode toward the tables, Renée following with quick, nervous steps. His eyes swept the gathering, and his first words were, "Where's Mom?"

He had addressed Cousin Helen, since she was the person nearest him. "We don't know," she said limply.

"What d'you mean, you don't know?"

"Nobody has seen her since we found your father."

Wilson had come forward. "Mr. Egstadt?"

"Yes."

"My name is Wilson. Sheriff's office. Will you and your wife step over here?" He motioned toward the folding canvas chairs deserted under one of the trees.

As he followed the man David demanded, "Are you doing anything about finding my mother?"

"Everything possible. Don't worry. She's probably just off by herself, resting."

"At six o'clock! She wouldn't wander away from the party that long."

"Our men are looking for her, and several of your own party are too." He gestured for the couple to sit down and took one of the chairs himself. "When I find out a few things from you, it may help us to figure out where your mother is. Now, when did you last see your father?"

"When we left to go down to the beach. He was lying over there."

"And your mother?"

"We said good-by to her about four o'clock."

"She was here when you drove away?"

"Yes."

"Where? I mean specifically."

"She was sitting at the end of the table there the last time I saw her."

"Was there anyone else here in the picnic site when you left?"

"No, just the three of us."

"How long were you three here together?"

"Ten minutes maybe."

"What did you talk about?"

"Nothing in particular. Just—good-by, and don't forget to write, and come to see us—that sort of thing." David pulled a handkerchief from his pants pocket and wiped his damp forehead.

Renée's eyes were large and intent.

"You didn't wait to say good-by to your father?"

"We didn't know where he was, and we had to get going. It's a long drive."

"You didn't get along very well with your father, did you?"

"We were not very close, but we got along all right."

"When you talked to him during the day, what did you discuss?"

"We didn't have a chance to speak privately." David had squeezed the handkerchief into a ball in his palms.

"Have you any ideas as to who might have quarreled with Mr. Egstadt today?"

"None."

"You must have some ideas as to the reasons for this unfortunate occurrence."

"Well, I haven't. I was flabbergasted."

Renée listened apprehensively but shrewdly. There had been no witnesses to their last meeting with Esther. She surmised that the detective suspected Maurice had participated in the scene and that its aftermath had been the man's death. Obviously they had not yet talked with Esther. Where was she?

A county car with the sheriff's insignia on the door pulled in beside David's sedan, and a uniformed officer approached the group under the tree. He stood a few feet away and communicated silently with Wilson by a jerk of his head. The detective rose and went to the man. In a moment Wilson came back and spoke to David.

"You can put your mind at rest. Your mother is O.K. She's in the car over there. Our men picked her up several miles down the road toward town."

David had risen as Wilson talked, and the detective addressed him restrainingly, "You can see her after I talk to her. Just stay where you are. She's perfectly all right."

Wilson turned decisively and strode toward the machine, watched by all the party. He got into the rear seat while the driver remained in front and the other deputy stood nearby.

Esther sat back on the leather cushions, her hands lying loosely in her lap. What make-up she had put on earlier in the day had worn off, and her hair was frowzy. She looked very tired, but her eyes were calm.

"I understand the officers found you sitting off at the side of the road under a tree."

"Yes. I walked a long ways. Several people offered me rides, but I wanted to walk. I finally got too tired to go any farther. While I was resting there under the tree I saw David's car go past, headed this way, and I wanted to start back, but"—she glanced down at her dusty shoes—"my feet hurt."

"Where were you going?"

"Nowhere. Home, I suppose. I must," she said indifferently, "have been suffering from shock."

"What gave you a shock?"

"Everything that happened this afternoon."

"Tell me what happened."

"Surely you know," she responded with a wondering glance. "My husband, he's dead, isn't he?"

"Yes. You witnessed the event?"

"Of course. I shot him," she said matter-of-factly, and then regarded the man more perceptively. "You knew that, didn't you?"

Taken aback, Wilson murmured, "We weren't sure."

Esther looked past the shoulders of the man in the front seat and out through the windshield to the people clustered around the tables.

"None of the rest of them would do such a thing," she said dully, "only me."

"Why did you do it?" Wilson asked softly.

She let her eyes rest reflectively upon him. "You wouldn't understand. It's much too long a story."

"You—er—disliked Mr. Egstadt?"

"I hated him. Just as so many others did." She sighed and folded her hands together. "I suppose you'll lock me up now."

"Yes, we'll take you in to the courthouse."

Her gaze traveled past him, out the side window to where David paced nervously back and forth under the trees. "Before we go I want to talk to my son. He seems very upset."

Wilson considered her and answered slowly. "Well, I guess that's all right."

"Alone, please," she added rather imperiously.

"Well, I don't know about that."

"I think you could at least grant me that much," she said quietly.

Wilson surveyed the woman, reflecting that she seemed perfectly sane and composed. The state of shock she spoke of had obviously worn off. She certainly didn't act as if she were going to try to pull any fast ones.

"O.K. I'll call him over."

He stepped out of the car and hailed David with a wave of his hand, then jerked his head at the deputy in the front seat. They withdrew a few paces as David climbed into the car and took his mother in his arms.

"I'm sorry, Mom," he whispered hoarsely. "I shouldn't have blown my top at you the way I did."

"It's all right, Davy. You were right. You finally made me see what I had been doing all this time." She patted his shoulder comfortingly. "You have nothing to reproach yourself for." She drew back and regarded him earnestly. "You understand, don't you? I had to show you that I knew I had done wrong, had to prove I was on your side, not his."

Frowning, David studied her. "Show me?" he muttered thickly.

"It was more than that, of course. All of a sudden, it all came over me. I couldn't contain it. What he had done to me. I should have fought him as I went along, but instead, all the fight—for all the hurts and subtle insults and the constant domination—rose up all at once in me. And it was too strong. There was too much of it banked up, so that when it came I was overpowered. As if all I was was one concentrated force of resentment and rage. Afterward, as soon as the explosion died out, it was gone, and there didn't seem to be anything left of me. I just—dropped the gun and walked away." She smiled faintly. "I was a little surprised when I found myself way down the road. I was awfully warm, from the sun," she finished casually.

David stared at her, stunned. Then his eyes darted toward the men a few feet away. "You didn't tell the detective!" he said hoarsely.

Her shoulders rose and fell slightly. "Of course. What else could I do? I wanted to be sure you understood that I had finally and completely repudiated—him. I wanted you to know that when it came right down to it, even if I had betrayed you as you said, it was not forever. That in the last analysis I was wholly on your side."

David made a gasping sound and hugged her to him frantically. "Oh, Mom, Mom, you shouldn't have done it! You shouldn't have told him."

David's face stiffened with thought. He looked off urgently, his chin on her hair, and then drew back, eying her firmly. "Look, don't say another word. We'll get you an attorney, and he'll tell you what to say. You've got to deny you ever said anything to this Wilson."

She smiled at him faintly. "You're sweet, David. It makes me feel good to have you want to protect me. But there's no use. What could life possibly hold for me now? Even if I could fool the courts and the public, I couldn't fool myself. I know what I've done."

She twisted her hands together, and her face seemed to sag. "That's one thing that happened this afternoon. I quit fooling myself. And I can't begin again. I'm so tired—so awfully tired. You have no idea, Davy, how much it takes out of you in the long run, deceiving yourself. I just haven't the strength to start it all over again."

As her son watched her with a baffled expression, Esther went on meditatively, her eyes upon Alison over by the tables, "I thought about Arthur today. Before, and later when I was sitting by the road. You were too young to remember your uncle Arthur, Alison's father. He tried to persuade me not to marry Maurice. But I wouldn't listen. I see now that he was right, clear down the line.

"'I'm telling you, Tess,' he said, 'that man is riddled and consumed and filled with hate. God knows what the psychologists would say caused it. Probably it's not even his fault. I don't suppose he even knows that he hates everybody. But it's there. And a person like that will destroy you. He'll corrupt you. Someday you'll get just like him. Either that, or you'll have to go through a lot of suffering and misery to break away from him.'"

Esther shook her head sadly. "I didn't understand what Arthur meant then. But I do now. It's true. Maurice weakened me; and all the time I've lived with him he was filling me up with hatred too, a hatred like his. Hatred of *him*. And today it showed its ugly face. And when it broke through my defenses and took me over at last, I was no better than he. In fact, I was worse. I committed the final act of hostility. I killed another human being. I don't think Maurice ever did that. He drained his ill will off in little acts of malice against others. I let mine pile up for a big and irrevocable cruelty."

Wilson came to the door with a somewhat diffident air. "It's time to go," he said quietly.

As Esther looked at her son, tears welled into her eyes. "Give Renée my love," she said. A thought seemed to strike her, and she leaned close to whisper in David's ear. "Don't say a word about the letter. There's no need to bring all that into this."

He hugged her close with an inarticulate sound.

Over by the tables every eye was on the car. They had discovered that Esther was there and, without having to be told, the relatives suspected the truth. When David stepped out of the machine with his head bowed, a hand up to his eyes, they had no further doubt. Esther had done what many of them had sometimes wished they dared to do.

At first it was incredible. But after they had been told outright that

Esther was being taken to the courthouse to be charged with the murder of her husband, it soon became less astonishing.

"I guess we misjudged Esther," Marvin said slowly. "She must have always just been putting up a front for the rest of us. From a kind of a 'I've made my bed, now I have to lay in it' attitude."

"Something happened today," Fred said slowly. "I'd bet on it. Something that was more than even Esther could take."

"Well, I suppose we'll find out before it's over," his wife said morosely. "It's going to be just terrible. All the publicity. I *don't* know what Esther could have been thinking of."

Alison spoke up miserably. "We've all got to stand by her, that's all. I'm sure she had justification." Defiantly Alison lifted her head and looked from one to another of the group. "How can any of us blame her? She only did what most of us have wanted to do at one time or another."

"The rest of us had better sense than to do it," Jane retorted sharply.

This second shock had jarred Jocelyn's opinions back into line after the scrambling the first one had given them. She spoke up dogmatically. "Well, I for one am certainly going to exert every effort to see that Tess gets out of this. That man was a walking incarnation of wickedness. If anybody deserved to be struck down it was Maurice Egstadt. Poor Tess was only an instrument of divine justice. And I certainly intend to speak out on the stand until there'll be no doubt in anyone's mind that if ever a man deserved what he got, it was that one."

Bea had been sitting by the table with her head on her arms. Now she straightened and bent a petulant look at her sister. "Oh, Joss, don't be ridiculous. Whatever her provocations, she had no right to kill him unless it was actual self-defense. That's what we'll just have to hope and pray for—that he was threatening her." She leaned her forehead in her hand and said heavily, "That girl never did have any sense when it came to dealing with people. It's just like her to get in a tight spot and just naturally do the wrong thing." She shook her head in anguish. "Poor Tess."

Peggy had been standing wide-eyed at the edge of the group. "Will she get the death penalty?" she asked in horror.

In the police car on the way to the county seat Esther sat slackly, her eyes unseeingly fixed upon the soiled nylon skirt stretched over her knees. She knew that it didn't really matter what penalties the state decided to impose. As far as she herself was concerned, life was already all over. Arthur had been right. She was destroyed.

TEN
Wilson

Deputy Sheriff Wilson slept that night the sleep of the just, a man who had fulfilled his day's work to his own satisfaction, with no loose ends left over, no troublesome details unexplained.

He entered his office the next morning briskly, hardly thinking of the Egstadt case. The coroner had the body, and by now the autopsy would be completed. Esther's detailed, logical statement reposed snugly in the files. True, the question of motive was a little vague.

"I hated the man," she had stated calmly. "I didn't want him to live anymore."

Well, these husband-and-wife homicides often did sound just about that nonsensical to outside ears. Temporary aberration or something. And there were no loopholes in her account of the actual event. It figured.

After her brother Fred left her, Esther had stood up, walked to her husband's car, taken out the revolver, come back toward the tables, and seen her husband approaching from between the cars parked by the road.

"I may not have this part verbatim," she had said with a deepening of the vertical lines between her brows. "As I remember it, I was in a peculiar state, almost like a trance. I knew what I had to do, and other impressions just didn't register very well. But I think Maurice spoke first. 'What in the devil are you doing with that gun?' He was—oh, thirty feet or so from me. And I said, 'I have to kill you. You have done enough damage to other people.'"

At that point Wilson interrupted her. "Just what did you have in mind—damage?"

"My husband had an unfortunate compulsion to hurt other people. Where I was concerned it was in little ways. Belittling me, disregarding my feelings. Always criticizing our son, never approving of anything the boy did. If you care to check among the members of my family, you will find that Maurice had cheated and taken advantage of, or at least made most of them very uncomfortable."

Wilson regarded the woman wonderingly. Confessions of murder were not usually so lucid, so dispassionate. At his prompting she continued:

"So he stopped when I said that. I don't think he could believe his ears. I think he said, 'My God, Esther, what's happened to you? Have you gone crazy?' I decided I had better do it immediately if I was going to, so I lifted the gun and fired. He looked astonished. I had unconsciously expected him to fall instantly, and it was disconcerting the way he stood there with that odd look on his face. For an instant it was as if all life were standing still.

Then it was like"—she lowered her eyes, frowning as if in an effort to reconstruct—"like the world resuming its motion; the shot seemed to echo in my ears, and I saw Maurice jerk as if something had struck him backward; and then I could see the hole in his forehead. He staggered and fell forward, his arms out as if to catch himself."

She put the palm of her hand against her forehead. "After that I don't remember so well. The gun dropped from my hand and I went away. I couldn't look again at what I had done."

Mentally Wilson checked the position of the body against Peggy's and Leo's story of where they had picked up the revolver. The bullet's point of entry had been on the left side of the forehead. With the two squarely facing one another as they had undoubtedly done, a good marksman should have hit him dead center on the brow, but Esther admitted she had no skill with firearms. Everything figured neatly.

She had an attorney, and no doubt today the woman would be subjected to intensive sanity tests. But anyhow Wilson felt complacently that he had done his duty. If her lawyer pled insanity, he, Wilson, was still in the clear. He had his evidence.

He was hardly seated at his desk, ready to tackle the day's new developments, when his phone rang. The voice he heard was the coroner's.

"Hi, Joe, whadda you know?" Wilson greeted him jovially.

"Well, one thing I know is the stiff we picked up yesterday had a .22 rifle bullet in his brain."

Wilson was momentarily speechless. "Egstadt?" he said hoarsely after the pause.

"Yep."

"But the .32 we have here, it's been fired."

"Maybe so, but there ain't no .32 bullets in this boy. Not anyplace."

"Well, I'll be damned." Wilson face clouded, and he proceeded truculently, "You guys examined the body there on the spot. How come you couldn't tell what kind of a wound it was then?"

"We ain't magicians. Could of been either one. And everybody was waving that little Colt at us. So naturally I figured same as you did; it musta been the weapon."

Wearily Wilson asked, "What d'you figure the distance from where the shot was fired?"

"Fifty-sixty feet. It lodged against the skull in back. He had thick bones."

"Keep this under your hat. Don't let the news get outside the lab."

"Sure thing," Joe replied cheerfully.

Wilson set the phone in its rack disconsolately. Here went his day, all shot to hell. He had planned to lunch at the Elks' Club. They were having a special speaker. And he'd thought maybe he could duck out early for a swim at the country club before dinner. Some days it just didn't pay a man to get out of bed.

Before going into action he sat back to survey the situation grumpily. He pulled Esther's statement to him and turned to her account of the shooting. Did she or didn't she know there was another shot? They must have been almost simultaneous. Was she protecting someone? Had she perhaps fired into the air *after* the fatal shot and conveniently left the revolver there to confuse things?

Scowling, he read the transcript of her statement. No, Wilson mused to himself, he was sure the woman was telling the truth about her part in the affair. Maurice had stood there looking astonished, as well a man might if his wife suddenly pulled a gun on him. And then Mrs. Egstadt in her wrought-up condition heard something like an "echo" of the report, saw the man "jerk backwards," and saw the hole in his head.

So somebody, probably to the right and behind the woman, had been watching the whole thing. Someone who knew Esther couldn't hit the side of a barn ten feet in front of her, someone who had taken pains to finish the job she had bungled.

Did Esther know this had happened? That was the sixty-four-dollar question. Wilson thought she did not know.

He sighed, flipped a lever on the intercommunication apparatus, and asked for "Charlie."

Thank God he'd had sense enough, just to be on the safe side, to have a message included in radio and newspaper accounts of the event asking that anyone who had been at Sycamore Canyon Park between four and four-thirty the day before and who might have information relevant to the murder to please communicate with the sheriff's office. You could never have too much evidence, and Wilson figured that if he could get a witness to the exact time of the shooting or someone who had seen Esther or others near the scene of the crime, it would bolster the district attorney's case.

Succinctly and rather bitterly he told Charlie the news from Joe, concluding glumly, "So now we have to find out who had a .22 rifle handy."

"Well," Charlie said innocently, "we know that."

"We do?" Wilson reported sarcastically.

"Sure. When you were questioning the sisters, I asked that woman, Mrs. Farmer—cousin, I think she is to the rest of 'em; you know, the one that made coffee—well, I asked her if there were any other firearms in the party. Just routine, you know. And she said her little boy, Bradford, brought his .22 along unbeknownst to his folks, and they took it away from him and put it in the back of their car."

"Did you see the gun?"

"No, I didn't think it was necessary. We had the revolver and knew it had been fired."

Wilson leaned back in his chair and placed the tips of his fingers together across his chest.

"After this," he said sweetly, "when we're working on a case and you pick up any fascinating little tidbits of information on your own, how about letting me in on them, h'm? After all, I'm supposed to be in charge of this particular investigation."

"How was I to know it was important?" Charlie protested. "We *knew* it was the revolver."

The box on the desk buzzed, and Wilson flipped a lever. "Yes?"

In the squawking tones of the intercom system a voice came through. "We've got a man here who says he and his wife can swear to the time the shot was fired in the Egstadt case."

"Bring him right in." Wilson looked at Charlie more hopefully. "Now maybe we'll get somewhere."

A young man entered after the door was opened by a deputy in the outer office. He was bareheaded and wore a waist-length leather jacket above khaki trousers.

Wilson took his name and address and eyed the newcomer sharply. In response to his query the young man said, "My wife and I had been for a walk. We were coming along the road from the direction of the entrance, and she had just said, 'I think we oughta get started home, don't you?' and I looked at my watch and it was exactly fourteen minutes after four. It was right then I heard something that sounded like a shot. I couldn't tell what direction it came from, didn't even try to, as a matter of fact. I don't know why, but it seemed as if, out in the country like that, shooting was sort of normal. You know, you associate trees and everything with hunting. Well, I was just saying to my wife, 'It's only four-fifteen'—I was making it even numbers, see?—when I thought I heard another report, only fainter. I figured it was a car backfiring. And I never thought no more about it. We were around the first curve from where it happened, toward the entrance, and one car had just passed us going in, and another went by going out just after I spoke; so it was sort of noisy, and I'd never of thought of it again if I hadn't read in the paper this morning you folks wanted anybody that heard the shot to come in."

"You heard two shots?"

"Well, I think so. The second noise might have been an echo, outdoors that way."

"You walked past the scene of the shooting?"

"Yeah, and this woman passed us, walking down the road toward the entrance. I don't know whether we could identify her for sure or not. We didn't pay no attention. You expect to see people afoot in the park. But I suppose it must have been Mrs. Egstadt."

When this informant had been dismissed after signing a statement,

Wilson dispatched two men to Sycamore Canyon Park.

"See if you can find the .32 bullet and a cartridge case from the rifle. Mrs. Egstadt probably hit the tree on the other side of the stove."

He regarded Charlie glumly. "Now we've got everything to do over again. You can come with me." He consulted the list of names and addresses in his hand and observed, "They're scattered all over hell of course. Suppose we better start with the son. He and his wife stayed at the Egstadt place on Santa Rosa Street last night."

As they pulled up in front of the pleasant English-style bungalow where Maurice and Esther had lived, a hot-rod type vehicle turned in on the driveway just ahead of their car.

"Isn't that the kid that found the body?" Charlie said as Leo stepped out of the low-slung coupe.

"Yeah, looks like it. Leo Mallory. Well, that's a break. We'll have a word with him before we see the others."

Leo was regarding the county automobile uncertainly as Wilson opened the door. He hailed the boy, and they met on the flagstone path leading to the house.

"We're doing a little more checking," Wilson began casually. "Did you see anything of any other firearms out at the Park yesterday?"

"No. I never saw any guns. At least—well, not since in the morning. Bradford had his new .22 along; but his folks took it away from him."

"What time was that?"

"I don't know. Before dinner."

"Was everybody there when he brought the rifle out?"

"Yeah, we were all there." Leo paused and added, "Everybody but Dave and Renée. It was just before they came."

In a mild effort to befog his intentions, Wilson asked a few more questions, concluding with, "Anything particular you had in mind to take up with your cousin?" He nodded at the house.

"No. I just thought I'd come by and see how they were."

"We'd like to talk to them. Mind postponing your call?"

"No. That's O.K."

With a somewhat reluctant air Leo withdrew toward his car.

Wearing one of Esther's housecoats, Renée met the officers at the door. She called David from the rear of the house, and he joined them in the living room. When Wilson had apprised them of the fact that he was merely checking up a little further, they answered his seemingly desultory queries with a suspicious air. The detective was soon convinced that neither of the pair knew that Bradford had had his rifle at the picnic. The young couple, he could see, were warily determined to divulge no more than they had to, probably on the advice of the attorney they had already engaged for Esther.

Wilson made a quick decision. He spoke quietly. "In order to get your help I'm going to give you some information which you must promise me not to divulge to anyone until I give you the word, not even to your lawyer. Stevens you've retained, haven't you? How about it, will you trust me, and give me your word not to reveal what I'm going to tell you? It will be to your mother's advantage, I assure you."

Both the young people were alert, their eyes fixed upon him.

"This sounds pretty irregular," David replied curtly. "I don't see how we can make any promises like that."

"Maybe this will help you make up your mind. We now have reason to believe your mother might not be guilty of the murder. That's why I'm starting out again to go over the facts. If she isn't the one, you may be able to help me find out who is."

"I don't get it."

"Give me your word that you won't let out this information, and I'll tell you what the facts are that have changed the picture. The only reason I'm making this offer to let you in on the inside for now is that—one, I feel you have a real interest in finding out for sure who killed your father; two, you want to save your mother if possible; and three, I think we can rule you and your wife out as suspects. For one thing, we now know for sure what time the shot was fired, and the manager of the park told us last evening that he saw a small English car pass the office going out about fifteen minutes before the time we now believe to be the critical one. Mr. Black, the manager, couldn't swear to seeing you two in the car, but yours was the only machine that small in the park except for an M.G. with no top; so he is positive it was you leaving then, and he knows you did not return in your car. He doesn't let anybody get by without paying."

"You think," Renée queried slowly, "it may not have been Esther?"

"It may not. Which makes it necessary that we look into other members of the party more closely." Wilson smiled. "Frankly, I don't like hard work anymore than the next one, and I believe you can make this phase of my job easier."

David and Renée exchanged glances.

"O.K.," said David. "What's the deal?"

"It's this. Your father was killed by a .22 rifle bullet. Now, Mrs. Egstadt could be a very clever woman and have used the rifle herself and be using the revolver story to confuse the case and so get herself off. But I'm following a hunch. I think she believes the story she told."

"I'm sure she does," David said thickly.

"If this is true, we must find the person who fired the rifle. That's where you can help. By rights I should have hopped over to Los Alegres first and got hold of that gun at the Farmers'; but, being lazy, I didn't want to have to come back here afterward. I'll probably have a lot of calls to make, seeing your folks in Los Alegres, so I decided to catch you first."

"But how can we help?"

"You know the score about your father and the other people at the picnic. I need filling in on their relationships. We only had time for a superficial check on that aspect of things yesterday."

"You mean—motives?" Renée interposed.

"Exactly."

"You won't get far along those lines," David said heavily. "Nobody liked Dad."

"What I want to know is: who *hated* him? To whom was he a menace in some way at the present time? Or are any of your folks sort of— unbalanced—in their feelings, likely to fly off the handle and pick up a convenient weapon? All of that would give me something to go on."

"I don't like to implicate people who might be innocent. You don't necessarily kill somebody just because you hate and fear them."

"One of them 'implicated' your father—permanently; and left your mother holding the bag."

David nodded, frowning.

"Let's go at it this way," Wilson suggested. "There are a number of people who can vouch for one another's presence from—say four o'clock until four-thirty. They were together in groups, not out of another's sight during that time. Three of the men were together at the ball game from three-thirty on. And all the women were together in two different groups on the beach. We can account pretty well for the children also. And for the moment I'm eliminating the pair who discovered the body. If they're lying, both of them are, and that doesn't look likely."

Wilson pulled out a small notebook and leafed through till he found the right page. With his eyes upon it, he remarked, "Tentatively I'm setting aside Alison Mallory and Orville Gray. They alibi each other, and Gray never met Mr. Egstadt till yesterday, he says." He glanced up questioningly.

"Alison and Dad hardly ever saw each other in recent years," David volunteered.

"Now, here are the people who were alone all or part of the time around four-fifteen: Fred Mallory, Jocelyn Mallory, Marvin Nelson."

"Well, Fred never had trouble with Dad, as I recall. They weren't chummy, but they got along O.K. Aunt Joss had a tiff with him years ago over some property Dad inherited that she thought should have come to her, but they haven't quarreled recently that I know about. And Dad and Uncle Marvin were on bad terms once when I was a kid, over a business deal they went into together, but that's been over and forgotten for years."

"Did any of these three seem moody or otherwise unusual yesterday?"

"Not that I noticed."

Wilson glanced inquiringly at Renée.

"I don't think so," she said slowly.

"Any squabbles or emotional disturbances during the day?"

"N-no," Renée said thoughtfully. "Of course Maurice lay down and went to sleep after he ate, so he was out of the way. And we didn't arrive until just before they all sat down to eat."

"Any of the family interested in hunting?"

"I guess all the men did some occasionally. Deer season, or quail hunting. The only one really hipped on it is my cousin Grant, Aunt Bea's son. But he was with Les and Wilbur at the ball game most of the afternoon."

"How about his father, Marvin?"

"Uncle Marvin went sometimes, but I never heard of him getting any game. Uncle Fred is more of a sportsman than Uncle Marv. Belongs to the Rod and Gun Club, although he isn't very active."

"He knows how to handle guns though?"

"Yes, but the only crack shot in the family is Grant, if that's what you're angling for, and Grant is alibied."

"Hitting the target at fifty or sixty feet doesn't require expert marksmanship, just fair competence. How about your aunt Jocelyn?"

"I doubt if Aunt Joss ever fired a gun in her life."

Wilson continued to prod them with questions and, when he left, warned the young couple once more to retain the secret of the bullets.

"It's just for a few hours," he said. "I may be back this evening to check with you again. By then we will probably be ready to release the information publicly. Just remember, you're helping Mrs. Egstadt by keeping quiet about it."

"We'll keep still," David assured him.

In the car once more, on the way to Cousin Helen's in Los Alegres, Charlie observed, "Did it strike you the son and his wife don't seem very upset over Papa kicking the bucket? And it seemed to me they acted nervous themselves, as if there was things they hoped wouldn't come out."

"Everybody's like that in any investigation. They're all scared you'll stumble over the closet with their particular skeleton in it. I don't doubt they hated Egstadt's guts."

"He wasn't a real lovable character. I didn't know him personally. Just saw him around town once in a while."

"Same here. But I know what you mean. Had a reputation for being a big horse's ass. Wise-guy type. Whatever these kids had against him, though, I don't think is important to the case. The manager, Mr. Black, made it his business to catch every car that came into the park, to get their dollar admission. And the young Egstadts were well away before the shots were fired."

"They could have parked outside and walked back."

"It'd be quite a hike, especially without having somebody see them. We'll keep that in mind though. The thing to remember today is that one of the people we'll talk to knows damn well the rifle finished off Egstadt and knows that we know it too by now. We've got to watch attitudes and reactions to get a line on who we have to bear down on."

With a bewildered air Cousin Helen produced the rifle, which had been locked up in the coat closet off the living-room entryway. Bradford was being deprived of its use for a while as punishment for smuggling the gun into the picnic.

"Why do you want it?" she demanded.

"We're supposed to pick up all firearms on the scene of a homicide."

Helen was the sort of person who fussily notices all behavior within range of her own hearing and eyesight. Wilson checked again on her recollection of the late-afternoon events. Helen recounted the comings and goings on the beach precisely.

"—and then after Esther followed her kids, it was—oh, I'd say fifteen minutes before Marvin joined us. Came down the steps above the beach. He stayed around a few minutes. He seemed restless yesterday. I can't say just when he left, but the last I saw him he was standing by the end of the dam. Before Marvin took off, Jocelyn got up—to go to the rest room, I think, and a few minutes later I glanced around and saw Fred coming down the steps. I can't say exactly about just how much time there was between all them coming and going. Fred laid down on the sand with us women and pulled his cap down over his face. It was pretty flushed. I remember Jane told him he shouldn't have stayed out in the sun so long."

"How long was it then until you heard about Mr. Egstadt?"

Helen pursed her lips. "Oh, I'd say fifteen minutes or so. Leo came down. He said Marvin sent him. He told us in a low voice so other people wouldn't hear. Marvin told him to do that. Marvin was wonderful. Stayed so calm and sort of took charge till you folks got there. The men in the car, I mean. I guess you, Mr. Wilson, were a little later arriving."

All day Wilson and Charlie worked in Los Alegres, looking up Marvin on his job, finding Cousin Wilbur at his work, going from one house to another, questioning and collating the information obtained thereby.

All the questioned were wary, all put on a surprised expression when asked about the rifle. All were co-operative, however, seeming to take it for granted that the police would still be checking over the previous day's events.

Only Jocelyn took the offensive, so to speak.

"I don't care what you got her to admit to you, my sister never deliberately killed that man. If she did happen to make the gun go off, it was sheer accident."

"I'm sure Mrs. Egstadt's attorney will bring out anything of that kind,"

Wilson rejoined equably. "If her counsel makes it look as if someone else did it, have you any ideas who it might turn out to be?"

Jocelyn looked at him blankly. "Why—why I hadn't thought."

Wilson smiled cryptically. "When a man gets killed, it's usually his wife who has the best reasons for doing it."

"Esther could see no wrong in anything Maurice did," Jocelyn retorted.

"Apparently, though, he did do wrong occasionally."

"He was a wicked man. His death was a judgment from on high."

"Who," Wilson came back quickly but dispassionately, "do you think was the human instrument for delivering that judgment?"

"It might have been an accident."

"Performed by someone other than your sister?"

Jocelyn frowned as she stared at the man. There was a pause before she returned, "How should I know?"

By late afternoon Wilson had interviewed all the witnesses in Los Alegres, and he and Charlie hurried back to Valdale and from there out to Mountain Springs, the suburb in the foothills where Fred and Jane lived. Haste was necessary, because there could be little further delay in giving the coroner's report to the press and in changing the charge against Esther to one of assault with a deadly weapon.

Fred lived in a flat-roofed modern house whose angled walls followed the brow of a low rise off the main road. He was at home, reading the evening papers on the shaded terrace at the rear of the house. Jane ushered the officers out there and took one of the reed chairs herself.

"Leo told us you saw him this morning," she remarked.

Wilson smiled. "I'm sure some of your folks in Los Alegres phoned to warn you we would be around."

Jane flushed slightly, and her lips tightened.

"Perfectly natural," Fred put in. "You have to tie up all the loose ends, I suppose." He sighed. "Poor Tess, I tried to see her today, but they wouldn't let me." He regarded Wilson unhappily. "Anything new?"

"Very little."

Wilson had checked with the office on his return from Los Alegres and, as a matter of fact, there was quite a bit new. The sheriff's men had found the .32 bullet in the oak tree as predicted by Wilson and had also found the cartridge case of the rifle bullet on the ground at a spot which they estimated had been on the side of the Farmers' car, away from the tables. Furthermore, and perhaps most important, an elderly woman had come in with a piece of observation.

The lady's name was Mrs. Thyssen, and she was pretty deaf, even with her hearing aid. She had been lying down asleep in the back seat of her married son's sedan, which was parked by the road in the parking area where the Egstadts' and the Farmers' cars also had stood. Mrs. Thyssen had not consciously heard anything, shots or otherwise, but she had awakened rather abruptly and, rising on one elbow, found her glasses on the floor of the car. She put them on and sat up, shaking her head to clear it of drowsiness. Then she consulted her wrist watch and found the time just past four-fifteen. Glancing diagonally out of the window to her right, she had seen someone moving at the other end of the lot. Since the automobiles were parked three deep in parallel rows facing the stream, the glimpse she had of the person was between other cars and across the hood of the machine in front and to the right of the automobile in which she sat.

"My eyesight is perfectly good," she had asserted, "and I can swear I saw a person, but I wasn't interested for one thing, and for another, there were at least two cars in between me and whoever it was. The angle just happened to be right so that I could see a figure moving away from where I was. I only saw him for a second, and all I can swear to is, he had a cap on."

The interviewer at the office had leaped upon this last remark. "What kind of a cap? What color?"

"I couldn't say. All that sunk in on my mind was that the person was not bareheaded. I wasn't paying attention, you know."

"But it was a man?"

"That's the impression I had, I recall. But I couldn't swear to it."

On the way out to Fred's, Wilson had said ruefully, "Wish we'd had Mrs. Thyssen's testimony before we started out this morning. If it was a man, and if it was a cap, that makes it Fred Mallory. Marvin wore a straw hat."

"Jocelyn Mallory had a hat on too."

"Yeah, but it had things on it. Feminine stuff."

"Just a veil wound around it. I doubt if this old dame sees as well as she says she does. She wears glasses, you know."

"I know. But a woman's hat would register with another woman."

Wilson was working very carefully now. It seemed to him the case had narrowed down to Fred Mallory or Marvin Nelson.

He brought up the matter of the rifle to Fred Mallory with an ingenuous smile. "We slipped on that point yesterday. It's in the book of rules, you take notice of every firearm at the scene, even when you have the murder weapon in hand."

"I don't see how young Brad's gun can have any bearing," Fred rejoined innocently.

"Well, we have to get the facts. For our records. Now tell us what happened before lunch in regard to the kid's gun."

Casually Fred told the story of Helen's and Wilbur's altercation with the boy.

"Where were you when this happened?"

"I was standing over by the tub of beer with Maw and his boy, Grant."

Wilson made a mental note that this spot was parallel to the far end of the tables, beyond the stove and the water faucet.

"What did Wilbur do with the rifle?"

"He took it away from the kid and carried it to his car."

"Where did he put it?"

"On the floor in the back."

"It was in plain sight, then, if somebody glanced through the window?"

"No, he threw Helen's coat over it."

"I've asked this before, but I'll ask again: when you left Mrs. Egstadt sitting at the table, did you see anyone at all as you passed through the parking lot?"

"Not a soul."

"You went through the lot? Not around it?"

"Yes. There was plenty of space between the cars. I cut through the trees along to the steps."

"Meet anyone in the space between the cars and the steps?"

Fred pursed his lips. "I didn't *meet* anybody, but there were people around, I think. Kids running back and forth maybe. You know the rest rooms and dressing rooms are down that way, hundred feet or so from the parking lot. I wasn't paying attention, but I'm sure there were people in sight going toward or away from the buildings down there."

When they left the Mallorys, the officers drove back into town and went to the Egstadt home. Orville Gray's car was parked in front, and they found him and Alison in the living room with David and Renée.

Wilson smiled at them in a friendly way. "Glad to find you here. Saves us a trip to Coast City."

Alison's eyes fastened on him anxiously. "You wanted to see us—again?"

"I've been seeing you all today, rechecking."

Renée spoke up. "We just heard on the radio. Maurice was killed by a bullet from Bradford's rifle. They've already checked the barrel or whatever they do."

"Markings on the bullet," Wilson elaborated calmly.

"Does that let Aunt Esther out?" Alison inquired thinly.

"Can't tell yet. Of course she still has a charge of attempted murder against her."

"But they won't do anything to her for that," David queried tensely.

"Depends on the judge." Wilson smiled amiably. "I wouldn't fire the lawyer yet if I were you." He leaned back more comfortably in the chair he had taken. "Now we can concentrate on this rifle. I understand you were present when Mr. Farmer took the rifle away from his son," he observed to Alison and Orville.

Each nodded.

"Where were you standing—or sitting—when this took place?"

"We were at the end of the table toward the parking lot, talking to Flo and Aunt Jossy," Alison replied.

"That was roughly how far from Farmer's car?"

Alison glanced helplessly at Orville.

"Twenty–thirty feet," Orville volunteered.

"You watched Mr. Farmer put the gun away?"

Alison frowned. "I don't think I did. Aunt Bea spoke to me, and I turned around, as I remember."

"I saw him," Orville said slowly. "He opened the back door of his car."

"Where did he put the gun?"

"What d'you mean, where?"

"On the seat? On the floor?"

"It seemed to me he laid it on the floor, but I couldn't say for sure. He had his back to us, and the doorway was hidden by his body."

"Then you couldn't actually see what he did with it?"

"No." Orville smiled faintly. "Wilbur's pretty broad in the beam. He makes a better door than a window."

As they rested on her boy friend, Alison's eyes lighted fondly in appreciation of his little joke.

Wilson reflected irrelevantly that this couple would probably be a very happy one. Men were suckers for women who overestimated their sense of humor.

ELEVEN
Guilty

As the officers returned to their car Wilson sighed heavily. "I need a cup of coffee. I kept wishing they'd offer us one."

The two men had dined hastily at the Caballero in Los Alegres, and Charlie observed, "Yeah, it's been a long time since we ate."

"Let's drop in at the Sunny Spot on our way back to the office."

"Suits me."

"What do you make of it now?" Charlie ventured.

"Quite a lot. But don't talk for a while. I want to think."

So they were silent until the car was parked at the curb in front of the Sunny Spot. Gracie was on the evening shift this week, and the café was empty at the moment except for her and the cook, whose tall white cap could be seen through the square opening above the shelves behind the counter.

"Well, if it ain't the law!" she greeted the men brightly.

"Hiya, Gracie."

"Hi," Wilson added abstractedly.

"What'll it be, boys?" she inquired, spreading open a cellophane-covered menu and laying it between them on the counter.

"Just coffee for me."

"Give me a couple of them sugared doughnuts," Charlie ordered, adding suspiciously, "They fresh?"

"Just came in this afternoon." As she set their mugs of coffee on the counter Gracie observed sociably, "I read in the paper you guys are workin' on the Egstadt case."

"Keep right up on things, don't you?" Charlie quipped.

"Well, gee, I'm interested. Mr. Egstadt used to come in here all the time. And me and Dave Egstadt was in the same class in high school."

Wilson looked up at her. "Guess you knew the family pretty well then."

"I didn't know her, Mrs. Egstadt. 'Cept by sight, of course. I heard on the radio you guys think now maybe she didn't do it. And I'm glad. She always seemed real nice."

"Know any of the rest of the family, the Mallorys?"

"I know Fred. He eats here a lot. Good friend of mine. But I don't know none of 'em in Los Alegres."

"What did you think of Egstadt? Maurice, I mean."

Gracie had leaned back against the metal ice cream containers and lighted a cigarette. "I liked him," she said. "Jolly, he was. Too bad. I sure hope you catch whoever done it."

"I guess a lot of people didn't like him."

"I know Fred didn't cotton to him much. Oh, they was friendly and all that, don't get me wrong. But they weren't pals like you'd expect brother-in-laws to be." She held her cigarette to one side and smiled in rueful reminiscence. "Reg'lar card, that Mr. Egstadt was. Always kidding. Like when he'd leave me a tip. Never just stuck it under the rim of the plate like anybody would. He'd hide it in his crumpled-up napkin or drop it in the water glass. Once he put it under the crust of bread on his plate, and it damn near got thrown in the garbage."

"You *liked* that?"

Grade's eyes widened. "It was a joke. That's the way he was. A great big tease. Like he'd hide his pat of butter and swear I never gave him none and then go and bring out the first one when I rustled up another."

"Guess you liked Egstadt better than Fred, h'm?" Wilson prompted.

The girl's expression became guarded. "I wouldn't say that. They were different types."

Wilson made an inspired shot in the dark, grinning roguishly. "Guess both the boys kind of went for you, eh, Gracie? Rivals for your attention, huh?"

"Rivals?" She looked blank. Then she uttered a short laugh. "Brother, you got Mr. Egstadt all wrong. He wasn't no wolf. Didn't have no personal interest in me no more than any other dame. He used to pull the same stunts on Shirley, the girl that works the other shift from me. With tips and all, I mean. It was just his way. He'd kid around with any girl. I'll bet if a dame ever made a real pass at Mr. Egstadt, he'd of run like a deer, scared as heck."

"I've seen guys like that," Charlie put in sagely. "Put on an act like they was reg'lar hellers with women, but it's all front. Comes right down to doing something about it, and they're away like a shot."

Wilson was perplexedly revising his ideas. Intuition hinted to him that Gracie's observations on the two men and her attitudes toward them held some clue to his problem, but he could not quite catch the significance of what he sensed in her manner. He decided just to keep talking. Lighting a cigarette, he remarked casually, "Guess Fred Mallory was a horse of another color though."

"Fred is a gentleman," Gracie said primly. She moistened the tip of her forefinger and ran it nonchalantly over her eyebrows.

Wilson picked up his spoon and stirred the quarter of a cup of coffee left in his mug. Then with a grin he said idly, "Bet Fred wouldn't run. If a dame made a pass, I mean."

Gracie gazed over their heads and said loftily, "I'm sure I wouldn't know."

Suddenly it came to Wilson that one thing which had caught his attention was the way Gracie referred to Maurice as "Mr. Egstadt" but spoke of Fred always by his first name. Yet it was Maurice who played practical jokes and indulged in persiflage when he came to the Sunny Spot, while Fred was just a gentlemanly customer. One would think the girl's terms of reference would be reversed in the two cases.

Wilson made another reckless riposte, feeling his way toward clarification. "Oh, come on now, Gracie, don't try to kid me and Charlie. We've known you too long." He winked teasingly. "You and Fred have got to be pretty chummy here lately. Now, haven't you?"

"You cops don't miss a thing, do you?" she said coldly.

"Bet that gave Mr. Egstadt something else to rib you about."

"It was Fred he gave a bad time—" She broke off to eye Wilson sulkily and lowered her voice. "Look here, I don't know how you happened to know I was dating Fred sometimes. I suppose you cops don't do nothing but run around sticking your noses into other people's business. But I hope you ain't gonna go spreadin' it around. I got my reputation to think about, and people in a small town like this are so narrow-minded they don't understand how a girl can be friends with a guy that happens to be married."

"We won't mention it, Gracie. It's like you said. We're always buzzing around town and we find out a lot, that's all. Guess it must have worried Fred some, having his brother-in-law wise to his running around with you."

"Naturally he didn't like it. Mrs. Mallory is one of them narrow-minded types like I spoke of, and Fred was afraid Mr. Egstadt might let something slip sometime, him being such a kidder." She smashed out her cigarette on the counter ash tray. "But," she said carelessly, "now that the poor guy's dead Fred's got nothing more to worry about."

Wilson regarded the girl speculatively. Her expression was unconcerned.

When the officers were on the sidewalk again, Wilson observed, "That was a lucky cup of coffee."

"Not much of a motive," Charlie demurred.

"On the face of it, no, but there may be more to come out. At least we've got something to go on. I'm going to go down and get a warrant. Then we'll pick up Mr. Fred Mallory and get down to cases. No use fooling around talking to him on his own ground anymore. By morning we should have it all spelled out."

"There's a lot of little points to add up against him," Charlie mused. "For instance, nobody else said they knew the rifle was on the floor of the car. They couldn't tell that from watching Farmer put it away. And Fred was the only one said it was covered by Helen's coat."

"Nothing we have is proof. But everything points his way. Get him down to the office where we can really bear down, and we may get somewhere. I won't use the warrant unless he's troublesome. We'll get him downtown just for questioning."

When the sheriff's deputies left the house after their call early in the evening Fred had felt an inordinate relief. Certainly they must have known for some time that the rifle had killed Maurice, yet they obviously didn't have enough information to make them definitely suspect him. They would probably never find out the exact time the shots were fired, and so their list of suspects would remain too long and unwieldy. But Esther would be cleared. She might get a short term in prison for what she *had* done, but the poor kid had a future now, even if she had to serve out a sentence first. And they'd all pitch in and help her to get back on her feet afterward.

Fred ate his dinner that night with relish. It was the first meal he had been able to sit down to in a relaxed manner since the picnic the day before. He realized now that he had not fully estimated the terrific tension he had been operating under since the shooting. The sudden relaxation of that tension made him almost giddy with relief.

It was, therefore, a shattering shock to find Wilson and Charlie standing under the winglike roof projection outside the front door when he answered the bell about nine o'clock. Fred's defenses had been dispersed by the sense of security that had crept over him, and he grabbed desperately for the semblances of concerned innocence with which he had been masking his guilty knowledge. If he had not been caught so unprepared Fred might have refused to go with the officers unless formally arrested, after which he would have sought the protection of legal counsel immediately. But by the time he had regained some inner composure, Fred was already at the courthouse with his elaborately polite escorts. It was then that he began to bluster—when it was too late.

"We just want to go over the facts with you," Wilson explained with guileless patience, "here where there won't be any interruptions."

"I've told you all I know."

They had ushered him into Wilson's office, and the sheriff himself had joined them. He sat negligently on the edge of Wilson's desk, a pudgy, semibald man with a fatherly air, who surveyed Fred regretfully in a "this hurts me more than it does you" manner.

The door had been left ajar, and Fred glanced up uneasily to find the district attorney striding in briskly. He was a slender man with straight dark hair combed back uncompromisingly from a broad forehead over black-rimmed spectacles.

"You know Mr. Summers, the district attorney," Wilson remarked offhandedly.

"I believe we've met," Summers stated sonorously. He was the sort of man who seemed to take everything big. Even in announcing that it looked like rain today, Mr. Summers' deep voice would sound as if he were addressing a jury.

Fred was conscious of unalloyed panic. He had never been mixed up with the police before, and he was learning that in concentrated form like this they were a terrifying aggregation. He had never felt so alone in his life.

It was the district attorney who took over. "We'll be frank with you, Mallory; we have an overpowering array of facts which point your way in the Egstadt murder."

"I demand a lawyer," Fred retorted brashly.

"All in good time. Perhaps if you can explain a few matters to our satisfaction it won't be necessary."

"I always got along with Maurice." In his desperation Fred prematurely threw out his trump card. "I had no motive. I'm just unlucky that I didn't happen to be with somebody every minute of the afternoon yesterday."

Summers glanced sideways at Wilson, and, as the latter spoke, Fred had a frightening impression that his adversaries had rehearsed this interview.

Wilson casually inspected the nails of his right hand. "Charlie and I had a little talk this evening with Grace Tuttle."

"G-Gracie?"

Wilson's gaze bored into Fred's astonished eyes. "Looks as if Egstadt knew too much for your comfort."

For the second time in half an hour Fred's composure was annihilated. He cast a hunted look around the circle of waiting faces. These men were beginning to seem like magicians.

"What—what did Gracie say?"

"Quite a bit," Winters interposed suavely. "I'm afraid your contention of 'no motive' won't hold up, Mr. Mallory. Egstadt was in a position to cause you considerable inconvenience, and from what we know of Mr. Egstadt he was just the type who would enjoy telling your wife the whole story."

Fred's lips had parted, and his mouth remained open for some seconds. Jane! All night and all day today he had never once considered the possibility of Jane's finding out about Gracie. His only fear had been that somehow the police would find evidence to convict him of the murder. That anyone would discover or connect his affair with Gracie with the shooting had never crossed his mind.

Jane could not, must not know about him and Gracie. Jane would be able to stand up under the disgrace of a murder charge. Eventually she would be able to hold up her head again, even if he were convicted of killing Maurice. It would be a terrible blow to her, but Jane had been in the family long enough to understand and forgive anyone for shooting Maurice, as only one of the family could understand. But the humiliation of learning that her husband had been sleeping with a tart like Gracie would not only be beyond Jane's comprehension, it would be a mortal blow to her pride. Jane would feel disgraced, debased. Fred knew Jane. That *her* husband could even want another woman, let alone one so much her inferior as she would consider Gracie to be, would be an injury to her self-esteem from which she could never recover.

He had known that when he first took Gracie out and had been frightened at himself that he could run such a risk of hurting Jane. But it had seemed as if his appetite for the girl's young flesh had been as irresistible as a dope fiend's craving for his shots. The gratification of his desire for a woman as different from Jane as Gracie was had been possible only because he kept telling himself there was no way for Jane to find out just how far he had gone with the girl. If someone did happen to see him with Gracie, he could always lie and convince Jane they had merely stopped to have a drink together. That was how he had told himself he could handle it.

But if his affair with Gracie entered into a murder trial, it would be in all the papers. Everyone would believe he had been unfaithful. In jail, he would have no chance to lie himself out of it to Jane. And even if he could convince Jane that the story was false, she would still have to face the fact that the whole community considered her a betrayed wife. And to be put in that light would crush Jane, whether she believed it herself or not. Her standing in the eyes of others meant everything to Jane.

An overwhelming wave of guilt in regard to his wife left Fred limp and impotent. It was strange, but at the moment he dreaded the effect of his infidelity upon Jane more than he feared these representatives of the law who could imprison and kill him. Fred simply did not dare to cause this breakup of Jane's front to herself and to the world, the front of the perfect, all-desirable, invulnerable wife.

"You can't," he burst out hoarsely, "you can't bring this all out—about Gracie. I've got a family. A daughter, and a son in high school. Why, I'm a grandfather. Think what it would do to my family to bring Gracie into this!"

"We didn't bring her in," Summers interjected smoothly.

It struck Fred that his nerves were in worse shape than even he had realized. But after all, he didn't kill a man in cold blood every day.

He looked about at his audience frantically. "Look, I'll make a deal with you. Keep Gracie out of this, don't let her even be mentioned, and I'll give you the whole story. You must protect my wife and family."

"If the rest of your motive is sufficient to hold up, we'll do that," Summers agreed. "You did have other reasons, I assume."

"We all had reasons," Fred declared bitterly.

The sheriff had stepped to the door. He motioned with his head, and a male stenographer entered, seating himself beside the desk and drawing out the writing board.

"All right, tell us about it," the district attorney instructed quietly.

"I knew my sister Esther was disturbed when I came across her there at the table. You have to know the whole story to really understand, but it's too long to go into. Maurice was a son of a bitch. We found that out as we went along. He wasn't very bright, just had a lot of gall and push. He was mean in a peculiar kind of way. Seems as if even when he wanted people to like him, he couldn't seem to stop himself from doing things to make them hate him." Fred looked wearily thoughtful. "I guess he was really a tortured person. He antagonized all of us. Some of us he pulled real dirty tricks on. But me, I kept out of his way. I guess that galled him, that he'd never been able to get under my hide. And when he found out I was running around with Gracie, he was tickled to death to have found some way to torment me at last—" Fred halted and looked at the stenographer's flying pencil.

"Strike out the last two sentences," Summers commanded quietly.

"Well," Fred resumed dully, "Esther stood up for him no matter what. But yesterday, like I said, she had a funny look. As if she had—flipped, as they say nowadays. I don't know what had happened. Well, I walked off because she told me she wanted to be by herself. But I was worried. Tess is the baby of the family, and I'm—I've—well, I care a lot about her. I stood back between the cars and watched. She stood up almost as soon as I left her, and she went over to their car and took something out of the glove compartment and turned back toward the tables. I moved around and stood on the other side of Cousin Helen's car; and then I saw she had Maurice's gun in her hand."

Fred paused and wiped the palms of his hands on his thighs. "I don't mind telling you it scared me. Esther doesn't know much about firearms, and I couldn't imagine what she was up to. Then I saw Maurice coming in from the road, past Orville's car—the guy with Alison. Esther pointed the gun at him and said something, and he hesitated a minute and said, 'What the hell are you doing?' or something like that, and came right on with a mean look on his face."

Fred rubbed his hand over his forehead. "I had several reactions, real quick. Can't say for sure just what went through my mind. But one thing, I was scared for Esther. She hardly knows one end of a gun from another, and I had some idea she might get hurt if there was a fracas, if he tried to take the revolver away from her, for instance. Anyway, at the same time I remembered young Brad's rifle, and I opened the door and pulled it out fast. I got it up and aimed over the hood of Farmer's car, not actually meaning to do anything, but more just to be ready to yell out and warn Maurice if he tried any funny business with Esther. And then, by God, I heard the shot. I looked to see Maurice recoil. It should have knocked him down at that close range, even if she only winged him. But then I could tell she had missed. Well"—he spoke slowly—"it was almost reflex action. I sighted and let him have it. Afterward I tried to sort out what went through my mind, why I did it. Partly," he said honestly, "I guess, deep down, I just wanted to. He'd been such a miserable bastard, and if he'd finally driven poor little Tess to the point where even she was ready to kill him, I guess I just figured—why not? Knowing my sister, I figured that if he'd pulled something so raw that it made her want to shoot him, he probably ought to be killed. But partly, since she'd already started shooting, I suppose I figured—well, the fat's in the fire; she'll probably fire again so I might as well do the job properly for her. And partly I was scared for Tess. Really scared. If she kept missing and he got hold of that gun, it would be curtains for Esther. He'd turn it on her in self-defense."

Fred closed his eyes and let his back relax against the chair.

"Why didn't you come forward and speak to her after the shooting?" Summers asked.

"I was in a daze, so to speak, and I stood there a minute sizing things up. I saw her drop the revolver and just walk past him, stiff-like. I knew you guys would eventually find out it was a rifle bullet killed him, and it struck me that if you didn't find out—say, if the bullet went clean through and was lost, how would you even discover who fired the revolver? I figured for the time being it was best to sit tight. So I put the rifle back and wiped my fingerprints off it with Helen's coat, and wiped the door handle with the tail of my shirt, and got the hell out. Afterward, when I looked at the body before you guys got there, I saw there was no point of exit for the bullet; so I knew that even if Esther got held for shooting off the revolver, she'd be released because you'd find a .22 bullet in his head."

Fred sighed. "Is that enough? You'll keep"—he glanced at the stenographer—"the other—out of it."

Summers and the sheriff's officers exchanged glances. "I think your explanation as given in this statement will be sufficient." He smiled ruefully. "Mr. Egstadt seemed to be the kind of man who roused murderous impulses without half trying."

"You can say that again," Fred agreed bitterly.

The following evening several of the family met in mournful conclave at Jane's. Esther had been released on bail, and Renée was staying with her at the Egstadt house while David had joined the others in consoling Jane, who alternated between tears and ejaculations of rage. Cousin Helen had come over with the Nelsons. She sighed repeatedly and kept wringing her hands. The fact that her son's rifle had done the job oppressed her with a sense of guilty responsibility.

"That it should be Fred, of all people," Bea moaned for perhaps the fifth time. "Fred was always so level-headed and so cagey about keeping clear of Maurice."

Alison glanced worriedly at David. "Please, Aunt Bea," she murmured, "he was Dave's father."

"Don't mind me," David said despondently. "I know how Dad was. I can't blame the rest of you for the way you felt about him. And if Mom"—he swallowed miserably—"hadn't shot at him first Uncle Fred wouldn't have done it, and we wouldn't be in this mess."

Orville sat back a little from the others and watched sympathetically. Somehow the family circle had opened to include him. It was taken for granted that he should have driven Alison over.

Jane brought her eyes sharply to rest on David. "What I'd like to know is what got into Esther. Why after all these years she suddenly goes haywire and lights into Maurice. You needn't tell me, David Egstadt, that something didn't happen between you folks Sunday that blew the lid off. And with Fred in the spot he's in, I think we're entitled to know. It might help him."

"I think Mother's statement to the police explains her actions," David replied stiffly.

As Jane spoke Jocelyn had straightened to an even more upright position in the occasional chair where she sat. "Anyone would think, Jane," she said tartly, "that you and Fred were the only ones involved in this. Don't forget that, whatever his faults, Maurice was this boy's father, and as such deserves some loyalty from David. If David prefers to conceal the man's final infamy—whatever it was that opened Esther's eyes—it is our duty to see that the boy is allowed to keep out of it. There will be quite enough testimony to show that Maurice bred hatred in every person whose life he touched closely. *I* intend to talk, and Marvin will tell his story if necessary, and even Alison is willing to testify to how he has persecuted her for years. All that will explain why the man aroused such violent passions in other people. So just leave David out of it."

Jane looked sulky and dabbed at her eyes with a Kleenex.

"If only," Cousin Helen groaned, "Brad had left that rifle at home."

Several people stirred impatiently. This was perhaps the fifth time Helen had expressed this sentiment.

"What beats me," Marvin put in anxiously, "is why Fred went and confessed, even if it looked as if they had the goods on him."

"Mr. Currier, our lawyer," Jane quavered, "wanted him to repudiate his confession, but Fred refused point-blank." She sniffed and raised her head proudly. "But that's Fred. He's so *honorable*, poor dear."

"He's sensible, too. And practical," Marvin insisted. "And it just ain't practical not to follow your attorney's advice. You don't have to stand by a confession the cops worm out of you in the middle of the night when you're all upset and scared."

"He probably thinks he's protecting Mother," David offered gloomily.

"Well, Mr. Currier said," Bea maintained bravely, "that he can't possibly get murder in the first degree. At the very worst it'll be second degree. And he'll get time off for good behavior—"

"If the jury has any sense at all," Jocelyn interrupted firmly, "Fred won't get anything. He was only defending his sister."

Marvin shook his head dubiously, and Alison rose to say her farewells.

When she and Orville had gone, Bea observed ruefully, "Well, there's one good thing came of it. This time it looks as if Alison's going to get her man. Seems as if tragedy brings people together. At least, this one seems to have speeded things up for those two."

"It's sort of poetic justice," David said sadly, "Dad's death helping out Alison's romance, after the way he always picked on her boy friends."

When David had taken his leave, Cousin Helen spoke up. "I didn't want to say anything in front of David. Goodness knows he's had enough to bear. But the improvement in Alison's love life isn't the only good thing that's come out of all this horror. At least we're rid of Maurice at last."

"I can't say I feel very good," Marvin reproved heavily, "about the way we all feel actually glad he's gone. I get a guilty feeling that in some ways we're no better than he was, or we wouldn't feel like that. It's as if he'd—affected—all of us, made us resemble him. Esther tryin' to kill him, Fred actually doing it, and the rest of us secretly applauding 'em, and not concerned about anything but getting Fred and Esther out of the trouble they're in." He shook his head. "It ain't quite decent someway."

"I'm sure," Jocelyn asserted priggishly, "nobody could be blamed for wanting to be rid of that man."

Marvin stared at her with a detached expression. "He was guilty of a lot. But I can't get over the feeling we're all guilty too. We shouldn't have let him—infect us."

"You're right," Jane said sharply. "That's what gets me. In one sense Fred is taking the rap for all of you. And yet he's the least guilty of the whole bunch. Maurice never did anything to us. Fred didn't hate him—personally, the way you—or Jocelyn—did."

"I wonder," Marvin murmured. "I wonder."

On the way back to Los Alegres Marvin expressed himself further to Bea. "I have a hunch there's a lot of things we'll never know about this whole business, no matter how it comes out in court."

"I don't see how you can say that. Everything has come out. Both Esther and Fred walking right up to the cops like big simpletons, saying 'Sure, I done it.' Honestly, if they'd only both had sense enough to deny *everything!* Nobody ever would have known which one of us did it. Because, like you said, in our hearts we're *all* guilty."

"Maybe Maurice himself was the guiltiest of all," Marvin mused aloud. He uttered a choked laugh. "You could almost call it suicide. By the way he treated us he made actual or potential murderers out of all of us."

THE END

THEIR NEAREST AND DEAREST

BERNICE CAREY

For Bill and Danny,
who were born in Salinas

CHAPTER ONE

Stanley West's dark blue business coupé stood in its usual place beside the flight of wooden steps to the office door. But the bookkeeper, pulling into his own parking spot just ahead of Stan's, was surprised. He was early himself, and the boss did not usually show up until nine or later.

The shed workers' automobiles stood in glistening ranks farther down across the driveway to his left; and a towering truck lumbered past toward the loading platforms at the rear, its slatted walls crammed with crisp green lettuce fresh from the fields. As Earl dismounted from his sedan, one head jarred loose from the load and bumped along the ground at his feet.

Ordinarily Earl unlocked the outside door whose window was lettered in green and gold: Golden West Produce Company. This morning, since Stan had evidently preceded him, Earl did not get out his keys. The door held, however, when he turned the knob. Slightly puzzled, the bookkeeper pulled the key ring from his pocket and let himself in. The night lock was on.

The windows were to the north and west, their venetian blinds still drawn against yesterday afternoon's glare. In the outer office there was the usual morning air of suspended animation, the desk tops clear, the waste basket empty, the filing-cabinet doors closed, the Petty calendar girl displaying her sleek legs, her smile just as inviting as if it had not been wasted upon darkness through the night.

Earl jerked the cords of the blinds so that the slats lay horizontally, flipped the pages of his desk calendar to the current August day, and then glanced at the frosted-glass door leading out to the sheds, from behind which he could hear the dull roar that meant work in progress. No sound came from behind the frosted-glass panel in the room's inner partition, the door whose window was modestly lettered in the lower corner, *Stanley West, Private*; but it had occurred to Earl that Stan might have entered directly from the shed instead of from outside.

As his eyes rested for a moment on the neatly cleared desk under the front windows, Earl breathed an imperceptible sigh. He was busier than usual this week with Dorothy away. Instead of taking her vacation in late June when things were slack, their office girl had coyly requested two weeks in mid-August when shipping was in full swing; for that was when her fiancé, Herman, who was a lineman for the telephone company, got his vacation; and after a two years' engagement, she and Herman had decided, as Dorothy put it, "to take the plunge," and use his two weeks' leave for a honeymoon, after which Dorothy would return to her typing and filing and telephone answering "just as if," she had informed Earl and Stanley, "nothing had happened."

Stan had granted the inconvenient vacation time, remarking privately to Earl, "When a girl looks like Dorothy, it would be inhuman to put obstacles in the way of her getting a man."

She wasn't very decorative, but neither Earl nor Stanley minded. Her competence and good nature made people forget a rather thick-lipped mouth that seemed too full of teeth, eyes that squinted a little behind thick-lensed glasses, and a series of constant and unsuccessful experiments with light tan hair.

Earl seated himself and opened drawers and began to arrange his work materials, consulting the memos clipped together in the wire basket brought up from a deep drawer, glancing at the letters waiting beneath the memos, resurrecting his typewriter from the desk's nether regions.

Then he turned in his chair and looked again at the inner door, with a sudden urge to know for sure if Stan was there. He rose and tapped lightly on the glass.

"Stan?"

There was no answer.

"You there, Mr. West?" There was no rule about what form of address Earl used toward his boss. Some ultra subtle distinction in circumstances dictated whether it was to be "Stan" or "Mr. West" or just "Hey, boss."

The doorknob turned in Earl's hand, and he was facing the center of the room, where he often met Stan's eyes across the rectangular desk top.

The verbalization that crossed his mind, rather foolishly, was, "He's there all right. He sure is there."

Stanley West's head and shoulders lay forward across the wide, dark green blotter that was blackened in an irregular design almost to its outer edges.

The thought never crossed Earl's mind that Stanley West might be alive. Perhaps it was the hands with the spread fingers, palms down on the top of the desk.

Earl put his left hand out and braced himself against the doorjamb. Behind him the cacophony from the work area increased in volume, then diminished simultaneously with the sound of the door's closing.

"Stan still here?"

It was the voice of Ralph Musio, the shed foreman.

Earl turned mechanically, his movement revealing the smaller room beyond him. "I just," he said in a flat voice, "found him."

Ralph took a step forward, his eyes widening. "Christ Almighty."

Earl turned again, and both men stood staring.

Ralph pointed. "His gun." It was a statement with a trace of question underlining it.

"Looks like it."

They stood together in the doorway, their eyes upon the vicious .45 revolver lying at the edge of the desk just in front of Stan's thick, greying hair.

"Suicide?" Ralph breathed.

Earl's eyes met his with the glazed expression they had taken on when he first opened the inner door. "Suicide," he repeated flatly; and they both recognized that the way Earl pronounced the word dismissed its validity.

"We better do something."

"Yes," Earl agreed helplessly. "Yes." He looked vaguely around the outer office until his eyes fell on the telephone. He walked stiffly toward it, picked up the speaking tube, and poised a finger over the dial.

"The number. I forgot."

"Look in the book. It's on the first page."

Earl turned back the cover of the slender city directory and muttered, "Oh yeah, I remember now."

When he had replaced the telephone he sank weakly into the desk chair.

"You need a shot," Ralph said abruptly. "Got a bottle around?"

Earl swallowed. "Not in here." He nodded toward the inner door. "Stan's bar—"

Ralph's eyes darted to the door and back. "Better skip it."

Earl nodded at the telephone. "They said—don't touch anything."

Ralph pulled a package of cigarettes from the pocket of his blue work shirt and, shoving them toward Earl, commanded, "Here, take one."

Gratefully Earl busied himself with lighting the cigarette. Ralph went to the window and looked through the barred blind at another truck pulling two trailer loads of the fresh, clean green stuff from which they made their living.

"What happened?"

"How do I know? I saw his car outside when I pulled up. But the outside door was locked. I never thought anything, just went ahead gettin' things out for the day; and then, I dunno, something just seemed to tell me: Better find out if Stan's in there. So I knocked and then I opened the door, and you came in." Earl raised his head. "Was his car here when you came down at seven?"

"Yeah, and I thought it was funny, him bein' here at that hour. But what the hell, you know how it is first thing in the morning with the crew coming on and a million things to see to gettin' lined up for the day. I never thought of lookin' him up."

"I wonder—how long."

"It's God damn funny. He wouldn't be down all that before seven; and if he was here all night, why didn't the patrolman investigate his car bein' there?"

"Well, he could leave the business car parked here, and drive off with a friend or something."

"If he was gone all night, how come his wife wouldn't notice?" Earl moved his hand apologetically. "Maybe that's nothing unusual, him bein' away all night."

"You got somep'n' there," Ralph agreed. He looked at the door. "It must be his own gun all right. Nobody else'd leave theirs there. Must," he added slowly, "have stood in front of the desk and plugged him, right in the ticker."

"How would somebody else get hold of his gun?"

"He kept it right there in the top right-hand desk drawer."

"Sometimes he carried it in the car," Earl contributed aimlessly. "He—he kind of liked guns. You know, home, he's got everything—shotguns, rifles—the works. Racks for 'em in his den."

"I woulden know," Ralph said shortly.

"He's got other type revolvers; but this one, he kept it here mostly."

"I still say, how the hell's anybody gonna get it off him? He wouldn't give somebody a chance to reach in the drawer and take it."

Earl rose and stood two feet away from the inner door, looking into the room.

"Look here," he said to Ralph, who joined him.

While the outer office floor was covered by a tile-patterned linoleum, the inner one was carpeted to the walls. At the left of the desk a whiskey shot glass lay on its side on the green broadloom. On the desk top above it stood a heavy tumbler half full of water.

"He could," Earl said slowly, "have gone to the bar over there to pour a drink, and while his back was turned somebody took the gun out and concealed it. So when Stan sat down at the desk the other guy had his chance."

"How come he'd be drinkin' alone, if somebody was with him?"

Earl regarded the small bar on the room's back wall. One of its doors stood open, revealing shelves full of bottles. The door concealing glasses was closed.

"Maybe he wasn't. Maybe the—the—other party cleaned up his glass and put it away—"

The telephone buzzed behind them, and Earl started. He spoke mechanically into the mouthpiece, "Golden West Produce Company." He frowned uncertainly, then said efficiently, "I'm sorry, Mr. Harper, Mr. West is not—available. No, no, it's no use to call later. We're—we're tied up."

He set the instrument back and looked at the foreman. "I wasn't going to tell him. It's going to be hell around here," he said despairingly, "when the news gets out."

His eyes rested wildly on the desk. "Right now when Dorothy isn't even here. It'll all fall on my shoulders. The business."

"Is that something new?"

"No. No, but I'll be *responsible*."

"So what? You'll do all right." Ralph glanced out of the window as a businesslike sedan with red spotlights pulled up. "Well, here we go. Get hold of yourself."

Earl pulled the back of his hand across his forehead. "It's a relief. Being able to turn it over to them."

CHAPTER TWO

The Stanley West home was in a quiet way one of the show places of Salinas. It stood in the constricted little residential area that blossomed unexpectedly between the helter-skelter auto courts and service stations along El Camino Real, and the older and more prosaic bungalowed neighborhood west of Main Street and the business district. In the few square blocks where the West residence stood, the lawns and the back yards were kept by professional gardeners, while hired girls saw to it that the two-story houses were always in a state of shining tidiness.

The West house was a pleasant architectural compromise between the ranch-house and the Spanish-hacienda schools of thought, done in cream-colored wood with a shingled roof and a narrow two-tiered veranda set between the side wings facing the street. The second story of the veranda had a railing crowned by colorful potted plants behind which french doors led to the upstairs hall. At considerable expense flourishing live oaks had been brought in from the hills, roots and all, and set out at artistically suitable intervals on the front lawn.

At six-thirty that morning Laverne West had come foggily awake for a few horrible seconds, had groggily swallowed two aspirins ready on the bedside table, washing them down with copious draughts of water, and had thankfully sunk into unconsciousness once more.

When she reawakened at approximately a quarter to nine, she felt almost good. She frowned as she saw that the other twin bed with its studded, pale leather headboard was undisturbed beneath the heavy linen spread. She couldn't remember what Stan had told her he would be doing last evening. He usually told her his plans—although she knew the plan and the actuality did not always coincide. His absence could mean an all-night poker game, or—her jaw muscles hardened—a girl, or a simple decision to stay at somebody's country place all night if the hour had grown unduly late over a business talk or a bull session.

Through the windows open over the garden at the rear of the house she could hear the voices of her twin thirteen-year-old sons, already busy at whatever "project" was under way. Last week it had been the construction of an outboard motorboat destined hopefully for use on Monterey Bay.

Patty, her eighteen-year-old daughter, was, she supposed, still asleep in her room in the south wing.

Languidly Laverne noted that the sun was out, something one hardly expected on a morning in August when ordinarily the fog that had been funneled up by the mouth of the river during the night hung sulkily over the dry river bed for several miles inland. At least this morning she could wear something that was not only appropriate to a summer day but comfortable.

The chartreuse cotton, she decided, with the tiny sprigs of pink in it, a square-dancing dress actually—though she wouldn't have been caught dead at anything as corny as a folk dance—with its low, gathered neck, its short, puffed sleeves, its flounced skirt. The flat gold sandals, she decided, the ones that were practically all straps. Maybe the gold junk-jewelry necklace fashioned like a chain of maple leaves. No earrings, she guessed. And her hair brushed up all the way around so it stood out loose and fluffy.

She lifted herself to a sitting position, moving experimentally. No, her head was all right, didn't feel as if her brain were a loosely cohesive mass of ball bearings joggling around unanchored inside her skull. She had risen so she could see her hair in the mirror of the dressing table to her right. It was only a week since she'd had it touched up, and it was reassuringly still a uniform, soft, light bronze clear to the scalp. She hadn't meant to look at her face. She tried never to see it in the morning until after her circulation had been stimulated by a shower; but it was hard to inspect one's hair without inadvertently noticing the area beneath it.

Almost briskly she swung out of bed, draped the matching negligee over her lacy white crepe nightgown, stuck her feet into pink mules, and padded to the bathroom as if to escape the dominating expanse of looking glass.

It was really quite a pretty face whose dark blue eyes surveyed its reflection after a half hour spent in the bathroom and before the dressing table. There were only two little lines between the brows, and faint depressions in the flesh between nostril and lip, foreshadowing the permanent grooves which would settle there someday. Deliberately Laverne smiled so that the corners of her mouth lifted. She had to watch that. In certain lights the flesh at the corners of her lips seemed to be adopting a downward slope.

She went downstairs to the kitchen, passing the colored maid, Lula, who was pushing a carpet sweeper over the Persian rug on the polished hall floor. Laverne announced with a smile, "I think I'll take a tray out on the terrace for breakfast. Can't waste this lovely sunshine."

A janitor service came once a month for heavy cleaning, but Lula did all the work otherwise; so Laverne and Patty waited on themselves for such things as breakfast and straightening their own rooms if they weren't otherwise busy.

Laverne sat in an awninged chaise with her tray on a metal table. With her fair skin and delicate hair, she was not a sun addict, although most of her friends made a fetish of broiling themselves to a sort of golden-oak shade and staying that way all winter if possible.

The twins in Levis and Hawaiian shirts went in and out of the narrow door at the back of the garage, preoccupied with lengths of board and bits of wire. Sounds of hammering were interspersed with periods of altercation carried on in shrill voices. Laverne wondered idly what in the world they were making now.

She had brought the previous evening's newspaper out with her, and as she ate, her eyes traveled desultorily over the front page spread out on the table beside her plate. War in Korea as usual had usurped the headlines. She lifted her eyes in the direction of the garage. If only there would be peace by the time the boys were eighteen. There was an item about a hit-and-run automobile accident west of town as a result of which a farm laborer had died during the afternoon without regaining consciousness. There was the usual box giving the total shipments of lettuce the day before. And the threat of a railroad strike. And an airplane crash in New Jersey.... Lots of news, she thought, and all bad.

When she was down to her coffee and a cigarette in an ivory holder, Patty came sidling through the screened door, bearing her own tray, which was more heavily laden than her mother's had been.

Patty's hair was streaked by the sun from a light brown to an almost platinum blond. At the moment it was parted on the side and drawn back to two short pigtails tied with blue ribbons. She wore faded and very tight pale blue pedal-pusher pants and a red and yellow strapless bra, the ensemble set off by run-over, scuffed brown loafers.

Her mother said without asperity, "You look like hell." And then she sighed. "To think that I too could once look cute got up like that."

"You're plenty sharp now," Patty replied cheerfully. "For a middle-aged woman."

"I am thirty-eight years old, which I do not consider middle-aged." Laverne eyed her daughter. "Where were you last night?"

"Around."

"No. Not really. I thought," sarcastically, "you might have stopped off on Jupiter's seventh moon like those silly radio programs the kids used to insist on hearing while we ate dinner."

"I went to the show. California. Where were you?"

"Who went with you?"

"Oh, some of the kids. You and Dad go out?"

"Your dad, you ought to know, was off on business somewhere, now that the fall deal's under way and the market's unsteady."

"Is it?"

"Is what?"

"The market unsteady."

"Did you ever know a time when it wasn't?"

"What did you do? Sit at home by yourself?" Patty checked herself, and chuckled. "Silly me. As if the, quote, popular, attractive Mrs. Stanley West, unquote, ever sat around by her little self of an evening."

"You needn't be offensive, Patty." An aggrieved note came into Laverne's voice. "Sometimes I think you actually resent my being young. You'd rather I suppose, that I was old and fat and grey-headed and had false teeth. Like Mrs. Ricco."

"No. It's fun, having a mother like you." Patty regarded her strangely. "Less restricting, I think. The old fat ones like you spoke of would probably 'mother' a girl to death, try to live her life for her; but someone like you, they're usually too messed up in their own affairs to pay much attention to *what* little daughter's up to."

Laverne looked taken aback. Noticing this, Patty glanced aside quickly and said with a throaty chuckle:

"Skip it, Mom, skip it. I think you're awful cute and I love you like crazy."

Rather stiffly Laverne declared, "I'm sure I've always tried to be a good mother to you kids."

Across the yard Kerry was yelling into the workshop end of the garage to his brother Terry, "Not that way, you dope, not that way! The other end up."

Laverne's face was turned in that direction, away from her daughter. She *had* tried, too. Read all the books and spent endless hours talking about her children to her girl friends and sat through countless awful school programs and P.T.A. teas. And what was the result? She and Patty were on easy, affectionate, superficial terms with one another; but they had never had a deep closeness. Very young, Patty had quit telling her things, intimate personal ones, that is.

And the twins. Well, she tried. But what could they do—together, she and the boys? They liked rough things like riding, and fishing trips where you camped out. They loved being taken with their father out to the fields, where all anyone could do was stand and look at a row of lettuce made even more startlingly green by the moist brown dirt on either side of it; and when you'd seen one row of lettuce you'd seen them all.

Some women did seem to make their children their life. But it wasn't her fault that she hadn't been able to, that somehow, for instance, Brian had crept into that life. Her expression went blank, concealingly, as her eyes came to rest on the vivid cerise blossoms of an oleander bush.

It was a mess, a horrible mess, with Brian becoming ever more demanding, insisting she do something definite. It was her fault, of course. All she had to do was make up her mind. And it was childish not to be able to. But it was all very well for Brian to be so—settled—in his mind, about planning a future course. Clarice was in Reno right now. And Clarice didn't even know that it was serious between Laverne and Brian. Clarice was suing Brian on simple desertion grounds, and anyway Clarice was already tied up with that broker in San Francisco. She *wanted* to be rid of Brian. But Stan, even though he sometimes seemed hardly aware that his wife was alive, was piggishly determined to keep her his wife.

It would be simpler if she hated Stan, in a sweeping and satisfying way. But she didn't. While neither, of course, did she love him. Or did she? In some peculiar, devious way? Was that why she could not make her decision?

Brian put everything so simply, so reasonably: He loved her; she loved him; and they were not getting any younger. It was not as if the children really needed her. Patty was eighteen, ready to start living independently of parental guidance. The twins would soon be in high school. Their father's protection was all they needed. They were on the verge of adolescence, would soon rebel openly against the bonds of dependency on home and mother.

Their voices cut across her thoughts, young and shrill and supremely vital. They seemed to cut through into a great hollowness within her. Being twins, their emotional dependency was upon each other, not upon their mother. In a little while they would hardly notice that she was gone.

So why was she immobilized, pointlessly going along from day to day? Was it simply because that was what Stanley wanted her to do, because he did not want the pattern broken?

Her eyes swept over the white wall of the three-car garage where the Belle of Portugal rose climbed to the shingled roof. She might be able to keep her own little car if she divorced Stan; but at least for the present, if she married Brian, there would be no three-car garage, no gracious two-story house.

The painted white brick walls traced with the green of Paul Scarlet rose vines stood eight feet high against intrusion on their back garden with its rectangle of lawn making a verdant pool in the center. The pretty walls seemed to enclose and embrace Laverne too in rich physical comfort.

She glanced down at the little watch on her wrist, the face encircled with sapphires. Her coffee cup still sat on the table beside her chair. By no standards was there an excuse to have a drink this early. But she thought longingly of the little bar in the dining room and the bottle of her own brand of bourbon. It didn't take long with the help of whiskey. Your mind stopped going back and forth from yes to no. It soon began to seem all right to wait, to put off, eventually even to forget that there was a decision which must be made.

She reached for the package of cigarettes on the table, and moved restlessly in her chair. If it weren't for the help of a few drinks now and then, she didn't know what she would do. If she lived in the city she thought perhaps she'd go to that man who had psychoanalyzed Grace Bailey. He was marvelous, Grace said, made a new woman out of her. Wryly, Laverne thought to herself, "And that's just what I need, to be made a new woman. God knows the one I am doesn't seem to be much good, to herself or anyone else."

Patty's voice broke in upon her. "Do you really think Dad'll break down and buy the Corral de Tierra place?"

"He's weakening," Laverne said, lightly for Patty's benefit. "We have a date with Chuck Willet to drive out and see the place again at two this afternoon."

"Boy, that would be neat." Patty pushed her plate away and leaned back in her chair with her tanned bare legs out stiffly in front of her, heels braced against the flat sandstones. "Our own pool, stables, a guest house. That would be really living."

"It would be nice," Laverne agreed. "But of course we'd have to sell this place first. The other is so much more expensive. Chuck says he can sell this for us; but he doesn't have a real prospect; I can tell."

"What are you dealing with Chuck Willet for? Why not the Eastons or the Bonnet Realty? They're sort of friends of ours too."

"Well, Chuck had this place out there and brought it to your father's attention. I know Chuck is a little—crude; but at the same time the Willets are accepted. And Dora is a nice person."

"Oh, she's all right. But him. That butter-wouldn't-melt look on his fat face doesn't fool me. There's a look in his eyes that says different. Well, however it comes about, I do hope Dad lets us buy this place. Everybody lives in the country nowadays. It's the thing to do."

Laverne let her thoughts dwell on the Ormsby place, as it was called because originally it had been built for and occupied by that family. Its shake-covered exterior with a log trim gave the house a rustic appearance that belied the luxurious modern appointments within. She would love living there, with its view of Mount Toro and its rose garden and its winding drive through a meadow up to the main grounds. It would make her feel like a lady of the manor. And it would be a marvelous place for parties.

It was almost as if Stan were using the Ormsby place as a bribe to keep her, even though he couldn't know for sure how serious it was about

Brian—unless—unless Brian had carried out his threat to go to Stan and tell him straight out. But he wouldn't be so reckless. He couldn't. It would leave her in such a bad bargaining position. And Brian was a lawyer. He knew better than to do such a thing where a divorce was involved.

Through the open hallway doors they heard the front-door chimes, but neither Patty nor Laverne stirred in response. Lula was in the front of the house.

In a moment she appeared at the terrace door. "Cass Huggins wants to see you, Mrs. West," she announced with a rather surprised air.

No one thought it strange that Lula had not said "Mr. Huggins." Cass Huggins was city chief of police, and nobody ever referred to him except by his full name.

"Cass Huggins?" Laverne echoed incredulously.

"Yes, ma'am."

Laverne rose. "Well, show him out here. Now what do you suppose *he* wants?"

Patty straightened and put the soles of her feet on the floor. "Selling tickets to the policemen's ball probably."

Laverne glanced toward the garage. "I hope the twins haven't done something delinquent." She turned to the doorway as a man in a blue uniform, carrying a visored cap, appeared there. "Good morning, Cass," she said brightly. "This is a surprise. Seeing such a busy man so early in the morning."

Although he had been two years ahead of her, Laverne had gone to high school with Cassius Huggins; therefore she was taken aback when he spoke gravely, "This is a tough assignment, Mrs. West. I'm afraid I've got bad news for you."

Laverne's whole body went still, and Patty's blue eyes widened at the man. Unobtrusively, before he went on he moved a little closer to the woman, as if to be in reaching distance in case she needed support.

"It's going to be a shock, but there's no use in beating around the bush. Stan has had an accident."

"Oh." It was a faint, sighing breath; and Laverne's mind leapt to the empty bed upstairs. "He's—he's—hurt?"

Patty's slender brown hand had become a tight fist on the white metal table top.

"I'm sorry, Laverne"—the policeman's humanity came to the fore and he called her by her first name without thinking—"he's dead."

"Oh-h." Again the soft, sighing escape of breath. She swayed almost imperceptibly.

Cass took her arm and gently guided her to a low-backed canvas chair.

"Take it easy," he muttered. "I know this is a hell of a way to break it to you; but there isn't any easy way, I guess." He peered at her. "D'you want a drink of water or something?"

She shook her head numbly. "What—what happened? How—"

"He was shot, Mrs. West. In his office. Earl found him this morning."

Patty sat rigid, her hands clasped in a tight ball between her breasts. There was a hysterical note of desperation in her voice as she demanded, "An accident?"

Cass turned to observe the girl. At first glance when he came out to the terrace he had thought of her as a child, what with her pigtails and those short pants; but now he was reminded that Stan West's daughter was at least eighteen, maybe almost nineteen, and that she was a woman.

"We're trying to find out," he answered her question quietly.

Laverne repeated in a harsh, mechanical voice, "What happened?"

"We're not sure," Cass returned cagily. Without being invited to, he pulled up a chair that matched Laverne's and sat down between the women. Now that he had dispensed with the unpleasant duty of breaking it to them, he was intent on his real job, to find out, if he could, what they knew.

"In order to get the whole thing straight I have to ask you a few questions. What about last evening, Mrs. West? When did you see your husband last?"

Laverne closed her eyes against the exuberant sunlight and tried to think. "I haven't seen him," she said slowly, "since night before last."

"Night before last! Can you explain that?"

"There's nothing to explain," she said impatiently. "The last I saw Stan was when we went to bed that night. I didn't wake up until after he'd gone in the morning. He always has lunch out, and he wasn't at home for dinner last night."

"I see. Did you speak to him during the day?"

"Yes." Laverne closed her eyes and tried to remember. There had been the cocktail party out at Peabody's. She had gone with the Jardines, and Brian had dropped in, but he'd had to leave, some family affair, his aunt's birthday or something. How awful, how terribly awful that she was not very clear on anything from five o'clock on. No lunch, and a couple of drinks before she left home, to put her in the mood, and then the martinis at Peabody's. But before that, yes, that was it ...

"He phoned me at home, during the afternoon. Something about dinner with an Eastern buyer, at the hotel downtown. I believe he dropped in here at home late in the afternoon while I was out, to shower and change clothes before dinner." Rather appealingly she looked at Cass. "He and Earl are busier than usual right now, with Dorothy away. Our stenographer, Dorothy Sprague. She just got married, you know. It's always busy this time of year. So much to see to. They get to talking, brokers and so on. I never expect Stan to keep regular hours."

"I know," Cass reassured her. And it did check. Earl Fowler had mentioned Stan's dinner date with the head buyer for a chain of wholesale produce markets in the East. "But wasn't he home, during the night?"

"I don't think so. His bed hadn't been slept in."

"Didn't that strike you as unusual?"

Laverne's eyes darted toward him warily. "Well, yes and no. I guess I thought he might have been late and—and just turned in at the hotel downtown."

Cass's eyes were speculative. The hotel she meant was not more than a dozen blocks from this house. Hardly a trip to deter a man, even if he'd been drinking. But he turned to the girl.

"When did you see your father last?"

While Cass Huggins talked to her mother, the girl had slumped. She sat huddled now with her hands in her lap, her shoulders drooping. She looked a little sick.

"Day before yesterday," she said dully. "At dinner. We all ate together, alone, the family."

As if the effort of speaking had exhausted her, Patty put her elbow on the table and leaned her head on her hand.

"Did Mr. West have any particularly pressing worries right now?" he addressed Laverne again.

She met his eyes blankly. "The business—it's always a worry. You know that, Cass. The market. If the crop's bad, that's bad; you don't have enough to ship. If the crop's too good, that's bad. No price—"

She realized that she was babbling, and she caught herself harshly. "I don't know of anything—unusual that way," she said flatly.

"Anything personal weighing on his mind?"

Patty broke in. "You—you think—*suicide?*"

"It's possible."

"Stan—commit suicide!" Laverne exclaimed involuntarily.

"We don't think he did. Do you know of anyone who might have had a grudge against Stan?"

Laverne was regarding him fixedly. "Cass. Was Stan—murdered?"

"We think so."

Again Laverne's eyes closed, and she leaned back in the chair. There was no headrest, and her head wobbled slightly.

Cass put a firm hand on her arm. "Steady, Laverne."

With a visible effort she opened her eyes and stiffened her neck muscles. She looked at the policeman unseeingly. Then she pushed herself up out of the chair with her hands on the armrests.

"I think I'd better lie down."

Cass rose. "I know it's a shock."

From the rear of the yard rose a scream. "Terry, bring that back here. I gotta have that screwdriver."

Like a robot Laverne turned and looked toward Kerry facing out in the rear doorway of the garage. Slowly a look of intelligence came into her eyes, and her shoulders squared.

"I must tell the boys," she said dully, and walked away down the terrace steps.

The two on the sunny flagstones watched but could not hear as she called the twins up to face her beside the doorway. They saw her put a hand on each shoulder in its raffish printed shirt, saw the boyish faces turned to hers only an inch or so above them.

Cass looked down at the girl. "This is tough on you folks. Believe me, I'm sorry. If you want me to, I'll speak to the maid on the way out and tell her to call your mother's sister and ask her to come over. Sort of take charge for you."

"Thanks."

The boys, looking subdued and frightened, followed Laverne across the grass. She regarded Cass Huggins with an air of detachment.

"You'll have to excuse me. I can't take any more." She passed him on the way into the house.

"Shall I have your maid call the doctor? You feel all right?"

She paused, half turned toward him. "I'm all right."

She mounted the stairs with one hand on the railing, leaning on it as if she were old and weak.

Carefully she closed the door to her room, but now that she was there, alone with her unmade bed and the disorder of her dressing table and her filmy robe over a chair and the pink mules in front of the long wardrobe whose sliding door was open, she didn't know what to do. Couldn't think why it had seemed such an ineluctably desirable goal, to get off alone here in her room. Stan's smooth bed. Unused. The closed doors of his wardrobe closet. His photograph on her desk, one taken seventeen years before— when they had still been mad about each other.

Thoughts assaulted her mind, collided, ricocheted off in irrelevances.

Stan. Shot. And she didn't even know where. In the head, or the body. Or whether he had died instantly. She leaned back in the chair with her head against the upholstery and went limp. Tears began to seep out between her lashes. And she was surprised to notice that she hadn't cried before. You always cried when someone died. She had known she would, sooner or later. And sure enough she was doing it now. Gasping a little, and snuffling, she stumbled up and got a handful of cleansing tissues and fell across her bed face down, feeling at her waist the roll of the blanket where she had turned it back on arising and the smoothness of the undersheet beneath her bare arms.

She made no effort to stop. She was willing to keep on crying and crying; but at last she lay still and spent with her cheek on the damp percale pillow case.

But in a moment she rolled her face in agony against the yielding pillow. It was too much, too much. She couldn't stand it.

Brian! Brian. Right away she had known. But she hadn't let the knowledge emerge, rounded and definite. She writhed upon the mussed bed, recoiling from her thoughts. Thoughts in which now there was neither love nor hatred, only horror, and an unlocalized fear, fear that pertained to Brian himself—because he had killed, to herself—because she had loved a man who would kill. Her whole being was scooped out into a shell of horror by the recognition that she was not really unprepared to learn that Brian had shot Stanley. He was impetuous. Impatient. It was, in fact, the uncalculating, freely given quality of his emotions that had drawn her into friendship and more with him. And he had a taste for the dramatic. He saw everything as if it were an act on the stage.

Who but Brian would, when he felt things had reached an impasse, go direct to his inamorata's husband and say: Look here, Laverne hasn't the guts to make a decisive move; so I'm putting it to you. Things can't go on this way. Let's be civilized and practical. You've stepped out on her enough so that she has the goods on you if she has to use it.

And yet cagey enough to be sure there were no witnesses to the conversation—in case it didn't work out as he planned. Nobody but Brian would act like that.

She had kept telling him it wasn't as simple as he thought. That even though Stan was no longer madly in love with her, the thought of divorce had never crossed his mind.

Brian thought Stan was phlegmatic, a cool, practical man. Stodgy, Brian considered Stan. Well, he had found out how stodgy Stan was. Brian should have known—a man who loved guns as Stan did, who took every opportunity to go hunting. He should have known there was a cool taste for violence there.

She crushed her head between her palms, almost seeing and hearing the scene in the office where Brian had sought Stan out. Stan's harsh, insulting anger. (He had never really cared much for Brian, even before anything developed between herself and the young lawyer. Stan thought Brian was a dandy—even slightly effeminate.) And then Brian flaring up, the quarrel growing, growing. And a gun coming into it. Brian, to her knowledge, didn't own one. Cass Huggins hadn't said. It must have been the .45 Stan kept in the office.

She breathed a little more quietly. It might have been self-defense. There might be that to consider on Brian's behalf.

She came up on her right elbow and pressed the back of her left wrist against her forehead.

Murder. Cass Huggins. They would look for the murderer. Motives. *Motives*. Even she—

How many people knew about her affair with Brian? Really knew, that is. Everybody, all their crowd, anyhow, knew that he and she were friends, that they paired off at dances and dinners and so on. They were supposed to think though that it was just—playing around.

Thank God, she had never confided in anyone. Not even to Edith, her sister. Nor to Joan, her best friend. And Brian. He wasn't the type to bandy a woman's name about, not when he was crazy about her. And if Stan had suspected anything, he hadn't known how serious it was; he too would have thought it was just a flirtation.

Laverne sat on the edge of the bed, thinking hard. Evidence. For police to find. Evidence, that is, about her and Brian.

There was that motor court. She didn't even remember just where it was. Somewhere in the Santa Cruz mountains. But Brian had given a false name; and it wasn't the sort of place to be fussy about taking license numbers. You paid your ten dollars and no questions asked. And a hotel in San Francisco. Twice. But different hotels, not famous ones, and false names again.

And they had never written each other letters. No, Cass Huggins might have his suspicions, but he couldn't prove anything....

She put her elbows on her knees and bent forward with her head in her hands, feet spread ungracefully apart on the pale rug.

The woman who earlier had risen from that bed, avoiding sight of her reflection in the mirror would have recoiled in dismay from the image the same glass reflected now, the hunched, ugly pose of a creature sunk in self-examination and despair. But it never occurred to Laverne to look up nor to care how she appeared from the outside.

There was a knock on the door, and her sister's voice. "Laverne. It's me, Edith."

Heavily Laverne straightened herself. "Come in."

Edith, who had never been as pretty as Laverne, had a look, beneath the horror and the commiseration, almost of satisfaction, a look common to those who love opportunities to "take over" in times of others' misfortunes.

"Darling," she intoned vigorously, "darling, it's awful."

From the way Laverne looked up at her sister, Edith might have been a stranger; but she allowed her head to be cradled on the other woman's shoulder; and in a moment she found herself crying again, sobbing, "Poor Stan."

CHAPTER THREE

When she raised her head again Laverne mumbled, "Patty, I haven't even spoken to her since—since—"

"She was in the dining room with her head on the table bawling when I got here," Edith volunteered, "with Lula patting her shoulder and crying too. The boys were on the terrace. They look scared."

"I'll have to—go to them."

"I talked to the twins, told them to go back and work quietly on their boat. That's what they said they'd been doing, building a boat. I told them it was better to keep busy, whether they felt like it or not."

Laverne surveyed her sister's sensible face and was grateful. They were rather different, for sisters. Edith had married a dentist; and all the way around she lived a more sensible life than Laverne. She was active in the P.T.A. and the Women's Civic Club; and she didn't have as much money to spend as Laverne did. Bob was doing all right; they had a pleasant house and a part-time hired girl; but Edith worked harder over her two children and her house and garden than Laverne did over her family and home.

"Now, just don't worry about anything," Edith said. "I'll stay all day. Mrs. Trumbull had come to do the ironing; so she's with the kids."

"I'll go speak to Patty."

When Laverne came out of her room Patty was ascending the stairs. They met one another's eyes uncertainly; and the girl's were covertly appraising. Laverne was guiltily thankful that her own eyelids were suitably puffed and pink, the flesh around her eyes slightly swollen.

"Patty," she murmured, "I'm sorry I rushed away like that, without a word to you. I didn't know what I was doing."

"I know," the girl said dully.

She suffered Laverne to embrace her, and they stood with their heads pressed together for a moment, Patty's hands on her mother's waist. Then the girl pulled away.

"I'm going to go and dress, more suitably. There'll be—people—around."

She walked away without looking back. Laverne's eyes followed the girl's bare shoulders until her bedroom door closed. Patty seemed so withdrawn, so unresponsive. Could it be— Did she suspect—that her father's death was tied up with her mother's actions? Did she feel that Laverne was somehow responsible?

Another part of her mind had registered the sound of the front-door chimes, and now she became aware of Lula on the stairs looking up at her.

"Mrs. West"—Lula's voice lowered conspiratorially—"it's more policemen.

They want to go through Mr. West's things. They want to go in his den."

"It's all right. Has to be, I guess, whether we like it or not."

Through the open door of her bedroom she could see Edith capably hanging things away. The bed was already made. She glanced down at her gay, girlish frock. She too would have to change into something more suitable.

She felt calmer now, more able to cope with the coming hours. But she had also an urgent need to take advantage of this clarity that had followed her tears and her recognition of the real state of affairs. She wanted to be alone for a bit before people impinged upon her for the rest of the day. Her eyes roved over the paneled doors in the corridor with its row of french windows to the west. Patty's room down to her left, the twins' room at her right, and ahead of her on the northwest corner of the house, the guest room. Quietly she crossed the hall, went in, and closed the door, pressing the button in the center of the knob to lock it.

She went to the street window and pulled up the blind. For a moment she looked down past the foliage of the oak tree at her right, into the sunny paved street, across to the grey, English-style house on the other side. She lowered herself into the wing chair and stared unseeing through the window between the ruffled organdy curtains.

Brian seemed to have faded to shadowy importance just now, while the past with Stan had taken on an immediacy, a realness it had not held for some time.

How short a while it seemed now. How quickly the years had passed. Yet it was almost twenty years since she had married Stan. She had been nineteen, and the folks had thought her too young. And in less than a year she'd had Patty. How young, how very young she had been. Stan was only ten years older than she; but looking back, it did not seem as if he had really been young in the same sense that she had been in those early years. During all the thoughtless playing and helling around, Stan had had a firm grip on himself and on his goals.

She had been a home-town girl, and Stan had been one of those lettuce men who suddenly came from nowhere in the late twenties, leasing land, sometimes buying it, throwing up flimsy corrugated steel sheds along the railroad tracks, eventually transforming the quiet little country town, and finally—rather to their own surprise—finding that they dominated it completely.

Her father, a pharmacist with his own drugstore, had been moderately prosperous for the time. But her marriage to Stan had opened up a new world to Laverne, one that, except for the ties with Edith, soon obliterated the social orbit she had followed before. All Stan's friends were also business associates; and with their wives they made up a world of their own, almost completely isolated from the former society of this valley whose traditional modes of agriculture they were transforming into an industry. It was partly that in those days many of them came and went with the seasons, moving almost in a body to El Centro, to Arizona, and back to Salinas with the crops. Of necessity they turned in upon their own group for company. They didn't have time to become integrated in the community.

Nor, in those early days of the thirties, had they really gauged their strength, the lettuce men. They had known only that in a nation frazzled by depression, they occupied a fortunate little oasis blooming with the tight green spheres that rolled away in strings of refrigerated freight cars and lolled back in the green of U.S. currency. Oh, there had been failures, men who lost their shirts. There had been what they then considered lean years; and seasons when nobody made a dime, but you always lived on the loan against the next season; and somehow you survived; and anyhow, all of them, even when they lay awake at night in terror of the falling market price, knew they were living better than they ever had before. For that was the odd thing. Most of them had been nobodies before. A few had even been itinerant workers themselves before they got into the game. Although a few had come from old, landed families and had been somebodies to start with, and some had had their own capital, enough to start up on a shoestring, none had been as well off as they were after they became produce men.

Stan was perhaps typical. His folks had been ranchers near Santa Maria, people who just got by, who never sank to poverty nor rose to opulence. Stan had not gone beyond high school in his education; and he had never really settled in a line of work, although his jobs always centered somehow around agriculture. He had been one of the earlier ones to take hold in Salinas, around 1927.

With a little frown Laverne realized that even now she didn't know just how Stan had got his start. He was not a loose talker; he knew how to keep his affairs to himself. And it was one of his beliefs that a woman should not be burdened with business worries. When she met him in the early thirties the Golden West Produce Company was already an established concern of two or three years' standing. The banks, of course, must have financed him for leasing land, erecting a shed, as they had almost everybody else. What Stan had had for security, or who went good on his notes, she didn't know.

Anyhow Stan had survived when others went under or were forced to merge with more powerful partners. And he had done well. The Golden West Produce Company might not be one of the big sheds, but it was one of the biggest and sturdiest of the small outfits.

And fun! There was a trace of bitterness in the smile that curved her lips. Oh hell yes, they'd had fun. She had always been able to park Patty with

Mamma, or with Edith, or with a baby sitter.

Laverne thought of an article she had read lately about the 1920s. It had started out talking about some writer who had been a big shot then and whose wife later went crazy; and the idea had been that the twenties were a heck of a gay, carefree, sort of hysterical time. It had struck Laverne that the mood described had been exactly that of the years before the '36 strike in Salinas. She had wondered then about the validity of the article writer's conclusions. Was it really the twenties that were so different, or was it just that the people who wrote of them were looking back at their own twenties? For with her those years when she was in her twenties—falling by the calendar in the 1930s—had been as mad and as thoughtless as the time that writer spoke of.

The lettuce balls at Del Monte at the close of the fall season every year with the produce crowd overflowing the Bali room and drinking themselves blind in private rooms rented for the night upstairs. And the women all with new formals and crushed-velvet wraps and fur coats. Fun! Oh my God yes, she thought bitterly. Some clown always jumped into the patio fountain or was forgotten and turned up sleeping on the ledge of the swimming pool the next morning. Or somebody had an irresistible urge to feed the swans on the lake and got marooned in a rowboat out in the middle. And you were never sure *whose* car you came home in.

And Big Week of the rodeo. Every house an open house. And people bringing home live geese from the carnival set up opposite the railroad station. And that character—she couldn't even remember his name now—who always made long-distance calls to New York or Seattle or Phoenix when he got lit, calls the hostess seldom knew about until she got her phone bill.

And the trips by train to Stanford and Berkeley for the Big Games. By train because everybody knew nobody would be sober enough to drive home afterward. And the loud partisanship for one university or the other, though most of the crowd had never set foot inside a college classroom. That was all changed now, of course. Everybody's kids went to college, whether their fathers had or not.

It all came back so vividly, so vividly, now. She had been like a little princess, so gay, so vivacious. And cute! Her hair was a natural ash-blond then, and her nose turned up a little and her cheeks had a doll-like plumpness. And Stan ... Well, she had thought it was one of those storybook deals, the real McCoy. She danced and laughed and flirted and sometimes men kissed her and made passes at her. But she knew what it was, just play. It was her and Stan—as far as that sort of thing went. Stan always poised, self-contained, sure of himself. She had never questioned Stan's perfection, his perfection in every way. If Stan said something, for instance, that was it: gospel truth. She remembered that her favorite song had been "One Alone" from *The Desert Song*. Romantic she had been. Sentimental. No, "naïve" was the word.

There were divorces in their crowd, and much-discussed marital crises, most of which boiled down to nothing finally. She knew some of the guys did step out on their wives, that one or two even played around with trimmers from their own sheds, or with entertainers at the cheap night clubs which thrived on the edge of town. And, of course, everybody had heard about Mattie's out north of town, which was planes above the horrible little houses at the edge of Chinatown, where on Saturday nights you could actually see the lines of Filipino men waiting outside.

And she knew Stan liked to gamble and that some of his men friends were—well, a little rough. Like Chuck Willet, for instance, who was reputed to have won and lost thousands in a single night at blackjack.

But it just never occurred to her—about women. And even then, she had to give Stan credit. It wasn't high-class prostitutes. And he didn't take advantage of the position of girls who worked for him.

Laverne pressed her hands over her eyes, her head against the chair back. No, the first one, the first one she knew about anyway, had been irreproachable socially. A house guest, in fact, of the Harpers, an old school friend of Wilma. Marcia, Marcia Allen. From the South. Tennessee.

Laverne's face creased with pain. Even now, fourteen years later. That adorable southern drawl. "Lawd help," with the *l* in "help" not quite pronounced, had been Marcia's favorite expletive. Curly brown hair and round blue kitten eyes, and a figure that—well, Laverne would like to see it now. Curves like that always went out of bounds sooner or later.

It hadn't taken her long to grow jealous over Stan's notice of the stranger; but she had never dreamed—And then the night he hadn't come home—

"Like last night," she thought irrelevantly. And she had learned for sure he hadn't played poker with Chuck and the boys as he had told her. So that she became watchful and caught him in one lie after another. And then—it had been at a week-end house party in the Carmel Valley, and she had run across them necking in the patio after dark, necking in such a way that she wasn't to be put off by protestations that it was just the casual sort of thing that did happen sometimes after too many drinks. Inside the house the radio had been playing a current hit song, "All I Do Is Dream of You." Always afterward the sound of that thumpy, repetitious rhythm made her feel physically ill.

Laverne had thought she was going to die; but it was Sunday night, and they were leaving early in the morning and she didn't really know the hosts very well—they were people just moved up from Phoenix where the husband was a big shipper in the Salt River Valley; so she didn't make a scene.

That was one thing, Laverne told herself defensively; she might be verging on alcoholism and she might be an adulteress, and even almost an accessory to murder; but she had always behaved like a lady.

But alone at home she had called Stan on his relations with Marcia; and his denials did not convince her. On the contrary, they enraged her.

It was, in fact, the first time she had ever been in a real fury with Stan.

His calmness, his reasonableness, his air of, "Now look, you're a silly, sweet little girl who's getting all excited about nothing," had driven her frantic until she had screamed at him, "What kind of a fool do you think I am? I know what it means when I find you and that bitch wrapped around each other like—like pair of rolled-up stockings."

Stan had surveyed her with his steady brown eyes as if she surprised him; and then with a maddening air of patience had taken his departure.

It went on for several days; and when his composure never cracked, Laverne decided to get a divorce. *That* had hit him where he lived; and surprisingly his attitude changed. He dropped the air of adult forbearance and met her on terms of equality. He even admitted to misbehavior with Marcia.

"But, baby," he had protested, "you know how those things are. Men, after all, are men; and it doesn't mean a thing. I don't give a whoop in Hades for Marcia Allen, wouldn't care if I never laid eyes on her again."

Before he was through he was pleading, promising. But somehow Laverne's attitude had changed too. The anger abated, and only the pain was left. She couldn't bear it, her little storybook world gone like a burst soap bubble. If Stan could want somebody else, even temporarily, she couldn't bear it. She wanted the Great Romance—or nothing. And he had not lived up to it; so why go on? Even his coming around to humbling himself by imploring her not to leave him added to her distracted sense of betrayal. She wanted the old strong Stanley, the Stan without flaw. For a period then she had almost really hated him.

Laverne glanced at the closed guest-room door. Then, as now, was Edith who stepped in. Stan had gone to her for help. You would have thought Edith would have been on her sister's side, taking up the cudgels in behalf of outraged virtue. Edith, the pillar of respectability, and her husband an elder in the Methodist Church.

But Edith had said, "I know. I don't blame you a bit, honey. I'd be furious myself. But Stan's really broken up about it. I could tell from the way he talked to me. I really think he's learned a lesson; Honestly, I don't think he'll ever do anything like this again."

And that, Laverne now reflected cynically, showed how much Edith knew about human nature.

Then, however, Laverne had stared at her sister incredulously. How could Edith fail to understand? It wasn't how good Stan might be in the future. It was what he *had* done. That was what had ruined everything.

"You have to consider Patty," Edith had pointed out. "A broken home. You struggling along trying to bring her up alone. What would you *do*, Laverne?"

"I'd have alimony."

"That's something else to consider," Edith had proceeded cautiously. "Stan's doing very well. You're very comfortable."

Then they hadn't yet built this house; they had been living in a six-room bungalow closer to downtown.

"You can look forward to a nice comfortable life with Stan," Edith had pursued inexorably. "And he'll behave in the future. I'd gamble on it. This has scared him. He doesn't want to lose you."

In the long run it had been these mercenary arguments of Edith which had been decisive. She *was* comfortable, and it would be difficult—and lonely—bringing up a child all by herself. And as it turned out Stan had behaved from then on. At least, Laverne thought cynically, when he started slipping again, later, he had been irreproachably discreet about it. She had never incontrovertibly *known*.

He had even, very quickly, resumed his old air of assurance, of tolerant perfection. He had become again, in the actual practice of their daily life, at least, the wise husband and father whom nobody contradicted. He was even perhaps a little kinder, a little more indulgent to Laverne.

Somehow they had just gone on. Partly to salve her wounded pride, partly, she supposed, as a private gesture of defiance, she had had a brief affair herself—with Pete Garroway, the Jardine Brothers field man who had been an eligible bachelor then. No one, she was pretty sure, had ever known, for sure, that it was an affair. She hadn't wanted open defiance somehow, more a reassurance, for her own satisfaction.

To tell the truth, she hadn't enjoyed it much. She remembered now, with a sort of compassion for her younger, rather pathetic self, how she used to bring up questions to Pete, offhandedly, she thought, as to how she compared with other women he had known. In bed, that is. Pete was always evasive, seeming embarrassed, being vaguely jocular about it. She never got a direct answer. But it was something that had bothered her. It was something a woman could never find out for sure, how she compared with other women; and it had taken on an importance in her mind. After the trouble with Stan.

And then the twins came along and they built this house; and life was different somehow, more dignified, more—well, settled, as if they had found their place and relaxed in it.

She had thought it was because of the changes in their personal life. But, looking back, she could see that it had been something the same for the whole crowd. It had really begun after the big strike in '36. Nothing had ever been quite the same since. It was as if the strike had shown them their strength, shown them dramatically that they didn't have to feel like *nouveau riche* intruders but that instead it was *they* who were the backbone, the leaders in the valley, potentially even the social aristocracy, that the old-time political and pioneer figures here in the county seat must, when it came right down to it, dance to the produce people's tune—not vice versa. What had really produced this change, this feeling of holding a place of authority and prestige, was, she thought, the way the great financial interests and the real political powers of the state had moved in and helped them win in the showdown with labor back there in '36.

Anyhow, gradually Laverne had realized that by imperceptible degrees she had become a Somebody, right here in the town where she had grown up. Her name was of value on committees pertaining to community activities; her parties were news. During the war she handed out coffee at the USO to soldiers from Fort Ord; she lent her name to bond-drive rallies. She never, however, became as much of a clubwoman as Edith did. She let people use her name on letterheads sometimes; and she appeared at large functions; but lately that was all.

Oddly enough, she had been happier during the war probably than at any time since the early days of her marriage. Stan had been frightfully busy and made a lot of money, and the kids and the USO and civilian defense had kept her busy and then everything in general had been so exciting.

Stan had been surprisingly intense about the war. She remembered how, at the very first after Pearl Harbor, the black-outs and the air-raid drills had been fraught with a real sense of danger. If bomber planes could reach Hawaii, might they not also reach the Pacific coast? She had nearly forgotten it now, but there had been almost a revival of real intimacy between her and Stan in those years. He had seemed to welcome the chance the war provided to feel a personal responsibility for the fate of the United States; and in that mood of heightened awareness of larger issues, he had paradoxically seemed to come closer to her. Perhaps, she reflected, it was because winning the war had been a large, objective purpose that they sincerely shared.

But when after victory the tension and the excitement died down, life went back to what it had been before—just living.

It took a year or so after the war was over for her to recognize what had happened, that a sort of loosening process had set in, that her spirits were getting flabby, that she didn't seem to give a damn much, one way or the other, about anything.

Edith, strangely enough, was the only one who had seemed to detect that something was wrong.

One afternoon, when Laverne had dropped in at her sister's on her way home from shopping, Edith had eyed her across a button she was sewing onto one of the kids' shirts, and said bluntly, "You look kind of peaked. What's the matter? Are you bored or something?"

Laverne raised her eyebrows in astonishment. "Bored! Heavens no, I'm too busy to be bored."

"Busy with what?"

"Why—socially. We've got something on every night this week, to say nothing of two or three luncheons I'm invited to."

"Oh—play. Except for having the kids, that's all you've ever done, 'Verne, is play."

"What else should I have done?" Laverne retorted dryly. "What's life for if not to enjoy it?"

"You ought to get active in something."

"Such as?"

"Well, there's the church."

"And what does that amount to but more luncheons and ladies' 'circles'? No thanks. I find my own friends livelier company."

"Well, there's politics. You could join Pro-America. A lot of women in your set belong."

"Politics scare me," Laverne retorted flippantly. "They might make me think."

The words had tripped out unthinkingly; and suddenly she fell silent, her eyes following Edith's needle as it went in and out through the button's holes.

Irrelevantly she thought of Vic Bailey laughing over a cocktail glass a few evenings previously, responding to some bit of badinage, "I don't ask questions; I just have fun."

Why had she said: "It might make me think," and then thought of Vic Bailey's quip? Were there repressed questions in her, questions that might dislocate her among her friends, that might interfere with her "fun," necessitate readjustments all the way down the line in her life?

She rose abruptly, with a little laugh. "You think that if everybody doesn't live just the way you do, Ede, their life must be all wrong. But I assure you, a lot of people would give their eyeteeth to be able to lead the kind of life I do."

It wasn't actually until a year or so ago that she realized she was drinking too much, actually depending on it. So she had started watching it.

And somewhere along the line she had become aware of Brian. She'd known him practically always. The Rhodes were an old family in the valley, and after the war Brian had started a law practice in town. Since Salinas was the county seat, the town was full of lawyers. Brian was going in more for the criminal end of things, defending some very weird characters—robberies, and knifings, and a murder in one of the Filipino camps, and a truck driver out in the Alisal who had clubbed his girl friend to death in a drunken fury.

Laverne had attended one of his more sensational trials, and knowing Brian socially, she had been surprised at his personality in court. She had known he was volatile, uncomfortably direct in his approach to life—impulsive perhaps. These had not seemed quite the traits which would be an asset before a judge or a jury; and it had been an eye opener seeing how he made these characteristics valuable, by harnessing, channelizing them. There was nothing reckless, nothing slipshod, in the way he deliberately put emotion—passion, you might say—to the use of his client, in the spirited way that he wrangled with and infuriated Keith Coletto, the district attorney. And Laverne realized dimly that the difference lay in the fact that in court his mind was in complete control of the emotional side of his personality, that he deliberately used his own temperament, while outside, socially and personally, he didn't always bother to—as the saying went—use his head.

Laverne sighed. Well, however it had happened, somehow it had. They had found themselves in love. At first it had been hard to believe that the young—Brian was only thirty-six—dashing, popular attorney had fallen in love with her. What, she had asked herself, do I have to offer? But whatever it was that appealed to some subtle psychological drive in the man, answered some insistent emotional need, apparently she had it.

But now she was immobilized emotionally. She was free, and free with all of Stan's financial assets in her hands, except for possible trust funds for the children, and Brian would soon be free of Clarice. She could marry Brian and still enjoy the proceeds of the business, not have to give up the Ormsby place and two cars and a fat checking account. But if Brian had obtained all this for her at the price of murder— Her mind balked, refused to go on, either with acceptance or rejection.

Suddenly she felt the need of a drink. It was odd that she hadn't craved one before, when Cass Huggins came, or when Edith arrived. But now she needed a stiffener.

She was rising from the chair when she heard a tapping on the door and Edith's nervous voice, "Laverne. Laverne!"

"I'm here," she said, and turned the doorknob, unlocking it.

"I couldn't imagine where you'd gone," Edith breathed with relief.

"I had to get off by myself for a few minutes."

"Of course."

Both looked toward the stairs as a man in a business suit appeared, mounting them.

"We're making a routine check of your husband's effects, Mrs. West. Will you show me the bedroom he occupied?"

Laverne pointed. "There."

She and Edith met one another's eyes as he disappeared into the room.

"I'm going down to get a drink," Laverne announced abruptly.

"Do you think you should—today?"

"If I ever needed one, I need one now. Don't worry," she added dryly, "I'll stay sober."

"I'll go in and see how Patty's making out," Edith said.

Descending the stairs, Laverne thought that she ought to have repaired her make-up. That man, a city detective, she supposed, would see her before he left the house. Still, perhaps a ravaged face was more in keeping with her position.

CHAPTER FOUR

Their real bar was in the rumpus room in the basement; but there was a smaller one in a sideboard in the dining room. As Laverne traversed the living room, through the open french doors overlooking the driveway to the south, she saw a shabby yellow station wagon pull up, the front door swing open, and a lean figure in slacks and a boyish plaid shirt emerge from it swiftly.

The sight of Joan gave her almost as much of a lift as a drink would have.

"Darling," Joan cried, "I've just heard. It's ghastly, perfectly ghastly."

They met before the doors and embraced frantically. When they broke apart Laverne's lips trembled and she brushed at her eyes again.

"Hal phoned me from the shed. He'd just heard."

"Joan, I'm so glad you came. Edith's here, but she isn't like you. I needed someone of my own kind."

"Of course you did, sweet."

"I was just on my way to have a pickup. I'm shattered. Absolutely shattered."

"Have you had anything this morning?"

"No, not a drop."

They were in the dining room and Laverne queried, "You?"

"No. Nothing for me. And listen, pet, just one to pull yourself together. Today may be just when you need it. But you mustn't. You've got to know what you're doing."

Laverne swallowed a full shot of whiskey, and took a quick drink of water. As she set the tumbler down she felt warmer, more competent. Psychological perhaps, since all she could possibly feel so far was the heat of the alcohol in her gullet; but she felt pulled together.

"There are police in the house. Already," she said. "Let's go in the living room. I think we'll be uninterrupted there. For a while anyway."

She sat near the fireplace in a small chair covered with heavy silk; and Joan sank to a hassock by the hearth. Laverne took a cigarette from a box on the table beside her. Joan had already pulled her own package from her shirt pocket, but she leaned toward the table lighter Laverne held forward.

Laverne surveyed her friend with a sense of gratitude. Good old Joan, breezy, casual, the kind all the fellows called "a good scout." Her hair was darker than Patty's, but tawny and careless-looking, like a girl's. Joan wore it shoulder length, but now it was dragged back and twisted in an untidy knot high on the back of her head.

Their friendship had started somewhere back in those days when they had all had such a good time. Joan had been a bride too, and her only child, a boy, Jack, was just a year older than Patty. He was now in Texas, taking training for the Air Force.

Because of the girls being so congenial the two couples had run around together quite a lot, although Stan had never cared too much for Hal, even though the two men had known each other before they came to Salinas. Hal had also come from ranching country farther south in the state. Laverne could see how it was. Hal wasn't Stan's type. Pleasant, agreeable, but not much force to him. And he tried too hard, socially. Laughed indiscriminately at everybody's jokes, careful never to offend anybody. Considering Joan's vitality, he seemed like rather a weak sister to be her husband. But Laverne believed that Joan was genuinely fond of Hal in an unexcited way.

She felt a moment's pity for Joan. It had been such a nip and tuck struggle for the Schmidts, all the way along. Once Hal and Greg Harper had been partners; but somehow Hal got squeezed out. He "sold out his interest to Greg" was the way the Schmidts expressed it. But everyone knew Greg Harper simply got rid of him.

And then Hal started up for himself and went disastrously broke. Somehow he got financed again after that, and he had hung on. But the Schmidts never seemed to be really in the chips; and now, Laverne knew, Hal was on the ragged edge again. Stan had told her a little about it. Jardine Brothers, the biggest outfit in the business, were willing to buy Hal out; but he was fighting desperately to maintain his business as an independent.

"If it weren't," Stan had told her with a queer look in his eye, "that you and Joan are such bosom pals, I'd try to get hold of the Schmidt shed myself, expand a little. I could use a shed on the Market Street string. But it would cause hard feelings; so for your sake I'm keeping clear of it."

"Stan!" she had exclaimed. "I'd die if I thought you took a hand in breaking poor Hal. Why can't he get more financing?"

"Ever hear of pouring money down a rat hole? The banks are through, and nobody'll go on his notes anymore."

"Well, I would," she had said idly, "if I had it. For Joan's sake."

Stan had contemplated her with the faint gleam in his eyes, the smile with closed lips that she had once found thrilling, his strong, silent-man look, but which, ever since the trouble over Marcia, invariably kindled in her the beginnings of an impotent fury. As if he knew and understood things she didn't know and hence held some unknown power over her. Frequently she had recognized the signs of concealed antagonism between her best friend Joan and her husband.

With a slight sense of shock she remembered now that the very last time she had talked to Stan—on the telephone yesterday afternoon—he had again betrayed that antagonism. She had reminded him of the cocktail party at Peabody's, two miles west of town, and when Stan said he couldn't make it she retorted acidly, "Well, naturally, you wouldn't have time to take me anywhere. I suppose I'll have to bum a ride with Joan." Stan had countered dictatorially, "I'll give Bill Jardine a ring and ask him and Rose to pick you up. I don't want you riding out with her. Understand?"

Laverne swallowed miserably, recalling this, her last conversation with her husband, and how she had murmured sarcastically, "Yes, Master," and hung up with a bang.

There was something about the way Stan always seemed to be submitting to the friendship with the Schmidts, as if he were doing his wife a favor, throwing her a sop, so to speak, that both perplexed and secretly nettled her. She didn't like having her friendships treated as if they were harmless, childish whims to be indulged by her betters.

Joan knew all about the early crisis over Marcia Allen, had been the first to know of Laverne's pregnancy with the twins, and Joan knew of her friendship with Brian, although she had not told even Joan how far that "friendship" had gone. Something had held her back, a strange intuition that it wouldn't set well with Joan, hearing that her girl friend was really in love for the first time since the early days with Stan. Her reticence to Joan on this matter had given her a disturbingly guilty feeling, as if she were betraying her friend. Laverne did not understand it.

But now she was thankful Joan did not know the truth about her and Brian. For once she had been smart. It was a protection to him, that no one knew.

"Have the cops talked to you yet?" Joan demanded in a low tone.

"Not really. Cass Huggins came around to tell me. And he sent men over to go through Stan's things."

"They'll want to know where you were last night."

Laverne's eyes were startled. "Where *I* was!"

"I know you didn't do it, pet, but Hal said the word was out that Stan was—well, murdered. Naturally they'll check up on you."

"I never thought of that," Laverne said weakly. "I got pretty tight," she said fretfully, "out at Peabody's. No lunch, and those martinis. It's awfully vague. I know I'd remember if somebody told me."

A pained frown distorted Joan's features. "I wish they'd never had the damned party. When I think that it was just yesterday morning I was out there helping Liz with the hors d'oeuvres and flowers, and we felt so—gay. And now—" She shook her head almost angrily and regarded Laverne whimsically, adding dryly, "I'll say this for you. You can carry your liquor. Anybody that didn't know you; they'd never catch on. But I knew you were a goner. Any time you start walking around smiling sweetly but otherwise making like a zombie, your friends all know, darling; you're gone."

"I went on to dinner. In a car. With somebody." Her face brightened. "With Rose and Bill Jardine."

"Right. Hal and I left before you did; but that was the plan shaping up. The Jardines and Wilma and Greg. You were all going to Monterey. You hadn't settled on a restaurant."

"Yes. Yes, we did. That Spanish place over there. I remember Greg wanted a fish dinner on the wharf, but they voted him down."

"That's O.K. then. You're alibied for the evening anyhow. But what happened after dinner?"

"I came home. That's all I know. They dropped me off, Rose and Bill. And after that, I don't know. I went to bed, of course."

"What time?"

"I don't know."

Joan came to her feet in lithe movements. "I'll phone Rose right now." She crossed the oriental carpet into the front hall and dialed efficiently.

Laverne sat dumbly, trying to assimilate this new aspect of things. If Stan was murdered, would they suspect his wife? But that was fantastic.

In a few moments Joan came back. "They got home about ten, she says, and came straight from letting you off. She said you were pretty well saturated but still navigating under your own steam. Bill saw you to the door and into the front hall. You all had wine with the dinner and liqueurs afterward. I guess that's why you stayed in such a fog."

Laverne slowly nodded her head. "Then I went straight to bed and slept almost eleven hours. That's why I didn't have a hangover, that and the aspirin I took way early this morning."

"When I think of how yesterday afternoon when I talked to him, it was for the last time; and I didn't even realize it!" Joan shivered slightly.

"You saw Stan yesterday?"

"Yes. I told you, at the party. Guess you didn't pay any attention. Hal and

I stopped by to see if you wanted a ride. Hal waited out front in the car. You'd already gone, and Lula let me in, but Stan was in the study. Said he came home to get cleaned up before he dashed out again."

"How—how did he seem? Was he upset? Worried or anything?"

"Not that I could tell. That's what's so chilling. He was so absolutely normal—and now—"

Joan stood before the hearth, fitting the arch of her shoe over the edge of the stones.

"This is the horrible part about dying the way Stan did. I feel terrible about him. But this—it doesn't give you a chance for clean, honest grief. Right away you have to start thinking: Who did it? And figuring how you can show the police *you* didn't. Unless they find out right away, they'll be questioning everybody that knew Stan. And me and Hal, for instance, I don't think we have an alibi."

Laverne frowned. "Come to think of it, Cass didn't even tell me when it happened."

"It must have been sometime last night, probably the early part of the night."

"What did you mean," Laverne asked hesitantly, "you and Hal don't have an alibi?"

"Well, we went home from Liz and Hank's party, had dinner, and Hal went back to the office at—oh, eight-thirty or so. Had some reports to go over that he forgot to bring home. I went to bed and read and fell asleep before he got in. Early. I was dead tired. All I know is he was there in bed this morning. Not that it will matter. We certainly had no reason, either one of us, to kill Stan. But as I said, it makes you think. Especially if they should ask questions

The telephone in the hall rang, and Joan said, "Want me to get it?"

"No. I will. I can't stand just sitting like this. It's better if I—do things, as if—as if things were normal."

Lula was at the door at the rear of the hall, and Laverne waved her away. She picked up the instrument and said, "Mrs. West speaking."

An unctuous voice came over the wire, "This is Chuck Willet, Laverne. We've just heard the terrible news; and I couldn't resist calling. Seeing as how we'd had an appointment, you and Stan and I, this very afternoon—"

She remembered. The Ormsby place.

"I wanted to let you know how shocked I am. If there's anything at all me or my wife can do—"

"Thank you; it was good of you to call." Laverne frowned. There would be a lot of this sort of thing. And Chuck Willet, of all people, to be first.

"Wonderful fellow Stan was. Wonderful. I wanted you to know you have my heartfelt sympathy."

"I know. I—well, it's good of you—"

"I won't keep you. I know you must be all broken up—"

As Laverne set the instrument back impatiently, she met Joan's inquiring eyes.

"Sympathy. From Chuck Willet."

"Isn't that like him, pushing in the first thing."

Laverne pushed at her hair over the temple and sighed wearily before she said with a sardonic chuckle, "He might not be so effusive and friendly if he knew what Stan told me last week end. I suppose you've heard by the grapevine, Chuck's thinking of running for the Board of Supervisors next spring—"

"What crust!"

"I gather he hadn't come right out and said anything to Stan yet; but when we were dressing to go out last Saturday evening Stan and I were talking about the Ormsby place and Willet handling the deal; and Stan said Chuck was going to be in for a shock if he expected Stan to swing any support to him."

"Stan didn't intend to back him, eh?"

"No; and I gathered Chuck assumed that Stan would just naturally help get the produce people behind his campaign."

They turned as Edith came down the stairs. "Hello, Joan," she said matter-of-factly, and to her sister, "I wouldn't bother with the phone or the door, Laverne. Let Lula or I handle it. No use to wear yourself out."

At the foot of the stairs she glanced upward cautiously, and added conspiratorially, "They've been asking me questions. Made me leave them alone with Patty now. Honestly, it's awful." She eyed Laverne thoughtfully. "You'll be next, I suppose; so you'd better be prepared. Just try to stay relaxed."

Laverne was gazing upward anxiously. "They shouldn't bother Patty, poor kid. She's terribly upset. I'd better go up."

"No use. They insist on talking to everybody alone—"

Abruptly the door chimes broke into their little tune, and Edith sighed, "Not more cops, I hope."

When she opened the door it was Brian standing there, in a light summer business suit, his dark hair uncovered.

"'Lo, Edith," he said shortly, while his eyes sought and found Laverne. He came toward her, his hands outstretched. "Darling, I just got the news. I had to come over. This is hell for you."

It was then that the two officers came stolidly down the stairs. The group by the fireplace could see them through the entrance to the living room. Although Laverne had deduced that they were what books called "plain-clothes men," she felt vaguely surprised that the Salinas police force should include such a category. To her knowledge she had never seen either of the men before. It just went to show how the town had grown.

Detectives, no less. Perhaps they were really attached to the sheriff's office at the courthouse downtown and could be called on when needed. And wasn't it strange, she thought; they really looked like the police detectives you saw in movies, flat and uncommunicative of visage, their bodies unobtrusively sturdy of build.

The one with the uglier face spoke: "I'm Captain Farwell, Mrs. West. County detective force. Would you mind stepping into the den for a few minutes? We're going to need your help."

She rose composedly. "Not at all."

The detective noticed Brian's step forward, the abortive movement of his hand toward restraining the woman.

"You're Mrs. West's counsel?" he asked phlegmatically, making it apparent that he recognized Brian.

"I don't need any counsel," Laverne countered sharply.

"She didn't summon me," Brian added in explanation. "I'm a friend, and I stopped by to offer condolences. However, since the Wests' own attorneys aren't here, I'd be happy to be present during this interview, representing Mrs. West."

"That's sensible," Edith interposed.

Laverne's spine stiffened. "Let's get this straight. I don't want protection against the police. My husband has been murdered, it seems; and that puts me on their side. Anything I know that can help them they're welcome to."

Edith looked anxious; Joan's eyes upon her were unfathomable; and Brian looked concerned. She met his eyes levelly. Surely he knew she was not fool enough to tell these men that he was her lover. And how else could they find out? Anything else they asked, however, she would tell them.

She realized now that, although all the romance had long been gone from her feelings toward Stan, actually she had been very fond of him, that, along with financial considerations, this affection had been one of the deterrents to breaking with him. She hadn't wanted to hurt him.

And now Brian had hurt him beyond recall. While she was still not capable of turning Brian in for it, while even this terrible action of his could not abruptly kill her feeling for him, neither could she bring herself to becoming a silent, acquiescing partner to his act by joining up with him through accepting his protection from the police.

She was no fool. She knew as well as they did it was desirable to have a lawyer beside you in a situation like this. But under the circumstances, not Brian.

On her way to the door, she turned to Edith. "See what the boys are doing, will you? Nobody seems to be—caring about them."

"Of course, dear."

Joan spoke up. "How about my taking them home to lunch with me?

Then I can take them out to Jan Peabody's this afternoon, let them ride the palominos. That will take their minds off things."

"Fine," Laverne agreed.

The officer spoke up, to Joan. "Will you wait until we've interviewed Mrs. West? Since you seem to be a close friend of the family, you may be able to shed a little light on things. And," to Brian, "you too. We'd like to talk to you before you go."

"I left an office full of work," Brian protested. "Can't you catch me later in the day? I'll be there."

"We're going to have a full schedule ourselves," the captain said flatly. "Won't have time to run around to offices. Tell you what I'll do. I'll talk to you now." He nodded at the women. "If you ladies will step out. Then I'll take you next, Mrs.—" He was looking at Joan.

"Schmidt," she supplied shortly.

The other man spoke deferentially to Laverne, "If you'll come this way."

Dully she followed him to the den and preceded him inside. They sat down a few feet apart. "Smoke?" the detective said politely, offering her a cigarette from his package. She accepted, and they sat awkwardly, smoking.

"Fine collection of firearms," the detective observed, nodding at the rack over the mantel.

"It was sort of a hobby of my husband's. He liked hunting."

The detective nodded at a deer head and a moose head mounted on opposite walls of the room, and let his eyes come to rest on a stuffed wildcat with venomous glass eyes that stood atop a set of bookshelves.

"Trophies, I guess?"

"Yes." Laverne looked at the snarling bobtailed cat; and her eyes filled with tears. She fumbled inside the low, gathered neckband of her dress for the Kleenex she had cached there.

"It's rough," the man said sympathetically, "something like this. Makes it worse, bein' what it is. But you want to try to look at it this way, as if it was no different than as if he'd been in a plane crash or fell over in a heart attack. Them things happen and you just gotta take it."

Laverne mumbled and blew her nose.

"It won't be long," the detective said. "The captain'll just ask them a few questions. He'll be in in a few minutes."

It was more than a few minutes. They had time for a second cigarette before Farwell opened the door.

First of all he took her over the previous day and evening, eliciting the same information she had given Edith and Joan.

"Weren't you surprised this morning when his bed hadn't been slept in?"

"No ..." Again she explained. A possible poker game, a late business conference, a possible hotel room.

"Didn't you think it might be a woman?"

"If there were other women in my husband's life," Laverne said calmly, "I didn't know. And I doubt it very much. We—were devoted," she lied calmly.

"I see. How about enemies? Know of anyone who had it in for Mr. West?"

"I think he was rather well liked."

"Any business rivalries?"

"I suppose everybody in the business is a rival in a sense. But they don't think of themselves that way. I've always thought the produce people worked together very well."

"Ever hear him speak of anybody in his own organization he didn't get along with?"

"No-o," she said thoughtfully. "But Mr. West didn't discuss his business with me. It always seemed to run smoothly, however."

"Um ..." The detective spoke slowly, "Do you know anything about what his plans were for this day? Who he was expecting to see? If any deals were cooking, or anything like that."

"I told you. I wouldn't know about his business affairs. And when the season is on I often don't—didn't see much of him, he was so busy. All I can tell you about his plans for today is that this afternoon we were going out with Chuck Willet to look at a piece of property in the Corral de Tierra; and this evening I was having two couples in for dinner. The Schmidts were one of them, the Baileys the other."

"Would you say Mr. West had seemed worried lately, had anything out of the ordinary on his mind?"

Laverne's eyes steadied on the man's face, and gradually their expression blanked out.

It was true. She hadn't seen much of Stan in the past week, but she realized now that his manner had indicated that something might be on his mind. Was it possible that somehow he had found out something definite about her and Brian? Had Brian approached him even earlier than last night? Had last night perhaps been a final showdown between them, with the lid being blown off? It was consistent with both their temperaments that they could have been high-handedly settling things—about her—without even consulting her.

She was suddenly angry with Brian. She had been horrified, shocked, in a sort of trauma about him before; but now she was disturbed in a different way. Being made a bone of contention behind her back. Her delicate chin and jaw were again hard beneath the soft flesh.

But she answered the detective's question in a soft, reflective voice, "No. No, I wouldn't say so."

In a few minutes then he let her go. Farwell could tell when he had obtained all he was going to for the time.

CHAPTER FIVE

Afterward it seemed as if Cass Huggins and Farwell had asked questions for hours, not only while people were examining Stan's body and messing around in the room with cameras and other equipment, but even after the hearse had taken Stan away, although actually it couldn't have been more than an hour and a half all told.

When he was finally left alone, with the inner-office door locked against him, and against everyone else, Earl sat at his desk, feeling whipped. The morning had taken everything out of him. The fact that emerged most clearly from his soggy thoughts was that now everything would be up to him, all the decisions pertaining to the business. Until the estate was settled and Mrs. West sold out. Meantime, he supposed, technically she would be in authority. Which was a meaningless state of affairs. Laverne West knew nothing. All she ever had on her silly little mind was clothes and cocktail parties and gossip.

The sudden responsibility disconcerted Earl. He had never been one to want it. There had always been Stan somewhere in the background. Of course, he comforted himself, Ralph was an exceptionally good shed foreman. He'd see to that end of things. Without even being told or asked Ralph would assume more authority in matters of production, to take up the slack left by Stan's absence. And their field man, Bob Wakely— Earl's lip curled a little. This would be Bob's meat. Now he would really throw his weight around. He was the type who chafed under orders, even from Stan. Now Bob would go his own sweet way.

But when you came right down to it, it was the paper work that tied it all together, the columns of figures which Earl controlled that really "ran" the business. And now, even under an executor of the estate, he would be really in charge.

Earl sighed and resigned himself to the role. If he was anything, he was conscientious.

His eyes wandered over the office, the filing cabinets, Dorothy's desk, the door to the lavatory in the corner. Only one thing was lacking of essential office equipment. The safe. And it stood locked in a corner of Stan's private office.

The officers had let him take the petty-cash box and the bankbooks out of it. There was little else there. A few deeds, licenses, contracts, and leases in heavy envelopes, that was all the officers found in it.

The telephone had been ringing all morning. Earl lifted it off its cradle and leaned his forehead on his hands. He had to have a few minutes to collect himself. The morning mail had come in, and his eyes fell on a colored post card depicting an automobile driving through the trunk of a redwood tree. From Dorothy. Now probably in Vancouver, British Columbia, which had been the goal of her wedding trip north. A fine time, that's all Earl could say, a fine time she picked for being away.

It wasn't until Farwell had been half through questioning him that it dawned on Earl that the detective did not rule him out as the killer. They would be going over the books very thoroughly; he knew that. But they would find nothing wrong there.

The questions had been specific. When had he last seen Stanley West?

"He was still here yesterday when I left a few minutes after five. I looked into the office to say good night. That's the last I saw him."

"Then what did you do?"

"I went home."

"Where'd you go in the evening?"

"Nowhere. We have a new television set, and we ate dinner on a card table in the living room so as not to miss any of it—"

"We? Who is that?"

"Why, my wife, and my daughters, Penelope and Pamela."

"How long did you watch television?"

"Till ten o'clock. Then we all went to bed."

"Did you hear from Mr. West again? By phone perhaps?"

"No. Not a thing."

"His daily schedule of engagements here ..." The officer nodded at the desk calendar from Stan's office. "There's a dinner appointment; but I don't see anything else for the evening."

"No, there wasn't anything. Not to my knowledge."

"Did he say anything about being at the office in the evening?"

"No, but he wouldn't have mentioned it necessarily. He often dropped in late to go over something. And we're both extra busy now with our stenographer being away."

"I understand the shed closed down at five last night."

"That's right."

"Now about yesterday. Aside from this list on the calendar and including it, will you go through the people who saw Mr. West yesterday afternoon? I understand he was out in the fields all morning."

"That's right. He came in about two. Had a late lunch at a restaurant on the highway, he told me."

"O.K. Take it from there."

"Well, he was in his office most of the afternoon. He wrote a couple of letters himself, our girl being away. Just routine stuff. You can see the carbons if you like. Then he did some phoning. I wouldn't know who to; I was busy myself. And then the first person he saw was Bill Jardine. You know—Jardine Brothers. I think it was more a social call. The door was open, and they seemed to be just chewing the fat about general conditions and Association affairs—Grower-Shippers, I mean."

"Yeah. Then who?"

"Then, let's see, Hank Peabody came in. You know, used to be a big rancher in the old days. Leases his land out now. Well, Mr. West has a lease on some acreage of his out toward Castroville. That was some of the property he was out looking at yesterday morning. They're discussing terms on a renewal."

"He leave the door open during that call, too?"

"No. But ordinarily he doesn't. Makes a better impression during a business call if he seems to shut me out. Makes it seem important."

"O.K. Who else? According to this calendar Peabody was the only one he had a real appointment with."

"That's right. The others just dropped in. There were gaps of anywhere from ten minutes to half an hour between all these calls, you understand? And Ralph Musio was in shooting the breeze with both of us along the middle of the afternoon. Let's see. Hal Schmidt was here. You know Schmidt—"

"I know of him. What did he want?"

"Nothing, as far as I know. He's a friend of the family. Guess he was just out this way and stopped to pass the time of day."

"Wasn't closeted in the inner office with West, eh?"

"They talked in there with the door closed, if that's what you mean."

"West tell you what they talked about?"

"N-no."

"O.K. Who else?"

"Why, Chuck Willet came by. I understand he's trying to sell the Wests a place in the country. I think that's what he called about."

"You hear what they said?"

"No, the door was closed."

"Now, about any of these calls, you notice anything unusual, loud talking, or signs of anybody being—say—disgruntled as they came in or went out?"

Earl pondered for a moment, remembering. He supposed you could say there had been a rather unusually quiet look on Chuck Willet's face when he went out and that Stan had not looked too pleased when Earl took the letters in to be signed immediately afterward. Stan was probably not too anxious to buy the Ormsby place and was getting pressure from both his wife and Willet.

And Hal Schmidt had walked out without speaking to the bookkeeper, although Hal was usually almost embarrassingly friendly. And Stan, coming out to go to the washroom just after Hal left and before Willet came on in, had said wryly, "You ever have trouble, Earl, with your wife making friends with people you can't stomach?"

This was perhaps unusual enough to repeat to the police, but Earl decided against it. "No," he said, "I don't remember anything unusual."

Then there had been a siege of questions about possible enemies of Stan, about his domestic and social relationships.

Now Earl sat with his head in his hands and wondered if he had done right. He told himself that he had, because after all he didn't *know*. He only suspected, albeit with increasing conviction. But if he were wrong it would be a terrible thing, throwing suspicion on an innocent man.

Stanley West had held Hal's note for ten thousand dollars, a personal note that was long overdue. It was one of the papers in the safe that the police had carefully catalogued and which was waiting now to be turned over to whoever would be the executor of Stanley West's estate. The time had come for Schmidt when there was no more getting credit at the bank. Stanley had been reluctant about the loan. He had spoken to Earl about it, to the effect that "that's what you get for having friends."

And now everyone knew that Hal Schmidt was on his way out—once again. Had he come to Stan for another loan, or to ask for still another extension of time on the one Stan already held? And had Stan turned him down? Had Stan perhaps gone further than that? Had he decided it might be nice to add another shed to his holdings, and had he put the squeeze on Schmidt?

Their conversation in the inner office had been in normal tones, out of which Earl could not have distinguished words if he had tried. But one thing was sure; Hal Schmidt had not left the office yesterday in a happy mood. Through the window Earl had seen Hal encounter Chuck Willet, who had just driven up. They had stopped, apparently to pass the time of day, and even then Hal's expression had been glum. And there was Stanley's remark about one's "wife's friends." Laverne West and Joan Schmidt were thick as thieves. And Laverne West had no sense—in Earl's estimation. With Laverne controlling the West finances Hal stood a chance of having that loan extended and perhaps of getting enough more money from Laverne to tide him over the fall deal.

Another failure would be crippling to Hal Schmidt's ego. Who could say that he might not kill a man to avert it?

But then why had he not taken the keys from Stan's pocket and opened the safe and removed the note to destroy it? Because, Earl decided laboriously, too many people knew it was there. Himself, Laverne probably. Its disappearance would be suspicious; and Schmidt counted on Mrs. West's intervention when the estate was settled. Phillips and Bixby, Stan's attorneys, were to be the executors. They were old family friends as well as legal advisers to the Wests. If Laverne insisted on holding out Hal's note, they might shut their eyes to the lapse. At any rate, these things took time, probating a will, settling an estate. The very legal processes could give Hal the extra months he needed—if the administrators did not immediately start settling up loose ends such as this, which they might well do unless the chief heir, Laverne in this case, instructed them to hold off. All in all, for Hal Schmidt, Stanley West had died at a fortunate time.

CHAPTER SIX

The news did not get out into the working area of the shed until after the police cars arrived, and then it would have been hard to trace exactly the route by which it traveled. Within half an hour of Earl's finding the body, however, the word that Stan West had been killed was passing up and down the packing line.

Bonnie Maffey saw her partner turn her head to listen over her shoulder to the trimmer who stood at her back. Bonnie's own eyes expertly inspected the firm green ball her left hand lifted from the tilted metal basket between them. The slender-bladed knife in her right hand was already slashing off the butt end to which earth still clung, allowing the coarser outside leaves to drop away into the cull pit beneath the slatted floor, while her mind automatically assessed the head as free from slimy tipburn and of proper symmetrical shape and weight to go on the "hump"—the long table between the two trimmers and the packer they served.

Ray, their packer, was using only "fives" and "fours" today, heads of a size to make four dozen or five dozen to a crate. A light wooden box lined with heavy waxed paper stood to each side of him; and his quick hands stowed each head in its appropriate crate.

Radio programs screeched constantly from a loud speaker at the end of the shed. And still the workers were able to hold protracted, connected conversations in normal voices, even the men packers across the hump entering into talk between the trimmers who faced each other at closer quarters—as if their ears were able to pick out the sounds they wanted to hear and to tune out the others.

When Bonnie's partner Freda brought her head around after hearing what Doris in back of her had said, the radio was going—for the third time that morning—"tweedle-de-dee, twiddlede-dee-dee, it gives me a thrill, to wake up in the morning—" And then all of a sudden this paean of joy was broken off sharply by the turn of an unseen dial.

Bonnie glanced at Freda while she paused for a moment to pull the chain which tilted their emptying basket higher. Freda exclaimed, her greenish eyes dilated under a fringe of sandy hair which frizzed over her prominent forehead, "Guess what, kid! The boss got bumped off!"

"Stan West!"

"Who else? Doris just told me." She turned her head. "You hear that, Ray? Stan got killed. Right in the office, Doris says."

Ray put a hand on the edge of each of his crates and leaned forward. "The hell you say. When?"

The packer beyond him called, "What's up?" and the word traveled on, crisscrossing back and forth down the line in a herringbone pattern.

Bonnie stood transfixed, her hands pressed to the front of her black rubber apron.

"How come?" she croaked. "What happened?"

The rump of the trimmer behind her brushed hers as the girl demanded over her shoulder to Freda, "Who says so?"

"I dunno," Freda called back; "but you notice Ralph's been out of circulation now for quite a while. Doris says Jim saw him step in the office, an' he ain't been out since. And that was a little after eight-thirty."

Their words brushed back and forth across Bonnie, and she felt the movements behind her as Alice jiggled about, trying to hear from each direction in case any new facts passed along.

"Jesus," Ray remarked, "I wonder what happened." He looked toward the loud-speaker. "Guess that's why they turned off the music. It ain't fitting—in the circumstances."

Jerkily their work resumed its former rhythm.

"Personally," Freda observed, standing with a head in one hand, her knife poised in the other, "I think they oughta give us the day off—out of respect."

"And lose all that time?" Ray exclaimed.

"With pay, naturally, you dope."

"And let all this hay rot?"

"There'll be more tomorrow."

"If it's to show respect to Stan, we keep workin'. That's what he'd want, to hit that market fustest with the mostest."

Like a mechanical doll Bonnie picked up a head, saw that it was a runt, and released it to roll into the trough below the table.

Freda had glanced out between the huge baskets, and now she declared, "Well, I'll be a ring-tailed baboon. There's Sandy—on her way to the can *again*. Honest to God, that's the third time this morning, by actual count."

"Maybe she's got the runs," Ray contributed good-humoredly.

"Runs, hell. You heard me say Ralph's been off the floor most of the morning. She's just takin' advantage of it."

Dully Bonnie had glanced in the direction Freda indicated, toward the girl with flaming red hair that blossomed in a cluster of ringlets over her forehead and fell in a cascade of more curls in the back. Her hip movement was sufficiently limber that the skirt of her black apron swung from side to side over her legs in their tight blue jeans. Ordinarily there would have been whistles and wolf calls from the packers who faced in Sandy's direction as she sauntered down the floor, but now no one seemed to notice her. They were all too busy asking one another questions to which no one knew the answers.

"She sure is proud of herself, ain't she?" Freda said without rancor. And to Bonnie. "How about it, kid? How about you and me takin' five." She wriggled her shoulders. "Sure does get you through the shoulders, don't it?"

"Just hold it," Ray demurred. "Only ten minutes till relief time for everybody. And you gals get some stuff up here for me to start on when we get back. I don't want to be held up waitin' on you."

"Listen, sweetheart, any time we can't keep up with you. An-ny time." Ray good-naturedly made an impolite noise with his tongue.

"I wonder," Freda mused, "who done it."

"How do you know anybody did?" Bonnie said weakly. "All Doris said was he was—killed. It might of been an accident."

Freda surveyed her doubtfully, and turned her head. "Hey, Doris, din't you say Stan was murdered?"

"*I* didn't say. They just said he was dead. Earl Fowler found him in the office."

Freda looked back at Bonnie and asserted confidently, "He was murdered all right. Stands to reason."

"Sure," Ray chimed in, "Fred here"—he nodded toward the packer at his right—"says he heard the driveway out in front is lousy with cops."

"Can you beat that. Murder. Well, it just goes to show," Freda remarked sententiously.

"It sure does," Ray agreed soberly. "And he was a good guy too." He paused in his work and pursed his lips judiciously. "I wouldn't be surprised this is the best shed in the valley to work for."

"Well, they don't ride you. You can say that," Freda seconded.

"All in all," Ray continued thoughtfully, sprinkling crushed ice from a small scoop, "he had a good name in the game, Stan West did. Wasn't no bastard like some of 'em."

"My old man," Freda supplied, "he's an old-timer. I've told you that. Goes back to before '36. He was here, right down there the day they gas-bombed the labor temple, and he like to got his head knocked off, right down there on the corner of Gabilan and California Street the day the vigilantes rushed the picket line—"

"Yeah. We know, we know," Ray interrupted. "You already told us. Five or six times—"

"I was leadin' up to a point," Freda said coldly. "My dad said even back then Stan West behaved himself better'n some of the rest of 'em. I ain't namin' no names; but you all know who I mean. Well, Pop said Stan West at least kept out of sight durin' the whole thing. Didn't serve on no committees or get his name in the paper or run up and down Main Street with no deputy sheriff's arm band and a six-shooter on each hip. 'Course he was in with the Association. Had to be; and on their side naturally; but what I mean to say is, he didn't throw his weight around."

"I wonder," Ray said meditatively, and lifted a crate onto the moving table behind him. "Suppose he wasn't popular with the rest of the lettuce crowd? So one of the boys rubbed him out?"

"I wouldn't *think* so," Freda said consideringly. "The Wests were *in* everything. Real big shots in town."

"I'd sure like to know."

Just then the whistle for relief time ripped through the other sounds reverberating through the shed.

"Well, be seein' you, girls. Don't take too long to powder your noses."

Bonnie did not join the stampede toward the rest rooms and the snack bar which dispensed hot coffee and candy bars. She walked over to the open side of the building and stood leaning against the edge of a huge sliding door. The sun fell upon her and she closed her eyes for a moment, relaxing in its warmth. From the pocket of her boyish blue shirt, she pulled out a package of cigarettes and lighted one.

Down at the far end of the shed she could see her brother Rex leaning against an empty basket talking to a man in grey clothes and a cap. She wanted very much to talk to Rex, now; but this was no time to seek him out. It might be dinnertime before she had a chance to speak to him. How she would get through the day she didn't know.

Her gaze went out across the railroad track and a vacant lot golden with dried weeds to the uneven wooden wall of an auto-wrecking yard farther down the highway. Her spine pressed against the edge of the door. She was so frightened that instinctively she sought support.

Again her eyes went back toward Rex. He was laughing now, and she could see the gleam of his white teeth. He had left the basket and was moving away, toward the platform alongside the refrigerator car. His shoulders swayed in a little swaggering movement, and there was a just perceptible roll in his walk. Showing off as usual.

Sandy passed, on her way back to her station, her bosom thrust out, her apron tied so tight around her middle that her little round stomach was outlined by it. Sandy had made quite a play for Rex when he came here to work. Bonnie wished, all of a sudden, that Sandy had made out with him. But perversely Rex would have none of the shed siren.

Bonnie dropped her cigarette and stepped on it, her lips twisting resentfully. She ran the fingers of her left hand around the back of her neck, digging into the flesh as if to relax the muscles there, and then flipped her hand through her short brown hair.

She was tired: abysmally tired. And not from working either. She was tired of the load she had carried for ten years. And when you stopped to think that she was only twenty-three now. She'd had too much on her shoulders, too much, that was all. And now this. Her nerves curled with fear.

Maybe she ought to wash her hands of the whole thing. Forget about Rex. Just not care. Just not give one good God damn. But that didn't help. She knew she couldn't give up. She had cared too long. It was a habit.

She thought of Nancy, and glanced at the electric clock on the ribbed silver wall at the end of the shed. Ten o'clock. Well, she just hoped Nancy made it to the soda fountain on time. A girl seventeen had so little sense of responsibility. Ten until four, and then the regular man soda jerker at the creamery out on Alisal Road came on for the evening shift and Nancy could go home.

It was bad leaving Daddy alone all that time, with only Mrs. Meggs running over every hour to see if he was all right. Of course, since his last stroke he just lay there. And they couldn't afford a nurse; and if Nancy was to have decent clothes for school this fall, she had to work part-time this summer as well as helping in the house.

Bonnie made Rex fork over a good big hunk of his pay check for his share of the groceries; but you couldn't get too much out of a twenty-year-old kid. He might leave home entirely if she cracked down too hard; and she needed his help in keeping the family together. But you had to let him keep enough to buy tires for his old heap and to take out a girl occasionally. And naturally—at twenty—clothes were important, although she didn't think he had really needed that Palm Beach suit this summer. He had a good brown suit and two pairs of slacks and a nice maroon corduroy jacket.

Of course, he was generous with Nancy, slipped her an extra five now and then for home-permanent sets, or junk jewelry.

By noon the versions of Stanley West's death were becoming more exact. To eat her lunch Bonnie sat in the spot where she had stood for a cigarette. Another trimmer, a widow of thirty who had two little kids, sat on the edge of the floor with her feet hanging over, and a man who was married and had a little boy and was expecting another baby, sat opposite Bonnie with his knees drawn up and his black lunch bucket open beside him. Only the three of them, out of the whole crew of nearly a hundred, were left in the suddenly quiet steel shell, where hidden machines still muttered *sotto voce* as they marked time, waiting for the resumption of full speed. You could tell a lot about people, Bonnie sometimes thought, by watching to see which ones frugally carried their lunches. The single girls and fellows, like Sandy and Rex, and the young married couples who were both working rushed out to the lunch counter on the highway or jumped into their cars to go to a drive-in restaurant. The scattered few who put up egg or bologna or liverwurst sandwiches at home, to save money, were people who had to help support other people, like herself and her two companions.

Bonnie listened carefully to the others as she devoured her tuna sandwich and peeled her orange and ate it section by section and stripped the waxed paper off the bottom of her boughten cupcake.

The story was coming out clearer all the time. Stanley West had been shot at his desk sometime during the night. With his own gun. Ralph Musio had let that fact out to somebody, and it had got around.

"I wonder who they suspect," said the trimmer who was letting her feet dangle.

"Hard to say," said the man.

"It was probably a burglar. Whether they got anything or not. You reckon they did?"

"Don't think so. The money that was on hand was all still in the safe. That's what Joe told me Ed Brogan told him Earl Fowler told Bill McElroy."

"Well, it's a terrible thing, anyway you look at it. Wonder what'll happen to the shed now. Who'll get it."

"Well, of course Mrs. West'll come into everything. Suppose she'll sell though."

After hearing the news that morning Bonnie had discovered that her head was aching. She took an aspirin before she ate her lunch; but when she resumed her position for work at one o'clock her head still ached. Ralph Musio was back on the floor, and she thought of telling him she was too sick to work and asking to go home; but she rejected the idea even as it occurred to her. This was no time to draw attention in any way to the Maffey family.

Sometimes out of the corner of her eye she caught a glimpse of Rex going past, propelling a full basket with the help of another man, or alone, pushing away one of the empty bins; but he never looked at her.

CHAPTER SEVEN

The whole story went through her mind like scenes from a movie, although actually she had never participated in person even in one scene, except for between-the-acts conversations with Rex. But she could imagine it all as clearly as if she had stood beside the two men in the final fatal climax.

Rex, by working summers as Nancy was doing now, had been able to graduate from the high school downtown. Bonnie had not quite made it. She dropped out in the middle of her junior year. It had been drop out or flunk out. Her grades had seemed to be on a downward slide. Stubbornly she told herself that it wasn't that she was dumb. But she had been tired even then. The other kids helped. They washed dishes every night and made the beds. And Daddy did the grocery shopping and helped cook; but it seemed as if a disproportionate amount of the work had fallen to her lot. Because she was the oldest. It was the school homework that had defeated her. Maybe she *was* a little lacking mentally too. Couldn't concentrate when there was too much else going on around her. And there always was, at home.

They lived in the same house then that they did now, a duplex two blocks off Alisal Road. They had the south half of the house. And it had two bedrooms. Nancy had shared one with her, Rex the other with Daddy. Then there was a small living room and the kitchen, which was too small to eat in. They ate on a gate-leg table in the front room. She had never been able to study in the living room, because Daddy either had some of the neighbors in talking or somebody had the radio on. And Nancy was always in and out of the bedroom or was actually preparing to go to bed just when Bonnie settled down to study. And anyhow, through the plasterboard walls you could plainly hear Rex and one or another of his pals guffawing in the other bedroom or you could hear every word of the adult talk in the front room.

But that was neither here nor there. Rex somehow had made it. Maybe he was brighter than she was, since he had seemed to get all his work done in study hall at school. And Nancy was going to make it if Bonnie had to stand over her with a horsewhip to see that she studied.

Patty West had been in high school at the same time Rex went. She was two years behind him, but each had known who the other was; for Rex had been on the varsity basketball team. But Patty naturally was one of *the* crowd. Socially Rex was in another world.

The story began, and Bonnie could see it as if she had been there, last winter at a basketball game. Rex sometimes attended games in the high school gym, even though he was out of school now.

That evening he arrived while the preliminary lightweight game was in progress. Bonnie could visualize him standing on the steps between the seats, his hands in the pockets of his slacks, his black leather jacket hanging carelessly open, glancing about with conscious sophistication at the rowdy, shrieking crowd of spectators and the long-legged boys under the bright lights below, leaping and racing over the slippery hardwood floor.

He saw a vacant seat down front and stepped over the intervening feet and legs to drop into the place. Rex was seated before he noticed that the girl screaming and jumping up and down beside him was Patty West.

Two other girls and one of the senior boys were with her, in a row beyond Patty; but as the lightweight game ended and the varsity team ran out onto the floor with a great show of speed and vitality and naked shoulders and thighs, Rex found himself talking more frequently to the girl beside him. She recognized him as a former varsity man himself, and Rex was soon delivering expert opinions and leveling constructive criticism at the players on the floor—for Patty's benefit.

As they pushed out through the doors with the vociferous after-game crowd, Patty said, "We're going down for a milk shake. Why don't you come along?"

"O.K. Guess I might as well."

It turned out that Patty and her friends were on foot; so Rex grandly offered to drive them down in the used car he had bought on time during the fall season at the sheds. It was not a very grand car, being a Chevrolet sedan that had seen several paint jobs and fender-straightening operations in its ten years of service; but Patty and her chattering companions seemed not to notice.

More friends joined their group at the soda fountain on Main Street, with much yelling over the backs of booths and blasé lighting of one another's cigarettes, which they smoked with self-conscious nonchalance.

These were members of the set that really counted in the Salinas Union High School, a set Rex had never been able to penetrate when he went there; and although now he was a man of the world making his own money and at last possessed of his own automobile, Rex was still no more than two years older than the oldest of them; and his spirits expanded at this belated inclusion in the "most popular" crowd.

He took them all home, the ones who had been at the ball game with Patty, dropping each at a pleasant house separated from its neighbors by lawn. With Patty, he walked up to the front door and waited while she unlocked it.

"Maybe I could see you again sometime," he ventured with a smile that was bolder than he felt.

"Maybe." Patty grinned. "We're in the phone book. Give me a ring."

As he went back to his car Rex looked about thoughtfully at the darkened houses and the night-softened shrubbery and the pools of darkness under the great live oaks, contrasting the size and spaciousness of the grounds with those of his own neighborhood. The Maffeys lived in the old section of the Alisal district, the one lying closest to downtown, the part originally dubbed Little Oklahoma.

There was no space there. The lots had fifty- or thirty-five-foot frontages, and often supported as many as three or four separate dwellings to a lot, each constructed with economy and utility, rather than charm, primarily in mind. Even now there were few trees, and lawns were a rarity, although here and there flower beds bloomed hopefully under front windows and along driveways. Although it was better than it used to be, there were still too many unpainted auto courts, and shacks that had never been given the finishing touches, and stucco walls that were cracked and stained. Even with the houses that had been kept up and improved, it still looked like Little Oklahoma, an island of squalor between downtown and the newer residential subdivisions expanding in standardized smartness toward the foothills.

Bonnie did not learn of this encounter with Patty West until sometime later; but it was on that evening that Rex, as she put it, "began to get ideas."

He waited for a week before he telephoned; and then he made a date with Patty to go to a drive-in movie. She met him at the door herself, and he waited in the entrance hall while she got her coat. There was no one in evidence in the softly lighted living room to his left. He peered into the room with seeming casualness, and was impressed and surprised. The room looked neither like a furniture-store window nor like the pictures in magazines; for it was neither sparsely modern nor fussily antique; but it did look expensive, with the long sofa framed in narrow dark wood and covered with a satiny material, and the deep, soft chairs, and tables with curved legs, and the silk-shaded lamps.

Rex could tell that Patty was, as she herself might have said, "intrigued" with him; and he had decided to play it smart. He'd keep her guessing. No passes. No love-making. It might not work; but he figured such a program was safest.

Two weeks later she granted him a Saturday-night date. That evening he met her mother. Patty called him into the living room and introduced him. Rex thanked the gods that Stan West was not around. He guessed, correctly, that Patty had not told her folks her date was one of the workmen from the shed; and Rex wanted to tighten his hold on the girl before Stan found out.

Laverne West was mistily vague. She was dressed in something sleek and purplish with earrings and a bracelet studded with what looked like diamonds but which probably weren't. An empty long-stemmed glass stood on the coffee table. She too was going out later, he surmised, and was already primed with alcohol for the evening. Rex had not done much drinking himself, but he'd seen enough of other people under the influence to tell.

Laverne had only smiled sweetly, never thinking to question the background of her daughter's escort. The town had grown so big that nobody knew everybody anymore.

They drove to Capitola at the beach that night and danced in the public dance hall. Afterward they necked a little. It was almost a ritual necessity. She would have thought there was something wrong with him if he hadn't made some move in that direction. But Rex was restrained. Although he could tell that Patty was interested now, definitely, she was not yet securely enough hooked so that he dared to be natural and forget to scheme.

It was after this that he told Bonnie about his new female interest. At first she had been amused.

"Leave it to you," she said, smiling at him fondly over her coffee cup. It was during Sunday-morning breakfast that they had got to talking about it. Nancy had already departed with friends for a day on the beach at Santa Cruz. "Gettin' mixed up in society. Is she nice?"

"She's a good kid. And I think she likes me. Fact is, I think she likes me more all the time."

Bonnie put her head forward. "Rex," she said, "you're not getting serious about that girl!"

"I don't say I've fell for her or anything like that. But it's a good old American tradition, marrying the boss's daughter."

"Rex!" Bonnie stared at him aghast. "Are you nuts?"

"Nope, just not a guy to neglect an angle."

"Angle, hell. You go getting your hopes up like this, and you're in for a big disappointment, that's all. That girl will just play you for a sucker."

"Maybe. Maybe not."

Bonnie eyed him shrewdly. "I didn't hear you say nothin' about her askin' you out with her crowd. Havin' you to the house."

"Give her time."

"My God. I didn't think even you were that green. Know what she's doing? Slumming, that's that. I know these high-hat little bitches. Always looking for a new thrill. This time you're it."

"She ain't no bitch," Rex retorted truculently. "She's a damn nice girl."

"So you are falling for her!" Bonnie countered triumphantly.

"I like her, sure. What kind of a son-of-a-bitch d'you think I am, stringing a kid along if I don't have no respect for her?"

"Well, all I hope is," Bonnie said more quietly, "she don't give you a lot of grief."

"Don't worry about me. I can take care of myself."

So the friendship went on, with a date every week or every two weeks. But it was as Bonnie said. Patty did not include him in any foursomes or small groups, and somehow she avoided having him meet her father.

It was during Big Week of the rodeo that Rex finally asked about her father. Patty rode every day in the parade on her own pretty bay mare which she boarded at stables in the foothills. Rex had scrounged up a moth-eaten little cow pony from a rancher in the Prunedale district north of town, paying more than he could afford for the use of it. But all four days of the parade he rode up Main Street and out to the rodeo grounds and managed to head his horse in beside Patty's bay at the fence encircling the arena where they perched to watch the dusty events.

After the performance on this day they stopped at a highway lunch counter for hamburgers, leaving the horses tied to a post at the side of the building.

Patty wore a beige western riding habit with high-heeled boots, and her flat-crowned felt hat hung on her shoulders, held by the braided cord knotted around her throat. Rex wore a gay red and green plaid shirt, old, skintight Levis and a battered pair of field boots, with a hat rather like the girl's, except that the brim was curled at the sides from much handling.

"Does your dad," Rex asked abruptly as they finished their cokes, "know you go out with me?"

Patty's eyes left his and contemplated the crushed ice in her glass. "Why should he?" she said lightly. "I've dated a lot of fellows in my lifetime that Dad never happened to meet. He doesn't pay much attention to my doings."

"I was just wondering. Wondering if he'd approve of me."

"Why shouldn't he?" Patty's expression was too ingenuous.

Rex regarded her steadily and grinned sardonically. Patty dropped her eyes. She swished the ice around in her glass.

Her tone was consciously frivolous as she chided, "You must have snobbish ideas. I gather you're implying that Dad wouldn't approve of your seeing me—just because you're one of his employees."

"That's about it."

"Oh, that's ridiculous," she retorted flippantly.

"Is it?"

The weeks of the summer went on, and Patty was away on vacation trips, and they saw each other only once or twice.

And then it all happened in the week before Stanley West died. Rex told Bonnie about it one evening when they were both at home. He had spoken wryly, realizing that he was laying himself open to "I told you sos."

Stanley West had discovered that his daughter was running around with one of the receiving crew from his own shed. And a fellow who was not just working temporarily, to pay his way through school or something; but one of a fruit-tramp family from Little Oklahoma, long-time regulars in the game. He said nothing to Laverne; but one evening when his wife was out he called Patty into his den for a talk.

"What's this," he said, "I hear about you being seen all over town with some fruit tramp, a guy named Rex Maffey?"

For a moment Patty couldn't think what to say. Then she stated coolly, "I have a friend named Rex Maffey, if that's what you mean. I date him once in a while, not very often."

"Don't you realize people are going to talk if they see you hanging out with some cheap punk from Little Oklahoma?"

"He isn't cheap, and he isn't a punk; and it's not his fault his family can't afford to live in a ritzy neighborhood."

Stan's lips curved in their typical closed smile, and there was almost an approving gleam in his dark eyes; but he lowered his lashes to conceal it.

"O.K. Maybe my language was a little strong. But I'm thinking of your best interests."

"That's big of you," the girl said rudely.

"Now don't get sassy," he reprimanded curtly. "You're young, and you don't know the score yet about a lot of things. All I'm saying is you'll be safer if you stick to kids in your own set. People like the Maffeys, they're different from us, have different standards, different ways of looking at things, and you could get in trouble messing around with that type of people."

Patty was regarding him intently, paying little attention to his words. "Who told you about Rex?"

"I suppose a lot of people know. Apparently you've been seen with him in his car, and at soda fountains, and here and there."

"So? But who took it upon themselves to make a big deal out of it by telling you?"

"No big deal. Matter of fact the person that let it out to me assumed I knew. And I didn't really like learning about your friend in the way I did. A man doesn't enjoy having one of his friends jokingly say they hear he may have a new son-in-law one of these days, and find out that he's referring to one of his own trimmers' brothers."

"That," Patty said coldly, "was a gross exaggeration. Rex and I have never even discussed love, let alone marriage."

"You see, though, the impression people get."

"Just who was it that made this cute remark?"

"It could have been a lot of people. Apparently everybody knows about the affair but me. I expect your name is being bandied about up and down the line right in my own shed."

"No! Rex isn't the type to talk about a girl. Who told you this?"

"It doesn't matter. But it happened to be Chuck Willet who let the cat out of the bag."

"Chuck Willet! That evil-minded old hyena. Everybody in town knows what he is. And you'd listen to that—that crook!"

"That's just the point I'm getting at, Patty. Your conduct has laid you wide open to talk from people like Chuck. And I don't like seeing my daughter put in a position like that. That's why I'm asking you to break it off with this fellow. It's not doing you any good, honey. Can't you see that?"

"No, I can't, and you wouldn't either if you knew Rex."

"Why haven't you brought him around then? Why haven't you had him here to the house where I would meet him if you're so sure he'd make a good impression?"

Patty shifted her gaze so that it fell on the vicious face of the stuffed cat behind the man. Quickly her eyes dropped to a pile of *Field and Stream* magazines on the shelf below. She replied slowly, "I guess because I knew you'd be like this. I guess I figured you for a snob." She raised her eyes defiantly to his.

Stanley shrugged. "You see."

"Suppose," the girl said quietly, "I refuse to quit seeing him."

Stan pursed his lips. "There's not much I could do in that case—except have a talk with the young man myself."

"Daddy ..." Her voice and her eyes were pained. "That would be cruel."

"I don't think so."

"Well, I do. He—well, it would hurt him—unnecessarily."

"Then you'd better handle it yourself."

Patty stood up, her eyes lowered. "Can I go now?"

"If you want to. Think it over, honey. I don't want to seem harsh; but I'm older; I know more about these things."

At the door she lifted her lashes and shot him an impenetrable glance before she turned and went out.

Patty had been drifting along, getting a kick out of seeing Rex occasionally, partly, she realized, as a form of revolt against parental standards. She wasn't really in love with anyone right now, and certainly not with Rex. But something happened to her feelings after this talk with her father. A stronger partisanship for Rex grew out of it.

He picked her up at home one or two evenings later, to go for a drive; and while they were out she told him what Stanley had said. She had not really intended to. It wasn't the sort of thing you told a boy casually—that your father thought he wasn't good enough for you. Especially when in some ways you agreed with your father. But Patty thought Rex would not always be just a laborer in a lettuce shed. Lots of young fellows did manual labor—as a start in life. Her father seemed to look at it from the point of view that Rex would always be a shed worker. She did not question herself as to the means by which Rex might cease to be a fruit tramp, or consider whether she might be that means. Nor did she consider whether the boy's possible future in life would cut any ice as to how she felt about him or would feel in the future. The main things she felt with any clarity were that her father was interfering in her affairs and that she didn't like it. Telling Rex on her father was an obscure way of getting even.

Rex had parked the car on a hillside where they could look down upon the valley twinkling with lights.

"So what," he asked cautiously, leaning back in his corner, his arm along the seat back, "are you going to do about it?"

"Well, I'm certainly not going to pay any attention. I probably shouldn't even have told you, but it made me hopping mad. I thought in this day and age people didn't have to consult their parents about choosing their friends."

"Maybe if you just ignore it, he'll forget about the whole thing."

"No. Dad doesn't forget things." Patty stared through the windshield at the dull glow the city reflected against the foggy sky. She was silent for a moment while Rex watched her. "I think," she said slowly, "I'll say nothing. Just defy him. I was meaning to ask you anyway. Saturday evening on Labor Day week end I'm planning to have a barbecue supper in the back yard for some of the kids, sort of a last get-together before everybody leaves for school or one thing or another. I want you to come. I won't even mention to the folks that I've asked you; but once you've been our guest, well, the ice is broken. There's not much Dad can do about it. And that, in a way, you see, calls his bluff. He'll see he can't dictate to me."

Rex eyed her inscrutably. "What does this make me? A bone for you and your dad to fight over?"

"No, no," she protested hurriedly. "It's the principle of the thing. Whether I have a right to choose my own friends or not."

"I see. But when you get right down to it, you yourself don't think I'm really a—suitable friend."

"How can you say that? Of course I do. That's the whole point. I think Dad's attitude is ridiculous."

"I didn't notice you inviting me out with your other friends before, not until your dad forced your hand."

An uncertain expression was visible on the girl's features in the semidarkness. "But Rex," she said heartily after a nearly imperceptible pause, "I haven't known you very long. It—it just hasn't worked out that way—I mean, that—that we'd be going the same places and all—"

"O.K. It was just an idea. I only hope your dad doesn't get on his high horse about it. After all, I do work for him, and my sister too."

"Oh, Daddy won't make a fuss," she declared, but there was a faint lack of conviction in her tone.

Rex said no more. Things were working out the way he wanted them to. "This," he thought to himself, "will show Bonnie. Wait till I tell her I'm invited to a party at Wests'."

But Bonnie was not impressed. "You just remember what I tell you. You're heading for trouble mixing with those people. If Patty was in love with you, I'd say more power to you. But she isn't, and—"

"How do you know she isn't?"

"A blind man could see what she's doing. All she's thinking about is showing her father he can't tell *her* what to do. She doesn't care what happens to you in connection with it. And I'm just telling you, Stan West is nobody to fool around with. People just don't get in his way. He sees to that. Sure, I know he's a good guy. He ain't a big ignorant bully like some of these guys. But he's—well, he's got character. Nobody's going to shove him around. Not even his daughter. I haven't worked five years in Stan West's shed without finding out a few things." Bonnie's eyes became thoughtful. "Matter of fact, I wouldn't be a bit surprised if Stan West wasn't a lot more influential in this valley than anybody suspects. He's smart, Stan is."

"So what. For God's sake, he isn't going to whip out his power and use it on me."

"I don't know. You never can tell about people."

With an air of braggadocio Rex retorted, "Well, he better not try pushing me around. He does and I'll tell him what's what."

"I can just see you telling Stanley West where to head in at," Bonnie said scornfully.

"Maybe he ain't the only one that's got ambition. Maybe he won't like it; but maybe someday I'll be sitting in the chair in that office—when the old man retires."

"Rex, are you nuts! Do you really think you've got a chance to marry that girl?"

"If I play my cards right, who knows? Everything's sure worked out according to schedule so far. And I don't intend to have Mr. Big-shot West interfering with that schedule. So far, he's worked right in with my plans. Threw Patty over on my side." Rex moved his hand horizontally from the wrist. "Just as neat," he said smugly.

"You," his sister said coldly, "are going to come to with an awful headache one of these days. You mark my words."

CHAPTER EIGHT

The day before the night he died Bonnie watched Stanley West walk down the length of the shed, talking to the foreman, Ralph Musio. Bonnie's mind was worriedly concentrated on her reckless, scheming little brother, and she turned slightly to watch the boss, wondering how deeply it would bother him to have his daughter kicking up her heels in defiance.

Ralph stepped aside to speak to an inspector at one of the loading doors, and Stan stood alone, his eyes sweeping thoughtfully over his domain. Bonnie saw his gaze fall upon Rex, who was backing up after helping to swing a basket of lettuce into place for the trimmers. She was too far away to hear, but she saw Stanley lift his hand in a calling gesture and say something to Rex as the boy halted in front of him. Rex replied, and Stan spoke again; then Rex moved on. Stanley's eyes followed the boy as the latter moved off.

Bonnie meant to ask Rex what that interchange consisted of; but at home the dinner hour and the early evening were hectic and rushed; and in the morning nobody ever conversed over the hustle and bustle of breakfast and getting off to work.

So now all she knew was that Rex had been away until late in the night and that Stanley West was dead.

From the start she had tried hard to reject the thought that had come to her mind the first thing. Rex was a good boy. Heedless and impractical, but he was smart and a good worker. But suppose when Stanley West spoke to him yesterday it had been to ask Rex to see him last night. Suppose Mr. West had decided to act for himself in regard to his daughter—and it was just the sort of thing that he would do, take things into his own hands, tell Rex to lay off or be fired. And suppose Rex, getting cocky and also mad, talked back to the boss and the boss got tough. Bonnie knew, but Stanley West didn't, that you had never been able to handle Rex by getting tough. It only made him stubborn. It even led to kicking and screaming on the boy's part. And now that he was older, kicking and screaming would be translated into striking out with more adult weapons—such as a gun if there happened to be one handy.

Rex had a temper, naturally. Everybody had one. Bonnie never believed people who said they or someone else did not have a temper. It just took different degrees of pressure to release different people's tempers. She had lived too long at close quarters with other people not to know. Once the young married couple in the other apartment of their duplex, a couple who seemed all billing and cooing had had such a fight in the bedroom, whose wall was also the wall of hers, that she and Nancy had huddled together in their bed, hardly breathing from fright as they heard thuds against the wall and hoarse breathing and guttural words of counter accusations. And the next day the girl had a black eye.

And Mrs. Meggs next door. There wasn't a sweeter woman anywhere—when she was in a good mood. But Bonnie had heard Mrs. Meggs' voice raised against her own kids in a pitch of hysteria that indicated complete loss of control.

And those two guys on the other side of the driveway. Just last week Bonnie had been washing dishes and through the kitchen window had seen them go after each other with their fists until one had a bloody nose; and it all started over one of them telling the other that if "his God-damned kid didn't stop leaving his God-damned wagon in front of the God-damned garage door" every time the complainant drove in, he'd "drive right over the God-damned little brat's wagon."

And really they were both pretty nice guys. Accommodating and friendly. They had just both been on edge and overtired. She knew the feeling.

Bonnie knew how unpredictable was the line beyond which lay the realm of no control in human emotions. Maybe among people like the Wests no one ever acted like that. Perhaps if you had plenty of space for each person to live in, and more education to take up your mind, and a feeling that you were more in control of things that affected you, like how much money you could make and all, you didn't revert to a pure animal level so easy.

But she felt that Rex could go wild too—if Stanley West, for instance, handled him wrong, shamed him or threatened him, and kept rubbing it in. Especially when the kid was building up this big deal in his mind of getting out of Little Oklahoma by means of Patty West and settling down someday in Stanley West's own desk chair.

But not murder, Bonnie tried to think, not murder.

She and Rex rode to work together in his car; but he also carried three passengers to and from the shed, the last one living just across the street from the Maffeys'. They talked all the way about the murder, which was now a large black headline in the daily *Californian*. There was no opportunity for Bonnie to speak to Rex privately; for when they came into the house Nancy was in the kitchen putting away the groceries she had lugged home from the supermarket in obedience to a list left by Bonnie.

At last, after their dinner and the dishwashing and getting Dad settled for the night, when Nancy had departed for her girl friend's house, Bonnie stood in the doorway to the bathroom, where Rex was shaving in preparation for going out, and she spoke to him, her voice held low so as not to be overheard by the couple in the other half of the house.

"Rex. About this murder. Do you know anything about it?"

The little motor of the electric razor whirred as he held the instrument from his cheek and turned startled eyes toward her.

"What do you mean? Know anything about it?" And then he clicked the switch of the razor and looked at her. "What do you think I'd know?" he added with slow resentment.

"You were talking so big about what you'd do. How he wasn't going to butt in about the girl. Rex, you didn't have words with him—where anybody'd hear you?"

"You think I shot Stan West?"

"Hush! You want the people next door to hear you?"

"Is that what's biting you; you think it was me?"

"No, I don't think anything of the kind. But I—I'm worried. You were sore at him, and you know we wondered when we was talkin' about it if maybe he'd call you in and give you a talkin' to about the girl. And you were out all last evening, and I—I wondered if maybe he had—well, called you in for a showdown."

Rex studied his sister's plain, anxious face with the short, broad-tipped nose, the full pink lips. At first his expression was hard, but it softened under the gaze of her worried hazel eyes.

"Look, kid, forget it. What would I be doing in Stanley West's private office in the middle of the night, fooling around with his own gun? You think I'm crazy or somethin'?"

"No, not crazy. But—headstrong. You've gone and got your heart set on getting ahead through this girl. And I know how you are. You don't like to be crossed."

"Well, I don't go that far to get my own way. My God, Bonnie, what do you think I am?"

"O.K. I just wanted to satisfy my mind about it."

He pressed the switch on the razor again and resumed operations on the dark stubble at his jaw line.

"Where were you last night anyway?" she asked, trying for a casual tone.

"Down to the pool hall."

"Till twelve o'clock or after? I woke up at twelve and you weren't in yet."

He snapped off the razor again and regarded her coldly. "Look, Sis, I'm a big boy now. Remember? Maybe sometimes I go places good little girls aren't supposed to know about."

Bonnie frowned. "I suppose," she said wearily, "you've got to sow your wild oats, but if you mean what I think you mean, I should think you could find better ways to spend your money than helping build up Chuck Willet's bank roll."

Rex was shaving again, holding up his chin to get a few whiskers on its underside. His eyes slid away from the mirror for a speculative look at the girl.

"Funny thing, you mentioning Willet. I saw him last night."

Bonnie stiffened disapprovingly. "Rex, you *were* at one of those houses. I—I didn't really think so. Thought you were just—bragging."

"Relax, rela-ax, kid. I didn't go out back, if that's what's eatin' you. One of the guys we was with wanted to go to Mattie's out in the country. I ain't sayin' who it was; but he had a roll, wanted to splurge. So me and—well, never mind who the other guy was—anyway we went along and sat in the parlor and had a couple of beers while we waited for him. Hell, I can't afford the dames at Mattie's. So anyways"—Rex was coiling up the cord of his razor as he talked—"when we was coming out to get in the car along about twelve-thirty, this yellow Cadillac convertible swings in the driveway and past the house to park out back. Our lights was on, and we got a good look. It was our friend Chuck Willet all right."

"Alone?"

"Yep. But not for long, I guess."

Bonnie had relaxed against the doorframe, forgetting the murder in the pleasure of gossip.

"It sure is the limit, that guy strutting around as big as you please, into everything, and all the time raking it in from every whore in the district. All the pay-offs them places have to make, it makes you wonder if the girls themselves get anything for their work."

"Well, Willet's take is perfectly legitimate. He just leases out the property where they live. Nothin' illegal about that." Rex grinned mischievously as he took down from the rack the rumpled grey towel the whole family used for drying their hands. "'Course I understand it ain't healthy to even run a lottery or allow a poker game on your property unless he gets a rake-off, or first thing you know he *will* own the joint. Know what I heard? He's thinkin' of running for the Board of Supervisors next election."

"Oh, no!"

"That's what I heard."

Bonnie stood aside and followed Rex into the living room.

"How would he ever get elected? Everybody knows about him."

"Not everybody. And does anybody care? All these soldiers up at Fort Ord, they gotta have some place to go and meet women. So Willett owns the property where they go. That's just good business. And you've got to hand it to him; he's smart. He'd run things efficient. And he'd play ball with the Grower-Shippers. Have to, or they'd break him. I dunno, seems like sometimes the big shots like to have a few shady characters in politics. You can put the heat on a guy whose nose ain't too clean. And as for getting the votes, all you've gotta do to get elected to anything, seems like, is promise everybody everything, and then actually give 'em a few of the things you promised. F'r instance, out here if he promised to take our side on the Board right down the line, he'd get a lot of votes. People figure what the hell, they're probably all crooks anyway and you might as well have one you know and one that's put himself on record to hand you a little of the gravy."

"Well, I still don't think anybody decent would vote for him if he did run."

"Suppose there ain't much choice. Suppose it's Willet or some dumbbell. Anyhow what're we worryin' about? Did you vote last time?"

"No. I was tired."

"O.K. So there you are."

As Rex shrugged into his corduroy jacket, Bonnie said, "You shouldn't stay out too late. You'll get run down."

"Oh, I won't be late. See ya."

When he was gone Bonnie remembered the murder. She felt a little better. He had said he had nothing to do with it. But—she frowned—the subject had changed rather suddenly, to something juicy like whore houses. Which was bound to distract her attention. She closed her eyes and shook her head slightly. Too much imagination. Nerves, that was her trouble. She'd look in on Dad, and go to bed, get some sleep.

CHAPTER NINE

Chuck Willet's real-estate office was quietly just around the corner from Main Street; no ostentation, just a simple business establishment with lettered signs inside the windows concerning seven-room ranch-type dwellings that were going for a song at twelve thousand dollars.

Emma Bradley had presided over this office for nearly twenty years, as bookkeeper, stenographer, and receptionist. People assumed she was a widow, since she called herself Mrs.; but no one knew much about her. She attended the Catholic Church and belonged to the Business and Professional Women's Club and otherwise kept to herself. She was from out of town, had simply turned up working for Chuck Willet, and that was that. People finally stopped asking personal questions about her past and finally forgot that she might once have done something besides walk back and forth between the office and her apartment in the brick apartment house west on Alisal Street, near the post office.

Emma was invited to the Willet house sometimes, for Sunday dinner, or on Thanksgiving or Christmas; and Dora Willet seemed to look upon her merely as what Emma ostensibly was: her husband's trusted employee. Since Dora was liked and respected in town, other people accepted Emma on the same terms, lumping her somehow with Dora, as part of the respectable side of Chuck Willet's two-toned existence.

There was a difference, however, between Chuck's domestic woman and his office woman. While there was much about her husband's business affairs that Dora only suspected and rigidly repressed from conscious acknowledgment, there was nothing that Emma did not know.

On the day following the discovery of Stanley West's body, Chuck lifted his eyes to Emma, where she stood beside his desk, and instructed offhandedly, "By the way, find out when West's funeral is and have flowers sent. Put it on my calendar so I can plan to go."

Emma's square face beneath the combed-back, iron-grey hair did not change expression. Her voice was deep, a little roughened for a woman's; but it went well with the hundred-and-eighty-pound physique that was shapeless around the bosom and hips.

"Joe Farwell talked to you yesterday about the murder," she stated with her eyes on his face.

"Yes, it happened I'd been in to see Stan at the office the day he died. They talked to everybody that saw him that day."

His expression was bland as he raised his eyes to Emma's impassive face. "Terrible thing, losing Stan," he added unctuously.

"Too bad," she said flatly. "He was your most reliable contact in the Grower-Shipper Association. He could have clinched their support if you get nominated for the Board."

"I'm not worried about the produce crowd," Chuck said impatiently. "I stand in good with the lettuce people." His tone was petulant as he added, "I wish you'd stop needling me about politics. What's it to you if I want to show a little civic spirit?"

"There's an old saying: The shoemaker should stick to his last."

"If I'd always listened to you I wouldn't be where I am today."

"Probably not. About West, you can look at it another way. If he decided he didn't want you starting up the political ladder Stan could have thrown quite a monkey wrench in your plans, couldn't he? His word carried weight in the Association."

"Now why should Stanley West want to throw monkey wrenches into my affairs?" Chuck's voice was oily.

Emma let her eyes rest with a far-off look on the wall beside her boss's desk. "People are funny. Sometimes they get along in middle age, have a nice family, got enough money ahead to feel safe, and they get religion— in a manner of speaking. Come all over principles." She brought her gaze down to the man who was watching her narrowly. "See what I mean?"

She gathered up a sheaf of papers from the desk, turned, and stalked stolidly out of the small private office, in to her own domain in front.

Things were slow that morning, and Emma had time for thinking. Before noon Chuck went out by way of the rear-door opening into his private office. Time and again Emma's fingers slowed on the typewriter keys, and she sat staring at the paper in the machine.

No one, now, except her and Chuck, knew how Stan West had got the money for his start in business. There were not even any records left. Old notes had been burned, old check stubs destroyed. But it was Chuck Willet who had financed West, back in the days even before Emma came here to work for him. The loans had been repaid with interest; but Stan was a good guy, that way; he didn't forget a favor. He remembered his old friends. And no matter what people said about Chuck Willet in later years when he extended his interests around town to take in investments that the stuffy people considered shady, Stan had always had a good word to say for Emma's boss, helped him, in fact, to get established as a solid citizen.

But this itch for prestige, for public recognition, that Chuck had developed lately, bothered Emma. She knew he considered a piddling little post as a county supervisor only an opening wedge toward eventual greater glory. And Emma looked upon political office holding as a spectacular means of getting oneself out on a most unsteady limb. It seemed, however, to be something Chuck's ego demanded right now.

It was especially reckless after the Senate crime investigations, which had reached clear down into local affairs and brushed dangerously close to their own activities. The whole business, what with newspapers and television and books—had jarred a lot of people, made them think.

And Stan West was getting to that age when people often got stodgy, and hungry for the essence as well as the appearance of respectability. He had his money made, his business established; he didn't have to leave loopholes now for risky dealings in order to secure his financial safety. Lately he hadn't been seeing much of Chuck—for evenings with a bottle and a deck of cards or some carefully chosen girls.

And Chuck had counted on Stan for a strategically placed word here and there in furtherance of his ambitions. The Wests, through Laverne's connections with the old-home-town crowd, could swing weight not only among the produce people but among the hard core of old-timers.

Emma drew a cigarette from the package lying on the desk's pull-out board and inhaled deeply when it was lighted. The small chair creaked as she leaned on the adjustable back.

There was not much reason that she knew of—and Emma knew a lot—for anyone to shoot Stanley West in cold blood.

Stan West was not a weak character. Straight to the point, with no ifs, ands, or buts. If he made up his mind to something he came out with it, cold turkey. Suppose he had made up his mind to drop Chuck Willet. Suppose Stan had, in fact, turned against him—on account of Chuck's political ambitions. As she had told Chuck, people were funny. You couldn't always be sure what would make them suddenly break out in a rash of ideals. Suppose Stan had a hidden streak of sentimentality about—of all things—Americanism.

Emma remembered the war years and how everybody had gone around exhibiting sentiment about the flag and the President and the Constitution—as if they welcomed an excuse to indulge in an open love of country. The Wests had taken their part in the orgy as enthusiastically as anybody else, being air-raid wardens and buying war bonds and all that.

So suppose when Chuck decided to move out of straight business dealings which were close to open flouting of the law into the sphere of government where he would operate in just the same way, it was too much for Stan. Suppose Stan West had some hidden code of honor that made him believe that in theory at least government should be strictly on the up-and-up.

The fact that as a business man West would see nothing morally wrong about the produce people's attempting always to have a county board that would see things their way and protect their interests when those interests might conflict with those of some other group would have nothing to do with West's being, in theory, a staunch supporter of clean government. All the produce people quite honestly believed that what was to their best interest must inevitably be good for everybody else. But Stanley West could have developed a code of honor to bolster this philosophy, to give it a patina of virtue, a code which forbade allowing anyone who wouldn't play strictly according to the legal rules to sit in as the representative of his kind on the team that made up the rules.

Emma was able to understand that point of view; and she had tried to explain to Chuck why some of his friends cast a dubious eye on his methods of making money. Chuck was quite honestly bewildered by the distinctions between legitimate political pressure that paid off indirectly to the officeholder with contracts and preferred advancements and continuance in office, and the methods of a man like himself, for instance, who paid off directly in cash as a reward for a little eye-closing on the part of officials.

"What the hell's the difference?" he had asked her belligerently. "They're all out to make money. Right? So they all try to get in guys they can trust to make up laws that'll benefit themselves, guys that won't put any more stumbling blocks than they have to in the way of the businessmen making all they can. If some guy doesn't play ball they put up more money to elect somebody else that *will* run things the way they want 'em. Right?"

"Yes, but—"

"So O.K. A guy like me, it's the same thing. Same thing exactly. I just work from the other end, see? I don't pay 'em by keeping 'em on the gravy train by using my influence to let 'em stay in office. I just say, 'O.K.; so it's illegal for a girl to entertain her gentlemen friends for money. A little game of fantan's illegal. I don't ask you guys to change the law for me'—the way the produce crowd would expect 'em to change the law if it interfered with *their* business. No, all I ask the guys in politics is that they look the other way, and I'll make it worth their while. So what in the hell's the big difference? Like I said, business gets in guys to make the rules it wants; *I* pay guys not to notice if I'm breakin' the rules once in a while."

"Damn it," Emma retorted, "you know I don't give a whoop in Hades about the rules, not personally. But most people look at it different; and I can't see why you can't see it. You gotta have rules. It's the only way they can all keep getting their share. Most businessmen, they don't make their dough out of women and gambling so they're willing to tie that kind of business up in a strait jacket. Furthermore, people are queer. They like to have something they can forbid, put out of bounds. That makes the dirty tricks they pull themselves seem more—more virtuous. Gives them something to look down their noses at so they can feel superior. It isn't that they give a damn if you're in the line of business that's out of bounds. But they still want the rules there so they can operate inside them, and so they can blame the guys that are *outside* the rules if things go wrong."

Chuck shook his head at her. "You're getting too deep for me."

"It's just," she said wearily, "I don't like to see you butting your head against a stone wall. I'd like to see you be realistic about things, see you accept the fact that you're not in the same class with—say, Stan West, or Bill Jardine. They're respectable; you aren't. Why not face it, and not try to get into their league?"

"The hell I'm not as good as Stan West, or Bill Jardine, or any of them. And I'll show 'em someday too. Maybe someday I'll be telling them what to do."

"You should live so long. Look, this is all I've got to say; and it's my last word on the subject. You go getting those guys to back you and start you up the political ladder; and you'll do what *they* say, not the other way around. And if you don't, you'll wind up in San Quentin; that's where you'll wind up."

"You're crazy. Nobody's got anything on me. Nor ever going to have."

Emma remembered this conversation now. She had never been able to straighten Chuck out on this question. His mind simply couldn't grasp what she had tried to get over to him.

But Stan West would be quite capable of giving it to Chuck straight: No, I not only won't support you; I'll do my best to keep you from being elected. The County Board of Supervisors is no place for you.

Emma mashed out her cigarette butt until it was a mess of shredded paper and tobacco. Fantastic, yes. But again, people were funny.

The way Chuck was about these political ambitions, for instance. He had everything anybody could ask for: power, plenty of money, a nice wife, and enough standing in the community to get by; but nothing would do but that he must show people—the ones who looked down their noses at him behind his back. Show them that, all right, so I'm not good enough for you because a lot of my income comes from call girls and gambling joints, well, what do you think of me now, up there representing you in the courthouse and maybe someday in Sacramento, or who knows, even Washington?

Tough and ruthless and shrewd as he was, here was Chuck Willet acting like a little kid determined to have a new bicycle for Christmas and ready to hit and kick and lie down on the floor and scream if he didn't get it.

Only he was not a little kid. He was a grown man and could be dangerous if crossed about something as almost pathologically necessary to him as this nomination had become. Stan knew Chuck was dangerous; but he might not have known how insanely Chuck wanted this new phase to his career.

But Emma knew her boss. She could see as plainly as if she had been there, how Chuck could have opened the drawer while Stan's back was turned at the little bar. Chuck knew Stan so well that he would know where the latter kept his gun. How he could wait with the gun concealed until Stan sat unsuspecting at the desk and how Chuck could lift the revolver and pull the trigger. It would simply be a rather unpleasant task he had to perform. It might, in fact, not even be the first time he had had to perform such a chore. The first time in many years certainly; but there were those years before he settled in Salinas, and settled there with a stake whose source no one knew except that it dated back to the prohibition era.

Emma began resolutely to type again. It was not her funeral.

CHAPTER TEN

At the inquest held over Stanley West's body the facts that were made public did not add up to the naming of his killer. It was established that he had died "not earlier than 10 P.M. and not later than 1 A.M." from a bullet through the heart fired by his own gun. Evidence indicated that the shot had been fired from at least three feet away from the body, and the fact that there were no fingerprints on the gun ruled out suicide. The room otherwise had been such a welter of fingerprints that so far they had proved useless as clues. A janitor service cleaned the offices once a week; and it had been three days since the service was performed. Everyone who had entered the room in the meantime seemed to have touched some smooth surface in it.

Stanley's business affairs were in order; his will was only what might have been expected. Laverne inherited *in toto*. Generous insurance policies took care of the children, the funds to be held in trust until their twenty-first birthdays.

Nothing mysterious turned up among his papers. The overdue note to Hal Schmidt was duly noted, and that gentleman questioned until perspiration gathered in beads on his forehead. Despite Hal's lack of a real alibi for the hours in question and despite the possible motive if Stan were putting on pressure for payment of the money, there was no way of placing Hal at the office that night, and the motive seemed weak.

The police, although they did not publicly say so, were baffled. Simple robbery might have explained the case; but neither the bank, Earl Fowler, nor Mrs. West had any reason to believe Stanley had been carrying any appreciable sum of money. Moreover his wallet still contained nearly fifty dollars in bills.

Cass Huggins was nervous. The crime had happened within the city limits, and although the sheriff's office was co-operating fully, he felt that it was really his responsibility. And public opinion was going to be pretty damn critical if they just never found even a suspect.

Cass sat in his office with Joe Farwell, head of the county detective bureau, and reviewed developments.

He bit the eraser of a yellow pencil and fumed, "If we could just get a line on why he was at the office. Now this guy he had dinner with at the hotel. He says Stan left him about ten o'clock after a couple of drinks at the bar; and the bartender and a bellboy confirm that. Saw him walk out through the lobby alone. Then—pfft!—nobody sees him again, except the night watchman on that string saw a light in the office at ten-fifteen when he made his rounds and Stan's car outside. Didn't pass the front of the Golden West shed again till one o'clock. Light out and the car still there. Tries the door, and it's locked. Thinks nothing of it. Figures West must have left with somebody else. But the damn fool didn't notice any other cars there."

"Well, he's got quite a long beat," Farwell excused the watchman. "And you don't keep an eye on the front right along the highway the way you do along the railroad tracks and the sides."

"The way I see it," Cass insisted, "West had an appointment with somebody at his office. If we could just find out who."

"Not necessarily. An appointment, I mean. There was a light in his office and his car alongside, both in full view of the highway. Suppose somebody saw them and just dropped in. Surprise visit." The detective's eyes narrowed, and his lips pursed. "If somebody was laying for West, waiting for a good chance at him, that would do it. The other guy could park further along, walk in, get him in conversation, accept the offer of a drink, and let West have it, wash up his own glass, and walk out. Or he could turn in on the other side of the Valley Value shed next door, drive around back to park, and walk up from the rear. On the other hand, it might have been unpremeditated. A chance call like I've indicated, a disagreement—over something important. And that's that. The guy gets away without anybody noticing his car had been there. Nothing open along there that time of night. The lunch counter down the road closes at ten."

"But what in the hell would West be doing there at that hour?"

"He'd just come from a conference with an Eastern buyer. His business would be on his mind. Stopped to check something. Papers or figures."

"The only lead we've got is this guy Schmidt, owing West money," Cass said with a discouraged air.

"We're still working on that angle. The Schmidts are pretty close to the Wests. Even if the loan angle's no good, through them we may get a line on some private trouble in West's life. I'm going to talk to the wife and daughter again today. We're checking on Laverne pretty thoroughly—pretty thoroughly. After all, that's always the first place to look—the wife."

Cass frowned. "It isn't professional of me to look at it this way; but damn it, I've known Laverne West most of my life. I just can't see her bumping her old man off."

"Maybe not; but it looks like they each pretty much went their own way; and we've found out she hits the bottle pretty heavy. All that doesn't add up to a nice, cozy, happy home life. And she's not alibied."

"Well, go to it," Cass said wearily. "We better arrest somebody, and pretty damn quick. First thing you know people'll be saying we're deliberately protecting somebody. And Keith Coletto wants action. He plans to run for district attorney again. He figures it won't look good for him if we let prominent shippers get bumped off and he don't prosecute *somebody* for it."

"Yeah, he was already on the prod about this hit-and-run accident the other day. Giving us county boys hell for not finding the driver for him. He's scared people will start saying violent death is run-of-the-mill stuff in his territory, and nobody ever gets hauled in for it."

"Well," Huggins said sardonically, "run out and find him a defendant."

Farwell took with him the detective who had accompanied him the first day. Lula admitted them and ushered them into the living room. Laverne was in her room, dressing to go out. There were, she found, matters to attend to with her attorneys downtown now that she was sole owner of the Golden West shed.

The preceding three days had wearied her. She was pale and there were shadowy depressions under her eyes. She felt that she looked years older.

When Lula knocked at her door she was dressed in a plain dark silk coat dress fastened with black buttons set diagonally down the skirt.

"Again?" she sighed in response to Lula's announcement. She turned to the full-length mirror and fluffed up her hair on one side, deciding not to renew her lipstick. For the police it was better to look a little faded.

She smiled at the men as she entered the room downstairs. "I thought," she said ruefully, "you fellows had already picked my mind clean."

"We're only trying to find your husband's murderer," Farwell reminded her soberly.

Laverne sat down. "Yes," she agreed.

In previous interviews they had harped on Stan's friends, on his relations with everyone he knew; so Laverne was not surprised when they began on her social activities for weeks preceding the murder. But as always they came down eventually to That Night, and she found them asking about her own car, the little English-made convertible Stan had given her the previous Christmas. When she had driven the car last before Stanley's death, how often she herself went to his office—to which the answer was, "Practically never," and questions about the physical arrangements of the office. Irrelevant, darting, seemingly pointless questions of all kinds.

She answered steadily, carefully. And finally Farwell asked if they might speak to Patty again.

Laverne frowned. "Is it really necessary? My daughter is so young, and this has been such an ordeal for her."

"We'll try to make this the last time," Farwell promised.

Laverne held herself straight and stepped gracefully on her high-heeled pumps as she crossed the hall and mounted the stairs. In the upper corridor she slumped a little. Her eyes rested regretfully on Patty's door. The poor kid. She had taken it hard, Stan's death. She had been so quiet, withdrawn. Distraught almost. Laverne had occasionally forgotten her own inner turmoil in a yearning to comfort her daughter.

She called softly and tapped on Patty's door. The girl opened it to regard her mother questioningly.

Laverne smiled crookedly. "I'm sorry, honey, but it's the cops again. I tried to steer them off; but they insisted. They want to talk to you."

"Oh no! Not again."

Laverne closed her eyes and nodded. "They do rather wear a person down."

"Poor Mom," Patty said impulsively. "I'm so sorry, about everything."

Laverne smiled wanly. "It's as hard for you as it is for me." She paused and added ruefully. "Well, maybe it is a little worse for me. I gathered from this interview today that they've got it into their cute little pointed heads that maybe *I* killed your father." The cords in her neck tightened as she swallowed convulsively.

"Mother! No?"

Laverne shrugged. "It's traditional, I guess. They always suspect the widow." With an effort at lightness, she added, "But you can rest assured, darling, it wasn't me."

Patty moved out of the room and clasped her mother's arm. "I know you didn't." They started down the hall together, leaving the door of Patty's room open. "But how awful for you," the girl murmured distractedly.

"I guess I'll live through it." At the head of the stairs Laverne disengaged her arm and patted the girl's hand. "Well, chin up, darling," she said facetiously, trying to reassure Patty. "Pip-pip, and all that sort of rot."

Patty stood a moment with her hand on the banister, looking after Laverne, who was proceeding toward her own door. She hadn't really noticed her mother in the last hectic, terrible days. But now she saw that the woman's face looked thinner, her skin transparent, stretched taut over the nose and cheekbones. Her eyes looked as if Laverne had not had enough sleep for days. And Patty hadn't seen her teed up since it happened. Something else struck Patty. Some of the—the—well, the silliness—seemed to have been washed out of her mother by the wave of trouble that had engulfed her.

She peered, terrified, over the banister, down to the lower hall. They thought her mother had done it. That was why they kept coming here. Sooner or later they might arrest her—for murder.

Her mother. Poor frivolous, unhappy little mother. But brave, too, as it turned out. Even trying to make little jokes to buoy up her daughter's spirits.

Patty's hand clenched on the railing; and then she went down.

She hardly heard Farwell's introductory remarks as she sat in a chair with a straight back, her hands clasped in the lap of her light-wool skirt. She looked at Farwell so straight and so unseeingly that he felt uneasy. After a few moments she tossed her head to shake back her tawny hair and blurted out, interrupting a question of his, "There's something I think I better tell you. It may not mean anything; but again it might. And I—I don't dare, now, not to let you know "

"Yes?" Farwell prompted softly.

"It's about me—and my father." She looked down and frowned, as if uncertain about how to make her disclosure.

"A week or so ago my father and I had a quarrel. About a friend of mine. A fellow my father didn't approve of. He told me to quit seeing him. I—I don't remember our exact words; but I—I think I defied him, said I wouldn't quit seeing this boy. And my father—well, he indicated if I didn't break it off, he'd see the fellow himself. So now, I don't know. Maybe he did talk to the boy. Maybe—maybe they quarreled. It's all I've been able to think of since this happened. I haven't seen the fellow since then. He sent me a sympathy card, that's all."

Her eyes had been glazed with determination; and now they went from the face of one detective to the other; and suddenly they became panic-stricken.

"It's just an idea. Probably nothing to it," she rushed on. "Maybe I shouldn't say it, implicate someone when I don't know. But if you're—if you— Well, it can't be my mother."

Soothingly Farwell took over, and in a few moments, reluctantly, guiltily now, Patty divulged the "fellow's" name.

When the officers had gone Patty went up the stairs and knocked at her mother's door.

"Patty?" Laverne's voice responded. "Come in. The bloodhounds gone?"

"Yes. And I think I've started them off on another scent."

Laverne straightened up on the chaise longue. "What do you mean?"

The girl dropped to a seat on Stanley's bed. "I held back something before, something that may have some bearing on—all this. When I heard they suspected you, I decided that even if it was a false scent, I'd better give it to them. And now, I don't know, I don't feel quite right about it. There's probably nothing to it, and I've just caused somebody a lot of trouble."

Laverne eyed her daughter curiously. And waited. Patty told her then about Rex and what she had told the detectives.

"You say I—met him?" Laverne prompted questioningly.

"Yes, in the hall one night. We were just going out."

"Funny. I don't remember any good-looking young fellow with brown wavy hair."

"I guess you—had your mind on other things," Patty murmured.

Laverne sat frowning at the floor. "It doesn't seem like the sort of thing that would lead to murder."

"No," Patty concurred unhappily. "I guess I should have kept my mouth shut. But I'm so tired of them hounding us. And it's been on my mind. I couldn't help wondering. After all, Rex is one person that I do know had a grievance against Dad. And there doesn't seem to be anyone else."

"Was he—this Rex—was he in love with you? But of course he must have been to take it so hard."

"I don't know. I don't really think so."

"Did he"—Laverne hesitated in embarrassment—"did he—well—make passes?"

"No." Patty looked down at her fingernail scraping the fabric of the bedspread. The color in her tanned skin had deepened. "We—well, he had kissed me, and like that. But it wasn't—heavy necking."

Laverne stood up, pressing a hand to her cheek. She walked to the window overlooking the back yard, where the twins sprawled on the terrace reading comic books. She spoke with her back turned.

"Of course, those people, they're different from us. You can't tell *what* they'd do."

"He didn't *seem* any different than anyone else. But, looking back, I can see it burned him, hearing Dad had forbidden me to see him again. Anyway—" Patty came to her feet. "I thought I'd tell you."

"Whether it means anything or not, I'm sure you did right, dear."

Laverne stood at the window after the girl was gone, pondering the situation. There was a possibility here. At first glance, it seemed a ridiculously flimsy motive, to kill a man because he told you to quit seeing his daughter. But this boy was one of those other people, and you couldn't tell what people like that would do. Their feelings and thought processes were a mystery.

For Laverne, people were divided into two classifications. On one side were the people like herself. This group began somewhere in the white-collar class, like bank clerks and schoolteachers and people who worked in offices; and from her own position it rose to include people in the economic status of a J. P. Morgan, the social position of a member of the Roosevelt family, and the intellectual category of an Albert Einstein. All such people, she considered, were fundamentally like herself, and therefore understandable. On the other side were all the people who wore dirty clothes when they worked and used their bodies to do that work. In her own immediate world this took in of course all the shed and field workers, and on a larger scale people who worked in factories, and—as a matter of course—practically everybody with darker skins than those of her own immediate circle, and naturally all the people from other countries who spoke with accents.

So—although it hardly seemed reasonable that Rex's motive was strong enough to induce murder—since he was one of those other people, Laverne quite honestly figured that you just couldn't tell what he might think or feel or do. Those people just weren't like ordinary human beings.

It was like Patty, though, not to notice this difference. She was still so young. At eighteen, one didn't know anything, really.

For no reason that she knew of, Laverne's mind wandered from the subject she had been pondering. It went back to an evening at the dinner table. Only last February it had been.

In the afternoon some little Japanese girl had come home with Patty. They were on a committee together to decorate the gym for a dance. Laverne had gone to her own room to write letters after they came in and had given no thought to her daughter's companion beyond noting that she *was* Japanese and thinking vaguely that they made a lot of noise coming upstairs. Both Laverne's and Patty's doors were standing open; and once Laverne had lifted her head to wonder if they were having hysterics in the bathroom; and later she had paused in her writing to wonder if she ought to go in and tell them not to stamp so hard on the floor. She could hear Patty's record player going; and they seemed to be trying out the recently revived Charleston. But she had decided not to bother. Somehow, Laverne reflected, there had been so many things in recent years that she just hadn't felt up to bothering about.

Stan had come home early and passed the girls in the downstairs hall. At the table later he accosted Patty superciliously, "I see you've taken to fraternizing with the Japs now."

"For cripes' sake, Dad, the war's over. Remember?"

"That doesn't make the Japs any more popular than they ever were around these parts."

"The rest of the United States doesn't see it that way," Patty muttered. "At least that's what I learned in school."

Stanley regarded her soberly. "I know. There's something to this talk that our public schools are riddled with radical influences."

Terry and Kerry had been listening alertly, as they always did to adult conversations; and now Terry piped up, "Maybe you just know ones you don't like, Dad. Japs, I mean. We got one in our class, Henry Tanaka, that nobody likes. He's a reg'lar kissee. Always makin' up to the teacher. But then there's Tommy Hirasaki, he's a swell guy. President of the student body this year and guard on the basketball team."

Laverne spoke up then. "Let's skip it, shall we. I hate arguments at the dinner table."

That was the way she had been. All she wanted was to be left alone, not stirred up by the children and Stan. Automatically, even in this petty disagreement, she agreed with Stan. What he thought was almost always what all the best people thought; and she supposed, looking back now, that it had always been simpler for her to let him do the thinking, since even if she had thought herself into different conclusions from his, he could have overridden her opinions anyway. He knew so much more than she did.

One reason, on that evening, that she had wanted to shut them up, was a disturbing, inchoate intimation somewhere deep in her mind that she herself was inclined to side with the children on the question under discussion.

Once a college friend of Rose Jardine's had visited in Salinas for a week end; and the friend had been inclined toward embarrassingly radical remarks. At a small evening party Rose had given in her honor, when the Japanese Question arose, the friend had created a terribly strained feeling by declaring bluntly, "You produce people might as well face it honestly, instead of pretending it's the Japanese *character* you hate. What you really hate them for is for being rivals in the same business. Secretly, of course, you all hate all your rivals, even the ones you call your friends; but the poor Japs can be segregated out easily on account of their appearance and their names; so the rest of you all join together and take advantage of the chance to expend your hatred safely on *them*. And, of course, when the country of their origin behaved in the abominable way it did, you forgot that these local people's ancestors had deserted that country to find a better way of life; you just used Japan's behavior as the final, perfect excuse to turn on your hated rivals."

The party broke up soon after that; and Rose never invited that friend to come down again.

But then, too, Laverne had guiltily felt that there was a grain of truth in what the woman said. She had not acknowledged the feeling, however, any more than she had the stirring of agreement for what the children said at the table. For dimly she sensed that an admission along those lines must lead to an examination of the whole bulk of her attitudes and thinking, a task that was beyond her strength.

When later in the evening Stan had broken a preoccupied silence by observing, "I've been thinking maybe we ought to stretch a point and try to send the boys to a good private school where they wouldn't be likely to pick up with so much trash," her reaction had been one of assent, encouraged by the thought of what an impression it would make on her friends when she casually referred to the twins being "away at school," just like an Eastern society lady in a magazine story.

Gradually her reverie dissolved into conscious recognition of the twins' immediate activities on the grass beyond the terrace. They were wrestling like puppies, squealing too, much like young animals at play. She resisted an impulse to push the window open and tell them to stop, that they might hurt each other. Instead, wonderingly, she watched their childish antics. They were entering that fantastic stage of growth where sometimes their postures, their movements startled one by the way they presaged the adult male that would one day emerge from the lanky boy's body, and then, in a twinkling, here they were, like this, tumbling over one another like two-year-olds.

Laverne sighed and turned back into the room, frowning slightly with a "Where was I?" feeling. Her teeth sank into her lower lip. Patty. This boy, Rex Maffey. The murder. Odd, how she could already apply the word to Stan's death, so matter-of-factly, so dispassionately.

But if it turned out that Rex Maffey had killed Stanley, it brought her own life into equilibrium again. She could relax and begin to adjust herself and try to plan. She would no longer have to shy away from thoughts about Brian. She wouldn't have to wrestle with fear and revulsion when she thought of him. In the past few days it had been impossible to believe that she still loved him—after what he had done; yet equally impossible to say to herself: I don't care for him anymore.

If this suspicion of Rex were true, what a relief it would be.

CHAPTER ELEVEN

The clatter and rattle and rumble of work proceeded as usual in the Golden West shed with the radio blaring irrelevantly over it all. Freda talked on apace, and Ray responded with joshing remarks, and Bonnie worked steadily, participating idly sometimes in the talk about high prices and the iniquity of withholding taxes and the qualifications of candidates in the union elections and whether it was true that Harry really only paid fifteen hundred dollars for that 1948 Chrysler he was sporting, and if so, how he managed to get it for that.

Earl Fowler came out of the office door and around the end of the line, his head raised to look down the length of the shed. Bonnie saw him lift his hand and beckon when he caught sight of Ralph Musio, saw Ralph head down toward the office and disappear.

Farwell was waiting, sitting with one haunch on the edge of Earl's desk.

"Still nosing around?" Ralph accosted him cheerfully.

"Still at it. I'm looking now for a guy named Rex Maffey. Got some questions to ask him. I understand he works here."

"Yeah." Ralph looked mystified. "But he's just a kid."

"Got reason to think he might've talked to West that day. Could you get hold of him for me?"

"Why, sure."

"Ever see Mr. West talking to this kid?"

Ralph wrinkled his brow. "Stan was out on the floor late that afternoon. I told you that. And now that you mention it," he added slowly, "I remember he did stop and call Rex over to him, said something, and then walked on."

"So? Didn't happen to hear what they said?"

"No. I had moved off."

"Anybody else close enough to 'em that they might have heard?"

"Don't think so. They was between the outside doors and the baskets."

"You notice Maffey after West went on? How he seemed to react to the exchange?"

"No. No, never occurred to me to look at him again."

"Well, send him in, will you?"

Farwell turned to Earl, who had listened intently. He jerked his thumb toward the inner office. "I'll talk to him in there."

Rex's every nerve was on guard as he stepped into the office. Earl opened the inner door and gestured with his head. "In here."

Farwell sat in Stanley's chair, looking across the desk as Rex walked in. Rex knew who the man was from having seen him in the shed the day after the murder, asking seemingly desultory questions.

"I understand," Farwell began, not inviting the boy to be seated, "Mr. West spoke to you last Monday when he was out in the shed late in the afternoon."

"That's right."

"What did he say?"

"He asked if I was Rex Maffey, and I told him I was."

"What else?"

"He said, did I like working here, and I said it was O.K."

"Why should he have asked you that?"

"I don't know. But he made a practice of speaking to the crew. He was always stopping to pass the time of day with some of the guys."

"No special reason for stopping to speak to you in particular that day—and asking for you by name?"

"Not that I know of."

"I understand you know his daughter, Patricia West."

"Yes, sir. She went to high school when I did."

"You've had some dates with her the last few months."

Rex wondered for a panic-stricken moment how this man had found out. Had Patty told him, and if so how much had she told him? Still, other people knew. Anyone might have mentioned it. He decided to use the truth up to the danger point.

"Yes, sir."

"Mr. West know that?"

"I don't know."

"What do you mean, you don't know?"

"He never happened to be home when I called for Patty. So—I don't know."

"She never said whether he knew or not?"

"Not that I remember."

"Do you think Mr. West would have objected to this friendship?"

"I don't see why he should."

"You don't? Where were you last Monday evening?"

"Home, part of the time. Out with some fellows later on."

"What time did you leave home?"

"Little after nine."

"Where'd you go?"

"Little Daisy pool hall on Alisal."

"How long were you there?"

"An hour or so."

"Then where'd you go?"

"I drove over to a bar."

"What bar?"

"The Lucky Spot."

"I see. That's just down the highway from here about a quarter of a mile, isn't it?"

"Yes."

"Alone?"

"Yes."

"You passed here, I suppose."

"Yes."

"What time'd you get there?"

"I don't know for sure. About ten-thirty maybe."

"As you passed the shed here, did you see a light, or Mr. West's car?"

Rex hesitated. "I think there was a light. I wasn't really noticing."

"O.K. Then what?"

"I ran into a couple of fellows I knew, and we had a couple of beers."

Farwell had been jotting down notes on a piece of paper during this last exchange.

"Name of the fellows?"

"Shorty Hendricks and Willard O'Hara."

"Then what?"

Rex twisted his cap and glanced down at it. He believed that the policeman was within his rights in asking these questions, and it never occurred to him not to answer.

"Will wanted to make a night of it, and they didn't have a car with 'em. They'd been drinking and they took a taxi out there. So they asked me to drive them out to Mattie's."

Farwell raised his eyebrows. "Mattie's, h'm? Pretty high-toned idea, wasn't it?"

"Well, Will had some money. He wanted to splurge a little."

"What'd he do, treat you guys?"

Rex was feeling like a schoolboy brought before the principal. "Not me," he said gruffly. "I don't like to be under obligations, fellow giving me money for something like that when he's tanked up. He's liable to be sore the next day because he got so generous. I waited in the parlor. I had a drink and played the juke box and talked to a—a—young lady."

"How long'd you stay there?"

"Maybe an hour. Maybe less. Then I dropped those guys off and came on home."

"What time'd you get home?"

"Quarter to one."

"What time did you all leave Mattie's?"

"About twelve-fifteen or twelve-thirty, I think. I didn't look at the time."

"There are a good many time gaps in your story," Farwell said coldly. "Times when you could have kept an appointment here with Mr. West."

"What do you mean? I was with people all the time."

"Except when you drove from the Little Daisy to the Lucky Spot. Except from the time you dropped your friends at their homes until you actually got home."

"You're crazy," Rex protested hoarsely. "Why should I have an appointment with Mr. West?" And immediately he realized that this rhetorical question was a mistake; for Farwell smiled.

The detective leaned forward suddenly. "Do you still deny that you knew Stanley West had forbidden his daughter to go out with you again?"

Rex's eyes wavered, but he declared stoutly, "Yes."

Farwell leaned back in the chair. "In that case we'll go down to the office and you can tell Chief Huggins."

"You can't arrest me," Rex cried. "I haven't done anything."

"I can escort you down to the chief's office for further questioning," Farwell stated silkily.

While Rex was being interviewed Farwell's companion had industriously obtained samples of fingerprints from the rear view mirror, the dashboard, and the door handles of Rex's car, and by the time Cass Huggins was ready to interview the boy, the officers knew that one of the prints on the visitor's chair in Stanley's office on the morning of his discovery matched the prints Farwell's assistant had found in the car.

The police felt relieved. Motive, opportunity—the boy by his own admission had passed the Golden West shed alone in his car late on Monday evening, and had also been out alone in his car sometime between twelve-thirty and one—and now a nice concrete set of fingerprints at the scene of the crime.

CHAPTER TWELVE

Bonnie watched and waited for Rex to reappear in the shed. When, after forty-five minutes, he had not shown up, calmly she laid her knife down, stripped off her rubber gloves, and sidled out between the baskets and walked up to Ralph Musio.

"Where is my brother?"

Ralph looked unhappy. "I'm sorry, kid. They took him down to the police station to ask him some questions."

Bonnie's eyes dwelt dumbly on the foreman's face. Then, still looking at him, she reached behind her and unfastened her apron. Without a word she turned, rolling up the apron absent-mindedly, and headed for the rear door and the steps down to the outside.

"Hey," Ralph called after her. "Where you going?"

She turned her head, and said expressionlessly, "To look after my brother."

"But you can't do that. You can't just walk off and leave your position empty."

"You can take my position and stick it," she said coldly. And added with a baleful look, "Stool pigeon."

Ralph followed her, protesting, "Now you look here, kid, I didn't have nothin' to do with them picking Rex up."

"It was you came and got him for 'em," she said tonelessly, without turning her head. "I seen you."

"For Chris' sake, kid. They just told me, 'Bring Rex Maffey in to the office.' What're you blaming me for?"

Ralph stood at the top of the steps and watched her descend them and head for the cars around the side of the building. He pushed his hat back and uttered aloud, to himself, "Shock." That explained it, he thought, her acting so queer and turning on *him*, for God's sake.

Bonnie sat in the driver's seat of Rex's car, and with her fingers on the ignition keys, which had been left in place, realized that she must stop and think. No good rushing off in all directions. And it came to her. A lawyer. That was what Rex needed. But who? There was a guy with an office out in Little Oklahoma. But he wasn't good enough. It had to be a good one. And then she thought of Brian Rhodes. She'd read about him in the papers. He handled things like murder, and assault and battery, all the nasty, unpleasant things. She pressed on the starter purposefully.

Bonnie took the old brown stairs three at a time, mounting to Brian's office above a store building on Main Street. A young woman with an upswept hair-do and long red fingernails regarded Bonnie superciliously from under arched brows as Bonnie rested her fists on the desk inside the door.

"I've got to see Mr. Rhodes right away. It's an emergency." The young lady nodded haughtily at two occupied chairs. "There are people ahead of you."

"But this is an emergency."

"I'm sorry. You'll have to wait." The secretary poised a pencil efficiently over a sheet of paper. "Your name please."

Bonnie moistened her lips nervously, glanced at the other two people, and gave in. She told the woman her name, and sat in a chair at right angles to that of the man who had a long nose and loose folds of flesh on his cheeks, and who stared at her from faded blue eyes with his colorless lips slightly parted.

Soon a fluttery, overly made-up woman in a green suit with vermilion accessories came smiling out of the inner office, and the plump lady with a fan-shaped feather on her hat went in.

It seemed hours before the man with the long nose was admitted, to emerge looking as glum as ever, making it Bonnie's turn next. By this time it was past the secretary's usual lunch hour, and she revealed it by the grouchy look she directed at Bonnie.

Brian faced inquiringly toward the hatless girl in jeans and a short-sleeved shirt who sat leaning forward from the waist in the chair beside his desk. She was obviously tense as a fiddle string and he granted her his professional smile and the light, easy tone of voice, "Well now, what's your trouble?"

"It isn't me. It's my brother. He's just been arrested."

"Well," Brian smiled reassuringly, "that sounds serious. Suppose you tell me about it."

"We both work at the Golden West lettuce shed. You know about Mr. West being killed. Well, the cops picked up my brother this morning. They're going to pin it on him. He's down at the jail right now. He has to have a lawyer right away. And I've heard about you, that you're supposed to be good. So I came right away. I can pay you. I'm working steady. I may have to make it in installments, but you'll get your money eventually. You can look up our credit rating. It's good. And so—please   " She stood up. "Come with me right now. It's been an hour already; and he should have had a lawyer the first thing."

The girl could have no idea of the unsettling effect her words had on the man. Already Brian was weighing, considering, balancing one advantage over a corresponding disadvantage. A case involving Stanley West's murder was one that discretion indicated he stay clear out of. If anyone suspected the true state of his relations with the widow, it would look funny, his defending a man accused of making her one. However, might it not be the safest way to divert suspicion completely? When, after a decent interval, he married Laverne, people might think they had surely fallen in love *after* the tragedy; for if it had been previously, then Brian Rhodes would never have defended Stan's accused murderer.

His countenance had become an unrevealing mask.

"Did the officers charge your brother with murder?"

"I don't know. But they took him away from work; and they talked to him first in the office. So, regardless, he needs a lawyer. And honest"—her eyes were imploring—"he didn't do it."

Brian studied the face emptied of all expression save innocence. He supposed she really believed this. Even if the close relatives of the accused secretly feared their loved one had done it, they always convinced themselves he hadn't, and said so with this same air of passionate conviction combined with a look of ingenuous candor. It meant nothing that the sister sounded convincing.

Brian lowered his eyes and then glanced up through his lashes. "This is awkward," he said with engaging frankness. "Perhaps you didn't know; but Mr. West was a friend of mine. On that account I hesitate to enter the case. And if I did, I'd have to be pretty thoroughly convinced of my client's innocence."

"Who am I going to find around here that didn't know Mr. West?" Bonnie demanded flatly. "Who that's any good anyway? If you were a friend of his I should think that would be all the more reason for not wanting to see an innocent man take the rap."

"That's an interesting point of view," Brian smiled, stalling. He was tempted, and against all reason and common sense. There was something shocking about defending the man accused of murdering his sweetheart's husband; but the unexpected, the slightly bizarre had always appealed to him.

He surveyed the girl more carefully. Her conservatively cut brown hair was ruffled. If she had worn make-up earlier it had all been rubbed off during the day. Her shoulders were square under the clean shirt with the boyish collar. There was something, he realized, almost restful about her appearance, no part of which bore the signs of artifice, of camouflage. He thought of his secretary, with her skin always concealed under a pinkish-yellow coating, her hair lifted to stand unnaturally upright, her lips distorted into a shape not their own.

A little frown etched creases between Brian's brows as he stared down at the desk top. It hadn't occurred to him before. But suppose Laverne believed this boy had killed her husband, how would she take it if Brian defended him? That was something else to consider.

Bonnie waited patiently, although underneath the patience she was wild at the delay. Again Brian studied her from under his lashes. He could tell that she was still strung up like a tight wire, and in passing he admired the self-control with which she simply stood, and waited.

"I can't promise you I'll take the case," he heard himself saying, "until I talk to your brother. But I'll talk to him. Then I'll see."

"Please, please hurry then," she blurted out, "before they start beating him up or something."

Brian smiled, raising his eyebrows. "In Salinas? Police brutality?"

"Let's cut the comedy, huh? It's my *brother*."

"It might be a good idea if I knew his name." Brian rose to his feet, buttoning his jacket.

"Maffey. Rex Maffey. You're going there, *now?*"

"Yes, I'm going there. Now. And don't worry, Miss Maffey. He may be released already."

"Optimist," she muttered.

"And now you'd better go have your lunch and then go back to work. Give me a ring here before six o'clock, and I'll tell you how we came out."

"I'm going with you."

"You can't do anything. Just leave it to me. I'll see that your brother's rights are protected today; and if for personal reasons I find that I can't handle the case I'll suggest a good man for you."

Bonnie regarded him measuringly, and said, "O.K."

When Brian arrived at the police station Rex had not been subjected to the third-degree methods which Bonnie had feared. True, he was hungry, and thirsty, and he wanted a cigarette and even a few seconds surcease from questions; but no one had touched him physically.

Cass Huggins raised his eyebrows. "I expected somebody sooner or later, but I didn't expect you."

"Why not? Somebody has to see that the public enjoys its legal rights."

"We've got a city attorney," Cass said dourly, "to see to that. Anyways, we haven't booked your friend. Not yet. Just interviewing him."

"Yeah? Well, his sister has hired me to be present at the interview."

Cass shrugged. "O.K. We don't want any trouble. You can talk to him now, before we take him before the magistrate."

Brian pushed out his lips slightly. "So? That's how it is, eh?"

"That's how it is."

When Brian walked into the sparsely furnished office where Rex had been and where he was now enjoying a cigarette after a long, delicious drink of water, the boy looked up mistrustfully.

Brian introduced himself affably. "Your sister came to my office a while ago and engaged me to look after your interests."

Rex smiled involuntarily. "She did? She's a good kid, Bonnie."

"Yes," Brian said, "she is." And thought of the sturdy, plain little figure in work clothes who had stood courageously beside his desk. For there had been courage in the way she hung onto herself, controlled her fear, her desperate haste, asserted her brother's innocence when perhaps she wasn't even sure of it herself.

And Brian knew that he was licked, knew that from the start he had wanted to take the case, that he had been only postponing a decision. It was a rash thing to do. It could lead to all kinds of trouble and complications. But he was always committing impractical acts.

He sat down beside the plain oak table and ordered, "Well, let's have it." As he spoke, he studied the boy. Better looking than his sister, but not as straightforward, as open in manner. Scared now, of course. Not a typical juvenile delinquent, however—if there was such a thing. Dressed up in a quiet way, he'd make a good appearance in court. Clean-cut American youth. Maybe a little on the smart-aleck side, the way he handled his cigarette and smoothed down his curly hair and watched the lawyer with wary but defiant eyes.

Brian smiled at him. "They say there are two people you should always tell the truth to: your doctor and your lawyer. Keep that in mind. If I'm going to help you, I have to have the straight dope, good or bad."

"This is on the level? You'll stick with me."

Brian took a deeper breath than normal. "We're in this together now, Rex. Come hell or high water."

Rex relaxed visibly. In the next moment he looked younger, vulnerable, as if he were throwing himself dependently on the older man's strength.

"Well, first of all, I didn't do it."

"Good."

"But—well, if you have to know everything, I was there that night, in his office. For ten minutes maybe. He—he spoke to me in the afternoon and asked me to come in."

Although he seemed at ease Brian was as tense now as Bonnie had been earlier.

"Why?"

Rex did not look up. His finger traced the grain of the wood at the edge of the table.

"It was—about his daughter. Patty, her name is. I've been going out with her some lately. He told me to lay off."

"Why?" Brian repeated unemotionally.

Rex looked up with a trace of spirit. "Because I ain't good enough for one of the Wests to associate with in public. He said it wouldn't do her reputation no good."

Unconsciously Brian began to trace the wood's grain with his own finger.

"There wasn't more to it than that—something deeper, more serious?"

"Not as I know of. And it burned me up, I can tell you that."

"Yes," Brian agreed slowly, "it would."

He would have to feel out the ground here. The boy, Brian felt, was telling the truth as he saw it. A simple case of Mr. West not wanting his daughter to get emotionally involved with someone beneath her station in life. And that could be quite simply all there was to it. Brian realized that he actually knew little about Stanley West's real nature. Laverne had always been vague about her husband, never voiced any specific criticisms of him. The most definite thing she had ever said was: "There just doesn't seem to be anything *there* between us anymore, if you know what I mean. I'm sure he's fond of me, but—" Her eyes had been childishly puzzled. "It doesn't seem to mean anything."

To know him socially Stanley West hadn't seemed like the sort of man who would resort to petty tyrannies, especially those based on snobbery; but now it occurred to Brian afresh that there must have been flaws in the man's temperament that would help to account for the fact that his wife had been gradually turning into an alcoholic. He couldn't blame Stan entirely for the collapse of the marriage. Brian knew that Laverne had her own weaknesses which had contributed to it. But Rex's story made him more sure than ever that Stanley had been a destructive influence on Laverne. There was something archaically autocratic about this way of handling an unwelcome suitor.

Brian brought his mind back to his new client. "Did you quarrel?"

"How could I quarrel with Stanley West? He was my boss; he's older than me; he's Patty's father. All I could do was clam up and take it, and get out. He tried to get me to say I wouldn't see Patty anymore. But I wouldn't give him the satisfaction. All he could do was threaten to have me fired if I kept on seeing her."

"Did you see anyone else around when you came or left?"

"No. But the outside door was unlocked, and I came right into the outer office. The door to his office was open, and he called me to come in."

Brian frowned. "We'll have to look into this about the door. I suspect it's a night lock. Anybody leaving could lock it without having a key. What time were you there?"

"About ten-fifteen. He told me he'd be there between ten and eleven, had some work to do."

"Does anybody else know you were there?"

"I don't think so. I wasn't—proud of the whole deal; so I kept quiet about it. Then the next day, naturally, I didn't dare tell."

Brian quickly elicited the rest of the night's program from Rex.

"When you passed the shed again after leaving the Lucky Spot, was there still a light?"

"Yes. I noticed."

"Good. The other guys with you, did they notice?"

"I don't know. I didn't say anything."

Brian smiled. "I'll talk to them, prod their memories, eh?"

Rex's eyes brightened. "That's right. The light was off in the morning when Earl came. If the light was still on when I went by later, he must have still been alive."

"That's it. Now, did you notice if there was by any chance another car parked in front?"

"Not in front. But they park around to the side; and I don't know"—he frowned—"I was driving, see, and I'd had a drink or two, and if I did see it, it didn't make any impression; I didn't think nothing of it; but I sort of have a feeling there was another car back of Mr. West's." He shook his head irritably. "But it's just a vague feeling."

"We'll work on it," Brian said dryly. "Did you tell the officers you were in the office?"

"I didn't aim to," Rex replied unhappily. "I was going to stick right to it that I just drove by. But they acted like they *knew* I was there, and the first thing I knew I was admitting it."

"Did you know Mr. West kept a gun in his office?"

"I wouldn't have been surprised to hear it. He was that kind of a guy."

Brian surveyed his client curiously. "This isn't pertinent; but just for my personal curiosity, what did you think of Stanley West?"

"I never thought much about him one way or another, until lately, since I got to going out with Patty." Rex considered before continuing, "He's got a good reputation. Good guy to work for. But this business about me and Patty—naturally he didn't show up so good to me." Rex frowned. "But maybe, if you're going to be absolutely fair about it, maybe you can't blame him so much." He looked down at his hands uncomfortably. "Maybe he figured I—I was just out for what I could get." Rex's color had deepened. "Thought I was more interested in what—in where I could get to—through the girl—than—than in anything else. And so, like I said, maybe you can't blame him so much. He was looking out for his own interests, the way anybody would." Rex met the attorney's eyes candidly. "I think he was a guy that liked to be in control of the situation, and didn't like to—to give things up. A strong character, I guess you'd say."

Brian nodded thoughtfully.

CHAPTER THIRTEEN

Later Brian ate his lunch alone in a hotel coffee shop on Main Street. It was imperative that he talk to Laverne. If she believed Rex Maffey had killed Stanley, she might feel bewildered and hurt by his representing the boy. He would have to explain, make her understand. Her withdrawal from himself since the murder had been hard to take; but after his first puzzlement he had understood. She was being ultra discreet.

He was pleased at the way she had taken the whole business, the way she had squared her shoulders and lifted her chin and made her own decisions. Heartless as it sounded, Stan's death had probably been the best thing that could have happened to her. As Rex had said, Stan had been a strong character, and strong characters sometimes have a deleterious effect on the weaker beings forced into close contact with them.

It was the strain of charming weakness in Laverne that had attracted himself, Brian suspected, and the unconscious recognition of its complement in her nature, the bravery that had revealed itself in this crisis. Only the weak could know the true meaning of bravery.

Up to now he had never paused to examine the process by which he had become entangled with Laverne West. Clarice and his own marriage had provided the actual starting point, he supposed. He had met Clarice in San Francisco during the war. She was sleek and chic and glamorous; and it had seemed like a swell idea to have a wife waiting for him while he was overseas. Even when he returned and they bought a house and he took an office in Salinas, it had seemed like a good idea. It was hard to pick out the exact date when he realized that he didn't even like the girl he had married in a flurry of romantic excitement the week before he sailed for the South Pacific. At about the same time he had also realized—and that was an even worse fact to face—that she did not like him so well either. For one thing, Clarice had wanted him to make money faster, to spend more time cultivating the "right people." If his wife had had her way he would have joined every veteran's organization, service club, and fraternal order in town. The number of unprofitable cases he took on had irritated her increasingly; and she had, furthermore, soon decided that Salinas was the back door of creation. She missed San Francisco.

Laverne, he supposed, had been a sort of antidote for his own unsatisfactory domestic life.

With his elbows on the table Brian clasped his hands over his plate and frowned at the decal of water lilies on the coffee-shop wall.

There was no particular reason that it should have been Laverne who caught him. No reason except that she was herself supremely bored, nebulously rebellious, and ready to be flattered into receptivity by any personable male who would take the trouble to woo her attention. Of course, she was pretty; she was charming; and, he soon discovered, delightfully warm-blooded.

All these factors had been sufficient to start them on the irresponsible, and if he were to be honest, rather sordid course they had embarked upon, a course, he reflected now, that had been marked all the way by an undefined element of defiance on the part of each of them. Whether the defiance had been covertly directed toward their mates or toward society in general he could not quite determine.

In the course of their adventure, however, a change had taken place in himself. She began to mean more to him than a disguised means of assuaging frustration and disappointment and restlessness. He found himself not only wanting but liking her. And he realized that a similar phenomenon had occurred in her.

Somewhere along the line he had become fired with the determination to "save" her, through himself to give her a fresh start in life, one that would allow her to develop her capacities for happiness and self-fulfillment.

He lowered his hands, emerging deliberately from his reverie. He must not jeopardize their relationship by allowing any misunderstanding to arise over the Maffey case. Whether she liked it or not, he decided that he would call on Laverne that evening, get things straightened out between them.

When he came out on the street, however, he had gone only a few paces when he saw Laverne walking toward him, a small black hat crushed down over her bronze curls, a long, flat purse under her arm. In her sober costume, she looked businesslike and assured. But her expression was startled, uncertain, when she saw him.

"This is what I call a lucky break," he began warmly. "I had just made up my mind to talk to you if I had to break down a door to do it."

"Well—I haven't much time."

"Look, can we go back to the cocktail room for a drink?"

"You do beat all," she said wonderingly. "I've been a widow for four days, and you expect me to be seen drinking in public with a man."

He smiled boyishly. "The point is well taken. There seem to be certain lines along which my mind doesn't work properly. But we can go into the fountain down the street and have coffee. Surely that's respectable enough." His tone became more serious. "Please, Laverne. I've got to talk to you; something really important has happened."

"All right." She turned and they walked down the sidewalk together to the fountain café, which was not yet teeming with high school students as it would be in another hour.

When coffee had been served to them in a booth, Laverne eyed him questioningly. "Well?"

"It will be in tonight's paper. A young fellow named Rex works at the shed has been arrested, charged with killing Stan."

"No," she uttered softly, her face still.

"Yes. You see, somehow they found out he had been dating Patty and that Stan disapproved—"

Laverne leaned her elbow on the table and put her hand over her eyes. "I know. Patty told Farwell that this morning."

"Patty! I thought— I didn't think they got it straight from her. I thought they must have picked it up around town. Rex mentioned it, wondered if she told them. He kept trying to deny it to himself, I think. Didn't want to believe she put the finger on him."

Laverne let her hand drop and regarded Brian. "How do you know so much about it?"

"That's what I wanted to tell you. Maffey's sister came to me, asked me to take the case. I went down and talked to the boy, and—well, I agreed."

"*You* are going to defend him?"

"I tell you, Laverne, I don't think he did it."

She stared at him with an expression he could not interpret.

"And so, even though the whole thing is damned awkward, well, I felt I had to."

"I see." She looked away, turned the cup in its saucer. "Yes," she said slowly, "I can see how you'd feel that way—obligated to get him off."

Brian sighed. "That's a load off my mind. I was afraid that if you thought this kid was guilty, you would resent my defending him."

"I should think," she said in a low voice, not looking up, "that you would have found it wiser to keep out of this case."

"I should have. God knows I should have. But I let myself get sucked in. It was the sister, I think. She touched my sympathies. A hard-working, sober little thing, scared sick for her kid brother. Somehow I wanted to help them."

Laverne uttered a wry laugh. "Galahad on a white horse. But then—I suppose that's why I was drawn to you." Again she gave him that odd look. Then she went on in an ironical tone, "And do you know why Patty gave the police this lead—on Maffey? It was to protect me."

"You?"

"Of course. Have you forgotten how you came charging over last Tuesday morning to protect me from the cops? Well, things hadn't changed—up till now, it seems. They were still looking for motives, for me. And being in bed in a drunken stupor isn't much of an alibi."

Brian regarded her anxiously. "Of course, I knew they'd be investigating you; but I knew damn well you hadn't done it; and I thought they'd satisfied themselves on that angle."

"Now, it seems, they have. Patty fixed it. But good." Her low laugh was harsh. "And now you will try to save the boy's neck. The whole thing is like—what do they call it?—poetic justice."

Brian leaned forward with a concerned expression. "Darling, you're all strung up. You've got to try to relax. Don't let it prey on your mind. Whoever killed Stan, you couldn't have prevented it. Maybe it will never come out; maybe it will; but in the meantime it's only decent to try to save this kid if he didn't do it."

"If?" she said dryly.

"Even if he should have, he has a right to a good defense. And now that I'm in it, the whole thing loses some of its personal aspects for me. I want you to understand that. It becomes just my job, and so something apart from my personal life. As far as the case is concerned, to me it's no longer a matter of what my attitudes were to Stan or to you or to anyone else. It's—well, it's moved onto a different plane."

"It's a good trick if you can do it," she said dryly. Moving sideways on the bench, she got to her feet beside the table. "I won't expect to see you again until the case is over."

"But that may be weeks!"

"You should have thought of that. After all, when you're representing a man accused of killing a woman's husband, you can hardly expect it to look right if at the same time you're seeing the woman constantly."

Brian had risen to stand beside her, the check for their coffee in his hand.

"Laverne," he said quietly, "there's something bitter about you today. It's not like you."

Her eyes wavered under his gaze, and her lips quivered. "Nothing like this ever happened to me before," she murmured. "Maybe I haven't learned how one is supposed to act when it does."

She turned and walked out quickly through the caramel- and coffee-scented air of the little shop, while with a slight frown Brian stopped to pay the cashier.

Laverne hurried along to where she had found a parking place on a side street. A brisk wind was bringing the fog in from the west; and she had to hold her hand against the full folds of her skirt to keep it from swirling above her knees. She had not noticed that her car was directly in front of Chuck Willet's real-estate office, but as she opened the door to get in, Mr. Willet came out of his office and crossed the sidewalk to stand smiling down at her, and she guessed that he had been deliberately watching for her return. Drawing on her gloves, she looked up at him, nodding reservedly in response to his greeting.

"It's good to see you getting out again," he said blandly. "I was just saying to my wife the other day, 'It's wonderful the way Laverne is bearing up.' And, by the way, we've talked about it, Dora and me, want to have you and the kiddies over for dinner with us one of these days. I expect it's pretty lonesome for you folks around the house there by yourselves," he finished dolefully.

"Thank you." Laverne regarded him with blank eyes. She had never had the slightest use for Chuck Willet. She had been decent to him on account of Stan. Because he was a friend—or anyhow a sort of crony, of Stan. It came to her now with a sort of shock that she didn't have to be nice to him anymore if she didn't want to. She had always been sort of sorry for Dora though, Dora who was a little stupid, but kindly and timidly friendly, and who made a pathetic pretense that her husband's business was no different than anybody else's.

It was with a strange sense of power that Laverne said crisply, "Tell Dora I would be glad to have lunch"—she stressed the word slightly—"with her someday."

Chuck's dark, affable face hardened; and their eyes met steadily. Then Laverne turned the ignition key and devoted herself to the car. The man's expression was unpleasant as he walked back into his office.

Emma regarded him shrewdly and returned her attention to the papers on her desk. Chuck looked through the window at the back of Laverne's car pulling away. "Slut," he said through his teeth.

As she drove home Laverne let the scene with Chuck Willet fade from her mind as Brian again took over her thoughts. It was, as she had said, a sort of poetic justice that he should defend the man accused of committing the murder that he himself had done.

But if Brian *had* done it, would he have undertaken Rex Maffey's defense? Was he not, in fact, putting himself on the spot if he were guilty? He hadn't talked or acted like a man with murder on his conscience. Yet Brian was funny. Perhaps he wouldn't let it weigh on his conscience.

As she stopped the car in the garage, Laverne sat for a moment with her hands on the wheel. But how awful, if Brian were not guilty, that she had instantly assumed he was. And why had she? She remembered a book condensation she had read in the *Reader's Digest*. It was about psychology; and she recalled the part about subconscious wishes, how people were willing to impute to other people actions and motives that they wouldn't admit were their own. Had she subconsciously wanted to kill Stan herself, and so found it easy to think that someone else, even someone she loved, had been capable of doing it?

She pressed her knuckles in their soft kid covering against her teeth. The police had tried to find evidence against her. The wife was always a suspect. If she had evil unconscious desires that she didn't even know about ...

She had been feeling resentful toward Stan last Monday evening. *That* had been conscious. Almost everybody else had been at the cocktail party with somebody. But Stan hadn't wanted to go. He had been too busy to bother about *what* she did that evening. And there were the blank spots in the evening that she had recollected only when somebody refreshed her memory afterward.

She didn't believe that stuff about people "not remembering a *thing*" after they'd made asses of themselves when drinking. It was vague sometimes, but you could always recall if you tried. But suppose your mind didn't want to recall. She was sure she remembered going to bed. But suppose between Bill Jardine's leaving her at the door and the crawling into bed, she had done something else, like going to see for herself if Stan was really working.

She picked up her purse and stepped out of the car. She had to stop this. What was the saying? This way madness lies ...

CHAPTER FOURTEEN

Patty was sitting on the terrace, a magazine hanging from her hand. This side of the house was sheltered from the wind. Laverne dropped into the glider and pulled off her hat. Opening her purse, she took out her cigarette case and used the lighter on the end of it. Blowing out smoke, she looked at the girl.

"Anything new?" Patty said listlessly.

"I'm afraid so."

"What?"

"I ran into Brian downtown. He'd apparently just come from the courthouse. They picked up Rex Maffey this morning, and this afternoon he was charged with murdering your father."

With a rustle the magazine dropped on the flagstones and Patty's hand hung above it with the fingers limp.

"Brian is going to be his lawyer," Laverne went on. "He thinks," she said with her eyes sympathetically on the girl, "that Rex is innocent."

"I never thought," Patty said hoarsely, "that he really did it. He—he was supposed to be a red herring." Her stricken eyes were on Laverne. "Oh, Mother! What have I done?"

"Well, of course, Brian may be wrong. Maybe Rex did do it. The police must have more on him than just what you said. And if he is guilty, why, you did only what you should. Anyhow, in a thing like this, we're not supposed to withhold things. It's—it's against the law. So you can't be blamed."

"He'll hate me," Patty said in an empty tone.

Laverne looked at her with speculative eyes. "Did you— Were you very—fond of him?"

Patty twisted her hands together. "I don't know. He was cute. He—intrigued me. He was different. I—yes, I liked him. I wasn't—gone; but I liked him."

"Do you think he was in love with you?"

Patty's manner was becoming less dazed. She pulled herself more erect in the reclining chair, frowning a little as she considered the question. "No. No, I don't think he was. Oh, I think he found me attractive; but he wasn't out of his depth. Now that I think of it, there was something sort of—calculating in his manner toward me."

"How did he take it when you told him your dad had forbidden you to go out with him?"

"He didn't like it. He didn't say much; but it—it didn't set well."

Laverne gazed out across the grass to the back fence. "It occurs to me—a little late, I'll admit—that naturally I knew nothing of all this. Your father didn't bother to consult me. He had to handle it in his own inimitable way, with all the subtlety of a steam roller. And now look."

"Well, you had met Rex, right here at the house. You knew, or were supposed to, and apparently didn't care," Patty rejoined with a slightly puzzled glance.

"That's right," Laverne said slowly. "But maybe that was wiser, after all. Not to notice. Although I'll admit I didn't deliberately plan it that way. But at least I gave you credit for sense enough to handle your own affairs. You have to start doing it sometime."

The girl's attention was fully upon her mother now. "You know something?" she blurted out. "You've changed, just in these few days." She frowned. "You're more—grown-up."

Laverne's eyes rested upon her daughter, startled. Then she uttered a dry laugh. "That, my darling, was a rather revealing statement. Maybe," she added more soberly, "it's the responsibility."

As she spoke, Lula appeared at the french doors behind them. "Mr. Schmidt is here, Mrs. West. He wanted to know if you were home."

"I didn't hear the chimes."

"He knocked on the side doors, saw me inside."

"Tell him to come on out."

When Hal appeared in the doorway Lula had vacated, Laverne called pleasantly, "Hope you don't mind being received out here. When I got home from downtown I flopped in the first chair I came to."

"Just thought I'd stop and 'Hello.' How are you, Patty?" He seated himself beside Laverne in the swing, and offered further, "Joan went to the beach this afternoon; and I knew she wouldn't be home yet."

"I know. She took the twins with her. Would you like a drink?"

"If you're having one. I guess it's about that time of day."

"Patty, would you go ask Lula to bring us a drink out here? I'll have bourbon and soda. What for you, Hal?"

"Same thing'll be fine."

With secret amusement Laverne mused that if she had chosen a Pink Lady, Hal would have said, "The same thing." Always agreeable, careful to be no trouble.

When Patty had gone Hal turned to Laverne with a solemn expression. "I didn't want to say anything in front of the kid. But did you know they've made an arrest?"

"Yes, I heard."

"Oh." He looked disappointed. "Well, I guess it's kind of a relief, at that. It was bad, not knowing."

"This won't be exactly fun either," Laverne responded shortly. "A trial and all that."

"No. No, I should say not. Especially"—he lowered his voice sympathetically—"since I understand Patty is involved—indirectly, of course."

"News does get around, doesn't it?" Laverne observed wearily.

"Is it true Brian's taking this fellow's case?"

"I wouldn't know. But it isn't surprising, I suppose, if he is. He seems to get most of the county's big criminal cases lately."

"I just thought, his being a friend of the family and all—"

"Primarily he's a lawyer, isn't he? It's his business, things like that."

"Well, yes; but—"

Lula came out carrying a tray which she set on the metal coffee table before the glider.

As Hal raised his glass, he said flippantly, in an attempt to change the mood, "Well, here's to conviction."

Laverne had always been kindly disposed toward Hal. She took him for granted as her friend's husband, with almost no emotional reaction to him. This afternoon, however, she found him strangely irritating.

"Arrest doesn't necessarily mean guilt," she snapped.

Hal changed his tune quickly. "No, of course not. Guess I spoke without thinking. A person should always reserve judgment in things like this."

Irrelevantly Laverne thought, "I wonder what it is he wants." And answered herself in the next beat of thought, "The loan, of course. Now, I hold his note, not Stan." It was surprising the way now she sympathized with Stan's position on the matter, when before she had thought that without question it was only right to keep carrying Hal—for friendship's sake.

He had apparently decided it would be wise to change the subject and began to talk about whom he had seen at luncheon in a new restaurant out on the San Juan road which specialized in broiled spareribs. Laverne let him run on while she pondered wonderingly on her change of attitude. Now that she was responsible for taking care of what assets the West family had, of seeing to it that those assets grew rather than diminished, things looked different. She could understand Stan's attitude better.

She was quite sure that Hal would get around to the subject before he left her. It was with an odd little feeling of triumph at the vindication of her hunch that she heard him saying, "There was something I wanted to mention to you, a little matter between Stan and me that you probably didn't even know about—"

"Yes?" Her eyes were blue and innocent.

"Stan let me have some money a year or so ago; and somehow we just let it slide. He didn't need it, and so I just put off paying—" He broke off and laughed. "Which was to his advantage, naturally. The interest I owe keeps growing, you see. Well, I meant to take care of it this summer; but I'll tell you, the way it is, I'd rather wait now until along toward the end of the year, when the fall deal's over. Gives me a little more leeway in the business, you see. So, if that's O.K. with you, when the estate's being settled, you can just let this ride a month or two the way Stan was planning to."

Laverne could not keep looking at him with her assumed childlike candor. When Stan had mentioned Hal's predicament to her, she had thought she felt sorry for the poor guy. But she realized now that her response then had been a facile surface sentiment that barely touched her real feelings. For now she felt something real and painful. The man's desperation had meaning now. She could feel it.

And that made it harder to handle. For now there was a real conflict of interest. If she found that Stan's financial affairs could not endure the absence of this outstanding money, to protect herself and her children she was going to have to foreclose the note and help to ruin her best friend's husband.

"I can't give you an answer right now, Hal. I haven't had time to go into our affairs yet. But next week I'm going to go over the books with Earl and with Mr. Phillips, Stan's attorney. I haven't even made up my mind whether to sell the business or to try to manage it myself."

"Well, whatever you do about that, I'm sure Stan left things in good shape, and there's not much doubt that you could afford to hold this note personally a little longer."

She made herself smile at him winningly. "You can be sure, Hal, that I'll give it serious thought. By the end of next week, say, I ought to be able to give you a definite answer."

When he had gone she sat slumped in the padded swing, looking little and tired in her dark dress. For the first time she missed Stan, really missed him. She had had no idea how much his presence had protected her from. How many problems, how many decisions. No conscious idea, at any rate. Perhaps, though, she had felt what he meant to her, felt the warm padding his strength and authority had wrapped around her. Perhaps that was why she had hesitated at making the definitive break with him that Brian had urged upon her.

CHAPTER FIFTEEN

Stanley West had considered Ralph Musio one of the best shed foremen in the valley. Besides supervising the whole operation of the shed itself, from the unloading of trucks to the reloading of refrigerated freight cars, a shed foreman must deal with inspectors, truck drivers, an assortment of unclassifiable wanderers in and out of the work area, and most important of all, his crew, over half of whom are women.

Ralph could be tough; he could be jocular; and on rare occasions he could administer sympathy if he thought it necessary. It was his girls upon whom it was most often necessary to exercise these various approaches. Women at work were more unpredictable than men. They got into squabbles that had to be refereed; they gave you to understand that if they weren't working at quite top speed on this particular day, it was because of mysterious ailments that a mere man could not be expected to appreciate; sometimes they sulked at their packers; they had been known to burst loudly into tears over a mild reprimand, or to turn on their foreman with invective delivered in a limited but colorful vocabulary that would have surprised anyone whose knowledge of the female sex was restricted to perusal of ladies' magazines. And they did these things with the smug knowledge of support from their trade union in case the foreman became arbitrary about firing.

But they turned out the work. And if Ralph was one of the more competent men in his line, it was because he never forgot that elementary fact. So, even in the face of Bonnie's anarchic behavior, he was prepared to overlook it when she showed up at two o'clock, having eaten her lunch and calmed down sufficiently to go back to her position.

"What d'you expect me to do?" he complained. "Leave Freda alone while you gallivant around town? I called the union and got a relief girl in. I didn't expect you back."

Bonnie shrugged. "O.K. So are you telling me I'm off for the afternoon?"

"I suppose I can let her stand by for the rest of the day, to relieve dames goin' to the can. But, I'm telling you, if it was anybody else, you'd just lose a day's pay, that's what. But I realize the circumstances are unusual. So go on back to your place."

As she turned away, he queried, "Uh—d'you find out anything? What's the score?"

"I dunno. All I know is I got a lawyer for Rex. He went down to the jail an hour ago. I'm supposed to call him up after work."

"Tough," Ralph commiserated. "Personally, I don't get it."

"Neither do I."

"Well, say—" Ralph seemed slightly embarrassed. "If you want to call this lawyer, later on, to relieve your mind, it's O.K. Just go on in and ask Earl to use the phone."

Bonnie smiled. "Thanks." She started to turn away; then looking over her shoulder, she halted. "You know," she said with a little chuckle, "you ain't so tough, Ralph."

"Gwan!" His tone was rough, but he grinned.

The girl who had taken her place relinquished it willingly. "This is a break for me. Now all I gotta do is wait for some dame to have a hemorrhage or get the high-strikes."

"What got into you?" Freda demanded. "All of a sudden oopsy-daisy!— you've took off."

The girl behind Freda, and Alice at Bonnie's back, turned sideways to listen.

"You probably know," Bonnie said dully. "They took Rex to the station to question him about Mr. West."

"That's what we heard," Ray said.

"What would *he* know?" Freda prompted avidly.

"Don't ask me, I didn't get to see him. But I hired a lawyer to go down and get him out. Brian Rhodes."

"Good deal," Ray approved, his hands never missing a movement in their precise handling of the lettuce heads. "He'll spring 'im, O.K. That's allays the first thing to think of if you get tangled up with the cops. Keep your mouth shut and demand a lawyer. You shouldn't never tell 'em nothing."

"God, though," Freda observed, "Rhodes. He costs money. What'd he nick you for?"

"I don't know."

"You don't know!"

"I forgot to ask."

"She forgot to ask. Well, blow me up and call me a balloon."

"You don't think about money when your kid brother's in a jam," Bonnie retorted.

"Kid, I *always* think about money. It don't pay not to."

"I don't think Rhodes is so bad that way," Ray put in encouragingly. "Ain't lawyers kinda like doctors, fit their fee to your pocketbook?"

"That ain't the way I heerd it," Freda denied. "Blood suckers, that's what they are, reg'lar blood suckers. Any time you need a lawyer, they know they got you by the short hairs, and brother, they make the most of it."

After a while Bonnie was afraid it would be she who would go into the hysterics the relief girl had anticipated that afternoon. They meant well, Freda and Ray, and the two girls on either side of her and Freda; but they would not get off the subjects of why Rex had been picked up, of how cops conducted themselves, of the shortcomings of the legal profession, and always the refrain of Money. It seemed indecent to think of money at a time like this; but Bonnie found herself doing so. As Freda had suggested, the cost—especially if they had arrested Rex and if he was to be tried— would be appalling. And with Rex in jail, it would all be up to her. Still holding the trimming knife, she pressed the cold rubber back of her glove against her forehead. Bonnie wasn't the type to cry easily. It had been a long, long time since it had done her any good to cry; but now she felt like leaning against the metal basket and bawling her head off.

At a quarter to four she felt that she had waited long enough; and she left her post to walk down to the office, conscious of the eyes that followed her, all with curiosity, most with sympathy.

Earl Fowler had courteously offered her his own chair while she made the call, tactfully fiddling with papers in the filing cabinet and keeping his back turned.

When he heard her say "Good-by," he turned to look at her. She just sat there, and narrow bars of fog-diluted sunlight from the venetian blinds made stripes across her faded blue shirt. Earl moved forward.

"Bad news?" he asked gently.

She raised her eyes to his dully, and nodded, and kept looking at him. "They've arrested Rex—for murder."

Earl saw her eyes become shiny, and just as he realized it was from tears, a drop formed and rolled down her cheek.

"Gee, kid, I'm sorry." He touched her shoulder.

She put her hands over her face then, and her shoulders began to shake.

Earl watched her uncomfortably. "You just go ahead and cry," he said unnecessarily after a moment. "I—I'll get you a drink of water."

She was fishing a wrinkled handkerchief out of her pants pocket when the door opened to admit Ralph. He regarded her worriedly and raised his eyebrows at Earl who nodded unhappily.

Ralph, too, patted her shoulder; and after Bonnie had blown her nose Earl handed her a paper cup full of water. He wasn't quite clear as to why he thought she needed water; but Earl figured that when a woman cried you had to give her something.

She sipped at it and handed the cup back. Hoarsely she said, "He never did it. Never." She controlled her face, and said quaveringly, defiantly, "The bastards."

"It's a tough break," Ralph commented inadequately.

Suddenly Earl spoke up as if against some inner deterrence, "I don't believe he did it."

Bonnie lifted her eyes to him gratefully.

Ralph's tone lacked conviction; but he seemed to feel Earl had established the etiquette for the occasion. "Sure he didn't." He paused, at a loss, then went on heartily, "You got a good lawyer anyway. If I was you, honey, I wouldn't worry. Rhodes'll get him off. Tell you what, you just pull yourself together and run along home." He looked across at Earl for confirmation. "We'll fix it up so you get a full day's pay."

"Sure," Earl concurred. "Sure. You go home and get some rest, and we'll see you in the morning."

Bonnie had risen after wiping her eyes. She stuffed the handkerchief into her hip pocket with a boyish gesture.

"Thanks, you guys." Her tired face pulled itself into a sardonic grin. "Looks like I'm going to need every damn day's pay I can get. And overtime too."

"Here, go out this door," Earl offered hospitably.

When she had gone the men looked at one another.

"They must have somep'n' pretty serious on him. Tough on the kid. Old man's an invalid, and there's another kid younger'n' them, still in high school."

"I don't believe he did it," Earl repeated himself.

"O.K. then. Who do you think did?"

"I got my own ideas," Earl said doggedly, "but I'm not talking."

"If you know anything you ain't told, you damn well better spill it to the cops."

"I don't actually know anything; all I got is ideas."

"Well, I dunno. It could have been young Maffey. He's a cocky young devil. Thinks he's plenty hot stuff. Him and Bonnie ain't no more alike than nothing."

"Well—maybe."

CHAPTER SIXTEEN

When Bonnie did not come back to her place, it was as good as telling the other workers what had happened. Talk buzzed and soared and settled like a swarm of bees over the noisy shed. Nobody heard the ball game being broadcast over the radio. Speculation was rife. Had he? Hadn't he? What it finally boiled down to, however, was a rumbling undertone of resentment.

"Ain't it just what they'd do? Sure, it has to be one of us. Do they look around amongst his swell friends? Hell, no. Pin it on some poor working stiff. That's the easiest way out. Lay it onto some poor devil that can't afford a lot of expensive lawyers. You watch; they'll throw the book at him. And if it was Mrs. West or some of their society friends, hell, they'd be out in a year."

The redhead, Sandy, thrust her pointed breasts out more sharply under the bright green sweater and observed shrilly, in her slightly southern voice, "That sweet kid! Why, I just don't believe it nohow. He's nothin' but a baby. I just don't believe that sweet kid ever picked up no old .45 and fired it at Mr. West."

"I've thought all the time you was sweet on Rex Maffey," Fred commented smugly.

"Why, Fred Jackson, if you don't have the *worst* mind. A girl can't say a friendly word to a nice boy but you ain't ready to misinterpret."

"Nobody's misinterpretin' you, baby," Fred assured her equably.

Sandy shrugged haughtily. "It's just no use talking to some people. They got such low type of minds."

She turned so that her right shoulder instead of her bosom pointed at the packer, and retired into aristocratic silence. Gradually her plucked brows straightened to point at each other across two faint vertical lines above her nose. Sandy had less to say than usual in the hour before quitting time.

Sandy shared an apartment with another girl in a court north of the park on the west side of town. That evening after their dinner, whose main course had been canned beans and weiners, she sat in one corner of the Monterey-style sofa that opened into a bed at night, and looked over the evening paper. Frowning, she read the article about Rex's arrest, and her eyes paused on the line mentioning that Brian Rhodes was his attorney. That she had not known previously.

Sandy had taken off her loafer shoes and her socks, and she lowered the paper and watched her bare toes with their crimson nails wriggle against the plaid upholstery of the couch cushion. Through the bathroom door she could hear the water in the shower where her girl friend was cleaning up for a date.

She lifted her arm absent-mindedly and pulled back the net curtain to look out at an identical net-curtained window facing her across a plot of grass bisected by a cement trunk with narrower grey stems leading to the steps of each apartment.

She had seen Brian Rhodes around town and had learned somewhere that his wife was in Reno. All in all, with his looks and social position and his glamorous profession, Rhodes was an exciting man. And she liked Rex. He was just a kid, of course, and she had been a little piqued because he did not seem susceptible to her charms; but she still felt like giving him a hand. It was not smart though. But definitely not smart to go getting mixed up in this. Still ...

What she knew didn't amount to a lot; and it had never entered her head to go to the cops with it. It wasn't her place to do their work for them. But this was something else again. Her eyes became dreamy as she planned what to wear for the call on Brian. She went on to picture herself on the witness stand. Black, for the trial. In the movies they always wore black in courtroom scenes. But for seeing Brian at his office, her tailored brown suit and maybe the chartreuse blouse and the brown suede pumps.

She waited until morning to tell Connie, her roommate, that she was not going to work until noon.

"God, kid," Connie protested, "you've taken off twice already this month. Ralph ain't going to put up with it indefinitely. First thing you know you'll get the sack."

Sandy smiled complacently. "Don't you worry about li'l ol' me."

"Boy," Connie said wonderingly, "how you do it I'll never know. If it was me I'd of got canned a long time ago. Furthermore," she added accusingly, "how'm I gonna get to work, if you ain't drivin' down?"

"Call up Lil, and have her and Gerald stop by for you."

Sandy had her own car, a secondhand Ford convertible that she was still paying for. She drove downtown in it, and at nine-thirty, in the costume she had thought suitable, her bright hair glowing hatless above the snug shoulders of the brown gabardine jacket, Sandy presented herself to the haughty Gladys who in turn ushered her into Brian's private office.

When she had introduced herself and settled into the client's chair with her knees crossed, Sandy began, "I heard you're taking Rex Maffey's case."

"That's right."

"Like I said, I work in the Golden West shed. And I know Rex. So when I heard he'd been arrested, I just says to myself, 'Why, that little old kid never killed nobody.'"

Brian smiled. "That's my opinion too. I only hope we can persuade a jury to share it."

"From what I hear," Sandy said archly, "he couldn't have no better mouthpiece—uh, I mean, attorney."

"Thank you." Brian smiled again, and waited.

"What I got to tell you," Sandy said modestly, "may not amount to nothin'; but I reckon you never know. Some little old thing that you don't think much about at the time, well, it just could be an important clue."

"That's right."

"So I got to thinkin', and I says to myself, 'Well, I'm just goin' to go see Mr. Rhodes, and for what it's worth, tell him what I seen.'"

Brian pulled a sheet of paper toward him unobtrusively, his pen hovering over it.

"That night, last Monday, me and a friend had went to the show downtown, and we decided to go out and have a bite to eat at a place about a mile south of town. They have the best hamburgers there. 'Lettuce Inn' it's called." She paused to smile questioningly. "Get it? 'Let us in.' Kinda cute, ain't it? Well, just this side of the shed—on the other side of the street, of course—we was goin' south, you understand—my friend says, 'Christ, I believe I've got a flat.' The car was riding kind of bumpy like. So he pulled up to the curb, and got out, and walked around the front to look at the tires, but sure enough, he didn't have no flat atall. It was just them bumpy streaks of tar or something that they patch the concrete with. Well, we was parked sort of kitty-corner from the shed, and I glanced over, and I could see the side windows up front and the driveway alongside; and I thought to myself, 'Old Stan's sure sitting up late tonight.' The light was on in his private office, see; but not in the front office where Earl works. And then my friend gets back in and says, 'False alarm, thank God. I ain't in no mood to go changin' tires.' An' before he starts up again, he gets out his cigarettes, and we both light one— By the way," she broke off, lifting the flap of her purse, "d'you mind if I have one now—"

Brian concealed his impatience as he gallantly held the desk lighter to her cigarette, the while she smiled up at him through obviously false black lashes.

She exhaled and went on, leaning back in the chair. "So any-ways, I looked over toward the shed again, and the light went off right while I was a-lookin'. And then we pulled out."

"Were there any other cars besides Mr. West's in the driveway?"

"That's what I was fixin' to tell you. We was parked kitty-corner, like I said; and, you know, I saw it and never gave it a second thought. Stan's car right where it usually is, and just beyond it, parked right parallel with its nose to the building, like Stan's, there was another car."

"Good," Brian exclaimed softly, his eyes bright. "What kind of a car?"

"Gee, I don't know that. All I could see was the rear end. The closest light on the road was way back at the intersection. All I can swear to is that there was another car next to his."

"Well, can you describe its rear end? What kind of bumper and taillights it had, anything distinguishing about it?"

"No-o. No, all I can say is it wasn't dark like Stan's. His is dark blue, you know. It was a light color, that's all I know."

"What time was this?"

"A little after twelve?"

"How do you place the time?"

"Well, it was ten after when we came in the restaurant. I happened to notice."

"Fine."

She widened her eyes at him. "I sure do hope this'll be a help."

"It will. It will indeed. You didn't tell this to the police?"

"I didn't aim to get mixed up in it. Till now when I see they're making Rex the fall guy."

"You know you should have come forward with this information," he chided.

"Mr. Rhodes," she mourned, "you're not going to get little old me in trouble, are you, when I just wanted to help?"

"Don't worry. You are, in fact, going to be one of my star witnesses. I'll just call Gladys in now to get this down and she'll type it up for an affidavit."

"Won't I get to go on the stand?" Sandy exclaimed in disappointment.

"This is just a precaution. In case, well, of accident, in case for some reason you should be unable to appear at the trial."

"Oh, I'll be there," she assured him.

"Another thing. If you haven't told this story to anyone else, don't do it. It'll be more effective if the prosecution doesn't get wind of it."

"Oh, I wouldn't dream of breathing it to a soul. But, look, Mr. Rhodes, could you give the shed a ring and speak to Ralph Musio? Tell him you had to interview me about the case and that's the reason I didn't show up this morning?"

"I'll be glad to."

"I'd sure appreciate it, Mr. Rhodes," she purred with a cozy smile.

Sandy swung out onto the street jauntily after her talk with Brian. He was interested, she was pretty sure. His eyes had that appraising look, and he had smiled so often, and been so polite. Who knew, this might work into something. Sandy felt pretty pleased with herself. It had been a smart hunch, coming forward with this testimony. Smart all the way around. "All the way around," she repeated to herself complacently.

The windows of Brian's private office overlooked the side street. He stood before one of them, watching the red-headed girl as she took the few steps east toward Main Street, and crossed, going south.

A faint smile curved Brian's lips. Opportunity, if he had not missed the signs, had just knocked at his door. His face sobered. Had the same opportunity been offered to Stanley West, and had Stanley been more on his toes to accept than Brian had? After all, the girl worked for Stan. She might have used her job to catch the boss's eye.

Still, there had been no gossip about Stan along those lines. For his amusements he had been reputed to have restricted himself to carefully selected professionals. It was safer for a man who cared about his community standing. The girls with whom Stan West amused himself did not talk, after hours.

Brian's mouth tightened between set jaws; and he admitted to himself that he hated Laverne's husband, even in death. In fact, he disliked all people who were calculating in their personal lives. In business, in your work, yes; a man schemed and planned. But there was something repellent to him about a character whose personal emotions were ordered and pragmatically controlled, who never gave way to impulse, generous or otherwise. He had not quite recognized it before; but he was beginning to see that Stanley West had been one of those people who knew exactly what he wanted and had no compunctions about how he went about getting it.

He supposed that was why Laverne had been so wishy-washy about whether she would divorce Stan or not. He had achieved what he wanted in life: financial security, the respect of his world, a nice home, a nice wife, three lovely children. He did not want it changed; and Laverne had shrunk from pitting her own depleted moral strength against his stronger will, which in this case was set upon maintaining the *status quo*.

Brian hooked his finger in the blind pull and absently rolled the shade up and down, frowning into the street that crawled with slowly moving cars.

Laverne had wanted Stan to love her. But she had never realized it was a losing fight. Stanley could not live with anything he could not manage, and he could not respect anyone he could manage.

That was what had baffled Laverne. She was held captive by the knowledge that Stan wanted to keep her. Yet she sensed, without understanding it, that her husband's regard for her was like the feeling one might cherish for a beautiful Persian cat lying on a silken cushion, purring and arching its neck to a caressing hand. And as a human being she had revolted against the role.

CHAPTER SEVENTEEN

That afternoon Brian talked again to Rex. The boy looked pale, his eyes a little feverish, as if after twenty-four hours of confinement he had at last fully grasped the significance of what was happening to him.

Brian's manner was full of cheer and encouragement. "Things are coming along fine. We already have some fresh testimony. You know a girl named Cassandra Dooley?"

Rex looked blank.

"Good-looking redhead who works in your shed," Brian prompted.

"Oh, *Sandy*," Rex said in a tone of illumination. Then his eyes grew suspicious. "She gettin' mixed up in this?"

"In a way. Why? Don't you like her?"

Rex looked slightly uncomfortable. "Well, she ain't exactly a nice girl."

"That may be; but you'll see she's a good friend of yours when I tell you what she came to offer us." Brian then went on to recount Sandy's story.

Rex listened thoughtfully. "Gee," he murmured, "that sounds O.K."

"If we could just get a better description of that car. If we can dig up somebody else who saw it there. The trouble is, it was pretty well hidden from the highway, and in dim light."

"Light-colored, she said," Rex pronounced thoughtfully. "That ain't much to go on."

"No. But it's specific. It shows she did see a car there around midnight when the light went out."

"If only," Rex muttered, "we knew whose it was."

Brian bit at the inside of his lower lip, his mind reverting to Laverne, who had said that until Patty implicated Rex, the police had suspected her. So now, if he cleared Rex, might not a good many other people go back to suspecting Laverne? It would be neat, very neat, if they could pin it on somebody else. Say, the owner of that light-colored car.

Concentrating, he ran over the people he knew and whom Stan would have known whose cars were light in color. Bill Jardine, for one. He had a pale grey sedan. And the Schmidts' old station wagon; it was yellow. But surely any eye would register the difference between a station wagon and a regular automobile, even from the rear. With relief he recalled that Laverne's little foreign car was black, and that the Wests' family machine, a Buick, was light blue. There was her sister Edith; her and Bob's car was a light tan. But why would either Edith or Bob kill their brother-in-law?

"It's a needle-in-a-haystack business," he said ruefully, "looking for that car. But this girl Sandy's testimony may be just the feather's weight to get you off."

"Old Sandy," Rex said ironically, "never thought she'd be all that stood between me and San Quentin."

Brian ate his lunch alone and preoccupied at a hotel coffee shop on Main Street. When he was finished he drove out to the West residence. Whether it was discreet or not, whether Laverne liked it or not, he had to have help from Stan's family in getting evidence for Rex's defense.

He told Lula, who opened the door, that he wished to speak to Mrs. West. "On business," he added pleasantly.

Lula was quiet, self-contained, and sensible. Brian sometimes suspected that she knew more about the Wests than any of them realized she did.

"Yes, Mr. Rhodes," she now said imperturbably.

As he waited in the living room, pacing about and smoking, Brian realized with a faint sense of surprise that he felt better about Laverne because Lula was there. Lula came in only by the day, and somewhere down on the edge of Chinatown she had a residence that was the base of a life of her own. He had no idea what that life was. A husband perhaps. While she differed as much as it was possible to from the fat, ungrammatical, invincibly jolly stereotype of the female Negro servant of fiction and the movies, Lula did share one of that type's reputed qualities; and that was loyalty to her employer.

Brian stood before the long window facing the street and thought idly that Lula was probably in actuality one of Laverne's best friends. He smiled faintly, picturing the shocked look of surprise that would settle on Laverne's face if he expressed that thought to her. According to the standards that Laverne unthinkingly accepted from the society about her, it was impossible for either a servant or a Negro to be a personal friend of a woman like herself.

Yet Brian had gathered from casual remarks tossed off by Laverne what the actual relationship between the two was. She and Lula often worked together at household tasks, folding and putting away laundry, polishing silver, changing slip covers on furniture. They sometimes took morning coffee together, or ate leftovers for lunch in the kitchen. And they talked. Laverne inadvertently revealed their easy companionship by such offhand observations as, "Lula says I don't look well in green, makes my skin look sallow," or, one day when she was discussing Patty, "Well, as Lula said, it's no use worrying about your daughter's morals or her sex life. If she hasn't just naturally adopted her family's way of thinking on those things by the time she's sixteen, you're licked anyway."

And one day when he and Laverne had left the Jardine house together after having cocktails there, Laverne had commented laughingly, about the Jardine's maid, who was also colored and who had obvious bunions and who sang mournful hymns in the kitchen, "I don't see why Rose keeps that Martha. Did you notice how when she passed the tray she looked as if she wished the *canapés* were sprinkled with arsenic? Every time I see her at Jardine's I'm thankful for Lula, even if she doesn't sleep in, like Martha. At least Lula acts as if she *liked* us."

"Who wouldn't like you?" Brian had responded promptly.

It was a comfort now, though, Brian mused idly, to know that Laverne had someone unobtrusively in the background in her own house who did honestly like her, who was, whether Laverne admitted the status or not, a real friend of hers.

He turned from the window as he heard her step on the stairs. She halted in the archway, and frowned.

"Brian, for God's sake, I thought we settled it that you were not to come here. There's a limit to what I can take, you know."

"Look," he protested in a low tone, "this call is no more personal than if you were Mrs. John Doe whom I had never laid eyes on before. I'm trying to save a man's life; and I need help. I've got to have something to go on, and for me as well as for the prosecution, you're one of the main sources of information."

Uncertainly she advanced and sank into an armchair. "O.K., what now?" she said wearily.

He pulled up a small chair to face her and sat on it, leaning forward with his elbows on his knees.

"I can trust you not to mention anything I say to anybody?"

"Of course."

"Well, I've got hold of a. shred of information ..." And he repeated what Sandy had told him. "Now do you know anybody that knew Stan either personally or in a business way who has a light-colored car?"

"It's not much to go on," she said slowly. "So many cars nowadays are light grey or blue or a pale tan." Suddenly her gaze alighted on his face with a quizzical expression. "Your own car," she added softly, "is pale grey."

Brian clasped his hands and worked the fingers together. "Yes, but I've been thinking, those shades you spoke of, like my car, at night and not under direct light, they're simply neutral, don't give an impression of any color. I think what she saw would have been something with a yellow tinge, almost white."

"Bill and Rose Jardine's car, the one we were out in that night, it was yellow. Very sporty. But, my God, no one could tell me Bill Jardine killed Stan. The Jardine brothers, why they've got everything."

"It doesn't necessarily mean that whoever was there at midnight shot Stan; but it does mean that somebody saw him alive after Rex was supposed to have killed him—"

"Wait," Laverne said, and put her fingers to her cheek. "Bob Wakely, our field man; he drives a yellow club coupé. It's always a mess, dirty and muddy from plowing around on back roads and right out into the fields where the crews are. But Bob—Why, Stan trusted him. He's been with us for years."

"Look, can you find out for me if he has an alibi for that night, and if so what it is. The district attorney—Keith Coletto—he'll know; but they'll keep all the dope they can from me."

"I suppose all I'd have to do is ask him," she said hesitantly.

"Well, will you?"

"Yes."

"Ask questions, will you, of Earl, of your friends. Keep your eyes and ears open and tell me anything that might be a lead."

She smiled crookedly. "I'm no detective, you know."

"No, but who else is in a better position to find out things, who is closer to the whole thing than you are?"

Laverne leaned back and regarded the intent man with a whimsical expression.

"This is pretty weird, do you know that? You and me, of all people, hustling around trying to solve the—the murder."

Brian's eyes dropped. "Well, in a way, it's—fitting, isn't it? I suppose we both have a—well, some sense of guilt—about Stan; so maybe it's a belated form of atonement, trying to bring retribution to the person who killed him."

Laverne leaned forward with her hands clenched on the chair arms. "Brian," she blurted out, "right at first, I thought it was you."

"Me!"

Her eyes searched his startled face. "I was wrong. I see that now. It must have been that sense of guilt you just spoke of."

"Yes." He looked down. "It must have been. Because I can't even blame you for thinking that. Though why we should feel guilty I can't see. Maybe Stan stopped for a while—after this Marcia you told me about, when you threatened to divorce him. But there isn't much doubt he had another side to his life again, later, his—amusements, even though he kept them quiet so as not to humiliate you."

"I guess so," she said bleakly.

"So there's really no reason for any bad conscience on your part, or on mine."

She put her head against the chair back. "That's not the problem now though, is it? The problem now is to save this kid." She regarded Brian gravely. "The—girls, in Stan's life—if there were girls— I always thought it was the casual sort of thing—"

She looked down, embarrassed. "But could this, this business of murder, could it be tied up with that sort of thing?" Her eyes went here and there, not meeting his, revealing the difficulty she found in considering the subject. "'A woman scorned.' That sort of thing."

Brian stood up and jammed his hands into his coat pockets. "Your husband certainly led a complicated life."

"I guess we all do," she said.

That evening they let Bonnie see Rex at a little office sort of room at the jail. In some respects he was a favored prisoner. It seemed as if the district attorney was so self-satisfied at having a fall guy to take before the grand jury that they could afford to be magnanimous about his treatment ahead of time.

Bonnie noticed immediately that Rex seemed in better spirits. When they had greeted each other he leaned toward her conspiratorially across the table.

"Things are looking up; we got some new evidence."

"Thank God. Brian Rhodes dig it up?"

"In a way. Look, you won't say nothing if I tell you. We can't let it out what lines we're workin' on."

"Of course not." Her voice was tense.

"It was Sandy brought it in."

Bonnie's face clouded a little. "Sandy? I don't trust that little floozy. She's the kind that would lie when the truth'd do better."

"At a time like this you can't be fussy. And she can swear to it she saw a light in the office at midnight and saw another car parked beside Stan West's."

"Whose car?"

"We don't know. She just saw the back of it sticking out behind West's car."

"Then it was a longer car than his?"

"Yeah, and it was some light color."

"What light color? White? Yellow? Grey?"

"She don't know that either."

"Doesn't sound to me like much of a help."

"Well, don't you get it?" Rex muttered impatiently. "The cops figure I done it around ten-thirty sometime; so if she seen lights and a car there at midnight, it weakens their case."

"Yeah, I can see that. But what you really need is to find out who it was that was there, because ten to one that was the murderer. I wonder," she said soberly, "d'you suppose we ought to have Rhodes hire a private detective?"

"What are we going to use for money?"

"Well, I could sell your car."

"Nothing doing!" Outrage expressed itself in every line of Rex's face. "How'd I ever get enough ahead then for a down payment on another one?"

"You won't need one if you're in San Quentin—or dead."

"I'll get out of this. Rhodes is plenty smart."

"I wish," Bonnie growled, "that little bitch Patty West was in hell. If she hadn't of blabbed, they'd never of thought of you."

"I guess," Rex said dejectedly, "you were right—about me and her. I shouldn't never have messed around with them people. But, you know, I've been thinkin' ... At first I was sore as hell at Patty; but I've kinda come around to thinkin' it's partly my own fault. When you get right down to it I wasn't strictly on the level with the kid. I wasn't going with her first of all because she was a nice gal and I liked her. Mainly I was interested in what it could do for me, gettin' in with her. And I guess it never works out right, bein' friends with people for what you can get out of it. Where people are concerned, you should be on the level. Sincere, if you get what I mean."

"That's what I tried to tell you," Bonnie responded dully. "I told you, remember, that I wouldn't have a word to say if you were stuck on the girl. I'd of said, 'Hop to it and to hell with what her old man has to say.' But you were just out for what you could get. Like you said, whether you liked the kid or not, that was secondary. And," she concluded slowly, "I guess maybe you're right. You can't blame her so much. She could tell maybe she didn't mean much to you—for herself, I mean. It was who she was that counted with you." Bonnie frowned thoughtfully. "I guess that wouldn't give her any feeling she had to be loyal to you."

When Bonnie left him, Rex once more adjured her to secrecy about Sandy's evidence.

CHAPTER EIGHTEEN

Laverne had made an appointment with Earl Fowler for Monday morning. Wearing the dark coat dress and the plain little hat again, she set out with a feeling of reluctance for the shed. It was cool, and it seemed a little dim in the offices at the northwest corner of the building. Earl was polite, deferential, and very friendly.

Indicating his own desk, he inquired tactfully, "Shall we sit out here to go over things?"

Laverne glanced at the inner door. "No," she said slowly, "I'll sit at Stan's desk. There'll probably be interruptions out here."

The private office was nakedly neat, unused as it had been for the past week. To Earl, there was something chilling about the pristine expanse of green blotter paper in the center of the polished desk top; but its unmarked surface prompted no gruesome connotation for Laverne, who had not seen the old one soaked with Stanley's blood.

She smiled at Earl with deliberate girlish charm. "I want to know—everything."

"That's a pretty large order."

As he brought out ledgers and checkbooks and sheets of paper covered with columns of figures, and spread them out before her, Laverne concealed a qualm of dismay. But she listened with what she hoped was an intelligent expression as Earl began to explain the business and show her that it was indeed solvent.

He was interrupted occasionally by the telephone, and once Ralph Musio came in and spoke pleasantly but a little solemnly to Laverne, as if he could not forget her recent bereavement.

It seemed as if every time she glanced up from the papers, she met her own eyes in the photograph standing to the right on Stanley's desk, across from a group picture of the twins and Patty. It bothered her somehow. It was a new picture, a candid shot Stan had taken one Sunday afternoon in the back yard. She had been sitting on a rattan stool, and he had called from behind her and she had turned inquiringly. The lens had caught that look of smiling inquiry and Stan had had the snapshot enlarged. This was the first time she had seen it, framed and on his desk. He must have put it there only the day before he died.

With a slight frown, Laverne picked the photograph up, and folding the standard down, stuck it into a desk drawer. There was something accusing about it, proof as it was that, despite his defections, Stan had wanted her likeness close to him.

Once when Earl came back from speaking to someone in the front office, she confronted him with wide, questioning eyes.

"I don't understand," she said, tapping a document in front of her. "Are we in debt? Does this mean we owe the *bank* money?"

Earl glanced at the paper and smiled. "Well, yes and no. You see, our assets are clear; the shed, and the acreage down near Chualar, the trucks and equipment and all. But the actual funds for expenses during the season, they're supplied by the bank—"

"Then," Laverne said, aghast, "we're *mortgaged!*"

"Well, not exactly," Earl returned patiently. "Everybody, or almost everybody, does it this way. You see, Stan didn't believe in actually owning the land. All he really owned is the acreage at Chualar that I mentioned. For the rest he either leased or bought the crop direct from the grower. Understand? Well, that all takes a lot of dough, added to the payroll and operating expenses; and you don't get your full return until the season is over and you get paid for what you've shipped. So you don't try to maintain all that operating capital yourself. It ties up too much money. You get it from the bank, and then when they're paid back, what's left is profit. Understand?"

She shook her head. "But don't you have to pay them for using their money?"

"Yes, but it works out cheaper than using your own. The truth is," he added honestly, "you've got to be a damn big operator to *have* that much capital laying over from one season to the next."

"I don't like paying for the use of money," she maintained stubbornly.

"But everybody does it," Earl protested, on a note of exasperation. "Look, it's like this. In order to get a start, naturally, unless you've inherited a fortune from somewhere, you've got to get financed. Right? Well then, there's always that original—well, deficit, if you want to call it that; and what with expanding and everything and reinvesting, you never quite catch up. But that's O.K. if you come out with a profit at the end of every season. Get it?"

"All I get is," Laverne countered sharply, "that we're always in debt to the bank."

"So what? We're making money, aren't we?"

She looked down at the bankbooks and ledger and scattered papers. "It's weird," she said as if to herself, "absolutely weird."

Abruptly she looked up. "You know about this ten-thousand-dollar loan to Hal Schmidt? I gather then he couldn't get enough from the banks to carry him."

"That's right."

"Well, the way I see it then, if we get money all the time on credit in order to run the business, we're in no position to finance other people."

Earl's face was expressionless. "That's right."

"Then why did Stan do it?"

"Friendship, I guess."

Laverne frowned into space. "Friendship didn't mean that much to Stan."

"Well," Earl said patiently, "it's true Stan was paying interest on that amount, but on the other hand Schmidt would pay interest when he returned it; so the whole thing cancels out—"

"Except," she said slowly, "that it gave us that much less money to maneuver with."

Earl smiled. "You catch on quick."

Through the inner doorway they heard the outside door slam. Earl moved to look into the front office.

"Hi, Bob. Be with you in a minute. Wakely," he volunteered to Laverne. "I'll see what he wants."

Laverne stood up slowly and followed Earl through the doorway.

"Oh," Bob Wakely smiled. "How do you do, Mrs. West."

He was a large man in his early thirties, wearing a crew haircut, a leather jacket, khaki pants, and heavy black field boots with a single buckled strap over the instep. His face was very tanned; and he was the epitome of the bluff, outdoor type. Laverne eyed him narrowly. It was not hard to visualize him striding down the moist black dirt between lines of Filipinos in straw hats and neckerchiefs bending over the rows of lettuce to wield their short-handled hoes. She had never really thought of the Filipino crews as people; but now irrelevantly she wondered what those short, dark men thought of this big ruddy creature who was to them the big boss, with authority even over their own foremen.

The field man, of course, did much more than ride around watching to see that the field labor kept on its toes. He knew the land, the crops, who owned them, which would be good buys this year, which ones risky, when to plant, when to irrigate, how soon to start harvesting; but he was also the man who dealt most directly with field labor. And these particular laborers were men who seemed to sense that even though they did the hardest part of the work, they were permitted to do so only on sufferance, as it were. They were foreign; they were different; and they were never allowed to forget it.

Fleetingly Laverne was reminded that Stan was entitled to respect. He knew how to pick the right man for a particular job. You didn't need finesse to oversee the fields. It was in fact rather an advantage if there was something inhuman and brutal about the man in that position. Inside the shed, however, you needed someone who was fundamentally "a good guy," like Ralph Musio, someone who could get along with those people who either came themselves, or whose parents did, from Arkansas, from Oklahoma, from Texas, or from the arid Southwest, people who had a chip on their shoulder, who secretly chafed under their position on the lowest rung of the business's ladder, people who were fundamentally suspicious of bosses, people always spoiling for a fight, held in place only by the need for and their satisfaction in the pay checks they drew.

These were only nebulous, not fully formed thoughts in Laverne's mind as she looked at Bob Wakely. She had forgotten them even as they flickered past like shadows.

"Don't pay any attention to me," she said ingenuously. "Go ahead as if I wasn't here. I'm just trying to find out what goes on in the big outside world."

"Which," Bob said gallantly, "is no place for a lady." He laughed to show this was a joke. He turned to Earl. "We're starting to cut on the Peabody ranch tomorrow. I just came by to see how Ralph's holding out. Looks like it'll be all over by four o'clock today. Gettin' nothing but culls now off the Chualar field. I knew damn well they didn't do a decent job thinning there last spring; but that's Wendell for you. Last time we'll ever deal with that bastard."

"Who's Wendell?" Laverne asked.

"Labor contractor. Used Mexicans. But there ain't no substitute for Gooks in the field."

"Oh yes, Filipinos," Laverne said knowledgeably, keeping in contact with the conversation. Her voice broke off suddenly and her eyes steadied on the man. "You don't," she said parenthetically, "call them that to their face, do you—Gooks?"

"Hell, no. Ever since the war they've been getting as uppity as Oakies. Have to handle 'em with kid gloves."

"I just wondered," she said vaguely. "When you get through talking to Earl," she added, "could you come in and let me pump you a little—about—uh—the acreage and when it's ready to come off and all?"

"Why, sure thing. Right now, if you want to."

As Bob followed Laverne toward the inner office he raised his eyebrows at Earl and shrugged with the humorous resignation of one catering to a child's whim.

Laverne asked questions that she thought suitable and finally said ingratiatingly, with pretty artlessness, "I feel so responsible, since Stan is gone; and there's so much to learn."

"It's tough on you all right, bein' left alone like this—"

"It's been just awful. Police questioning and everything. I suppose they ran you through the wringer too."

"They asked me questions all right."

"I hope," she said whimsically, "you were alibied. Isn't that what they call it?"

"I didn't have to worry on that score. We had company to watch television that night, and then Anne served refreshments afterward, and we had a few drinks, and I'm damned if they didn't stay till almost one-thirty, just shootin' the bull. Al Fedora and his wife. Don't know whether you know him. He's a state inspector. New here."

"I believe I've met them," Laverne said brightly to cover her disappointment. One possibility gone already.

When she was ready to depart, Laverne told Earl as she drew on her gloves, "I'll just walk through the shed before I go. When I stop to think of it, I realize it's been years since I set foot out there."

"Want me to buzz Ralph so he can come and escort you?"

"No, thank you. I'll run into him."

The word that Mrs. West was in the shed spread as if it had been put on a teletype machine; but Laverne herself was unaware of the close scrutiny that followed her progress.

Why, she thought to herself, there's something impressive, something satisfying about all this activity, all these people accomplishing so much. For a moment she felt that she understood Stan's continuing fascination with what sounded rather dull if you said only "packing lettuce." To know you had set in motion and controlled all this purposeful movement was enough to give a man the exhilaration she had noticed Stan felt in his work. Perhaps it was no wonder he had seemed to feel so little need of her.

Ralph approached her as she stood musingly looking about her. When they had exchanged a few words, she asked in a low tone, "Which one is Rex Maffey's sister?"

Without turning his head Ralph replied, "Down to our right past this first basket, the one facing us, kinda brown hair and a blue sweater on."

Bonnie's eyes were fixed on her work. Neither she nor Freda nor Ray was talking. She had seen Mrs. West farther down the floor, and then she had not looked up again. As Laverne had come closer, all three of them had fallen silent, as if to guard against revealing anything to her.

"I wonder," Laverne pondered, "if I oughtn't to say something to her. But this hardly seems like the time."

"I wouldn't," Ralph agreed uncomfortably. "It would be conspicuous."

"And which one is the one they call Sandy?"

Ralph looked down at her quickly, but he replied in a casual tone, "Walk down this way. There, the one with red hair, with her back to us."

Sandy turned her head as he spoke, and over her shoulder stared at Laverne brazenly. Laverne glanced away, conscious of Ralph's questioning look.

CHAPTER NINETEEN

When she reached home Laverne went straight upstairs. The door was partly open in Patty's room, and she could hear the girl's radio turned on. From her own windows she saw the boys playing catch with a softball on the back lawn. Laverne took off her hat and laid down her gloves and purse. First lighting a cigarette, she went down the hall and tapped at Patty's door, pushing it further open.

The girl looked up listlessly from her position in the armchair covered in blue and yellow plaid. The back of her neck rested against one arm, her knees hung over the other.

"Hi," she said, and reached out to turn down the volume of the little table radio.

"I thought you had passed the age," Laverne said flippantly, "for making like a pretzel when you sat in a chair."

"I feel like a pretzel," Patty said dully. "Anyway I don't feel human."

"I guess none of us feel too chipper."

Patty dragged her legs off the chair arm and straightened her torso.

"What's bothering you particularly? Rex?"

"Yeah. I guess why I'm so low right now is Aunt Edith was here while you were gone." Patty lifted her eyes candidly. "Did you ever notice, Mom, she's so damned self-righteous?"

"Well, I never thought of Edith exactly like that. I guess I always thought she didn't have much imagination. That is, it didn't take much to satisfy her in life."

Laverne had seated herself on the edge of the bed, and she placed her cigarette between her lips and then held it away with a withdrawn look in her eyes. She was remembering, for no good reason, Edith's extremely practical arguments all those years ago about why she ought not to divorce Stan. They had all centered around financial security; and even though Edith had certainly been right—she must have been—there had been something a little repellent about her advice. But was self-righteous the word?

"She was so damned pleased about Rex Maffey being arrested that I thought I'd puke before she got out of here."

"Patty, your language!"

"I *feel* like saying ugly words," the girl retorted glumly. "And she thinks Brian is crazy, taking the case. She seemed to think that would end our friendship with him." Patty's eyes came back to Laverne anxiously. "Brian does think Rex is innocent, doesn't he?"

"Yes."

"I almost wish he didn't," Patty grumbled. "I almost wish he was guilty; because if he isn't it makes me an absolute heel. No one would have thought of Rex if it hadn't been for me." She rose and flounced to the window overlooking the street, hitching the waistband of her pleated skirt into place. "I keep thinking of what he must be thinking about me. And I don't know why I should care. Because the more I think about it the more I feel as if he was just trying to—use me some way. To better himself socially, I think."

Laverne surveyed the girl's back meditatively. "I believe," she said, "if it weren't for that, this mistrust of him, you could have gone for this boy in rather a big way."

"Looks that way, doesn't it?" Patty answered in a muffled voice.

"I don't know just what to do." Laverne spoke thoughtfully. "How to advise you, I mean, about easing your conscience about—about"—she chuckled dryly—"tattling on him." She rose and pressed out her cigarette in a dish on the table that held the radio. "I saw his sister today down at the shed. Not to speak to. It must," she said slowly, "be hard on her, the disgrace and all. Although maybe those people don't take things as hard as we would."

Patty turned from the window. "That's a phony remark if I ever heard one. They're human, aren't they, the same as we are?"

"Yes, but—their background and all."

"What makes you think we're so fine and noble and high-minded and all? It's one of us that got killed, isn't it; and Dad must have acted some way that made somebody hate him enough to do it. And look at me, throwing somebody else to the wolves to save our skins." She checked herself, and her tone became more reserved. "I guess you haven't done anything shoddy though. Maybe you're entitled to feel—oh, of finer clay or something; I don't know."

Laverne was still. She felt frightened. It all depended on what kind of standards you were using. But what about herself? How *did* she measure up? By anybody's standards?

"O.K., O.K.," she said harshly, "I suppose I'm no lily either. I just meant— Oh, the hell with it!" She regarded the girl ruefully. "Since when did you get to be a deep thinker?"

"It's not deep thinking. I guess I just feel guilty," Patty confessed shamefacedly.

"There's one thing maybe we could do," Laverne said doubtfully. "Maybe we ought to go and see his family, you and I, let them know we believe he's innocent. They'd tell Rex, and it might soften his feelings toward you, if what you're worrying about is that he's sitting down there despising you."

"I'd feel pretty awkward," Patty said slowly, "going out there. We could get the address from Earl Fowler, I suppose."

Laverne smiled. "We'll go this evening, shall we? Sort of a pilgrimage, for the good of our souls."

Patty smiled back shyly. Then suddenly she said, "You know, since all this, one funny thing has happened. You and me, we seem closer somehow." She looked down and ran her finger along a cord in the chair upholstery.

"It's me, I think," Laverne said with difficulty. "I seem more able to—to talk to you about—about anything serious." They were avoiding one another's eyes, and Laverne went on, beginning to forget her self-consciousness, "It's all rather strange. The first few days, before the funeral, they're sort of a blur in my mind now, as if I had been a little dead myself; but now I actually feel more alive, as if your father's death had brought me more life. That sounds like a terrible thing to say. I don't think I mean it quite like that. But it's as if—as if the world around me were opening up more, now that your father isn't there." Her eyes were blank but wondering. "As if he had stood between me and—and other things, like my relationship with you."

Patty was studying her with a frown. "You must have been all wrapped up in Dad."

"Was I? I don't know."

From the staircase a hearty voice called, "Yoo-hoo, where are you all?"

"What crust," Patty said involuntarily, "busting right upstairs without waiting for Lula to announce her."

Laverne was already at the door. "Oh well, you know Joan," she murmured. "Here I am," she called, and went down the hall to meet Joan, who stood at the top of the steps in a tweed suit and a beret, a large leather purse hanging on a strap over her shoulder.

"Not intruding, am I?" Joan said cheerfully, stepping forward to kiss Laverne.

"Of course not. Like to go downstairs and have a drink?"

"Well, if you twist my arm. How are you, pet? You look tired."

Joan linked her arm in Laverne's as they descended the stairs.

"How do you expect me to look, as if I just came back from a rest cure?" Laverne's tone was light but inexplicably edged.

Joan's fingers tightened on her arm. "Poor kid, you've certainly had your share of trouble."

As Laverne prepared a highball for each of them, Joan chatted lightly, recounting her day's activities. "I had a letter from Jack. He said he'd write you. He felt awful, hearing about Stan."

Laverne glanced over her shoulder to inquire, "How is Jack?"

"Oh, fine. All wrapped up in his work. You know," Joan went on casually, "right then you looked just like the photo on Stan's desk."

"Did I? Stan had a knack for catching people off guard. We have some nice prints of the kids. I'm giving Patty his camera. She wanted it as a— a remembrance."

"Poor Stan."

In comfortable chairs in the living room they faced each other with their drinks, and Joan used her toe to push off one of her spectator pumps. "Damn heels anyway. My feet are spoiled from wearing loafers and sandals all summer."

"That's right. It'll soon be September, won't it?"

Abruptly Joan said, "Hal tells me he spoke to you about our note, the one Stan held."

"Yes, we talked about it. Let's see, was it Saturday? Honestly time has been getting all mixed up for me lately."

"Poor baby, it's no wonder. After all you've been through."

Illogically Laverne felt irritated. Which was surprising. Joan hardly ever irritated her.

"Really, Joan, I'm hardly a baby. At least I'm beginning to realize I'd damn well better not be."

"Figure of speech, pet, figure of speech. But about this loan, I thought I'd better speak to you myself about it. Hal's no good at explaining anything, really getting it over, I mean. And I'm not kidding you, darling, that ten thousand bucks is the margin for us that means we squeak through or we don't. And I knew that if I put it to you straight out you'd understand. And I know how these things are when somebody dies, the whole thing has to go through an executor and all that, and they start right in cleaning up; so unless you step in they might crack down."

"Phillips and Bixby are the executors," Laverne said steadily, "and I intend to see that they do what I say."

"Well, then it's all settled, isn't it?"

"I don't know. I never realized until today what an ignoramus I was about finances. Stan never discussed that sort of thing with me; and I just didn't care. But while Stan had his faults—you know that—he did know his onions in a business way; and I intend to try to figure out what he was doing and go on the same way. Was he pressing Hal for that money?"

"Of course not," Joan retorted defensively.

"Because if he was, you see, there was good reason. It was because he couldn't afford to have it out any longer. And if that's the case"—she moved the hand that held her glass—"well, probably I can't afford to let it ride either."

Joan set her glass down carefully on the table beside her chair. Her eyes were piercing as she held her head forward slightly and demanded huskily, "After all we've meant to each other, you'd let me be ruined for a paltry ten thousand dollars?"

Laverne had been fairly certain that she would extend the Schmidts' loan; but with her new feeling of responsibility she had not wanted to be pressed into doing it; she wanted the decision to be her own. So now she felt little flickers of anger eating away at her composure.

"I'll help you if I can. I told you that. But, I repeat, I have to know for sure first that I can afford to. You must realize that I have three children to finish educating, that I myself have to live off the Golden West company for the rest of my life. Surely," she finished bluntly, "you don't think you mean more to me than my own children and myself."

Joan was staring at her uncertainly. She sank back in the chair and picked up her glass. "Sorry, pet, I didn't mean to be so—coarse about it. It's just—well, it's so damned important to us."

"I know."

Joan frowned into her glass, and then briskly changed the subject. "What's the matter with our friend Brian's head, I wonder? Taking on this Maffey case?"

Laverne sighed wearily. "He's a lawyer first, our friend afterward. And he thinks the boy's innocent."

"But it looks so queer, his coming in on this particular case. People may talk. Him going around with our crowd, and then defending the man who shot Stan."

Laverne said nothing. She was getting tired of explaining Brian to other people.

"Personally," Joan observed with a quick, shrewd glance at her friend, "I figured Brian was sweet on you."

"I hope no one else thought so."

"Darling, don't be naïve. Everybody noticed. I've never been sure that you didn't return the compliment where he was concerned."

"I've always liked Brian," Laverne said noncommittally.

"Did Stan know?"

"I don't think Stan would have cared, provided I didn't do anything—drastic about it. Like publicly having an affair, or breaking up our home." Laverne's tone was bitter.

"Poor darling—"

"Please stop," Laverne broke out sharply, "calling me 'poor' this and 'poor' that."

Joan sat arrested in the middle of a gesture. The ash from her cigarette fell on her skirt.

"I'm sorry," Laverne said wearily. "Nerves are getting me, I guess." And she drained her glass.

Without looking at what she was doing, Joan put out her cigarette in the ash tray and stood up.

"Of course," she said sympathetically. Crossing the rug, she bent and kissed Laverne's cheek. "Let's not fight, h'm? I know you're all tuckered out, and here I go prattling on and on."

As her friend's hand passed gently over Laverne's hair, it was all Laverne could do to keep from drawing away. But she stood up, smiling apologetically.

"I'll give you a ring tomorrow," Joan said briskly. "Now, get some rest and take care of yourself."

Again she bent and kissed Laverne, this time on the lips, before she strode out through the french doors to the driveway. Laverne went with her to the doors and stood on the steps.

As Joan opened the station-wagon door, she grumbled lightly, "God, I'm getting sick of driving this old thrashing machine. And Hal's old heap isn't much better."

Laverne was already beginning to feel a little remorseful over the sharpness with which she had spoken, and she murmured sympathetically, "The old wagon *is* a little battered. Isn't that a new dent in the front fender?"

"Oh heavens, no; that's been there as long as all the rest of them have. I take off part of the garage door every time I go in or out, but we never seem to be able to afford a fender-straightening job."

Laverne waved halfheartedly as Joan backed out, conscious of the veiled rebuke in Joan's remarks. Laverne had three cars now, and the Schmidts couldn't even afford to have their old one repaired.

Laverne's eyes were somewhat perplexed. What was getting into her? This vague irritation with Joan. And it had never occurred to her before to wonder if it wasn't a little—well, too much, this kissing at every meeting, when you saw each other every day. Of course she and Joan thought a lot of each other; but take Edith, for instance, her own sister. She loved Edith too, but they never thought of kissing except if one of them were going on or returning from some long trip. Laverne shrugged, dismissing these reflections, not wanting to pursue them any further.

CHAPTER TWENTY

Bonnie saw Laverne that afternoon, from a distance and between the heads of her fellow workers. After that she refused to see her again, keeping her eyes on her work even when Mrs. West passed within ten feet of her.

Even Freda's garrulity was quenched by Bonnie's taciturnity, although Freda continuously cast troubled glances at her partner as the afternoon dripped monotonously away.

When it was four o'clock, Freda offered brightly, "Say, kid, why don't you let your kid sister sit with your dad this evening and come on home with me for dinner? Maybe we could play cards or something after. You oughta get out, get your mind off things."

"Gee, I'd like to," Bonnie rejoined sincerely, "but I'm going down to see Rex after supper. They're pretty decent about lettin' me see him at odd times on account of me working days. Mr. Rhodes fixed it with Cass Huggins so I can see him early in the evenings. And, well, after that the evening's pretty well shot."

"How about coming out to eat anyway?" Freda persisted.

"Honest, I'd love to; but you know Nancy; if I'm goin' to be away I have to plan ahead. She's always got something cooked up with her friends."

"O.K. then, we'll plan ahead. Maybe Saturday night. We'll try to find a dance or something. Fix up a date for you. O.K.?"

"It sounds good," Bonnie assented with a smile that was unintentionally wistful.

Freda's husband ran the lidding machine which clamped shut the iced crates with their contents neatly secured in wide sheets of heavy waxed paper; and between the two of them they had bought a new home out in the Alisal Heights section where the houses had two bedrooms and picture windows and were brick halfway up and pale green stucco the rest of the way. Bonnie found it the height of luxury to be entertained by Freda and Jim. Freda's mother took care of the kids after school and during vacations, and although they hadn't yet furnished the house completely, still its hardwood floors and its painted woodwork shone newly; and there was even a fireplace in the front room.

It was what Bonnie dreamed of someday for herself; but it seemed as if the fulfillment of that dream was being constantly pushed further into the future. First it had been postponed in her mind until Nancy finished high school. Then Dad's paralysis put it off still further—until between the earnings of all three of his kids they could afford to keep him in a rest home or hire a woman to stay all day in whichever of their homes they kept him in. And now if Rex were to be removed from their family earning force, God knew when Bonnie would be able to look around for a man with whom she could seriously consider marriage and eventually a house of their own out in one of the new subdivisions. Men didn't care about saddling themselves with wives who had invalid fathers and dependent minor sisters, to say nothing of jailbird brothers.

Bonnie had never been hopeless, never really down, during all the ten years when she had been in effect the woman of the house. Taking hold and helping Dad to get the other kids raised had been just something you had to do and didn't think twice about. She had managed to have a little fun along the way, a few dates, steady boy friends two or three times.

But in the last two or three years she had thought more and more longingly of the time when Nancy should be a regular wage earner too, and when she could make the two kids, Nancy and Rex, sit down with her and dope it out, how they would share in caring for Dad, and outside of that be free to make new lives, each for himself.

But now it looked as if it was to be she and Nancy, and not even Nancy for another year or two.

So it was no wonder that she could not bring herself to look at Laverne West. It was his own affairs that had got Mr. West killed; and it was his daughter who had sicced the cops onto Rex.

That evening when she got home from visiting Rex, Nancy, in full make-up and a sweater and skirt, was waiting impatiently to be relieved of sitting with their father.

"Where you going this time?" Bonnie inquired.

"Just over to Jean's. We're gonna play records."

"Well, get in by ten-thirty. You've gotta get some rest or you'll be going into consumption the first thing we know."

"Oh, Bon-nie," Nancy disclaimed scornfully, and pranced away, letting the front screen door slam behind her.

Bonnie closed the wooden door, and went into her and Nancy's bedroom to hang up her jacket in the jam-packed little clothes closet. So she did not see the small English car that pulled to a stop in front of the house.

Laverne and Patty got out and gazed silently at the flat-roofed stuccoed house, with a small porch off which two doors opened. The front windows on one side of the porch were dark, but the paper shades of the others showed illumination behind them.

"I can't read the number," Patty said, "but this must be the house. I suppose we'd better try the side that's lighted."

"Sounds reasonable."

As they walked up the cement path to the door, in the house to the left of the duplex they could hear a radio quiz program, and from the frame house to the right a sudden burst of laughter. A sedan with wide glass windows all the way around turned in at the driveway and disappeared past the Maffeys' side of the duplex.

"There must be more houses in the back," Patty observed incredulously.

"Somebody," Laverne commented, "didn't believe in wasting space." They were on the porch, and she peered at the door casing. "There doesn't seem to be a bell."

Patty whispered, "I feel embarrassed."

"Too late for that now." Laverne knocked briskly on the wood beneath the net-curtained pane of glass in the door.

They heard Bonnie's step inside, and then as the door swung open they were bathed in the light of a naked globe set in the porch ceiling.

Bonnie stared at them blankly.

"How do you do," Laverne said, smiling. "I'm Mrs. West, and this is my daughter Patty. You're Miss Maffey, aren't you?"

"Yes."

"We've been rather concerned about you and thought we'd just drop in this evening. I hope you're not busy."

"No." Bonnie held the door back and stood aside. There was nothing else she could think of to do. "Come in."

A bridge lamp with a faded rayon shade illuminated the room they stepped into. Against the inner wall stood a rust-colored armless sofa that folded back to make a double bed at night. Across the room two overstuffed chairs stood in the corners, with a cabinet radio between them. A coffee table with a glass top stood in the center of the taupe rug which had a blue border and clusters of blue flowers in the corners. In the corner opposite the front door two straight chairs angled out carelessly at the sides of a half-open gate-leg table. A large picture of two white cockatoos in a glass frame hung over the couch. That was all the furnishings there were. It was all there was room for.

While she settled herself in one of the chairs, Laverne assessed the place with a housewifely eye. Tidy. No dust or rolls of lint. But there were spots on the impractically plain surface of the rug; and the couch material was worn threadbare on two places near the top of the back. The flowered drapes at the windows were faded, and the painted walls were dingy near the ceiling. Through the rear doorway she could see the corner of a gas stove and the sink with green-painted wooden doors under it. There was a smell that was not exactly dusty or moldy; but you were aware of substance to the air, an aura of too much living in too small an area.

Bonnie seated herself in one of the straight chairs by the table and eyed her guests with a waiting expression. Nervously she straightened the transparent plastic cover under whose slippery surface the printed design of a cotton tablecloth showed.

"We felt," Laverne began with her most charming smile, "that this was a time of trouble—and sorrow—for your family as well as ours; and Patty and I decided that we wanted to come and see you, and for what it's worth; to you, tell you that we believe your brother is innocent."

"I thought," Bonnie said huskily, with a slight nod at Patty, "it was her accused Rex of it."

Patty leaned forward, speaking quickly, "That's one reason I wanted to see you. I was afraid Rex thought that. And it isn't so. Please tell him that for me. It's true; I mentioned the—the misunderstanding I had with my father over my going out with Rex; but I never meant to get him in trouble. I don't know whether the police questioned you or not; but if they did, you know how they are. They just worm things out of you."

Bonnie was eying the girl uncertainly; and Laverne cast an inscrutable glance at her daughter, thinking that the kid was lying in her teeth, and so earnestly that she was probably even now convincing herself that the police *had* "wormed" the information out of her. Well, Laverne reflected, everybody had to lie to himself sometimes—to save his self-respect.

"If you don't think Rex killed Mr. West, then who do you think done it?" Bonnie asked slowly, her fingers absently lining up and realigning the sugar bowl and the salt and pepper shakers which had been left marooned on the table after the evening meal.

"If we knew," Laverne said earnestly, "we would come forward and say so. But we honestly have no idea."

"How is anybody going to find out?" Bonnie pursued doggedly.

"There's the rub," Laverne opined ruefully.

As she and Patty rose to depart, Laverne said apologetically, "I know it's what everybody says until it's meaningless, but if there's anything we can do to help, don't hesitate to call on us."

Bonnie had also risen, and suddenly she smiled; and for the first time since their arrival her face looked alive and young. "That's what I should be saying to you." Her expression sobered. "It's you folks that've had the real trouble, losing your husband like this. And I am sorry. At the shed we all liked Mr. West, respected him."

"Why—why, thank you." Laverne looked down at her hands; then she raised her eyes and said with resolution, "There's one thing I can do. Mr. Rhodes is a friend of ours. I'll talk to him, ask him to go easy on his fee. I imagine that's one of the worst burdens for you right now, the extra expense right when your brother is losing money by not being able to work."

Laverne's eyes suddenly steadied on the girl's face with a startled expression; and she said almost wonderingly, "That's right, I'm the boss now. Under the circumstances it's perfectly in order if I instruct Earl to keep Rex on the books, pay his wages while he's forced to be away."

"It would make a lot of difference," Bonnie breathed incredulously.

Patty talked in low tones as they went out to the car, but Laverne's mind did not register what her daughter said. When she was behind the wheel, Laverne murmured, interrupting the girl's voice, "Money is so much more important to people like them than it is to us, isn't it? As she said, it makes all the difference. I realize now that I never thought much about it. Your father always let me know how much I could safely spend, and that was that. It didn't really matter. It made the difference perhaps as to whether I could pay fifty or a hundred dollars for a spring suit, but it didn't make the difference between having any at all or not...."

Her voice trailed off, and she put her fingers to the ignition key. Her thoughts alighted for a moment on the Schmidts, Hal and Joan, their desperate concern over ten thousand dollars. She frowned through the windshield, not hearing Patty's answering remark. Now that she was reminded that she had never really thought much about money, her wits seemed suddenly sharpened in regard to it; and it struck her again that it was not in character for Stan to tolerate a deficit like ten thousand dollars, out of pure friendship. Could it be that there was something more behind this oft-renewed note of Hal Schmidt's, a hold of some kind on Stan?

"Be still," she said abruptly to Patty. "I'm thinking."

Hal Schmidt had been around for years. He and Stan had come to Salinas at about the same time, from somewhere in the central part of the Coast, where, she had been given to understand, they had known one another only casually.

But Hal couldn't have been blackmailing Stan; he just wasn't the type. And if people killed in connection with blackmail, it was usually the other way around; the blackmailer got killed.

However, both Hal and Joan had seemed very confident that she would extend the note, more confident of her than they were of Stan. Had they got rid of Stan—for ten thousand dollars? Laverne remembered Bonnie's phrase "make a lot of difference." To the Maffeys a few hundred dollars made all the difference; to the Schmidts it was those few thousands that would bridge the gap and make the difference between success and failure.

Laverne put her elbow on the steering wheel and rested her chin on her fist. She herself was willing to turn down their request and ruin her best friends to protect her own and her children's financial interests, a kind of conduct that actually went against the grain with her. Might not other decent people also do things even worse that went against the grain with them too? For assuredly someone had shot Stanley, and for a reason. And there weren't so many reasons why anyone would shoot Stan.

Timidly Patty's voice interrupted, "What's the trouble, Mom?"

Laverne raised her head. "The trouble is that I'm beginning to take a passionate interest in finding out who did kill your father. I've never said this to you before, Patty; but I hadn't been terribly happy with your father for a long time. Since he's gone though, I've realized that actually I thought a lot of him. And I'm beginning to feel a—a lust for vengeance. In spite of our—differences, I wouldn't ever have wanted this to happen to him. And do you realize, *I'm* the one who should know best who might have killed him? But I seem to know so little, as if I'd been walking around in a dream where, looking back, nothing seems quite real."

"Well," Patty said cynically, "I contributed my two bits' worth of information, and look where it got us."

"If everybody's two bits was put together, it might add up to a dollar," Laverne muttered. "I wonder. There's Earl. He sat in that office day in, day out. Everything went through his hands. It's too bad Dorothy was away when it happened. Sometimes a woman's intuition tells her things men don't notice. Of course, we can talk to her when she gets back next week. Meanwhile—"

She turned the key in the ignition. "We're going to call on the Fowlers right now."

CHAPTER TWENTY-ONE

At the corner they turned east toward the new subdivision near the army air base; and after cruising about the unfamiliar streets bordered by recently planted and still spindly young trees, found the rigidly modern five-room house with attached garage which Earl had bought last year. The front wall was made of two solid sheets of glass divided by a plain brown door. The roof slanted flatly back, and the garage jutted toward the street.

As they got out of the car Patty regarded the house moodily. "I must be a confirmed traditionalist; but this new architecture makes me think of nothing so much as a chicken coop."

In the dim light from the corner street lamps Laverne glanced at the houses on each side of Earl's, each long and low and unadorned, with barely sloping roof levels running into each other at odd angles above yards of glass curtained in unbroken expanses of tan casement cloth.

"It makes you wonder," Patty said, "if the American people aren't congenitally addicted to extremes. Fifty years ago they decorated the outside of houses with everything they could hang on them, cupolas, bay windows, fretwork, porches, stained-glass borders on windows. And then we went through a stage of bungalows that out-Spanished the Spanish and out-Englished the English; and now when they've decided simplicity is the thing, they're making them so simple that they look like a couple of cardboard cartons stuck together with sheets of glass."

The Fowlers' house was unlighted; but they could hear raucous voices, and the callers correctly suspected that the family were sitting in the dark watching television.

The door Earl opened for them led directly into the living room. He had turned on a floor lamp with a wide, shallow, coarsely woven shade. Mrs. Fowler rose from the end of the low sofa as she saw who was there; and the little girls, each crouched on a hassock some feet from the television screen, looked over their shoulders unwillingly.

"Well, come in, come in," Earl invited in a flurry of excitement. "Look who's here, honey, Mrs. West and Patty."

"This is a surprise," Mrs. Fowler gushed, stepping forward. "Sit down. Won't you let me take your coats? We were just watching television."

"Awfully sorry to interrupt the program," Laverne apologized.

"Oh, that's all right," Earl rejoined heartily, "it's nothing important."

"Say hello to the ladies," Mrs. Fowler reminded her children, a little sharply, turning on a table light which had a boxy base and a shade to match the floor lamp.

The little girls slid off the imitation-leather hassocks, nodded awkwardly, and waited to be excused from further attention to the adults. As soon as Laverne and Patty were ensconced in "sling" chairs whose lines looked uninviting but whose contours were surprisingly comfortable, the children sank back upon the stools and turned their eyes to the screen.

Earl stepped over to turn the sound down, and one of the girls uttered a low, plaintive cry.

"Don't turn it off on our account," Laverne protested.

"Turn it low," Mrs. Fowler compromised, "and you kids sit a little closer."

"Your house is lovely," Laverne offered graciously. "This is the first time I've seen it since it was furnished."

She kept an insincere smile on her face as she glanced about the room. A fireplace made of long, narrow bricks rose in an uncompromising bulky column to the ceiling between blank, combed-plywood walls. The rug was a plain pebbled weave the color of wet beach sand. The sectional sofa was cinnamon color, and rigidly rectangular, and the rather startling chairs occupied by herself and Patty were gold and green respectively. The two tables which served the seats were polished light-oak oblongs. All in all, it was a very smart room, with the spacious "underfurnished" look the most modern decorators now approved. It was a very suitable room, Laverne thought, for viewing television or for enduring brief social calls like this one; but it was about as homey as the ladies-room lounge in a railway station. There was something so geometrical about it. Laverne thought defiantly of her own Empire sofa and oriental rugs and the old-fashioned wing chair with the flounced footstool, and the bowl of ragged asters on the mahogany drop-leaf table against the inner wall of the living room.

She heard herself saying, "I really came to have a little private talk with Earl, if you don't mind, Mrs. Fowler. So you go right on with the program and Patty can watch too while maybe Earl can go in another room with me."

"Well—well, sure," Earl concurred uncertainly. "Is the kitchen all right? I guess that's the only other room there is, except the bedrooms."

She followed him through a narrow area that elled off from the main part of the living room and which contained a sideboard and a light-colored rectangular dining table.

Under the fluorescent ceiling light the kitchen emerged in a spic-and-span sheen of cream-colored paint and maroon tile. Earl pulled out a chromium and plastic chair beside the gold-topped table edged with silvery chrome, and Laverne sat in it, noting with approval the vase of wine-colored snapdragons on a Swedish mat in the middle of the table.

"I've just been out to call on Bonnie Maffey. It seemed like the decent thing to do."

Earl murmured noncommittally.

"At first I just felt it was too bad for Rex to be accused of this, if he didn't do it; but the more I get into it, the more I want to catch and punish the person who did. And it struck me that, between us, you and I should know quite a lot about Stan's affairs."

As Earl absently drew a package of cigarettes from his shirt pocket and offered her one, Laverne thought with a mental shiver, "How do I know it wasn't Earl himself?" The bookkeeper. Suppose there had been funny business with the books. This new house, completely outfitted in new furniture and a television set, represented a staggering outlay of money for a man who earned three hundred and twenty-five a month. But there had been an audit immediately, and according to her attorneys nothing queer had shown up. She decided that she must trust Earl. And perhaps pity him. The house and its contents represented, not embezzlement, but a colossal burden of debt that Earl would have to carry most of the rest of his life.

"I guess," she went on with a halfhearted smile, "I'm beginning to get my Irish up. I don't like to see somebody getting away with this."

"I know." Earl had gone to the cupboard to bring back an ash tray, into which he dropped the match that had lighted their cigarettes.

"So I thought that if you and I compared notes, we might get a hunch to go on."

Earl kept his eyes lowered uneasily. He had his hunch all right. Had had it right from the beginning. But it wasn't one he could tell her or that she would accept.

"Was there anything in the past few weeks that gave you an impression something was wrong? Anything out of the ordinary about Stan's behavior? I must admit I can't think of anything unusual."

Cautiously Earl began to speak, thinking that maybe if he sort of wove Schmidt in among other things, she might catch on for herself. "I've thought over and over that last day, trying to remember if there was anything significant about it. Some ways he had a lot of callers—for business hours. Bill Jardine came in, but they just chewed the fat, and I heard all they said. Peabody, of course, wasn't anything unusual. Then there was Hal Schmidt—"

"Hal saw Stan that afternoon?" Laverne interrupted sharply.

"Yeah. They were in the inner office together almost half an hour."

"What did they talk about?"

"I don't know. But I suspect it was about Hal's note. We could have used that money; and—maybe I shouldn't say this; but Stan was afraid Schmidt would go into bankruptcy this fall if things didn't break just right for him; and I think Stan thought the chances were against Schmidt pulling through; and if we hadn't been paid before he did go into bankruptcy, well, we could kiss that money good-by. And"—Earl smiled—"Stan wasn't one to kiss a dollar good-by, not willingly."

"Did he tell you that's what they talked about?"

"No, but he made a joking remark afterward—I hope you won't take it wrong, Mrs. West—about his wife's friends."

"Oh," Laverne said thoughtfully.

Earl cast her a quick glance, and decided he had made it as plain as he dared. He went on matter-of-factly, "And then a little while after Hal Schmidt left, Chuck Willet dropped in."

Laverne still seemed preoccupied. "Oh yes. He was trying to sell us a place in the country."

"That so?"

"I suppose he came to give Stan some more sales talk. It meant two fat commissions if he made the deal, one on the Ormsby place, and one on ours when he sold it."

"I didn't hear what they talked about. Stan closed the door a minute or so after Chuck went in. I guess Chuck's making money all right," Earl added idly. "I remember I was standing by the filing cabinet looking out the window when he pulled up in that new cream-colored Cad. Some class.

Hal Schmidt was just getting into his old Mercury, and he stopped to speak to Chuck—" Earl broke off, and then added slowly, "Come to think of it, Chuck looked kind of sour after Hal had spoke to him a minute. I was filing some statements, and I kept glancing out; and I remember now they talked for several minutes; and neither one smiled or laughed the way guys do if they're just passing the time of day."

Laverne was sitting tensely, her eyes fastened upon Earl. It was at the word "cream-colored" that she had come to attention. She tapped her fingernails on the hard table top.

Abruptly she stood up. "You don't need to say anything to anyone about this talk."

Earl looked up at her apprehensively before he too rose to his feet. "What are you going to do?"

"I'm not sure."

"It's none of my business, Mrs. West; but don't you think you ought to be careful? You know, whoever killed Mr. West is a pretty hard customer. It takes nerve to shoot a man in cold blood; and—and—well, you can't tell who it was. And—and you might say the wrong thing to the wrong party."

Laverne put her hand on his arm and smiled waveringly. "Don't worry about me, Earl. I think I know who the right party is—now. And I'm surprised nobody thought of it before. It's so obvious."

Back in the car, Patty inquired, "Well, did you find out anything?"

"Maybe." Deliberately Laverne pulled her mind away from its problem, instinctively feeling that it needed a recess. "Was the television good?"

"An old Western," Patty said indifferently. "This sure has been our night for seeing how the other half lives. You know, after seeing Rex's home, I don't wonder at him trying to get into our set. Who wouldn't want to get out of that hole?"

"I thought it might destroy a little of his appeal for you, seeing his background."

"It did—a little," Patty agreed slowly. "That picture! And with the frame made of mirror glass. Such taste. And I suppose he likes it. Still, at the same time, like I said, I feel less—resentful of his trying to use me to advance himself. I understand better."

She was silent a moment; and Laverne too seemed to be meditating uncertainly over her own attitudes as revealed in connection with the Maffeys.

"Did you ever wish," Patty said abruptly, "that you could start all over with somebody? Meet them again for the first time."

"Yes," Laverne answered hesitantly. "Yes, I've felt that way."

At Patty's question her thoughts had gone instantly to Brian. And she realized that, with her, as with Patty, Stanley's death had broken off a relationship in such a way that it could not resume and continue in the old way. Since her belief that Brian had killed Stanley, and the subsequent dispersal of that belief, with the self-revelation that had accompanied it for her, she could no longer think of herself and Brian as lovers. The events of the past week had ended that status for them—as far as she was concerned. Patty had said, "... that you could start all over with somebody," and Laverne realized that this was exactly what was happening with her and Brian. He might believe that at any suitable or convenient moment he could simply reach out and take her in his arms again; but she knew that this was not so. For her the past was broken, scattered like the pieces of a dropped china vase. She was starting all over. Brian had become once more just a friend, one she liked, one to whom she felt drawn, one she would like to know better, whom she thought she might come to love again. Would he understand when her actions revealed the way it was with her?

To the girl she said, "They always say you never have a second chance, that what's done is done, and all that; but I don't know. Sometimes it seems to me that all life is is a series of fresh starts. You can't repeat; that's true. Each new start will lead to a different result maybe. But, for instance, in this case of you and Rex. If you meet him again, what can you do but go back and start all over? Whatever was between you before, it's ended. It won't ever be the same again, your friendship with him. So it either has to be just gone, or started up on a new basis. And that, I suspect, will be up to you. If you want to find out if there is some—some affinity— between you, if there's something fundamentally congenial, you—well, you'll have to invite him to something socially, the way you wish, I guess, you had met him in the first place. To one of your parties, or to dinner with the family or something. And start getting acquainted as if he was just any boy you met that way. Then, sooner or later, you'll know whether he's a—a friend you want to keep or not."

With a feeling of exhaustion Laverne stopped talking. With a home, a family, a job like his, Rex was one of those other people, not the sort she encouraged her daughter to know; but what she had just said seemed like something she had had to say. It seemed as if, since Stanley's death, she had indeed had to make so many new starts, do so many things it would never have occurred to her to do before, but which now, unaccountably, seemed necessary, as if she must painfully begin even to make a new self for herself.

CHAPTER TWENTY-TWO

Laverne switched on the light in her room and collapsed at the head of the chaise longue, pulling off her hat and letting it fall to the floor. She pressed all her finger tips against her forehead as if to control the tumult in her mind.

This was it, the answer to the whole thing. Chuck Willet. He had misread Stanley West's character. He had thought that because Stan condoned his semilegal money-making activities, Stan, the good scout, the playboy, would unhesitatingly support his "old pal" for political office.

Laverne's thoughts wandered into recollections of Stan. The way he contributed regularly and generously to the party, not just through the Association, but personally. The Republican Party, of course. Laverne did not know anyone who was not a Republican. That was one reason it had been such a shock every time the Democrats won a presidential election—when one didn't know personally a soul who was going to vote for Roosevelt or Truman. You realized, of course, afterward, that it was done by all those other people who ranged downward below oneself economically and socially.

But Stan had always taken the elections seriously. She remembered the series of buttons in his lapel during campaigns, Landon, Willkie, Dewey, and the way he sat scowling through the radio broadcasts on election nights.

You could put it down that Stan was patriotic; he really loved his country. She supposed most people had some ideal, some principle that they would not compromise over, no matter how unethical they might be on some other matter.

Even she knew that there was crookedness in American politics, that there were many dishonest men holding down public offices, that people worse and bigger than Chuck exerted influence on government affairs. Stan knew that even now many local political figures played ball with Chuck Willet, let him dictate to them when it served his interest to do so.

But she could also see that Stan had reached a point where he could permit himself the exquisite luxury of quixotic behavior.

It must have been during the afternoon call that Stanley told him straight out: I not only won't try to get the Shippers' support for you; I'll actively campaign against you if you try to get the nomination.

It would have been a shock to Willet, Stan's denial of support. He must have fumed and brooded about it the rest of the day. Then, passing by, he sees a light in Stan's office; he stops in to discuss the matter further; they quarrel; he gets the gun while Stan's back is turned; and, in a fit of fury, kills him.

Laverne stared into space with frightened eyes. She must do something. But what? And how? Brian. He would know what to do. Her eyes fell upon the bedside clock. But it was too late tonight to see him. Yet how could she sleep with this knowledge tearing up and down through her mind?

She took two sleeping powders when she was ready for bed; and in the morning when she awoke at eight-thirty she felt rather dull. When she came downstairs, the boys and Patty were finishing their breakfasts in the kitchen, all three attired in Levis, plaid shirts, and cowboy boots, the boys' broad-brimmed hats hanging on their backs, held by cords knotted under their chins. Laverne regarded them with faint perplexity.

"Why the costume-party effect?"

"Don't you remember?" Patty demanded resignedly. "I was invited up to the Jardines' ranch in the valley for the day. And I don't know why, but you insisted I get the brats invited too."

"We like to go someplace too sometimes," Terry protested.

"And I'm taking the Buick," Patty announced.

"O.K., O.K.," Laverne agreed. "So I forgot. Just drive carefully and get back before dark."

"You want to sit down now, Mrs. West?" Lula inquired from the sink.

"I'll take my orange juice, but I'll wait till the kids go before I have anything else. I need," she added with a rueful grin, "a peaceful atmosphere while I eat."

From the back steps she waved good-by to the children and came back in to the scrambled eggs and hot toast Lula had ready. Just as she started to sit down, the telephone in the hall rang, and she said, "I'll get it. It'll probably be for me. We must," she murmured as she went down the hall, "get an extension in the kitchen someday."

It was Joan, and Laverne said, "Listen, dear, I was just sitting down to breakfast. Call me back, will you?" There was a pause, and she said, "Yes, that's all right. O.K. Do that."

As she returned to the table at the south window in the kitchen she explained to Lula, who had begun to wash dishes, "Mrs. Schmidt. She's going to drop by later. I've got important things to do today and don't particularly want her coming in, but what can you do?" Laverne spread the newspaper out beside her coffee cup. "I should be ashamed of myself, I guess; but honestly, close friends can be a nuisance sometimes."

She took a sip of coffee and said, "Seems as if I never get to look at the evening paper *in* the evening any more. I see the Maffeys, poor things, are still on the front page." She was silent for a moment, chewing toast, and then she went on absently, her eyes on a tiny item at the bottom of the page, "I guess they never caught whoever hit that man on the road out toward the Peabody ranch. Never will now, I suppose. It was in the morning before the night Stanley died. Someways it seems so long ago."

Lula had murmured unintelligible responses of agreement as she went about her work. She was drying silver now on a small towel, and she turned, leaning against the drainboard.

"You mentioning Mrs. Schmidt, I—it made me think of something that's kind of been on my mind," she said uncertainly.

"Yes?"

"It's bothered me, 'cause I suppose I *ought* to've mentioned it to the cops when they was asking me all them questions."

"What do you mean?" Laverne regarded the other questioningly.

"Well, you and Mrs. Schmidt bein' such close friends and all, I didn't want to make no trouble, and I figured it didn't really count anyhow—"

"Lula"—Laverne's tone was alarmed—"what happened?"

"Nothing, really. Nothing of any count. I've been wanting to tell you; but I didn't want to make you feel bad. Any worse'n' you already did. But that day, the day Mr. West was—the day he died—when Mrs. Schmidt came in to pick you up and you'd already gone. Well, like I told the cops, the study door was open and she went in to speak to Mr. West and I went on upstairs. I was fixing the linen in the hall closet up there. I told the cops all that."

"Yes, I know you did."

"Well, they came out in the hall down here, and I could hear their voices, and, Mrs. West, they were fightin'—"

"Lula!"

"Oh, not—not physical! Just—jawing back and forth. Well, I—" She paused uncomfortably, and closed the silver drawer. "I always knew her and Mr. West didn't hit it off so well; and I didn't think much of it. And I figured why make more trouble for you by telling them him and your best girl friend was on the outs when he died. She slammed the door when she went out."

Laverne relaxed against the chair back, letting out her breath with a relieved, "Oh!" She laughed shakily. "So that was all. No, Stan and Joan always did have chips on their shoulders for each other."

"Well, anyhow I feel better now that I've told you. 'Cause I did hold back. The cops asked me all about what I saw or heard and what I said to him."

"Did you hear what Joan and Stan were arguing about?"

"No, I couldn't—didn't," she corrected herself, "get the gist of it. But just before she slammed the door I heard him say, 'I'll wait till tomorrow morning, and if you haven't done it yourself before then, I'm going to report it.'"

"I don't understand it," Laverne said slowly.

"Well, I didn't either. That's why I thought I better keep my mouth shut."

Whatever Stan had been going to "report," he had died before he had the chance to do it.

Laverne's fingers groped blindly for her package of cigarettes, and she took one out and lighted it without noticing what she was doing.

He had died—no, he had been murdered. And Joan had been angry. She had not wanted him to "report"—whatever it was.

Laverne had folded the newspaper and as she got to her feet in uneasy preoccupation, she picked it up. She walked past Lula and went out through the rear hall to the terrace.

Blinking her eyes at the sunlight, Laverne shook her head slightly. Her mind felt queer, as if it were trying to think of a lot of things at once and couldn't.

Her eyes fell on a leather case lying on one of the canvas chairs; and she thought irrelevantly, "Patty meant to take Stan's camera with her today. She'll be annoyed when she finds out she forgot it."

Laverne's eyes shifted to a low rattan stool further forward on the floor of the terrace. Stan's candid shot of herself. She had never even seen it herself until—when was it?—the Sunday before he died. He had said, "I'm going to throw out that sweet-girl-graduate pose of you that I've had in the office all these years, and put my wife up as she is now." He had had only one print made. No one had ever mentioned Joan's being in Stan's office on the day after he put the picture on his desk. Yet she had said, "You looked just like the picture on Stan's desk...."

Laverne dropped into a chair, clutching the newspaper. Blankly she glanced down at it, and there was the item, NO CLUES TO DRIVER OF HIT-RUN CAR.

She stared at the little block of print with parted lips. West of town, on the road people took to the Peabody ranch. Joan was almost as thick with Liz Peabody as she was with Laverne. She had, in fact, been out to the ranch that morning. And Joan drove fast. And that afternoon—Stan commanding her over the telephone *not* to drive to the cocktail party with Joan. Laverne lifted her head and stared before her with a frown. They said Stan was out all morning driving around, looking over his acreage. He had extensive leases out that way. From Peabody himself.

"Report." You reported highway accidents. By late afternoon that day Stan would have seen the paper with the news of the man's having been run down on one of those roads.

Had it been Joan who hit the man? Had Stanley seen enough to implicate her?

The dent Laverne had idly mentioned on Joan's fender. It wasn't a sharp narrow indentation with scratched cut paint such as another fender or a garage door would make in contact. It was rounded and shallow with the paint unscarred.

Laverne put her hands over her face. Was she going crazy? First, Brian.

She had been sure it was Brian. Then she had thought maybe it might be Rex Maffey. Even Hal Schmidt. Stanley had turned him down on the note extension, and she had half wondered if Hal could have been so distressed that he— But she had quickly turned that thought off, not even considering it. And last night—because of his cream-colored car—she had been certain it was Chuck Willet....

She dropped her hands, revealing horrified eyes. The Schmidt station wagon was yellow.

And if she had dimly wondered about Hal and the note, was the loan not of equal importance to Joan? And Joan did not really like Stan, never had. It was only Laverne that she liked, and Joan knew that Laverne had been increasingly dissatisfied with her marriage.

It was beyond belief that one's best friend would shoot one's husband. But Joan knew the gun was there in his desk. All his friends knew it. If Stanley were going to turn Joan in for manslaughter, if he were calling for the payment of money they didn't have, if Joan furthermore thought her beloved Laverne would be better off without Stanley, was it not possible he had made her angry enough to shoot him?

Aimlessly Laverne rose and went back into the house. It couldn't be. She was going to pieces. Wildly suspecting everybody like this. She had automatically started out for the bar in the dining room; but in the hallway she stopped herself and turned in at the kitchen door.

"I need another cup of coffee," she said to Lula.

The maid talked about something or other while Laverne poured coffee. She never knew what Lula said during those moments. She took the steaming cup and walked out unhearing into the dining room, where she stood at the window, staring numbly at nothing while she sipped the hot drink.

As the nose of the Schmidt station wagon appeared down the driveway, Laverne started nervously. Turning, she set her cup and saucer down on the table.

How could she face Joan? What could she say?

She stood at the french doors as Joan leaped up the shallow steps. She was wearing faded denim pedal pushers and a sleeveless shirt, her feet in sandals, her hair tied up with a ribbon into a horse's tail at the back of her head.

"Kids all gone for the day?" Joan queried lightly, and dropped into the big chair beside the fireplace, shrugging the strap of her purse off her shoulder.

"Yes, I've been left all alone," Laverne replied with constraint. She sat down in the opposite chair, gazing at her friend with unconscious absorption.

"What's the matter? Has one of my eyebrows slipped its moorings?"

"What?"

Joan laughed. "You were staring at me so, I thought maybe something was wrong with me."

"Oh. Oh no."

"Well, how's everything going?"

"All right—I guess."

Joan straightened, her expression sobering. "You look so funny. Is anything wrong?"

Suddenly Laverne blurted out, "Joan, did Stan show you that new picture of me before he took it to the office?"

Joan's eyes grew still in her head. There was a tiny pause before she spoke. "Why, yes. Yes, he did. Why do you ask?"

"When? When did he show you?"

"When? Why, I don't know exactly— Oh. Yes, it—it was sometime the week end before he—died."

Laverne slowly leaned back in the chair. On the week end before he died Stanley had been in San Francisco on Saturday, returning only in time to dress and go out to dinner at the Harpers with her. On Sunday he had gone deep-sea fishing, and in the evening the two of them had been at home alone. Joan was lying, and with a dreadful feeling of relief, Laverne allowed herself to be convinced that her suspicions were correct.

She had no idea of what to do next. If only Joan would go. Longingly she thought of Brian, and the longing grew to feverishness. She would tell Brian. He would know what to do.

With a tremendous effort she forced herself to say carelessly, "I don't want to seem like an ungracious hostess, but I have an—an appointment downtown pretty soon."

In a voice that was cool and of fragile clarity, not at all like her usual tones, Joan said, "Maybe I could drive you down."

"Oh no, no, I don't want to bother you," Laverne returned hastily, and dropped her eyes before Joan's intent gaze.

"Who do you have an appointment with?"

"Why—why, my lawyers," Laverne answered, and then stopped, realizing that she had picked the wrong persons. Her fingernails scratched nervously at the chair arm. "About the estate," she appended quickly.

Suddenly Joan leaned forward a little further. "I thought you didn't see Stan all that day before he died."

"I didn't. I didn't," Laverne denied eagerly.

Joan seemed to reflect, her eyes never leaving Laverne's face. "But he talked to you on the phone."

"Yes, but—but just for a few minutes."

"He mentioned me."

"Oh no. No, he didn't. That is—" Laverne's throat tightened, and she stared back miserably.

Somehow it seemed as if everything that had happened during the past days had concentrated its weight upon this one moment: her grief, her own sense of guilt, the pressure of responsibility, the new demands she had tried to meet like a woman instead of a child.

She rested her elbow on the chair arm and bowed her head on her hand. In a low, trembling voice, she said, "Joan, we've been such good friends. Please—go home. I—I'm at the end of my rope."

She heard a movement in the chair opposite, but she did not lift her head until she heard Joan's harsh voice, "You always were a fool, Laverne. If you hadn't been, you'd have stood up to Stan and made him respect you. I've been fond of you anyway. But you ought to have had sense enough to know that I couldn't let my feeling for you stand in my way in a situation like this."

The flap of Joan's large handbag was open, and in her hand she held a .32 automatic. It was pointed at Laverne.

Laverne uttered a soft, startled scream.

"Be quiet! I can read you like a book, baby; and I knew almost as soon as I got here something had happened. The minute you asked about the picture, I knew that what had happened was something to make you suspect at last that I might have killed Stan."

"Put that thing away, Joan," Laverne quavered. "It frightens me."

Joan's expression softened involuntarily, but she quickly controlled it. "Poor kid," she muttered.

"How did you happen to have *that* with you?" Laverne asked faintly.

Joan glanced down at the gun. "I didn't used to carry it around with me—unless I was going on a long auto trip alone, or was alone in the house, but lately, I've been getting nervous. Odd that I should be nervous, isn't it?" she interpolated wryly. "But it was reassuring somehow to have the gun on me."

She rose. "Get up, Laverne."

"Why? What do you want?" Laverne whispered.

"You'll see. Come on. Stand up."

In spite of feeling half paralyzed Laverne got to her feet. Joan moved her head. "We're going into the study. Walk ahead of me."

Trembling, Laverne stumbled across the room and into the hall. Her eyes flickered toward the back of the house as she remembered Lula. But if she screamed she might be dead before the scream had died away; and if Lula came running out, she too might get a bullet in her brain; and then Joan would say she had come in and found them that way.

In the study Joan commanded, "Sit down there at the desk."

Laverne did so, looking up with terrified eyes. Joan stepped sideways and took down from its place on the wall the .45 revolver which matched the one in Stanley's office. She laid it on a small table, came to the desk, and pushed forward a sheet of note paper lying on the blotter pad.

"Take that pen," she said, nodding at the holder, "and write—"

"Joan! Joan, you can't!" Laverne cried out; and she thought of the open door behind the other woman. If only Lula would hear. Perhaps together they could overpower Joan.

Joan glanced at one of the open windows and the hedge across an expanse of lawn outside.

"Shut up." Keeping her own gun aimed at Laverne, she crossed and pulled the window closed. Then she wiped her forehead with the back of her free hand. "God damn it," she said hoarsely, "do you think I'm enjoying this? After all, I've loved you—for years. But I can't have you running to Brian Rhodes or Cass Huggins, blabbing. You're the only person in the world who knows enough little things, which, if they were put together, could put me in the hot seat. I never thought you'd ever tumble to anything; but obviously you have, and it's made you remember. God knows how many slips of the tongue I've made that wouldn't mean anything to anybody but you—"

"Joan, I don't—I won't— It's all a misunderstanding," she babbled in panic.

"Write on that paper, 'I can't take it any longer. I killed my husband. We were—' Let's see," she paused a second or so, "'We were not—happy together.' And sign it, 'Laverne West.'"

Laverne's eyes were wide with horrified comprehension. "Suicide," she breathed.

"Yes. With one of Stanley's own guns."

"You'll never get away with it."

"I have so far," Joan said simply, with a note of tragic resignation in her voice.

Looking at Joan, Laverne could also see the room and the half-open door behind her. The muscles in Laverne's face tensed in a supreme effort at control. She turned her head and slowly picked up the pen. She wrote as slowly as she could. She did not dare to look up again, but at last her ears heard a dull *Whack!* and a peculiar hoarse grunting sound. With a gasping exhalation of her own breath, she looked up into the surprised, fading expression on Joan's face, and she watched in speechless fascination as Joan swayed and slowly went down, the gun dropping from her hand as she fell prone on the rug, her shoulder striking a chair as she fell.

Only then did Laverne dare to look directly at Lula, whose face she had seen peering cautiously around the doorjamb a few moments before.

Lula stood now, one end of the heavy, old-fashioned rolling pin still clasped tightly in both hands as she stared dazedly at the woman she had felled with one carefully aimed whack on the top of the head.

Laverne had to close her eyes and draw a deep breath or two before she could speak.

"Oh Lula. Thank God. You heard!"

Lula regarded her with eyes still somewhat blank from shock. She moistened her lips. "I thought you were a goner," she said huskily.

Laverne glanced down at Joan. "Is she—dead?"

"I don't think so." Lula looked at the rolling pin she was still clutching, then thoughtfully laid it on a chair. "We better tie her up or something before she comes to."

"What with?"

Both looked nervously about the room. "The cords from the blinds," Laverne exclaimed.

"How we going to get 'em off?"

"Here, there's scissors in the desk."

"I'll do it."

While Lula sawed through the heavy cord with the shears, she proposed, "We'll tie her hands and feet together. Then we'll call the cops."

"What'll we do," Laverne whispered, "if she comes to before we get her tied?"

Lula looked over her shoulder as one of the cords separated. "Better hang onto the rolling pin. If she starts to come out of it, hit her again."

But Joan stayed out, snoring slightly, until Cass Huggins and a patrolman arrived. They listened with an air of dazed incomprehension to Laverne's and Lula's story, and then removed the reviving but still groggy Joan to the hospital.

CHAPTER TWENTY-THREE

At five that afternoon the children had not yet returned from their day in the country; and Brian sat with Laverne on the terrace at the rear of the house. He had just arrived, and she turned to him anxiously.

"You've been down there at the courthouse all afternoon. Tell me all that's been happening."

Lula came out through the french doors carrying a tray of cocktails, and Brian rose, eying her with amused admiration. "Our heroine."

Slowly Lula's face broke into a grin, and she rejoined facetiously, "'Twarn't nothin'."

They all laughed, and it felt good to be able to laugh. Brian turned to Laverne. "I think we should buy Lula a drink and let her hear the whole story too."

"A very good idea. Bring another glass, Lula."

The maid looked from one to the other of them; then she smiled quietly, and, as she set the tray down, said composedly, "Thank you. I would enjoy a drink."

As they sat in a ring with glasses in their hands, Brian began, "Well, you know, of course, Joan came out of it all right. No concussion. Just a bad lump on the head. And when she felt better she talked to Cass. After what happened here this morning, she knew the jig was up, and he got a full confession. Hal, of course, is completely crushed. He didn't know a damn thing about it. I think they're going to try an insanity plea.

"At any rate, this is how it went. The accident that started the whole thing happened at an intersection about a half mile this side of Peabody's ranch. Stan had turned off on a side road this way from the intersection and got out of his car to walk to the edge of the field there, one of his crops, and he was just taking a look-see at the lettuce to see for himself what kind of shape it was in. When he turned off there, he told Joan later, he saw this man walking west on the main road. A few minutes later, he glances toward the road and he sees Joan go by, driving like a bat out of hell, as he accused her. He got in his own car then and drove back to the road where Joan had passed, and looked both ways naturally before coming out of this side road. The pedestrian he had seen was gone; and it's very flat and open out there, you know. However, it didn't mean anything to him at the moment. Stan had only stopped for a few minutes, and the man should still have been in sight somewhere around the intersection. Stan only remembered not seeing him when he read in the papers in the afternoon about the hit-run victim found just this side of the intersection at the side of the road.

"So when Joan stopped in here that afternoon, he told her about having seen her there. Well, naturally she knew that if the police checked her car, they'd find it was traces of the station wagon's paint they found on the man's clothes.

"Stan told her he'd be at the office till late that night; and after Hal went to sleep, she phoned Stan and went down to plead with him to keep quiet. He refused, and apparently they both lost their tempers again. The final straw seems to have been his going to the bar in the room to pour himself a drink, and rudely omitting to ask Joan if she would have one. She says she thought of how he was refusing to extend their note, of how he had always secretly been jealous of her friendship with you, Laverne, and now he was determined to get her sent up for manslaughter! She thought in a rage, 'I could kill him!' He had opened the drawer for something earlier, and she had seen the gun. So when his back was turned, she took it out, stood across the desk with it behind her back, and when he insultingly seated himself and swallowed his drink, she did kill him."

The two women listened with sad expressions. Brian looked from one to the other of them as he paused, and added with a frown, "I can't understand how she forgot that Lula would be in the house when she decided to make a 'suicide' out of you, Laverne."

"People don't think about somebody like me," Lula said dispassionately. "We just don't count in their calculations."

"Well, I told her I was all alone," Laverne explained. "I meant the kids were away, was all; but she assumed I meant it literally."

"It was a risky thing though. I suppose she meant to give out a story that she came in and found you dead."

"She was desperate," Laverne said simply.

Brian surveyed them again, and shook his head wonderingly. "A rolling pin! Against a .32—and a .45."

"Well," Lula said stolidly, "it worked."

THE END